Emma felt breathless with anticipation.

But not from waiting to see the explosive colors that would light up the mountain sky. She'd always found fireworks romantic. It was sitting next to Jack on a picnic blanket beneath the stars that already had her heart in her throat.

A high-pitched squeal penetrated the silence, making Emma jump. It was a solid second before a splash of red covered the sky. Jack reached for Emma's hand. She swallowed but didn't look at him. She didn't pull her hand away either.

Instead, she leaned in toward him, absorbed in the moment. All her senses were bombarded by the experience, and she let herself get lost in it.

PRAISE FOR ANNIE RAINS AND HER SWEETWATER SPRINGS SERIES

Starting Over at Blueberry Creek

"This gentle love story, complete with cameos from fan-favorite characters, will enchant readers."

—*Publishers Weekly*

"A sweet, fun, and swoony romantic read that was both entertaining and heartfelt."

—*TheGenreMinx.com*

Snowfall on Cedar Trail

"Rains makes a delightful return to tiny Sweetwater Springs, N.C., in this sweet Christmas-themed contemporary. Rains highlights the happily-ever-afters of past books, making even new readers feel like residents catching up with the town gossip and giving romance fans plenty of sappy happiness."

—*Publishers Weekly*

"Over the past year I've become a huge Annie Rains fangirl with her Sweetwater Springs series. I'm (not so) patiently waiting for Netflix or Hallmark to just pick up this entire series and make all my dreams come true."

—*CandiceZablan.com*

Springtime at Hope Cottage

"A touching tale brimming with romance, drama, and feels! I really enjoyed what I found between the pages of this newest offering from Ms. Rains...Highly recommend!"

—RedsRomanceReviews.blogspot.com

"A wonderfully written romance that will make you wish you could visit this town."

—RomancingtheReaders.com

"Annie Rains puts her heart in every word!"
—Brenda Novak, *New York Times* bestselling author

"Annie Rains is a gifted storyteller, and I can't wait for my next visit to Sweetwater Springs!"
—RaeAnne Thayne, *New York Times* bestselling author

Christmas on Mistletoe Lane

"Top Pick! Five stars! Romance author Annie Rains was blessed with an empathetic voice that shines through each character she writes. *Christmas on Mistletoe Lane* is the latest example of that gift."

—NightOwlReviews.com

"The premise is entertaining, engaging and endearing; the characters are dynamic and lively...the romance is tender and dramatic...A wonderful holiday read, *Christmas on Mistletoe Lane* is a great start to the holiday season."

—TheReadingCafe.com

ALSO BY ANNIE RAINS

SUNSHINE ON SILVER LAKE

ANNIE RAINS

FOREVER

NEW YORK BOSTON

Forever
Hachette Book Group
1290 Avenue of the Americas, New York, NY 10104
read-forever.com
twitter.com/readforeverpub

First Edition: July 2020

Forever is an imprint of Grand Central Publishing. The Forever name and logo are trademarks of Hachette Book Group, Inc.

The publisher is not responsible for websites (or their content) that are not owned by the publisher.

The Hachette Speakers Bureau provides a wide range of authors for speaking events. To find out more, go to www.hachettespeakersbureau.com or call (866) 376-6591.

ISBN: 978-1-5387-0088-4 (mass market), 978-1-5387-0089-1 (ebook)

Printed in the United States of America

OPM

10 9 8 7 6 5 4 3 2 1

To Mom and Annette—the most caring and giving women I know

Acknowledgments

This book would never have happened without the help and support of so many people. Thank you to my family for so often being my sounding board when I'm writing stories, especially my husband, Sonny.

Thank you to my amazing literary agent, Sarah Younger, for wearing the hats of a cheerleader, therapist, confidante, and friend. I am truly blessed to have you on my side.

I would like to thank my editor, Alex Logan. You make my stories shine so much brighter than I ever could on my own. I would also like to thank the entire Forever team. It's a dream come true working with such a group of smart, savvy, and creative people.

Thank you to the women in my life who I count as writing partners and friends: Rachel Lacey, Tif Marcelo, April Hunt, and Sidney Halston. You inspire me in every way, and I'm so lucky to be on this publishing journey with you.

Since this book is about mom love in addition to romantic love, I want to thank my own mother for all her influence in my life. Being a mom is the toughest job in the world, and it's often thankless. So thank you, Mom—for everything.

Lastly, but in no way least, thanks a million to my readers. It's said that the average American reads two books a year. I know that most of you read so much more than that (which makes you extraordinary by those statistics), and I am so honored and humbled that you make the time to read the books that I pour so much of my heart into.

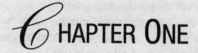

CHAPTER ONE

$\mathscr{E}$mma slid a cup of coffee across the counter as she tried, and failed, not to think about today's date. *Doomsday.*

"You okay?" her customer asked.

Emma blinked out of her zombie state and realized that it was Sophie Daniels, one of the regulars who stopped in the Sweetwater Café almost daily. "Yes, why?"

"Well, the first tip-off that you aren't okay was that you asked me what I wanted. You never ask. You always know." Sophie lifted a pale brow and then looked down at her drink. "And this isn't what I asked for."

Emma's gaze dropped to the caramel-colored cappuccino with a frothy top. "It isn't?"

Sophie gave her a worried look. "But maybe it's time for me to try something new." She started to pull out her debit card.

"I'm so sorry, Sophie." Emma held up a hand. "Your drink is on the house. And if you want something else, I'll make that too."

Sophie shook her head and took a sip as if to prove that she was completely satisfied. "Mmm."

"I'm just not fully awake," Emma explained. "I haven't had my own coffee yet this morning."

"Well, if that's the problem," Sophie said, "you deserve a break and a coffee of your own. Maybe one of those delicious pastries in that glass case too."

A break when she'd only just opened? Emma guessed that was her prerogative as the café's owner, but being the boss also meant she was responsible for every little thing that went on here, right and wrong.

Emma forced a smile as Sophie took another sip, obviously for show. "It really is good to switch things up every now and then. Maybe this will be my new drink of choice. See you tomorrow, Em," she said with a wave.

"Have a great day." Emma's smile fell flat as soon as Sophie's back was turned.

I should've stayed in bed.

She turned to call out to Nina as she put her belongings away in the back room. Nina was the only full-time employee here. The café also had two evening and weekend employees, one of whom called in sick as often as she came in. "Hey, Nina, do you mind covering the counter for me?"

"Not at all." Nina grabbed an apron and pulled it over her head of thick, black hair. At the café, she always wore it neatly pulled back. It was long and silky, and on their far-too-infrequent girls' nights out when Nina wore it down, she looked like she belonged on a Pantene commercial. All the guys wanted to buy her drinks, and all the women wanted to know her beauty secrets.

No beauty secret could save Emma this morning. She probably looked as bad as she felt. Emma was committed to always greeting her customers at the Sweetwater Café with a smile as potent as her coffee but today her smile felt like a weak decaf.

"You're a lifesaver," Emma said as Nina stepped behind the front counter.

"Says the woman who gave me a job and my first paycheck up front to keep a roof over my head."

Emma smiled. "Everyone needs a little help now and then." And right now, Emma was the one in need. She yawned as she prepared a cup of fresh coffee for herself and then retreated to a table in the back.

As she took a sip of the French specialty brew, she closed her eyes momentarily. It seemed like she'd had them closed for just a second before Nina tapped her shoulder.

"Are you asleep?"

Emma snapped awake. "No . . . Yes. Maybe." She looked at the clock and realized that the morning "rush hour" had passed. "Sorry, I didn't sleep well last night."

Nina frowned. "That bad review on the A-List site still bothering you?" she asked with a nod as if Emma had already confirmed her suspicion.

The A-List was a popular Sweetwater Springs website, intended to guide and direct tourists to the local hot spots. Emma had discovered a one-star review for the Sweetwater Café yesterday, but that wasn't what had kept her up half the night. Since she wasn't telling people today was her birthday though, it was as good an excuse as any. "I guess that's why."

Nina's lips contorted into a perfect pout. "Everyone gets bad reviews, Em."

This wasn't the first bad review the café had gotten, but Emma took every criticism seriously. Yesterday's review had complained of a lack of seating in the café. Well, that was only because the SC was a popular place to get a cup of coffee. It was a good thing, not a reason to avoid coming.

Just thinking about it made Emma feel worse. *Happy birthday to me.*

The bell at the counter rang.

"Want me to get it?" Nina asked.

"No, I need to earn my keep around here." Emma pushed back from the table and headed toward her customer. She stopped short when she saw Jack Hershey standing there in his park ranger attire. When women said they loved a man in uniform, Emma was pretty sure they weren't talking about the tan button-down shirt with olive-green cargo shorts that Jack wore. But that's the uniform that sent her blood rushing.

"Jack." In her exhausted state, she hadn't considered that he would come by today. But she should have. Jack hadn't missed one of her birthdays since they were kids. She held up a hand. "Don't."

The corner of his mouth quirked. "But it's tradition, Em."

"Maybe it's time we get a new tradition," she practically pleaded.

Thankfully, there was no one else at the counter. She stepped closer, glad that there was a counter between them because Jack had always stirred things inside her. They'd known each other since they were kids. Their moms, who were best friends, had joked about them getting married when they grew up.

Emma's throat grew tight as memories of her mom crashed over her, along with panic and dread. Her mom had died a long time ago, but Emma had been feeling her absence more lately as her thirtieth birthday drew near. And now the day had come. She was the same age her mom had been when she'd died. D-day.

"Okay. Here's an idea for a new tradition." Jack leaned against the counter. "Instead of me serenading you in front of all your customers, how about you agree to have a birthday dinner with me tonight? I'll take you out, and we'll catch up. It's been a while since we've done that."

Emma felt her face flush. Her mind raced along with her heart, searching for an excuse to politely turn him down. "Well, I'm afraid that I've already made plans with Halona and Brenna tonight." Halona owned the flower shop next door, and Brenna had worked down the street until recently when she'd sold her catering business. Now she was studying for her teaching degree, which was a lifelong dream of hers.

He looked down at his feet momentarily. "Right. Of course you have plans. There's no way you'd be sitting at home alone on your birthday, huh?" He reached into his front pocket, and she knew what he was grabbing. Her heart flopped hopelessly inside her chest as he laid three Hershey's Kisses on the counter. "I couldn't fit thirty in my pocket."

She rolled her eyes. "You are so predictable, Jack Hershey."

A smile curled his lips, reaching up to touch his blue eyes as he winked at her. His dark hair was a little tousled today as if he'd run his hand through it a dozen times already—he probably had. "Maybe you just know me really well."

She nodded and looked away for a moment to catch her breath. "Thank you."

"You're welcome. I'll serenade you another time. When it's just us." He turned to head out.

"Wait. Don't you want a coffee? Or something else?" She shrugged. "What would you like?"

He turned back to look at her, his eyes narrowing. "You

mean you don't know what I want? That would be a first
for you."

Emma's face grew warm. She really was out of sorts
today. "Right. Yes, of course I know. Just asked out of
habit."

He shook his head. "It's okay. I don't need a drink. I
just wanted to wish you a happy—"

She held up a hand. "Nuh-uh." She didn't want Nina or
anyone else in the café to overhear. She didn't want any fuss
made over her today. She just wanted to get through it.

"I just wanted to wish you a good day," Jack finished.
"Have the very best one, Em."

* * *

Jack got into his Toyota Tundra and headed back toward
his neck of the woods. He'd only come to Main Street to
see Emma. She always smiled when she saw him, but he
could feel the guard she put up whenever he was near. He'd
always thought she'd warm back up to him—forgive and
forget—but she hadn't yet. Not completely.

He turned at the stop sign and drove with the window
down, taking in the summer's breeze as it hit his face. It
was the end of June—the height of the season. Later this
week, there'd be Fourth of July celebrations. Once upon a
time, he and Emma had pretended those celebrations were
for her. Now she didn't want to celebrate at all.

Emma had turned thirty today, but he'd already surpassed
that milestone. He'd like to say it was just a number, but he
wasn't the same guy he'd been in his twenties. He stuck to
non-alcoholic beverages when he went out these days, and
he dozed off a good hour earlier at night, waking with the
birds, not the ladies.

Lately, he'd also found himself longing for things he never wanted before. A few of his friends were settling down, and a couple had kids on the way. Part of him envied those friends. The other part enjoyed being a bachelor when those very friends listed all the cons to being in a relationship.

He pulled into the lot of Evergreen State Park and cut the engine, looking out over the long pines with the rolling Blue Ridge Mountains in the far distance. After stepping out of his truck, he stretched for a moment before grabbing his radio to communicate with other rangers and authorities in the area. Sometimes he came across an injured hiker or ran into a situation with wildlife. Most recently, there was evidence of a squatter deep in the park. It was against the law to camp overnight at Evergreen State Park. He hadn't seen the person yet, but when he did, he aimed to have a talk with them. One warning, and after that, he'd issue a citation.

Jack walked to the side of the ranger station, where he kept his "toys." Half the lure of being a park ranger was in this outbuilding. He had a skiff boat, two four-wheelers, two utility vehicles, and a kayak. However, the ATV was his vehicle of choice on the narrow paths in the park. He climbed onto one and pointed it up Gray Wolf Trail, pressing the gas pedal and loving his job.

For the next hour and a half, he paroled the area, his mind bumping from nature back to Emma as the tires traversed the uneven terrain. He'd wondered if today would be hard for her. Judging by how frazzled she'd seemed, it was. He was glad she was going out with friends tonight. Hopefully they'd take her mind off things.

He slowed to a stop when he saw evidence of the squatter. He hopped off his ATV and walked over to a pile of charred sticks where someone had made a fire. Jack turned to scan the surrounding area. Just like every other time, whoever had been here was long gone. He was finding evidence about once a week.

Jack could understand the desire to stay overnight. Blue Sky Point was the highest overlook in the park, and it was breathtaking up here. From this location, you could see Silver Lake nestled in the Star Valley River. Silver Lake spanned beyond Evergreen's limits and stretched toward the downtown shopping area as well. If someone looked hard enough, from this point, you could see an eagle's nest built high up in a tree, an egret stretching its wings as it soared, and a deer running just as fast. The wildlife was the other lure to Jack's job.

As he breathed in the fresh air, his mind returned to Emma.

He fished his cell phone out of his pocket, relieved to see that he had a signal, and searched for Halona Locklear's contact. Maybe if he knew where Halona and Brenna were taking Emma for her birthday, he could stop in and buy Em a drink or a slice of cake.

He tapped Halona's contact and held the phone to his ear.

"Little Shop of Flowers," she answered after a couple rings.

"Hey, Hal," Jack said, leaning against a tall pine. "This is Jack."

"Hi, Jack. You need flowers?"

He chuckled. Sending flowers to Em might be overkill, and it would definitely cross that line that Emma's father had drawn in the sand between them over a decade ago. "Actually, Emma told me that you and Brenna are taking her out tonight for her birthday. I thought I'd find out where you're headed and try to stop in."

Halona was silent on the other end of the line.

"Hal?"

"Well, Brenna and I *offered* to take Emma out, but she refused. She said she had plans with you."

Jack straightened. "Oh. Yeah, that's right," he said. "I guess I forgot about that."

"You forgot?" Halona said, her tone sharpening. "Jack, it's a big birthday. Emma deserves something special."

Halona was exactly right.

"Good thing you reminded me, then," he said.

"Yes, it is. We don't need a repeat of the whole prom night fiasco," Halona pointed out. "I never thought she'd forgive you for standing her up the way you did."

Luckily, Emma was as forgiving as she was beautiful.

"So you're still taking Emma out tonight for her birthday, right?" Halona clarified on the phone now.

"Yeah. Well, we're staying in and celebrating at her house," he said.

There was another silence from Halona.

"It's not like that. I'm bringing over popcorn and a movie. Emma wants a quiet birthday this year." And apparently, she wanted to be alone.

Jack wasn't going to grant that birthday wish though. Today of all days, Emma needed to have someone by her side, and he wanted to be that person.

* * *

After a long day at the café, Emma dragged herself up her porch steps, unlocked the door, and shut herself inside. This was what she'd been waiting for all day. She just wanted to be alone.

Her dog, a West Highland Terrier named Barnaby,

barked to remind her that she wasn't exactly by herself. She dipped and ran a hand through his silky white locks, whispering hellos to him. Then she headed into the kitchen and put her purse on the counter before taking a seat on one of the stools and digging three Hershey's Kisses out of her pocket. She'd been saving them since this morning. This would replace the birthday cake she didn't have. She pinched their little paper flags between her fingers, making them stand upright and envisioning that they were candles. She supposed that would do.

Now all she needed to do was decide on a wish. Several came to mind. She wished that the one-star review hadn't happened and that she didn't care so much. She wished she felt up to going out with Halona and Brenna tonight. Or Jack.

Her cell phone rang inside her purse, making Barnaby stand at attention and bark ferociously. Emma grinned at her little guard dog, who was more likely to lick someone to death than bite them. "Thank you for alerting me," she said as she reached for her phone and checked the caller ID. "Hi, Dad."

"Happy birthday, sweetheart," he said. "How are you?"

"Great." It was just a little white lie.

"I decided to call you early before you went out for any celebrations."

"Good idea," Emma said. Her dad still lived in her childhood home and had remarried two years after Emma's mother had passed. He'd carried on with life as best he could, and Emma had done the same.

Emma chatted with her dad for a few more minutes, talking about his job and Emma's stepmother's newest cycling hobby.

"You should join us," he suggested.

"Do I have to wear those tight spandex bike shorts?" Emma teased.

"They're actually kind of cool."

Emma laughed. "If you say so."

"Well, I just wanted to call and wish you a happy birthday, Emma Grace."

"Thanks, Dad."

"Come over for Sunday lunch?" he asked. "Angel will cook your favorite for the occasion."

Emma hesitated before answering. Angel was a nice woman. She was kind, thoughtful, and beautiful. And Emma's dad deserved a second chance at love. Emma just didn't like the fact that his second chance came by way of her mom's hospice nurse. She didn't think anything had happened between Angel and her dad while her mom was still alive, but it still felt wrong somehow. "It's a holiday weekend, which means it'll be extra busy at the café. I might have to work. I'll let you know."

"Always working so hard. I'm proud of you," he said. "Talk to you soon, sweetheart."

"Okay. Bye, Dad." Emma disconnected the call. Then she sat on her barstool and stared at her Hershey's Kisses, knowing exactly what she wanted. "I wish today would just be over."

Leaning forward, she prepared to blow her pretend candles out and then stopped short when her doorbell rang. Barnaby charged in that direction, making a lot of ruckus for such a little guy. She considered not answering the door, but her car was in the driveway so whoever was at the door would know she was home. *A garage would be nice as well.*

With an exaggerated sigh, she followed Barnaby and lifted on her toes to look out the peephole. Her heart did a somersault. While she was listing her desires to her imaginary birthday genie, she really wished Jack Hershey wasn't standing on her porch right now.

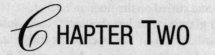

CHAPTER TWO

*J*ack offered a small wave as he stood on Emma's porch. "Hi, Em."

Her little dog came rushing toward him, barking wildly with his tail wagging. Jack moved a hand to pet Barnaby's head but kept his eyes on Emma.

"What are you doing here, Jack?" she asked.

"Well"—he pulled his hand from Barnaby and shrugged—"it's your birthday and someone should be here with you." He glanced down at the dog. "No offense, Barn."

Her eyes narrowed as he met her gaze again. "You spoke to Brenna?"

"Halona actually," he confessed.

She sighed and opened the door wider, gesturing for him to come inside.

Jack stepped over the threshold, Barnaby at his heels, and shut the front door behind him. He followed Emma into the kitchen, where he noticed she had the Hershey's

Kisses he'd given her earlier on the counter. "You were supposed to eat those," he said, taking a stool while she headed to the refrigerator. Barnaby huffed at the lack of attention and curled on the floor at his feet.

Emma glanced over her shoulder. "I was just about to. It's my birthday cake." She opened the fridge and grabbed some juice from the side door. "Apple juice? It's from the orchards at Merry Mountain Farms."

Jack's jaw dropped. "Hey, how'd you get some of that? I'm friends with the owner, and I don't have any in my fridge." Granger sold a variety of apples and berries in addition to the Christmas trees on his farm. But the apple cider his mother made was in limited supply, and they only gave it out to family.

"I babysat Abby and Willow last week," Emma said, referring to Granger's young daughters. "Granger paid me in juice."

Jack folded his arms over his chest. "If I'd have known it was that easy, I'd have offered to babysit a long time ago. Those girls love me. They call me Uncle Jack."

Emma grinned. "So your answer is yes to a glass of juice?"

"Yes, I'd love some. Juice and a chocolate Kiss sound perfect."

Emma carried two glasses over to the counter beside him and poured a healthy serving. "I never said I was sharing my chocolate Kisses with you."

"Fair enough." He gave her a long look, which was dangerous in his book because Emma had always stirred all kinds of desire inside him. It had nothing to do with her long blond hair and hazel eyes. It was something about the way she looked at him. The way her body responded to him being close. The way his body responded right back.

Emma slid into the seat beside him and took a sip from her own glass of juice.

"Wanna tell me why you lied to everyone?" he asked.

Her eyes widened. "I didn't lie."

He tilted his head and gave her a steady look. "You said you were going out with Brenna and Halona tonight for your birthday when I asked you to dinner. And Halona said you told her you had plans with me."

Emma's shoulders rounded. "Okay, I lied. Is it such a crime to want to spend your birthday alone?"

"No, but you don't usually spend it alone. The Emma I know loves a good party."

She met his gaze, sitting close enough to touch. There was something sad in her eyes tonight. He'd seen it this morning too. That's why he'd called Halona. He knew Emma so well. Well enough to know that something was weighing on her mind.

"Maybe I don't want to celebrate this time," she said softly.

"Because you're thirty?" he asked. The Emma he knew wouldn't care about leaving her twenties behind. Emma had never cared about spending the day at the salon or wearing designer clothes. She wasn't one of those women who didn't leave the house without makeup. He highly doubted she was troubled by getting a little older.

She reached for one of the Kisses on the counter and started peeling off the wrapper. "My mom was only thirty when she was diagnosed with breast cancer. It feels..." Emma shrugged as she stared at the mound of chocolate in her palm. "I don't know. Sad. I'm probably just being silly."

Without thinking, Jack reached over and placed his

hand on her forearm. "You're allowed to feel whatever you want. It's your birthday."

"And I'll cry if I want to?" There was a hint of a smile as she looked up at him. "Some part of me has been holding my breath. My grandmother died of breast cancer before she was thirty, and my mom died at thirty from the same thing. Now I'm here, relieved to have made it this far but also scared to death that I'm approaching a cliff and about to fall off." She groaned in frustration. "I'm being really morbid on my birthday, aren't I? It's just, I'm not finished yet. There are still things I want to do."

Jack felt an ache in his chest as she spoke. "What things?"

She shrugged, swiping a lock of hair behind her ear. "I don't know. I haven't traveled the world or climbed to the top of a mountain. I haven't gone skinny-dipping in Silver Lake." Her cheeks blushed lightly. "I don't want to, that's illegal. But my friends went in high school on a dare, and I was too chicken."

"I remember hearing about that," he said with a grin.

Something shifted in her gaze. "I also never went to prom."

Those words shot little barbs into his heart. He guessed that's what she'd intended.

Emma shook her head. "You see? I'm no fun to be around tonight, which is why I decided to spend my birthday alone. I sound like I'm whining into my drink completely sober. Can you imagine if I'd gone to the Tipsy Tavern with the girls?" Emma grabbed one of the chocolate Kisses and slid it in front of Jack.

"Sharing your cake with me?" he teased, hoping to lighten the mood.

"You're listening to my sob story so you've earned it."

Instead of reaching for the Kiss, Jack reached for his glass of juice and held it up. "A toast."

Emma's lips parted. She hesitated before lifting her glass to meet his. "Okay. To what?"

"To you," he said, tapping his glass against Emma's. Barnaby rose for the occasion and offered a soft bark, adding to the toast. "I hope the next year brings all your heart's desires, Em. You deserve the best of everything."

He held her gaze for a long moment, and then they both took a sip of their juice. Some part of him wished that he was on that list of her heart's desires, but he'd messed up his chance with her. And he didn't think he'd ever get another shot.

* * *

The next morning, Emma rolled toward her alarm clock as it shrieked just out of arm's reach. With a groan, she lifted halfway off the bed and whacked the button before collapsing back against her mattress. She felt hungover, even though she'd only had apple juice last night.

With Jack.

Her eyes popped open as she remembered the details of what had happened hours before. She'd been whiny and silly and...he'd been understanding and sweet. They'd talked for at least an hour before he'd gotten up to leave. Then she'd walked him to the door and said good night within a breath of asking him to stay longer.

Emma got up and headed down the hall to start the coffee maker. "Good morning, Barnaby," she said as the coffee brewed. She freshened his food and water bowls and then hurried back down the hall to shower and get dressed. When she was done, she prepared her first cup of coffee to go, unlocked Barnaby's doggie door so he could have free rein in her backyard during the day, and drove to the Sweetwater Café.

When she finally reached the store's front door to flip the OPEN sign, her first customer was already standing on the sidewalk outside.

"Jack," she said, opening the door for him.

"Happy—"

She held up a finger. Her birthday was over.

"I was just going to wish you a happy July," he said, giving her a wink.

"Right." She nodded. "What are you doing here?"

He walked in, carrying a shoebox and wearing an olive-green baseball cap with an SS embroidered on the front for Sweetwater Springs. She had one in lavender in her own closet. "Looks like I'm the first one here."

"Looks like. Your usual?" she asked as she walked behind the counter.

He grinned. "Back to normal, I see."

"Good thing you only turn thirty once." She turned to prepare his coffee the way he liked it. Her mental Rolodex may have been off yesterday, but it was working just fine today. She added enough sweetener to his coffee to move it more to the category of dessert than a beverage. Then she pressed a lid on the top and slid it toward him.

"Thanks." He reached into his back pocket and pulled out his wallet. Then he handed over his debit card.

"What's in the box?" she asked as she zipped the card through the reader and handed it back.

Jack shoved his wallet in his pocket and reached for his drink. "It's for you. I stopped by my mom's after I left your place last night. This box has been stashed in her closet forever. I asked her about it once, and she said these things were for you to have one day. Something told me that day had come."

Emma gave the box a curious look, aware that customers were starting to line up behind him. What on earth would Jack's mom have in her closet that she thought Emma would want? "Okay. My curiosity is up."

"I'll put it in the back, and you can take a look when things slow down."

"Thanks. And thank you for last night, Jack," she said quietly.

"Just being a friend," he said, stepping away from the register with the shoebox under one arm and his drink in the opposite hand.

None of Emma's other friends gave her heart flutters though. Just Jack. Emma refocused on the customer who was behind him. "Good morning, Halona."

"Thank you for last night?" Halona repeated in a whisper as she approached the counter. "Sounds like *someone* had a good birthday."

Emma's cheeks flared hot as she shook her head. "You know it's not like that between me and Jack." Emma grabbed a cup from the tall stack beside her. "Your usual?" she asked, moving the subject forward.

"Yes, please. I have a busy day at the flower shop, and I'm going to need this."

"Is Brenna meeting you here this morning?" Emma asked as she prepared the drink.

Halona shook her head. "No, she has the day off, and she's spending it sleeping in."

"I'm jealous." Emma placed a lid on Halona's cup and slid it toward her.

"Me too." Halona paid and then tasted her coffee. "Best coffee in Sweetwater Springs. See you tomorrow, Em."

Emma greeted the next customer who stepped in front of her. From the corner of her eye, she saw Jack walk back around the counter. He waved as he walked toward the front door with his drink. Emma waved back, a hot flash rolling over her as she watched him exit. No, none of her other friends or customers did that to her.

The rest of the morning went by in a blur as Emma served customers. By midmorning, all the seats at the café were full. The negative review on the A-List site was right in the sense that there was no room to take a seat with your breakfast.

"I can handle the counter," Nina offered. "If you want to take a break and go sit down. No napping on the job this time though."

Emma laughed. "Thanks." She poured herself a cup of coffee, her second today, and beelined toward the box that Jack had left her. There was a Hershey's Kiss lying on the top, which made her smile. She grabbed it, peeled off the wrapper, and popped it into her mouth, her gaze catching on the writing across the top of the box's lid: JENNY'S THINGS.

Emma's breath caught. Then she took a step backward, away from the box. Going through her mom's belongings at work wasn't a good idea. That was something that needed to be done alone.

* * *

Jack's rain jacket wasn't doing its job. He was drenched from head to toe, and even his boots were waterlogged as he walked along a trail in the park. A hiker had returned earlier, when the sky had just been gray and heavy with clouds, reporting evidence of a campfire near Blue Sky Point.

The skies had broken as Jack drove uphill looking for it. He'd slowed and had gotten off his ATV when he saw the pile of sticks, charred in the middle. Whoever had made it was no doubt taking shelter somewhere now. If they were on foot, they'd have very few places to go, and Jack knew all the places to hide. This was his territory, and he didn't appreciate someone putting the area and wildlife at risk.

He shrugged deeper into the shelter of his raincoat as he climbed back on his ATV and checked a few locations that might provide a reprieve from the rain, finding nothing. Then he came across a young woman with a small child in tow. He didn't think for a second that they were the culprit of the illegal campfire.

Jack slowed his vehicle beside them. Both were completely soaked and had obviously gotten surprised by the summer showers. "It's a good mile back to the parking lot. Want a lift?"

The woman looked relieved. "Yes, thank goodness." She hopped on his ATV beside him, pulling her young son close, and Jack took off down the trail, delivering her directly to her vehicle. Afterward, he headed back to the small ranger station where he kept an office—not that he was a desk kind of guy. The building was open to visitors and offered maps of the park, detailing the various hiking trails, kayak launches, and fishing sites. There was also a wall of pamphlets providing education on a variety of topics, including forest fire prevention and recycling, and there were nature-related handouts for identifying various plant life and birds that could be spotted in Evergreen Park.

Jack grabbed a set of dry clothes and stepped into the restroom to change. When he came out, he walked over to the front window to watch the rain outside. At least there was no reason to worry about an illegal campfire sparking a forest fire with a downpour like this.

His cell phone rang on his desk, and Jack headed to answer it. "Hello?"

His sister's voice greeted him. "Jackie."

Jack groaned. He hated his older sister's nickname for him. "Hey, Amanda." He sat in one of the lobby chairs and leaned back. His sister didn't usually call during his work hours. "Everything okay?"

"Yeah," she said, although he heard the note of hesitation in her voice. "I was just calling to ask for a favor."

"You got it," he said.

She laughed on the other end of the line. "I haven't even told you what it is yet."

Jack ran a hand through his damp hair. "Okay, what is it?"

"I need you to take Sam for a while."

Sam was Jack's nephew. He was fifteen and usually came to stay with Jack a couple weekends a year. Never longer than a couple of days. "You mean for a weekend or two?"

"Longer," she said. "He's been out of school for a couple of weeks, and he's already going stir-crazy here. I'm calling to ask you to take him, possibly for as long as a month."

"Just Sam?"

She hesitated. "That's right."

Jack stood and started pacing, his feet moving as fast as his thoughts. "Don't get me wrong, I'd love to spend more time with my nephew, but why? Where are you going?"

She was silent for a moment. "I'm not going anywhere. But I think it would be best for Sam if he wasn't here right now."

"And why is that?" he asked.

"I can't really answer that right now. I don't want Sam to overhear me," she said, lowering her voice.

Jack stopped pacing. "So I'm just supposed to say yes, no questions asked?"

"You already said yes, actually."

Jack wavered. "Amanda, are you okay?"

"I will be. But I need to have some time for myself. And I want Sam to have the summer of his life on Silver Lake. The kind of summers we had when we were young."

Jack didn't think kids in this technology age enjoyed running barefoot through the grass, swinging off ropes into swimming holes, or catching fireflies at night. Especially not the fifteen-year-old variety.

"Okay," he finally said without another word. But he'd be asking a lot of questions the next time he and his sister spoke.

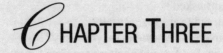

CHAPTER THREE

*E*mma headed to the back room as one of her evening employees took control of the counter that she and Nina had been working all day.

"You still haven't touched the box that Jack brought you," Nina noted.

Emma glanced at it. Maybe she hadn't touched it, but she'd been thinking about it all day. "I will when I get home. I think I need a deep glass of wine first."

Nina frowned. "Want me to join you?"

Emma laughed. "No. You have other, more important things to take care of. Like that new puppy of yours."

Nina rolled her eyes. "Why didn't anyone warn me that puppies were so much work? I had no idea. I thought it'd be easier to get a puppy than try to fill the void in my life with a guy. Now I'm wondering if it'd have been easier to find a date."

Working with Nina made Emma's days so much more fun. "I love the puppy stage, but I'm glad Barnaby is older now. Even if he still thinks he's young and feisty."

Nina laughed. "Maybe not so young, but he's still pretty energetic."

This was true. "Anyway, I'll be fine opening the box and drinking my wine alone." Emma had wanted to be alone last night, too, but she hadn't ended up spending it on her own. "I might stop at Home Décor and More first. I was thinking that maybe I could add a few tables outside on the sidewalk."

"Still thinking about that review on the A-List, huh?" Nina grabbed her purse from her cubby and pulled it over her shoulder. "I think tables in front of the café would be a nice touch. Do you need a permit for that or something?"

Emma shook her head. "I got it approved when I first opened the café. I just haven't done it. Halona might even let me put one in front of her shop next door. Coffee lovers can sit and drink while peering inside at her flowers."

"The reviewer was rude," Nina said, "but I'm glad you can take that negativity and turn it into something constructive. That is so like you. Well, that and your need to make sure everyone is happy."

Emma grabbed her purse as well. Then she reluctantly grabbed the box of her mom's things.

Nina tilted her head as she watched her. "And, while I'm a rip-the-Band-Aid-off kind of girl, it's so like you to put off something that might not be pleasant." She looked down at the box in Emma's hand. "Like procrastinating on finding out what's in that box. That's the real reason you're going shopping before you go home."

Emma nibbled on her lower lip. Nina had no idea how right she was. Emma had delayed a lot more than opening the box that Jack had left her today. She'd also put off her annual checkup at the Women's Wellness Center, canceling at the last minute.

That was unlike Emma. With her family history, she was extra cautious with her health. But turning the same age her mom had been when she'd died had really freaked her out. She'd started having heart palpitations and sweaty palms after lunch. She couldn't bring herself to go. At least not today.

It was just a minor delay, though. She'd reschedule tomorrow.

* * *

Half an hour later, Emma perused the aisles of Home Décor and More and found the perfect wrought iron tables to put outside her business. She would start with two at first, until she talked to Halona about putting an additional one in front of the Little Shop of Flowers.

Emma plopped down in one of the iron chairs on display and sighed. How was she going to get these tables and chairs to the café? She drove a compact car. She'd intended to get them ASAP, but that wasn't going to be the case. She could have them delivered to the café, but that was likely to take a week. In that time, the sourpuss reviewer might come back and leave another bad comment. Or worse, another customer might go without seating and do the same.

"Fancy meeting you here," a man said behind Emma.

She turned toward the deep voice, and her entire body sizzled in response. "I just can't seem to get away from you this week, can I?"

Jack shoved his hands in his jeans pockets as he stepped in front of her. "I'm doing a little home improvement this week." He pulled out the chair opposite her and sat at the display table.

"What kind of home improvement?" she asked.

"The kind that allows me to have a guest stay with me for an extended period," he said as he looked around the store. "Amanda called this morning and asked me to take Sam for a few weeks. Maybe a month."

Emma's mouth dropped open. "That's unexpected, I guess."

"She wouldn't tell me why, but I'm a little worried about her." Jack's gaze slid back to Emma at the table. "She's had a few rough patches over the last year. She got injured on the job last summer."

"I remember you telling me that."

He ran his hand through his hair. A trademark move of his. One that made her ache for some reason. "She was taking some heavy-duty painkillers for a while, but last I saw her, she seemed to be doing better."

Emma knew that Jack's father was an alcoholic, and his sister had struggled with her own substance abuse issues when she was younger. "Is she drinking?"

"I hope not." He blew out a breath. "But she asked me to help give Sam the summer of his life. If things were okay, she'd come too."

"The summer of his life," Emma repeated. "That's a pretty tall request."

"What am I supposed to do with him when I'm at work? He's a fifteen-year-old boy. I guess he can be an intern of sorts at the park, but that's not exactly giving him his best summer."

Emma grinned. "If I remember correctly, that would've been the summer of your dreams when you were that age. All you wanted to do was disappear into the woods."

Jack looked at her, his gaze sticking for a long moment. "That's true. Girls had nothing on nature. Most girls, at least."

Emma wanted to look away but couldn't. There was something magnetic in his eyes that held her attention. Something about him that made her mouth go dry and her body burn hot.

"Can I help you?" A store manager walked up to the table where they were sitting. For a moment, Emma had forgotten that she was seated at a store display.

"Yeah." Jack leaned back in the chair and kicked his boots up on the table. "Can we have a couple of lemonades and menus, please?"

The store manager didn't look amused. He frowned and looked over his small glasses at them. "There are plenty of restaurants around if you're hungry. I'm afraid this is not the place for social gatherings."

Emma straightened. "I'm interested in purchasing this set for my café on Main Street. I'd like two sets actually."

The store manager looked at her over his glasses now. She recognized him as one of her regular customers at the café. Marvin. He always came in for a tall, hot coffee. No cream. No sugar. He liked his coffee bitter, which seemed fitting for his personality.

Marvin seemed to recognize Emma as well. "You want to take the display model today?"

"Well, no, I don't have the means to take it home right now. I'll order it and have it delivered, I guess."

"Then you're not buying this set right now," he said, seemingly proving his point that they were doing something wrong. He looked at Jack's boots and back up at Jack.

Jack put his feet back on the floor. "I was just joking around by trying to order the lemonades." He pointed a finger. "Hey, wait. I recognize you. I've seen you at the park, haven't I? Are you the guy who tried to take my whole stack of bird-watcher charts?"

Marvin folded his arms over his narrow chest. "They were free. The sign said so."

"It said *take one*," Jack said.

Marvin shook his head, an annoyed sound escaping his mouth. "You asked me to leave your workplace, and if you're not purchasing today, I'm afraid I'll have to ask you to do the same."

* * *

Jack stood, towering a good foot over the store manager's head. He didn't like this guy. "We'll take this model and one more set. Today," he told him. Then he looked at Emma. "I have a truck. I'll deliver them to the café myself."

Emma looked at him. "Really?"

Jack nodded and looked at the store manager again. "We'll take those lemonades and menus, too, if you got 'em." He couldn't help himself.

The store manager's mouth pinched tighter. "I'll have someone load the tables up for you," he said curtly before turning and walking off.

"I almost hate to give that guy our business," Jack muttered.

"He's a regular customer of mine. His name is Marvin."

Jack looked over. "You have to see that guy every day?"

Emma laughed. "Some customers are easier than others. You learn to grin and bear it. Like right now. It's worth dealing with him in order to get these tables and chairs. They're perfect." Emma ran a slow hand over the surface of the table. "Thank you for helping out," she said, looking back up at him, her hazel eyes more green in this lighting.

"No problem. It's still your birthday week after all. What the lady wants, she gets."

"But you're here to get things for Sam's stay. Now there'll be no room in the back of your truck."

"Ah, it's okay. I couldn't find what I needed anyway."

"What were you looking for?" she asked as they headed for the check-out.

"Everything. A bed mainly. I suppose he can take mine, and I can sleep on the couch until I figure something else out."

They reached the register, and Emma paid for the table sets. Then they headed to the parking lot to wait at Jack's truck for a store employee to cart them out. That early morning rain shower had helped cool things down, but the temperatures were still higher than normal, even now as the sun made a slow descent.

"I have a spare bed you can take over to your place for the rest of the summer," Emma offered. She pulled her sunglasses from the front of her shirt where they were clasped and slid them over her eyes.

Jack noticed his reflection in her lenses. "I couldn't ask you to do that."

"No one ever uses it. It's fine. Just come by and get it one night," she said.

Jack had wanted to kiss Emma last night when he'd been alone with her in her house on her birthday. Going over to her house a second night this week might not be a good idea. They were friends, and he'd made a promise to her dad to never cross that line with her. After Jack had arrived drunk to pick up Emma for prom, her father had cut him off at the pass and said Jack didn't deserve her. And on some level, based on that one incident, Jack agreed. He wanted to be the type of guy who deserved Emma though.

"Thanks," he said. "And I guess if you're sure you don't mind, I'll take you up on borrowing that bed."

She smiled back at him, completely oblivious to his thoughts, and to the fact that he actually had shown up to take her to prom. And he wanted to keep it that way.

"I'm sure."

The store employee arrived with the boxes, and Jack loaded them into his truck. "I'll take them over to the café right now and set them up," he said.

Emma looked excited, which was a welcome change from how she'd looked last night in her house. "I'll meet you there. We can have those lemonades afterward."

"Sounds fitting for the best summer ever," Jack said. Even if his idea of the best summer included a lot more than a friendly lemonade with Emma.

* * *

Twenty minutes later, Jack pulled into the Sweetwater Café's parking lot and got out. "You want the tables set up out front?" he asked as Emma walked up beside him.

She nodded. "Yes, please. Thank you again. You're a lifesaver. I'll help you carry them."

He started to argue, but she rolled her eyes. "Put your alpha pride away and let me. I've been working out, you know." She flexed her biceps, and he swallowed. "That's impressive." And attractive.

10, 9, 8, 7…

He started mentally counting backward the way he did when he needed to cancel his thoughts and refocus his brain.

"What are you doing?" she asked.

He met her gaze. "What do you mean?"

"You just went blank. You completely disappeared."

He cleared his throat. "Sorry. I guess I got distracted."

She offered a hesitant smile. "Okay, well, as you can see, I can help with the tables and chairs. Let's do this." She grabbed the edge of one box and started pulling, not waiting for him to agree. He grabbed the other side. He could've carried it by himself. They weren't heavy but he didn't want to tell Emma no. He suspected she wouldn't have accepted no for an answer anyway.

"I have a toolbox inside the café," she said once they'd gotten the box to the front of the shop. "Be right back."

His gaze followed her as she disappeared inside the café.

10, 9, 8, 7, 6 . . .

"Hey, Jack."

He looked up as his buddy Granger headed toward him on the sidewalk with his two little girls, Abigail and Willow.

"Hey, buddy. What are you guys doing tonight?" Jack asked.

"I promised the girls a trip to Dawanda's Fudge Shop for a little treat." Granger looked at the front entrance of the Sweetwater Café and then back to Jack. "And what are you doing standing out here?"

Jack held out his hands. "Just helping Emma set up some new tables out here. No big deal."

"Yeah, right, Mr. Jack," Willow said, her perception way beyond her six years. "You like Miss Emma. Daddy told us so."

Granger shushed his daughter. "I told you it was a secret. That means you're not supposed to repeat it."

Willow looked proud of herself.

"Well, I like Miss Emma," Jack said. "But we're just friends."

Emma walked up behind him as he squatted to the girls' level. "That's exactly right," she agreed. "Good friends."

Jack straightened and turned to face her. "I thought you'd come back out the café door."

"I took the long way because I couldn't remember where my toolbox was." She gave him a strange look, her smile still hesitant. She lifted her chin slightly as she met his gaze.

What? They were just friends.

"Daddy says—" Willow started before Granger put a hand over her mouth.

"Daddy says if you want fudge, you better keep his secrets safe." Granger gave a sheepish smile. "Hey, Emma. How are you?"

She nodded. "Good, Granger. And you?"

"Just perfect. Happy belated birthday, by the way," Granger added. "Jack told me."

She slid Jack another look before returning her attention to Granger. "Thank you. I'm twenty-nine and holding."

Jack caught the hint of sadness in her eyes though. If anyone deserved to be happy, it was her. She deserved the world. And her father was probably right. She deserved better than a recovering alcoholic who was the son of a drunk.

Jack hadn't touched a drop of alcohol since he was twenty-one, but for two years before that, he'd gone down a path that he wasn't proud of. And he never intended to follow that path again. He wasn't naïve though. He'd watched his father relapse time and again. Had Amanda relapsed too? Recovery was a house of cards that one strong wind could destroy. Unlike his father though, if Jack ever got knocked down again, he wasn't taking anyone he cared about with him.

* * *

For the second night this week, Emma opened her front door and welcomed Jack inside. Sitting in a home improvement store was one thing. Hanging out at the café with other friends was another. But being alone in her home, just the two of them, was something completely different.

"Barnaby, get down." Emma scolded her little dog because he had immediately latched on to Jack's leg.

Jack didn't seem to mind. He took a moment to pick Barnaby up and lift him eye-to-eye.

"Watch out—" Emma started to warn, but it was too late. Barnaby lapped a tongue across Jack's cheek, leaving a shiny trail of drool. Emma's face contorted into a grimace.

"Whoa, you're a fast one, aren't you?" Jack laughed, and set Barnaby back on the floor.

"He's generous with his kisses," she said like she would to any of her friends. But using the word *kiss* around Jack made the space between them crackle. "Um, the bathroom is down the hall if you want to wash that off. And the bed is in the guest room," she said. "You can take it for as long as you need. I rarely have guests, and if I do, they can take the couch or I'll use the air mattress."

"Thanks, Em." Jack gestured to the bathroom. "I'll just be a quick second and meet you in the guest room."

She nodded and headed down the hall without him. A moment later, he appeared in the doorway.

"I can help you load it onto your truck if you want," she offered.

"Nah. I can get it."

She tilted her head. "I'm not sure how you survive with

all that alpha-ness going to your head. But fine. I'll go get dinner started."

"I get dinner too?" he asked, a light shining behind his eyes.

Her lips parted. That wasn't intended to be an invitation. Her plan was to get rid of him as soon as possible. "Well, what I have isn't much. Just a frozen pizza."

"Sounds perfect. You promised me lemonade at the café, but we got distracted," he pointed out.

Well, she guessed that was true enough. "I have lemonade in the fridge."

"I'll load the bed, and then we'll have pizza and lemonade. Maybe you can help me figure out what to do with Sam while he's here. And I can help you with that box I brought you this morning."

She hesitated. "I might need something stronger than lemonade for that."

"I'll stick to the lemonade," he said.

Something pulled in her gut the way it sometimes did when she was with Jack. Once upon a time, he'd enjoyed a beer or two, or even more than that. Then he'd casually started saying he wasn't in the mood. He'd order a soda instead or offer to be the designated driver. She hadn't thought anything of it at first, but after a while, she'd started to wonder. Why didn't Jack drink anymore? He hadn't just cut back. He'd stopped altogether.

"Pizza will be ready in twenty minutes," she said, turning away. "Let me know if you change your mind and decide to let me help."

He chuckled behind her. "Let me know when the food is ready, and I'll head to the table."

Emma walked into the kitchen, surprised that her dog chose to stay with Jack. *Traitor.* Then she got to work preparing dinner. She'd almost forgotten Jack was even here until he walked past her to the sink and washed his hands.

"Smells good, and I have to admit, I'm starving," he said.

An awareness buzzed through her. Through the window, she could see that the sun was down and it was dark outside. Fireflies started twinkling in the air, lighting up just like her own body when Jack was in proximity.

"Want me to pour you that glass of wine?" he asked, opening her fridge door.

"That'd be great. Sure you won't have a glass?"

"No, thanks. I've been dreaming of that lemonade for the last hour and a half."

"It's in the glass pitcher. Help yourself."

She pulled the pizza out of the oven and then grabbed some dishes from the cabinet. They both worked together to get the food and drinks on the table and then sat down.

She took a bite of her pizza, careful not to let the cheese string messily.

From the corner of her eye, she saw Jack lift a piece of pizza to his mouth too. "Kind of feels like a date, doesn't it?" he asked.

She coughed and then choked on her bite of pizza. "What?" she said when she could finally breathe again.

He looked at her with momentary concern as she reached for her glass of wine. "I just mean it feels that way. Not that it is."

She had difficulty taking in a full breath. "Why would it feel that way? We've eaten dinner before."

He shrugged broad shoulders. "I don't know. Honestly, it's been so long since I've been out with a woman, I don't even know what a date feels like anymore." He chuckled to himself.

"Me either."

Jack looked at her for a long second as if he might say something more. Why had he stood her up for prom, just when they were getting close? Why had he never shown interest in her ever again? She'd been halfway to being in love with him, and her senior prom was going to be the best night of her life. Instead, it'd been one of the worst.

His cell phone rang, and Barnaby pounced toward the noise, barking loudly. One shush from Emma silenced him. Jack chuckled as he shifted to pull the phone out of his pocket and glanced at the screen. "It's my sister. I better take this."

Emma nodded, relieved when he stepped away from the table. She closed her eyes for a long moment. Jack wasn't into her that way. The way she was into him. She was thirty years old. It was time for her to move on.

Barnaby announced Jack's presence as he stepped back into the room. "Hey, I'm sorry, Em. I have to go."

"Is Amanda okay?" she asked. She could already tell by the look on his face that she wasn't.

"I don't think so. She needs me to come get Sam tonight. It's a two-hour drive so I better get going."

Emma frowned. "That's four hours round trip. You'll be driving through the night. Can't this wait until tomorrow?"

Jack shook his head. "Amanda is addicted to a prescription drug she was on last year. She's trying to come off it, but she's having withdrawal symptoms. A friend of hers is going to stay with her tonight and drive her to a substance abuse facility tomorrow. But she doesn't want Sam to see her like this."

Emma took a breath. "Poor Amanda. Poor Sam...I'm coming with you." She pushed back from the table.

Jack looked surprised by her offer. "You don't have to do that. Barnaby needs you here, and I'll be fine."

"I'm sure you will. But just in case you're not, I'll be there." She grabbed her purse and headed toward the door, not giving him time to argue or herself time to second-guess. Barnaby followed behind her, apparently set on coming as well. "That's what friends do," Emma called over her shoulder.

CHAPTER FOUR

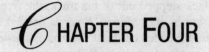

*J*ack wasn't sure what kind of help Emma thought she was giving him right now. She'd fallen asleep thirty minutes after leaving Sweetwater Springs, with Barnaby snoring softly in her lap, and hadn't stirred in the almost two hours since.

He chuckled to himself and sang along to country music on the radio. If Emma were awake, she'd protest. She was a girl who liked her soft rock.

Turning onto his sister's road, his good mood belly flopped as he pondered the reason he was in his truck. Amanda had followed their family's pattern of addiction. Jack understood why she wouldn't want Sam to know. Jack's perception of his father had changed as he grew up, watching him get drunk night after night. His father, who had once been a hero in Jack's eyes, was now just a guy who could keep it together long enough to make it to work sober. Soon as he left his job, it was him and the bottle. Nothing and no one else mattered, including his family.

Jack's foot lifted off the gas pedal, slowing and giving himself a chance to collect himself. He pulled into the driveway and glanced across the seat at Emma. She didn't move. As Jack stepped out of the truck, the front door of his sister's house opened, and Amanda headed down the steps to meet him. He could tell she was exhausted just by the way she carried herself, hands hanging at her sides and her feet dragging as she walked slowly toward him.

"Thanks for coming," she said in a barely audible voice.

Jack gave her a once-over. "You okay?"

She nodded, although she looked pale and shaky. Her eyes were bloodshot, and there were dark shadows underscoring and competing with their blue color. "I will be. Sam thinks I have the flu and that I don't want him to catch it."

Jack frowned. "It's not flu season."

"He's fifteen years old. His brain is too busy thinking about girls than whether his mother is telling the truth." She laughed softly. "I told him I'm going away with my boyfriend once I'm feeling better."

"Boyfriend?" Jack asked.

She held up a hand. "It's not the time for the overprotective brother act," she said wearily. "Sam is looking forward to staying with you on the lake."

Jack was looking forward to that as well, even though he wasn't thrilled about the reason. "Are you sure you'll be okay tonight?"

Amanda nodded. "My friend is inside. As soon as the doors open at the addiction facility tomorrow, she'll drive me there and I'll check myself in. I don't want to be like this. I want to be a good mom for my son."

"I have no doubt that you are."

"Thank you, Jackie." Amanda gave him a hug and then

gasped softly as she looked past him at the passenger seat of his truck. She pulled back to look at him. "Is that Emma St. James?"

"The one and only."

She covered her mouth with one hand, her eyes gone wide as she looked at him again. "I always knew you two would get together. It's about time."

"Actually, Emma just came along to make sure I didn't fall asleep at the wheel." He chuckled. "Good thing she wasn't driving."

Amanda's color seemed to improve. Even her posture was more upright. "This is awesome. I honestly felt kind of bad putting Sam on your plate. I mean, I don't want to cramp your bachelor's lifestyle."

He scoffed at that idea. "Oh, yeah. I'll have to cut back on the nightly parties I throw at the cabin," he said sarcastically.

She laughed quietly. "I am so proud of you, Jack. You have your life together, and you're finally with someone who will make you happy. That's incredible considering where we came from."

Had she not heard him when he told her he and Emma weren't a couple? "Emma and I were having dinner when you called. She wanted to come along and help," he said, trying to paint a clearer picture.

Amanda gestured at the passenger seat. "This gives me hope that you and I can be more than our pasts. That history isn't destined to repeat itself."

Jack frowned as he pulled back to get a better look at his sister. "Of course it isn't. Is that what you thought? That what's happening to you is because of Dad? You're not like him, Amanda. The doctors prescribed you pain medication that you needed at the time. Things may have gotten a little out of hand, but it's not your fault and you're getting help. So, no, history isn't destined to repeat itself."

Her eyes grew shiny as she listened. Then she looked down at her feet for a long moment. He hoped she wasn't crying. "Sam's not easy," she finally said, looking up again. Her eyes were dry. "He'll try to get away with things."

"I don't want you worrying about anything except feeling better, okay? Sam will be fine with me."

"With you and Emma," she said. Then her smile fell away, and she looked like she might get sick.

"Amanda? You okay?"

She waved off his concern with a hand. "Not really. I'll just tell Sam that you're here." She turned and headed back toward the house, leaving Jack standing at his truck. He glanced back at Emma, sleeping peacefully with her face pressed against the window. His heart squeezed, almost painfully.

"Hey, Uncle Jack." Sam came out of the house, carrying an overnight bag on each shoulder.

"Hey, bud. Where's your mom?" Jack asked.

Sam shrugged lanky shoulders. "Tossing cookies in the toilet. She's got the flu."

Jack looked down at his feet. "Yeah, she told me." He took Sam's bags and put them in the back seat. "Sorry to make you sit in the back. I don't want to wake Sleeping Beauty and her tiny beast over there."

Sam grinned, revealing a mouthful of braces. He still had that awkward look that Jack remembered from the last time he'd seen his nephew. The one teens got when they were still growing into their bodies. "Is that the coffee shop lady?"

"Yeah. Emma."

Sam climbed into the back seat and shut the door behind him. Jack got behind the wheel.

"I remember you flirting with her when I came to visit at Christmas. So she's your girlfriend now?"

Jack looked at Sam in the rearview mirror. "Where would you get that idea?"

"Mom said you had your girlfriend in the truck and that I shouldn't wake her."

Jack focused his gaze forward. If he corrected his nephew, Sam would correct Amanda next time they were on the phone together. For some reason, Jack's sister said it gave her hope to see him and Emma together. He couldn't just snatch that hope away from someone who seemed to be in short supply, could he?

Sam stirred quietly in the back seat. "Mom has been seeing someone too, you know."

"Yeah? Do you like him?" Jack asked.

Sam grunted. "I guess so. He's the reason I can't go home once her flu is gone. He wants my mom for himself and probably wants me out of the way."

Jack wished he could set Sam straight. It wasn't Jack's story to tell though. If Amanda wanted Sam to have a care-free summer, then that's what Jack would give him. "Your mom would never choose a boyfriend over you."

"Well, she kind of did. Anyway, she'll still be running my life even with two hours between us. She told me I had to check in with her every day and tell her every detail of what's going on. So in a way, I guess she'll be running your life too."

Jack felt an uneasiness in his stomach. "I wouldn't be surprised if your mom planted a nanny cam somewhere inside your bags." He was only half joking. "She doesn't need to worry. I plan to be on my best behavior."

He remembered what Amanda had said about Sam trying to get away with things. "And I expect the same from you."

* * *

Emma was wide awake, even though it was three a.m. That was partly because she'd taken a long nap all the way to pick up Sam and all the way back. She didn't wake up until Jack nudged her.

"Are we there yet?" she'd asked.

"Been there, got Sam, and came back, Sleeping Beauty," Jack whispered.

She'd had four hours of sleep, and now she was lying in her bed all out of sorts. She sat up and glanced over at Barnaby, who was sleeping in his dog bed below her window. The little dog was such a force to be reckoned with when he was awake, but once he fell asleep, he was practically in a coma. *Must be nice.* She draped her legs over the bed with a restless sigh and decided to get up, which was just crazy. This would make for an incredibly long day at the café.

She wandered around her house and thought about cleaning, but *nah*. She considered turning on the television or maybe reading a book. Then her gaze fell on the box that Jack had brought her yesterday. The one she still hadn't opened. The one that read JENNY'S THINGS.

She stepped toward it and, without letting herself think, started peeling off the tape that held the lid in place. Inside she saw that there were only a few things that barely filled the box. She reached in and pulled out a bandana with huge, pink magnolia flowers printed all over it. A memory flashed of her mom wearing it. She'd worn a lot of bandanas when she was in treatment, but this was her favorite. Her mom had loved bright colors, and she'd also adored flowers. Emma reached for the next item, a blue and pink jersey tank with white letters that spelled out JENNY on the back.

Emma tried and failed to remember what this was for. Her mom had loved to run. She'd done dozens of 5K races, loving a good cause as much as she did an excuse to put on her running shoes.

Emma ran her fingers over the white letters of her mom's name. It'd been a while since she'd remembered her mom as healthy, vibrant, and full of energy. Emma's eyes burned as tears threatened. She folded the jersey and placed it on the table beside the box and reached inside for the last item: a handwritten note. Or actually, it was more of a list. There was writing on the top of the page, followed by a series of starred items, some with tiny check marks beside them and some without.

Emma sucked in a breath and started reading.

My best friend Deb Hershey is sitting beside me, forcing me at nail file point to write this list. She says everyone needs a list of things to do before you die… even if you plan on living forever.

I got diagnosed with cancer today. This is my Life List.

Goose bumps rose on Emma's body. She sucked in an audible breath as she imagined her mom and Jack's mom huddled together while creating this list. She remembered the night her mom had first gotten diagnosed. That night, her mom had gone to see Deb, and Emma had come along. She and Jack had sat on the back porch, and Emma had cried while he listened to all her worst fears. That must have been when this list was written.

Emma blinked past the sting in her eyes and continued to read the items.

Run a marathon ✓
Swim across Silver Lake ✓
Fall in love with my husband all over again ✓
Be my own best friend ✓

A half dozen checked items followed on the list, ending with three that were left unchecked:

Start my own 5K
Save a life
Leave something wonderful behind when I die (50 years from now)

Emma reread the unchecked items, her heart reverberating with a deep ache. Her mother would never finish what she started. It seemed so wrong. Everything suddenly seemed wrong. And there was only one way to make it right. She had to finish her mother's Life List.

* * *

Emma was still thinking about the box and the items inside when she opened the café a couple hours later. She was thankful for the endless customers who seemed to file in and out. When the crowd finally lulled, Nina stepped over while preparing an order.

"I tried to call you last night," Nina said.

Emma poured a coffee for the customer she was serving and went to grab the creamer. "Oh, sorry I missed your call. Something came up."

Nina gave her a questioning glance as she made a cappuccino for the next customer in line. "Like what? A date?"

Emma scoffed. "When would I have had time to meet someone and plan a date without telling you first?"

Emma carried the drink back to her customer, an older woman, who offered her a debit card. She wasn't familiar with this customer, which made her wonder if she was the one who'd left her a poor review earlier this week. Well, if she was, there were two new tables in front of the shop to drink coffee, thanks to Jack's help.

Emma lifted her gaze to look out the window as she swiped the woman's card. Both tables out front were occupied, along with every seat in the café. Her smile faltered as she handed the card back to her customer. "I just added new seating, but it looks like it's full this morning too. I'm so sorry for the inconvenience. I'll be adding more seating soon." If Halona agreed to have at least one table in front of her flower shop.

The woman smiled sweetly. "It's fine, dear. I'm having mine to go anyway. It's such a beautiful day to walk and window-shop."

Emma relaxed a little bit, but her nerves came back in full force as more customers walked in. Where would they sit? They couldn't all be hoping to window-shop this morning.

Nina cleared her throat, and Emma moved so that she could ring up her customer. As the crowd inside the café died down, Nina headed back over to where Emma was making a shot of espresso. "You're still thinking about that bad review. I can tell."

"Guilty," Emma said without looking up at her friend. "I can't help it." She brought the espresso to her customer and took the payment. Then, with the first break in sight, Emma turned her back to the front of the café and faced Nina. "My mom always said that if you don't have anything nice to say, don't say anything at all."

Nina sighed. "Wouldn't the world be a much nicer place?"

"Speaking of my mom, I opened the box." Emma's hands started shaking just thinking about it.

"Well, what was inside?"

Emma sucked in a deep breath. "Not much. Just my mom's favorite bandana and a running jersey. There was also a list of things my mom wanted to do while she was alive."

"Oh?" Nina's brows lifted. "That sounds interesting. Like a bucket list?"

"Kind of. The list wasn't finished though. I think I want to finish it for my mom." She looked at Nina. "Or at least check off one of the items."

Nina nodded. "What item?"

Emma fidgeted with her hands as she talked. She was nervous and excited about the prospect. "My mom loved to run 5Ks, and she wanted to plan one of her own. I could do that for her. And it could maybe raise money for a good cause."

"You mean like for cancer?" Nina asked.

Emma shrugged. "There's already a group that does that in Sweetwater Springs. One of the unchecked items on the list was to save a life though. A fund-raiser with a good cause might do that."

"I think this is a really cool idea, Em. Maybe you can have your event at Evergreen Park," Nina suggested.

"I was thinking the same thing." Excitement swelled in Emma's chest. "I'll call in a bit and see if that's even a possibility. I want to get started right away."

"Well, let me know if I can help in any way. I'll donate my time and what little extra funds I have. Whatever you need."

Emma smiled at her friend and employee. "Thank you. That means a lot."

The bell at the front door jingled, and Emma sighed. The break was short-lived. She turned to greet Jack as he approached the counter with his nephew.

"Gotta quit meeting like this," he teased, his voice dropping to a low note that resonated in her belly.

"Am I going to have to spend my whole summer watching my uncle Jack flirt with his new girlfriend?" Sam asked.

Emma straightened and looked at Sam, not missing the subtle collective gasp from Nina behind her and Brenna who'd stepped in line behind Jack and Sam.

"What?" Emma asked.

Jack gave her a subtle head shake, his eyes pleading with her not to correct Sam.

"It was bad enough watching him try to catch your eye over Christmas," Sam went on, his bangs falling in his eyes.

Emma's gaze bounced back to Jack. *What in the world is happening this morning?* Emma had fallen asleep in the truck last night. Had she missed suddenly becoming Jack's girlfriend while she dozed?

"Uh, can I get my usual?" Jack asked Emma. "And Sam here wants a flavored coffee."

"I remember that about him," Emma said. Most teens she knew didn't order coffee, but Jack's nephew loved the taste. She always made his a decaf because fifteen-year-olds had enough energy to spare without adding caffeine to the mix.

"Of course you remember his order." Jack winked at her, and Emma heard Nina gasp again.

Nina whispered as they made coffees. "You specifically denied going on a date."

"I didn't have a date," Emma said.

Nina lifted a brow. "Well, maybe you didn't, but Jack sure did."

Emma carried Jack's and Sam's drinks to the checkout and rang them up. "Can I talk to you for a minute?" she asked Jack. "Alone?"

He gave her a sheepish look and then turned to Sam. "You mind staying out here a minute? A table just opened up over there." He pointed to a table against the wall. "You can do whatever it is you always do on that phone of yours."

"I need to text Mom back anyway," Sam said. "She's already nagging me about what I'm doing and who I'm with. I'll tell her I'm here with you and your girlfriend."

* * *

Jack felt like he was walking into the principal's office, which he'd had a lot of experience with growing up. He hadn't necessarily been a bad kid. It'd just taken a little extra persuasion to get him to follow the rules.

"What's going on?" Emma turned to face him, her cheeks flush against her ivory skin.

"Well," he said, feeling his lips stretch into a slight grimace. Guilt curled in his stomach because he'd brought her in the middle of this without her permission. And now he was going to make an inconvenient request. "My sister kind of got the impression that you and I are dating."

Her eyes widened. "What? Why would she think that?"

"Well, you were in my truck with me. At night. I told her that we were eating dinner when she called, and she just assumed, I guess." He scratched an invisible itch on the side of his jaw, looking for something to do with his hands.

"And you didn't correct her?" she asked, her voice rising an octave.

Jack held out his palms. "I did, but when Amanda gets something in her head, she doesn't listen. Then she said seeing you and me together gave her hope that she can be happy one day too. I want her to believe that. Especially now."

Emma nodded, even though she still looked like she might start yelling at him. "You were protecting her, just like you always have," she said quietly.

Jack needed Emma to understand his reasons behind what he'd led Amanda to believe. "Stress isn't good for Amanda right now. Not while she's in treatment. I thought I'd wait to tell her the truth about us until she's a little better."

"So you want me to pretend to date you for the whole town?"

"Not the whole town. Just Sam. If I tell him the truth, he'll want to know why I'm protecting his mom. He thinks Amanda is spending time with her boyfriend once she kicks the flu."

Emma drew a hand to her forehead. "I don't know, Jack. This seems messy. And Sam has already told people."

"We'll correct Brenna and Nina, and stop the rumor in

its tracks. Sam doesn't know anyone here, not really. This charade will just be for him, I promise."

Emma stared at him.

Jack needed her to say yes. For Amanda's sake. "I'm sorry I got you into this, but I'll make it up to you, I promise."

She lifted a brow. "How? A lifetime of Hershey's Kisses?" she said in a teasing tone.

"You already have that if you want it. What else do you want?"

She shook her head. "There's nothing I really want."

"Of course you do, Em. Everyone does."

Nina stepped into the room and cleared her throat. "She wants to organize a 5K."

Both Emma and Jack whirled to face Nina.

Nina held up a hand. "Don't worry. I'll keep your little secret safe."

"You were eavesdropping on us?" Jack asked.

"Of course I was. I had to see if what Sam said was true. And for the record, Brenna has already left the café, and she's probably called Luke by now. He's probably told the guys at the fire station, who've texted the news to their girlfriends, who are on the phone with their moms as we speak." Nina offered a satisfied smile.

Emma drew both of her hands to her forehead. "Oh no."

Jack tried not to take offense. "Would it be so bad if people thought we were dating?"

She looked up at him, and for some reason, he thought he saw hurt flash in her eyes. She'd wanted to date him once, and he'd broken her heart and her trust. He'd almost lost her friendship as well.

"Nina's right. I do want to organize a 5K. And I want to have it at Evergreen Park."

"It's July. The park is already booked for the summer,"

he said. "I can get you on the approved list for next year maybe, if I pull a few strings."

Emma frowned. "I was hoping for something this year."

Jack hated to disappoint Emma. "It's hard to say no to you. Always has been."

Emma stared at him a long moment. Then she looked at Nina. "If you're back here, who's watching the counter?"

Nina grimaced. "Sorry. I'll go do that." She disappeared back toward the front, leaving Jack and Emma alone once more.

Emma turned to face Jack. "I'll make a deal with you. I'll pretend to date you when we're with Sam if you'll find a way to get me on the schedule at Evergreen Park this summer."

He ran a hand through his hair. "You don't have to pretend. I'll get you on the schedule regardless."

"No, I want to." She nibbled on her lower lip. "And since you're my new boyfriend, maybe you can also help me organize the event too."

He chuckled under his breath. "Never guessed you'd be such a demanding girlfriend," he teased.

"And we're only just getting started."

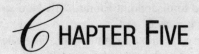

CHAPTER FIVE

What am I doing? "I can't do this. I've never planned an event before in my life."

Nina rolled her eyes at Emma as she wiped down the front counter. "No, but you run a café every day. It'll be fine. You can get that event planner who's always in here to help."

"Claire Donovan. Yes," Emma said. "Good idea." Her smile faltered. "Except it's wedding season. Claire is probably all booked up and has more on her to-do list than she can manage."

"She can still give you some tips. Relax. Take some deep breaths," Nina said.

Emma did just that. "Okay. I can do this."

"Yes, you can." Nina came and stood beside her. The café was quiet right now, which was welcome. "So Jack, huh?"

Emma felt her cheeks burn. "You heard us. It's just pretend."

"I thought I was your friend," Nina said, feigning insult. "I know better than to think you and Jack are just putting on a show." She narrowed her eyes, and it felt like she was looking straight through Emma. "Or maybe I know better, but you don't."

Emma shook her head. "You're not making any sense."

"Don't tell me you haven't thought about it. You two have crazy chemistry. I've been waiting for you guys to get together since my first day working here."

Emma sighed. "Well, keep waiting because that's never going to happen."

"Why not?"

"Because we're friends."

"So there's never been anything more? Not even once?" Nina pressed.

Emma looked away. There had been something once. Or so she thought. "This thing between us is temporary. I'll suffer through people thinking it's real, but at least I have you to vent to."

Nina put a hand on her shoulder. "Anytime. But I'm looking forward to the good details. Like what kind of a kisser he is."

Emma drew back as she returned her gaze to her friend. "I'm not going to kiss him."

"But . . . you're his pretend girlfriend. It's not believable if you don't kiss," Nina pointed out.

Emma hadn't thought of that. The thought excited her as much as it terrified her. She and Jack couldn't kiss. That would open a can of worms they didn't need, especially this summer when she was planning a 5K event that she hoped would be an annual thing. And Jack was caring for his nephew. They both had too much on their plates for kissing, real or pretend.

"Well, if you don't kiss, I for one will be disappointed."

Emma laughed, her gaze catching on her father as he

strolled in front of the café window. She pulled off her apron. "Do you mind if I visit with my dad?"

"And tell him about your new boyfriend?" Nina raised a brow, a teasing grin spreading across her face.

"No. I want to tell him about the race," Emma corrected, feeling a little burst of adrenaline. The more she envisioned the event, the more excited she got.

"Sure. I'll make the drinks," Nina offered. "I already know what you two want so go ahead and get settled."

"Thanks." Emma waved as her dad walked inside the café. She stepped over to him and went up on her tiptoes to kiss his cheek. "Hi, Dad. Do you have time to visit?"

He looked around the café with a nod. "I was hoping you'd be free."

"It's slowed down since this morning. And I can always spare time for you."

His eyes crinkled behind his thick-rimmed glasses as he smiled. "Good."

They moved to a table against the wall and sat down. Almost immediately, Nina slid two coffees and a plate of cookies in front of them.

Emma gave her a grateful smile. When Nina left, Emma looked back at her dad. "What brings you by?"

"Just wanted to make sure you had a good birthday."

She wondered if he realized how hard this one had been for her, given that she was the same age her mom had been when she'd died. He probably hadn't even put two and two together. "It was quiet."

"I thought you went out with friends."

Right. "I had a change of plans. One friend stopped by, and I had chocolate for the occasion."

Her father nodded. "Angel will make you a cake, and we'll put thirty candles on top. How does that sound?"

Emma forced a stiff smile at the mention of her stepmom. "Sounds nice." She rolled her lips together, wondering if now was a good time to tell him about the event she had decided to have. "Dad?"

He bit into a cookie and looked up. "Hmm?"

"I'm planning something. For Mom."

She watched the brightness of his blue eyes dull just a touch. "Oh? What do you mean?"

"Well, I found this list of hers. Deb Hershey had it in a box along with a couple of other things that belonged to Mom. She sent them to me this week." Emma left out the fact that Deb had sent them by way of Jack. "Did you know that Mom wanted to plan her own 5K?"

Her father's brow scrunched as he seemed to search his memory. "I remember her mentioning something about that. But it wasn't really practical at the time, with her being sick."

Emma nodded. "Well, I've decided that I'm going to do it for her." A surge of pride zipped through her.

Her father's brows dipped. "Sounds like a lot of work to me, sweetheart."

His lack of a positive response stung a little. "But worthwhile. It was something she wanted to do and never got a chance to. So I'm going to do it in her honor. I want to remind people that she was here," Emma added, remembering the unchecked item on the list about leaving something wonderful behind. This event could serve that purpose too.

Her father didn't look convinced. "You don't need to remind me that she was here. I remember her every time I look at you. You're the spitting image of your mother."

Emma looked down at the cookie in her hand. She and

her mom had the same hair and eyes, the same oval-shaped face and apple cheekbones. The resemblance was uncanny if you looked at photographs of them at the same age. "Will you walk for her? Or run?"

He smiled now. "Of course I will. Just tell me when and where."

"This summer. Evergreen Park."

"Evergreen Park?" her dad asked, his eyes narrowing. "How'd you manage to get booked there so soon?"

Emma shrugged a shoulder. "Lucky, I guess." Now wasn't the time to jump topics, especially since she knew how her father felt about Jack.

He took another bite of his cookie. "I'll talk to Angel about participating too."

"Great," Emma said with waning enthusiasm.

A few customers pushed through the front entrance, and she took that as her cue to stand. "Well, I better get back to work. A café owner's job is never done. But thank you for stopping in. It's always good to see you, Dad." She dipped and kissed his cheek.

"You too. Don't forget to tell me when you're available," he reminded her. "For cake and thirty candles."

"I will." Emma waved and walked back behind the counter. Well, Jack was working on booking Evergreen Park, and she'd just gotten her first participant. Two, if she counted Angel. That made it official. The event was definitely happening, and it was going to be amazing.

* * *

Jack slid his gaze over to his nephew, who'd been sitting on a bench and looking at his cell phone for the last hour. The phone was doing a better job of babysitting than he was.

Not that Sam was a baby. He was practically grown. Even so, Jack felt like he was failing this new job that Amanda had trusted him to do.

Jack returned his gaze to the calendar in front of him, which didn't make him feel any better about this whole situation. He'd made a deal with Emma to get her event on the schedule at the park, and all the Saturdays and Sundays were full.

He couldn't rightly cancel any of the bookings, and he doubted Emma wanted to do her 5K on a random weekday. He sighed and massaged his forehead, glancing back up at Sam who was still hunched over his phone and tapping his fingers rapidly on the screen.

"Girlfriend?" Jack asked.

Sam lifted his head. "No, just friends. They're not happy that I've left for the summer. I'm not all that thrilled either," he said. "Don't get me wrong, Uncle Jack, but this isn't really the hip place to be."

Jack sympathized. Even though Sam lived in a small town, he was only a short walk from city life. He had the best of both worlds at his teenaged fingertips. Sweetwater Springs didn't have that benefit. "It's not forever. Try to make the best of it."

Sam wasn't impressed with Jack's advice. "So I'm just going to be stuck here in this office, watching you work?"

"I do more than sit in this office." As if to prove a point, Jack stood. Obviously, the calendar wasn't going to change right in front of his eyes anyway. "Let's go."

Sam straightened, dropping his cell phone into his lap. "Where?"

"I need to patrol the woods," Jack told him. "I've had a squatter lately that I'm trying to find."

Sam stood as well and shoved his phone in his pocket. "What will you do if you find him? Arrest him?"

Jack chuckled. "They don't give cuffs to park rangers."

Sam looked disappointed. "Then what?"

"Well, I'll talk with the guy."

"Or the woman," Sam pointed out, following him to the front exit.

"Or the woman. And if I need to, I'll have the chief of police talk to him. Or her."

Sam followed him to the outbuilding holding ranger equipment. "Do I get to drive one of these today? Because that would make this job a lot more fun."

Jack shook his head, deciding on the ATV today. It wasn't as smooth a ride as the truck, but it would definitely add a little excitement to Sam's day. "Maybe next time. Take notes."

Once Sam had climbed on beside him, Jack set off down a trail and through the woods, driving for an hour before returning to the office.

"Hungry?" Jack asked, parking under the shelter.

"Starving. You forgot to feed me breakfast."

"Ah, geez." Jack shook his head. "I thought you were old enough to feed yourself."

Sam shrugged. "I didn't want to go through your stuff."

"You'll be at the cabin with me for a while, and if you expect to eat, you need to feel free to help yourself to my fridge."

"The beer too?" Sam asked as Jack pulled his truck keys out of his pocket and headed to his Toyota.

"I don't keep beer. Also, you're too young to even think about drinking." He glanced over, wondering if Sam had overheard him talking with Amanda about his past with alcohol. He didn't think Sam was baiting him. He wasn't that kind of kid. He was easygoing and friendly, and he deserved the best summer that Jack could offer. Which meant Jack needed to do better than this.

The best he could do right now was Joe's Pizzeria on Red Oak Street.

Jack climbed into the driver's seat as Sam hopped in on the passenger side. Jack had to carry most of the conversation as he drove because Sam was looking at his phone.

"So your mom has a boyfriend?"

"Reginald."

Jack looked over. "That's a name you don't hear too often. What's he do?"

"He drives an eighteen-wheeler," Sam said. "He's gone for several days, and then he's home."

"Home?" Jack looked over. "As in, home with you two? He lives in the house?"

Sam laughed. "Come on, Uncle Jack. They're adults. I'm sure Emma stays over with you all the time too. She doesn't have to stay away on my account, you know."

Jack wasn't sure what to say. He didn't want to lie, but he'd always been the overprotective brother. Amanda needed her health, and Sam needed his mom. "Noted," Jack said simply.

He pulled into the parking lot of the pizzeria, recognizing his buddy Granger's vehicle parked nearby. Hopefully he hadn't had his lunch yet. Then Jack could grab a table with him and at least have someone to help carry the conversation.

They headed into the dimly lit pizza parlor, laden with the aroma of Italian spices and pasta. Jack let his gaze roam around the room, and sure enough, Granger was sitting alone with an open menu.

"Come on, buddy," Jack told Sam. "I see a friend of mine."

Granger looked up as they approached the table. "Hey, guys. Is this Sam?" Granger asked.

Sam looked between them. "How do you know my name?"

Granger chuckled. "Your uncle is very proud of you. Want to join me?"

"I was hoping you'd offer." Jack plopped down in the booth next to his friend and gestured for Sam to take the bench. "Sam is staying with me for a while."

"Dude, that's bad luck," Granger told Sam in a teasing tone. Sam nodded in agreement, but Jack didn't think he was joking.

"What kind of job do you have?" Sam asked, grabbing a piece of bread from the complimentary basket that the waitress had laid at the center of the table.

Granger grinned. "I own a tree farm."

Jack slapped a hand on his back. "And if you get too bored with me, I'm sure Granger can put you to work."

Sam pulled back. "Seriously. Mom said I was going to have fun while I was here."

The guys laughed. When the waitress came to take their orders, they ordered an extra-large pizza pie to split.

"I'll have a Bud Light," Granger said.

The waitress nodded, took Sam's order, and then looked at Jack. "And for you?"

"Just a lemonade. I'm on the job," Jack explained.

Granger looked at him. "I am too."

Jack ignored his friend. "Just a lemonade," he told the waitress. He didn't need to explain himself. Granger had known him long enough to know he didn't drink anymore, but Granger had never asked why. Jack guessed most of his friends assumed it was because of his dad.

"So," Granger said, "Sophie Daniels was talking about you the other day in the Ladies' Day Out group."

The Ladies' Day Out group, or the LDO, was a club in town that served to get the local women in the community together for the sole purpose of having fun. Jack had often wished there was a similar group for men.

"Oh yeah?" Sophie owned a boutique on Main Street. She'd flirted with Jack before, and he had reciprocated, but it'd never gone any further than that.

Granger grinned. "The women were encouraging her to spend some time at Evergreen Park to get your attention."

"How would you even know this?" Jack asked on a laugh.

"My mom is in the group," Granger said. "What happens in the group stays in the group, except my mom has never been one to keep a tight lip."

Jack chuckled as the waitress returned and slid a drink in front of each of them. "Your pizza will be out in a moment," she said before walking to the next table.

Granger reached for his bottle. "So? If Sophie were to show up on one of your trails, what would you do?"

Jack chuckled to himself. "I have no idea."

Sam made a noise, and both men seemed to remember that he was even there. "Whoa. Uncle Jack, you wouldn't cheat on Emma, would you?"

Granger looked at Jack with a curious expression. "Cheat on Emma?"

Jack grimaced and looked over at Sam. "No, of course I wouldn't. I was just joking with Granger. I would never cheat on Emma."

Granger nearly choked on his sip of beer.

Yeah, Jack could tell he was going to have a lot of explaining to do this summer.

* * *

The next day, Emma sat outside her café at one of her new tables. The weather was gorgeous, the café was slow, and she had two employees working the counter. She, on the other hand, needed to get started on her to-do list for the 5K race.

She made a numbered list and started writing all the things she needed to handle ASAP. She needed to make up flyers to hang around town and in the café and possibly start a simple website where people could go to register. There would have to be T-shirts for people to wear to give the event a unified look as well. Maybe she could get Paris Montgomery to design the graphic and have the Print Shop complete the T-shirt order.

Emma clicked her pen and stared off into space trying to think of any other important issues. She wanted to keep the event simple this first year, and she'd have to anyway because she wasn't a planner and time was limited.

"Mind if I join you?" someone asked, snapping Emma out of her thought bubble. Mayor Everson rolled his wheelchair in front of her, wearing a collared polo shirt and some nice pants. He'd been a prominent member of the community even before becoming the mayor of Sweetwater Springs. The Everson family was wealthy and contributed that wealth to a lot of community events. Brian was the only one to really get his "hands dirty" by actually working. He and his wife, Jessica, organized a lot of the charities in addition to donating their money.

"Mayor Everson," Emma said in way of greeting.

He cleared his throat as he rolled his wheelchair under her table.

"Sorry. Brian. It's hard not to give you the respect you

deserve. Even if we went to school together and I know all your secrets."

He chuckled softly. "Haven't you learned? A politician has no secrets. Soon as you decide to run, all those bones are dug up."

"Not that you ever had any," Emma pointed out. "I just know about all the girls you've kissed and hearts you've broken before Jessica came along."

He grimaced. "And some broke mine."

Brian Everson had been a high school track star. Emma remembered that the girls had loved him and the guys had wanted to be him. The accident that had left him paralyzed in his senior year had brought his Olympic dreams crashing down around him. Even so, he'd risen above his circumstances and was now the town's head and heart.

"Are you here for a coffee?" Emma asked, setting her pen down. "I can go inside and whip something up for you."

"No. Looks like you're not working right now anyway."

"A café owner is always working," she corrected.

"I just saw you sitting out here, and I thought I'd say hello." He looked out on Main Street. "I like these new tables you've added. It's a nice spot to sit and watch the goings-on." He looked at her again. "Of course, I'm guessing you want only paying customers to sit here and do that."

She lifted a shoulder. "That would be best. I added the chairs because of a bad review on the A-List website," she admitted. "The review said that I didn't offer enough seating to actually sit and enjoy a cup of coffee." She still hated the thought of that review lingering in cyberspace and deterring potential customers from trying out her café.

He shifted around in his wheelchair, seemingly trying to

get comfortable. "I've grown a thick shell over the years. In my job, negative feedback is inevitable."

Emma watched a mother and child stroll by holding hands. And then a man walking his young puppy on a leash. "I have a soft shell, and my heart is exposed."

He narrowed his eyes as he leaned in to whisper, "Politics would eat you alive."

They both laughed.

"Good thing I have no intention of running for any kind of office," she said.

They sat awhile longer and chatted about the various things Brian had going on.

"I'm working on a new charity myself," Emma disclosed, after Brian updated her on his Mentor Match program. "This summer will be the first year. I'm still working out the details, but I'm all ears if you have advice."

Brian leaned back in his chair as he listened. "Jenny's Wellness Walk for Women. I like the sound of that," he said. "That's inspiring."

"But it's open to men and women, of course. Children too." Emma watched another person stroll by walking their dog. "And dogs. Anyone who can walk." As soon as she said it, all of the blood in her body flooded her cheeks. Her gaze dropped to Brian's wheelchair. "I can't believe I just said that."

"Relax. I'm not offended," he said easily. "You wouldn't believe how often someone says something like that and then thinks that I'm going to banish them from town. Thick shell, remember? Plus, I don't have banishment power. I'm working on that," he joked with a wink.

She nodded and released a pent-up breath. "My event is open to everyone," she amended. "I was thinking that people would pay twenty dollars to walk and that would also cover the cost of their T-shirt. The trail that borders Silver Lake through Evergreen Park stretches a few miles."

"You'll need watering stations for the walkers and runners. That costs money," Brian pointed out.

Emma picked up her pen and wrote that down. Then he pointed out a few more items that she added to her list. As she wrote, her heart began to sink. "That won't leave much money left to donate to whatever cause I decide on."

"You'd be surprised," Brian said. "Get some of the local businesses to be sponsors. I'll be one. Also add a place for donations on your website too. People are generous in Sweetwater Springs."

She continued to write. "Wow. Thank you for all the advice."

"Of course." Brian grinned back at her. "I'm sure Jessica would love to help. She has a lot of connections. I'm impressed that you're putting together something like this so fast. And shocked that you were able to book the park. That's no easy feat."

Emma pulled her lower lip between her teeth. "I have connections too," she admitted. And she had kind of traded her singlehood for the summer in order to make this happen. Although there were worse things than pretending to be Jack's girlfriend.

Brian rolled his wheelchair away from the table and slid the pair of sunglasses that were sitting on the top of his head over his eyes.

"Are you sure you don't want a coffee?" Emma asked. "It's the least I can do after all your helpful suggestions."

"No, thanks. Another time. I'll see you later, Emma." He waved and then continued down the sidewalk, leaving her with a bounty of new ideas and thoughts percolating in her brain. If she kept this event simple, she'd be able to pull it off. And in the process, she'd be able to help the community in her mom's name. Everything was falling into place.

Her cell phone rang, and she looked down at the number on her screen, immediately recognizing it as the Women's Wellness Center. They were probably calling to reschedule that annual checkup that she'd canceled.

Emma sat frozen, watching the screen until the call ended. She would reschedule. Of course she would. But not today. Today she was too busy planning something amazing.

CHAPTER SIX

Jack was back to staring at the calendar. He'd returned to it several times, only to come to the same conclusion: There were no openings in the schedule for Emma's 5K event. "Emma is going to kill me," he muttered under his breath as he ran a hand through his hair and tugged softly on its roots. He definitely felt like pulling his hair out at the moment.

"Got anything for me to do?" Sam asked, looking up from his cell phone. His teenaged body, tall and lanky, hunched forward over his device, shoulders rounded and his scrolling thumb primed to keep swiping up on his screen.

Jack started to shake his head and then reconsidered. "Yeah. Step over here for a moment." He waited until Sam was standing right beside him and then gestured at the calendar. "I promised Emma that I'd get her 5K on the park's schedule this summer. But look."

Sam took a moment to run his gaze over Jack's

handwritten notes in the large square blocks of his desk calendar. There wasn't one empty weekend block. Not even a section of white space in those squares to add something new. "Looks full," Sam said.

Jack massaged his forehead where a headache was wrapping its way around his brain. "That's my dilemma. Emma needs a spot, and I don't have one for her." Jack looked up at his nephew who looked so much like Amanda.

"Mom says you should never make promises you can't keep." Sam blew a bubble with his gum, making it pop loudly.

The sound penetrated through Jack's brain. "I was desperate."

"For what?" Sam continued to chew on his gum.

Right. Jack couldn't disclose his arrangement with Emma to Sam. "Doesn't matter," Jack said. "Emma and I had a deal, and now it'll be called off because I can't keep my end of the bargain."

Sam leaned farther in to look at the calendar. "So Emma wants to do some kind of 5K thing, right?"

"Yep."

"Why can't she do that on the same day as one of these other events?"

Jack shook his head. "It doesn't work that way, buddy. When I book the park, it's the whole park. The folks who are planning their event don't want to share."

Sam lifted his gaze. "Unless the two events help each other. Like, maybe Emma's event would somehow bring people to the park to enjoy the other event. And vice versa. Kind of like a symbiotic relationship."

Jack furrowed his brow. "A symbiotic relationship." He looked at the calendar again, and instead of looking for empty spaces, he looked at the actual events already in place. There was going to be a kite-flying festival. Walkers and runners would have to dodge kite-flyers. Not a good idea.

On another afternoon, a remote-control airplane event was planned. Not ideal.

There was going to be a dog appreciation day at the park, where dog owners brought their canines in for a bath, a treat, and a long walk along the hiking trails. Dog walkers would probably interfere with Emma's event.

There was also a kayaking race on Silver Lake and a Mentor Match picnic for Mayor Everson's latest charity.

Jack held out his palms. "I just don't see anything that will mesh."

Sam jabbed a finger onto the calendar for a Saturday in early August. "It's so obvious, Uncle Jack. This one is perfect."

Jack narrowed his eyes, following Sam's gaze. "The Women's Wellness Fair?" Jack remembered booking that one. The Women's Wellness Center in town was having a day of increasing awareness about women's health issues. They were doing free screenings and selling a few items to raise money to offer more free services to women throughout the year. "The Women's Wellness Fair," Jack repeated, trying to make sense of how Emma's 5K could jibe with that.

"What's Aunt Emma's 5K for again?" Sam asked.

Jack whipped his face up to his nephew. "Aunt Emma?"

Sam chuckled. "Just trying it out in case you two get married."

Jack massaged his face again, but his headache was now receding. "Emma is organizing a 5K race in honor of her mom. Entrants pay a fee, get a T-shirt, and the money goes to a charity. I don't think Emma has decided on what charity yet. She wants to make a difference in her mom's name." The hairs on Jack's arms began to rise. "Funding these free screenings that the Women's Wellness Center does would make a difference. It might even save a life." He looked up at Sam and patted the side of his arm. "You're brilliant."

Sam looked away and shook his head. "Anyway, is there a skate park or something here where I can ride my board?"

Jack patted his nephew's arm again. "Welcome to Sweetwater Springs. Where nature is your skateboarding platform."

Sam rolled his eyes in a playful way. "Can I go check things out?"

Jack waved him on. "Yeah, of course. Just be back before I leave at six. Call me if you need something. I'll have my phone on me." And Sam never went anywhere without his phone.

Jack heard the front door open and shut, but his gaze stayed glued to the calendar as he wavered on how to make this work. He'd have to convince Emma to raise money for the Women's Wellness Center, which seemed like a great cause to Jack. And the Women's Wellness Center would need to join with Emma's event. It seemed like a win-win union if they both agreed.

He leaned back in his chair. There was only one way to find out. He'd have to drop in and see Emma after work. If she said yes, their deal stood. If her answer was no, then they might be breaking up tonight.

*　*　*

Emma stared inside her refrigerator, her mood as grim as her dinner choices. She didn't feel like cooking, and one of the perks of being single was that she didn't have to. If she wanted to eat cold cereal for every meal, she could.

But she didn't necessarily want to. All she wanted to do was curb the hunger and go to bed. After standing on her feet all day at the café, she was beyond exhausted.

Cereal it is.

Emma grabbed a carton of milk and carried it to the counter before grabbing a box of Lucky Charms, a bowl, and a spoon. She poured a healthy serving of sugary, marshmallow-laden cereal and then twisted the cap off the milk carton and began to pour, stopping when she heard the doorbell. She wasn't expecting visitors tonight.

Per usual, her faithful guard dog stormed the front of the house.

Emma moved much more slowly, leaving her dinner at the counter and lamenting that it would probably be soggy by the time she returned. She walked to the door to peek through the peephole, and her breath caught the same way it did every time she saw Jack.

The doorbell rang again, and this time Emma heard Jack's voice. "Emma, it's just Jack."

She still didn't move.

"Em, I know you're there. Your car is in the driveway."

She could keep pretending. For all he knew, she was taking a hot bath right now. Barnaby lifted on his back legs and started scratching at the door. "Fine." Emma gathered her wits and opened the door. "I was going to answer. I was just making sure you weren't someone selling vacuum cleaners. I have a vacuum cleaner."

Jack offered a silly grin and raised both hands. "Not a salesperson."

She glanced beyond him toward his truck. "Where's Sam?"

Jack followed her gaze for a moment and then returned his eyes to her. "My nephew is a skateboarder. Soon as I parked in your driveway, he grabbed his board and headed down your street. He'll be around."

Emma continued to block the doorway. "And why are you here?"

"I have a proposition for you."

"Another one?" She lifted her brows. "I've already agreed to one proposition with you this week."

Jack seemed to pull in a deep breath, and something in his eyes told Emma he was nervous. She stepped back and gestured for him to come inside. "Come on in."

"I hope I didn't interrupt anything," Jack said as he followed her and Barnaby down the hall toward the open kitchen.

"Just soggy cereal. Want some?" she asked.

Jack inspected the box of Lucky Charms and her bowl on the counter. "Breakfast for dinner has always been my favorite. But I'll pass tonight. Thanks." He pulled out a stool and sat, folding his arms over his broad chest, which stretched the fabric of his T-shirt.

Needing distance, Emma leaned against the counter, mimicking his stance by folding her arms across her chest as well. "Okay, what's your proposition?"

He looked down at the floor for a moment, and she sensed his nervousness again. "Well, there's no spot available in the calendar for this summer."

She felt her heart drop as she plopped onto the other kitchen stool. "I see."

He looked at her. "But I made a promise to you, and I intend to keep it."

"It wouldn't be the first time you broke a promise to me." She cringed on the inside as soon as she said it. She kept promising herself to leave prom night in the past, but she couldn't seem to help herself.

Jack gave a small nod. "Fair enough."

"It's not fair. I'm sorry," she whispered. "I didn't mean to bring that up. You were saying?"

He hesitated for a moment, and she wondered if he was recuperating from the sting of her reminder. "I have an idea that just might work," he finally continued, his blue eyes lighting up. "Last we talked, you hadn't figured out where the proceeds from your event would go."

Emma let her arms drop down by her side. "To a charity that my mom would approve of. I'm looking at a few cancer-related ones and narrowing down my decision." She'd just decided yesterday to even have an event. Everything was moving so fast.

Jack grinned. "Well, I have a suggestion. The Women's Wellness Center is doing a full-day event in Evergreen Park in August, raising money and awareness for women's health issues, cancer included. I spoke to Dr. Rivers when she booked it."

Emma's throat grew tight as she listened. There was a slight ringing in her ears, and she could feel the blood rushing through her heart. She'd been avoiding the Women's Wellness Center. Fear had kept her from going to her yearly checkup, and it was also keeping her from rescheduling. What if the checkup showed the same results her mom had gotten at this age? What if this was it? What if...

"Emma?" Jack's brow creased as he looked at her across the kitchen island. "You okay?"

She nodded quickly. Then she forced herself to take a breath and smile to reassure him. "So what exactly are you suggesting?"

"Well, I haven't spoken to Dr. Rivers yet, but I thought

your 5K event would fit in nicely with that one. They're raising money and awareness for women's health issues, one of which took your mom's life. What if your event supported those screenings and consultations that could help other women avoid what happened to your mom?"

Emma shook her head. "I'm not sure, Jack."

He drew back. "Why not? It's perfect."

Emma felt weak and shaky. Perfect maybe, but it was hitting too close to home right now. How could she support and encourage women to do something that she couldn't even bring herself to do? Here she was trying to honor her mom's memory and the best way to do that was to take care of her own health—but she couldn't.

* * *

Jack had expected that Emma would be ecstatic over his suggestion, but instead she appeared to be on the verge of a panic attack. "Am I missing something here?" His gaze lowered to her fidgeting hands.

"I'm just not sure, that's all."

"This would be perfect for your event. A symbiotic relationship," he said, copying his nephew. Emma didn't look impressed.

"Didn't your mom go to the Women's Wellness Center?" he asked.

Emma nodded. "That was where they discovered that something was wrong. It was just a routine checkup." She looked down at Barnaby at her feet, and Jack could feel the emotion pulsing off her. Maybe he was wrong to think this was a good setup for her event. So many years had passed that he didn't realize this would be a painful suggestion, but obviously it was.

He got off the stool and stepped toward her. His motion seemed to startle her because she straightened from the counter that she was leaning against. Barnaby rose as well.

"What are you doing?" she asked, a note of suspicion playing in her words.

"Just trying to comfort you."

"By doing what?"

He stood only a couple feet away now. He took another step, closing that gap. "Any way I can. I thought this would be a good solution to our problem, but if it's not, I'll figure something else out."

The muscles of her throat tightened as she seemed to swallow. "Are there any other events I can join with this summer?"

His knee-jerk reaction was a grimace. "You can join with the Save the Bears Organization."

As he'd hoped, this made Emma smile. "I'm not sure that's a good fit for honoring my mom." She sighed and leaned over the counter again. "Maybe this whole idea is stupid anyway. I mean, she's been gone for eighteen years. If I hadn't seen that Life List of hers, I wouldn't even be doing this."

Unable to help himself, Jack reached out and put a hand on her arm, the touch of her silky soft skin firing up every cell in his body. She responded with that startled look of hers again, but she didn't pull away. "I think this is a great idea. I think she'd be happy that you're doing it."

Emma's throat seemed to constrict as she visibly swallowed.

"Most of the events happen during the day," he continued, "and we rarely book nighttime events because of staffing and the dangers of wildlife. But if you want to do your 5K at night, I can figure that out."

Emma considered the offer briefly but shook her head. "I want everyone to be able to participate. Nighttime makes it harder for families and older adults to join in. More people are likely to do this if it takes place in the morning."

"And we want as many people as we can get to go," he agreed.

The sound of the front door opening and closing had Jack stepping away from Emma and Barnaby darting off.

"Anyone here?" Sam called from the foyer.

"In the kitchen." Jack's gaze connected with Emma's, and he saw the disappointment in her eyes. He hated letting her down. That hadn't been his intention in coming here this evening.

Sam strolled in and looked between them. "Am I interrupting? I can go back out and skateboard some more if you two need some private time."

Jack felt the corners of his mouth lift into a smile. "Private time?"

"That's what Mom calls it." Sam shrugged a bony shoulder, looking slightly embarrassed. His hand went to pat Barnaby's head, which quieted the dog.

"We don't need you to leave." Jack turned back to Emma, who was smiling now.

"I just came in because I'm hungry," Sam said. "Lunch was hours ago, and I can usually raid the pantry at my house for snacks. You don't really have anything, Uncle Jack."

Jack massaged a hand over his forehead. "Right. I'm not used to having a teenager live with me. I've heard the rumors that they can eat you out of house and home."

Emma laughed, the sound making his heart skip around in his chest. Then he had an idea that would suit everyone— even though his ideas seemed to be striking out tonight.

"What do you say we all go grab something to eat? Something better than cold cereal."

She folded her arms over her chest. "I happen to like Lucky Charms."

"Me too, but I never turn down a free meal," Jack countered.

"Free?" She lifted a brow.

"I'm buying. It's still your birthday week after all. What do you want to eat?" Jack asked. "Anything at all."

Before she could answer, Sam did. "Burgers and fries. And not the fast-food junk. The real thing. I could probably eat two."

Jack turned to Sam, hearing Emma giggling behind him. "So it's true. You really are going to eat me out of house and home this summer. You'll be a foot taller and broader by the time I return you to your mom."

A sheepish smile swept over Sam's boyish face.

"Burgers actually sound amazing," Emma said. "I'm in."

Jack wanted to punch a victory fist into the air. He felt like she'd just said yes to a date, which of course she hadn't. This arrangement wasn't real. There was nothing more than friendship going on between them. It only felt like more.

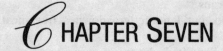CHAPTER SEVEN

*E*mma hurried toward her bedroom and changed into something fresh to go out in tonight. This wasn't a date so she opted for a pair of pale blue shorts and white blouse instead. Cute sundresses were reserved for dates, which she hadn't had a lot of lately. She was tired of dating. It never led anywhere—mostly her fault. She couldn't find a guy she was interested in. At least not one who was also interested in her.

She stopped in front of the mirror, powdered her face just enough to take the shine off, and brushed her hair. Then she hurried down the hall where Jack and Sam were waiting on her couch and giving Barnaby the attention he craved. "I know you're starving so I changed as fast as I could," she said.

Sam gave her a wide grin as he popped up off the sofa. She didn't know Jack's nephew well. He and his mom had moved away from Sweetwater Springs when Sam was a baby. Amanda was five years older, and Emma had hung out with Jack more than her. Amanda had always been sweet though. Emma regretted to hear that she was struggling with addiction these days.

Emma knew that Jack and Amanda's father had struggled as well. Jack never talked about it, but she remembered going to his house a couple of times when they were young and noticing that his dad wasn't acting quite right. Then there was the one time that he'd passed out on the couch, never stirring as they played loudly around him.

"Ready?" Jack stood from the couch as well and headed toward the front door.

"Just let me put Barnaby in the yard. A little fresh air before bedtime helps him sleep." Emma scooped up her dog and carried him to the back door. "Guard the house while I'm gone," she whispered as she always did, dodging one of his sloppy kisses across her cheek before putting him down. Then she walked back to the front of the house and followed Jack and Sam to the truck, slightly surprised when Jack jumped ahead and opened the passenger door for her.

"You're in the back," he told Sam.

"Oh, no, that's okay. I can take the back," Emma protested, stopping short when Jack gave her a look.

"The lady rides in the front. The teenager gets the back. Universal rules."

"It's okay. I'm used to it," Sam said as he climbed in. "I'm always in the back with Mom and Reginald."

"Reginald?" Emma asked. "Do you call him Regi?"

"No, he hates that," Sam said. "He's Reginald."

Jack chuckled to himself as he shut the door and got in on the driver's side. "I'm assuming you two want to go to Bear's for burgers," he said as he backed out of the driveway.

"Mmm, Bear's has the best fries. I haven't been there in ages. I assumed we'd go to the Sweetwater Diner."

Jack glanced across the seat. "The diner has burgers, but Bear's makes birthday burgers."

Emma scrunched her face and glanced at Sam in the back seat. "What in the world is a birthday burger?"

"You've never seen one?" Jack asked. "Well, tonight we'll fix that." He pulled up to a stop sign and looked over at her. "We'll forget our worries, relax, and celebrate. Sound good?"

She took a shuddery breath and nodded.

"Sounds perfect." Then tomorrow she could return to planning an event, running the café, and juggling a million other things, including what she was going to do about this slow-burning flame she'd been carrying for Jack for too long.

* * *

Bear's Burgers was a quaint little restaurant in town, specializing in every burger imaginable, including bison and vegetarian options. There was also every french fry variety imaginable, although Emma always went with the sweet potato fries topped with brown sugar and salt. She could be happy eating a plate of those and nothing else.

She followed Jack and Sam to a table along the wall and paused before sitting down. The options were to slide into the booth next to Jack, which meant close proximity for the next hour, or she could sit next to Sam, which meant more eye contact across the table with Jack. Both would result in those pesky heart flutters that she was trying to suppress.

"Are you going to sit?" Jack asked.

She nodded and slid into the booth next to him. She could feel his warmth, and some part of her wanted to slide in closer and soak it up.

A waitress stepped up to the table and laid out three menus. Emma looked up at her. "Ruby Jean."

Ruby had been working at Bear's since Emma came here as a teenager. She still wore her hair back in a tight bun at her nape, although the color had faded from blond to silver over the years. "It's been a while since you've been in," Ruby told Emma. She looked over at Jack. "You too. Even longer since you came together."

Emma and Jack had come here first with their moms and later, when Jack got his license, just the two of them. They'd always ordered a large bottomless plate of fries to split.

"And who is this handsome young fellow?" Ruby asked, looking at Sam.

Sam shifted in the booth across from Emma, offering an awkward grin at the older waitress. "I'm Sam."

"Sam is my nephew. Amanda's son. He'll be staying with me this summer," Jack said.

"Oh, how nice." Ruby gave a warm smile. "And where is Amanda? I haven't seen her in ages either."

Emma looked over at Jack, noticing the corners of his mouth dip subtly.

"She's taking some time to herself," he told Ruby.

Ruby seemed to wait for a moment as if thinking he'd say more. When he didn't, she pulled her notepad out of her apron pocket and reached for the pen tucked away in her bun. "Well, every woman deserves time to herself once in a while."

"She's not by herself. She's with her boyfriend," Sam pointed out.

Ruby Jean smiled. "Having the time of their lives, I'm sure. And I'm sure you'll have a great summer staying with your uncle Jack."

Sam heaved a sigh. "So far he's only had me working at the park with him."

"I'd hardly call what you've been doing work," Jack said, making everyone laugh, including Sam. Then they ordered three sodas, along with burgers and fries.

"We need a birthday burger," Jack told Ruby.

Emma let her face fall into her open palm. "Remind me to avoid you for all my birthdays for the rest of my life," she muttered, sweeping her gaze sideward to meet Jack's. Her heart stalled like an old car engine. Remind herself not to look over at him anymore tonight too.

"A birthday burger for the birthday girl, it is." Ruby tucked her pen back into her hair, like a knitting needle in a ball of thick yarn. "And how many candles should this burger have?"

"Thirty," Jack said, making Emma drop her face into her palm again.

"Aww, you're still a baby." Ruby patted a hand on Emma's back. "Thirty is just when things start getting good in life, darlin'."

Emma swallowed thickly. Her mom had missed that part of her own life. Thirty was when things had come to a sudden halt.

"Thanks, Ruby," Jack said before Ruby Jean walked away.

"Is she actually going to put thirty candles on my burger?" Emma asked Jack.

He chuckled softly, the sound a low rumble like thunder beyond the mountains. "I doubt Bear wants to light this place on fire tonight."

Emma drove her elbow into Jack's side, making him groan and chuckle harder. The touch made her body ache for more. What was wrong with her? Did thirty also come with soaring, out-of-control hormones?

"So you're a skateboarder, huh?" Emma asked Sam as they waited, needing to redirect her attention.

Sam had long hair that fell into his eyes. He seemed to hide behind it when he was nervous. She didn't think he'd be nervous now, but he peered across the table at her behind his overgrown bangs, a wide awkward smile sweeping across his cheeks. "When there's nothing else to do, I guess?"

"What do you do when you're home?" Emma asked.

"Video games mostly." Sam looked at Jack. "But Uncle Jack doesn't have any game systems."

Jack huffed. "When I was your age, I was outdoors anytime the weather was nice. Even when it wasn't nice, I was outside."

Emma nodded. "I can vouch for that."

"They probably didn't even make video games back then," Sam said.

Jack's mouth fell open. "Hey!" he said in a teasing tone.

Sam looked at Emma again. "I also hang out with my friends, who aren't here obviously."

"What about a girlfriend?" Emma asked as Ruby Jean set their sodas in front of them.

"Be back with the burgers in just a sec," she said, stepping away again.

Sam shook his head. "Not really."

Emma reached for her Dr Pepper and took a sip. "Your uncle Jack always had a new girlfriend every time I turned around."

Jack was the one who bumped her this time. "I wasn't

that bad." His voice dropped to a note that resonated through her body.

"Oh, you were." She met his gaze, forgetting that she'd promised herself to stop doing that. He was close enough that she could see the variations of blue in his irises. Close enough to lean in and press her lips to his. Close enough to know better.

She looked away, searching the diner for Ruby Jean. *Where are those burgers and fries?* Emma sat up a little straighter as she noticed a couple push through the restaurant's doors.

"What's wrong?" Jack followed her gaze. From Emma's peripheral, she saw him straighten a little as well.

Here came her father and Angel, heading straight toward them. Her father had never hidden his disapproval for Jack since her last year of high school. Judging by the grim line on his mouth as he approached their table, his feelings hadn't changed. How was Emma going to explain sitting here with Jack and Sam for dinner?

* * *

Jack's knee-jerk reaction was to tell Edward St. James, "This isn't what it looks like." His next reaction was to look down at his hands and hope to disappear.

Edward didn't like him very much, and that was putting it mildly.

"Dad." Emma stood and wrapped her arms around her father's neck as he reached their table. "Hi, Angel," she said to her stepmom next, her enthusiasm dropping a noticeable notch. Jack didn't think that was intentional, but he knew that Emma was a little bitter over the way Angel and Edward had met. Emma's mom had still been alive, which made for an awkward situation.

"Dad and Angel, you know Jack." Emma gestured at Jack sitting in the booth.

Jack offered his hand to Edward, noting the iron grip. Then he shook Angel's hand. "Nice to see you."

Edward nodded, his blue eyes steely. Edward had made it clear to Jack that he should never cross that friendship line with Emma. That was in Jack's college days when he'd started to drink too much, following a path that was all too similar to his dad's. Jack had done things he was ashamed of, like driving after one too many beers. Then there was that time he'd shown up at the St. James house drunk on the night of Emma's prom. Edward had met him at the door, frowned, and stepped out onto the porch with him.

"I'm here for Emma," Jack had said, probably slurring his words all over the place.

"No, you're not. If you think you're taking my daughter anywhere in your condition, you're mistaken. You're lucky I'm not calling the police," Edward said. Then he took Jack's keys and drove him home. The entire drive to Jack's house, Edward had lectured him. On drinking and driving, and dating his daughter. In no uncertain terms, he'd told Jack that anything romantic with Emma was off the table. "Your mom deserved better than the town drunk, and so does my Emma."

Jack met Edward's gaze now. It was pretty clear that he still thought Emma deserved better.

"And this is Jack's nephew, Sam." Emma gestured at Sam seated across the booth from Jack.

"Amanda's son," Edward said. "How is she?" he asked Jack directly.

Jack felt his body tense to a whole new level. She was

in a facility for addiction this summer. Amanda couldn't even take care of her own son. Yeah, Jack guessed his family was a bit dysfunctional in Edward's eyes. "She's great, sir."

"She's taking a vacation from me," Sam pointed out, the same way he had multiple times already since he'd arrived in Sweetwater Springs.

The group of them went silent.

"Not true," Jack muttered, giving Sam a stern look.

Emma cleared her throat and smiled. "Dad, Angel, we just ordered. Would you like to join us? I'm sure Ruby Jean can get your orders out at the same time as ours."

Jack inwardly groaned, once again wanting to look at her dad and say "This isn't what it looks like." Jack wasn't innocent though. He was enjoying sitting close to Emma, and he was enjoying spending time with her lately.

"Sure. That'd be great," Edward said, sliding into the booth next to Sam. Angel slid in as well, leaving Emma and Jack on the other side.

"At least now I'm not the third wheel," Sam quipped.

Jack's heart dropped in his chest. He wanted to give Sam another stern look, but the boy wasn't looking at him.

"I'm always the third wheel with my mom and her boyfriend. Then I come here, and I'm the same with Jack and Emma," Sam went on, oblivious to Jack's dirty looks.

"Oh?" Edward looked across the table. "Spending a lot of time together?" he asked Jack directly.

From the corner of Jack's eye, he saw Emma shift nervously. "Just a little," she admitted. "Jack has been helping me with the 5K I was telling you about. Since I'm having it at Evergreen Park."

"Oh," he said, seeming to relax a bit. "That's right."

"Edward told me about that," Angel said. "Emma, I think that's such a lovely idea. And I would really like to help you in any way I can."

Jack had to admit he liked Angel St. James. Angel seemed sweet and kindhearted, and she really seemed to make an effort to be friends with Emma.

"Thank you." Emma sighed softly next to him. "There's been a slight hitch in the plans though. There's no room on this summer's calendar for my event." Emma looked over at Jack.

"Well, no single slots," he said. "But I was thinking that maybe Emma could join her event with another one that's going on at the park this summer."

"Sometimes joining forces makes things stronger," Angel commented. "Right now, you just want to plan a 5K. But more people might come if there's another attraction. I just love an arts and craft fair," she added.

"But arts and crafts has nothing to do with wellness," Emma pointed out, her tone a little clipped.

Ruby Jean took that moment to return to the table. "Looks like I need to take a few more orders." She took the two new orders and promised to be back soon.

Jack looked over at Emma. "The Women's Wellness Fair is a great match."

Emma met his gaze, and he suspected, if she were to talk right now, her tone with him would be clipped too.

"Oh yes," Angel said. "A wellness walk for women. That name just rolls off your tongue, don't you think, Eddie?" She looked over at Emma's dad.

"Yeah. Sounds like a great teaming for your mom's event," he agreed. "Jenny really loved that center. They took great care of her," he said, his expression sentimental for a moment. "She even told me once that she wished there was a way to give back where they were concerned. To help them as much as they had helped her."

Jack could practically feel the tension rolling off Emma as she sat stiffly beside him.

"Really?" she finally asked. "I didn't know that."

Angel continued to carry the conversation, which thankfully turned to her new bicycling hobby.

Finally, Ruby Jean returned with a cart full of plates. She took them one by one and slid them in front of her customers. "There you go...This one is for you...And you. A growing boy needs his nourishment. Don't be afraid to ask for seconds," she added when talking to Sam. "I always give the kids seconds."

Sam's mouth fell open. "I'm not really...a kid."

Ruby Jean smiled widely. "Of course you are. When you're old like me, even your uncle here is a kid."

"I wouldn't turn down someone calling me a kid or giving me seconds," Jack advised Sam.

"And the birthday burger is for the birthday girl," Ruby Jean said proudly, sliding a burger twice the size of the other burgers in front of Emma. Thankfully, there was only one candle burning in the middle instead of thirty.

"Wow. That is a sight to behold," Emma said. "I'm not sure I can eat all of that."

Ruby Jean grinned. "You have to if you want a slice of birthday cake. That's the prize for eating the whole thing."

Emma laughed. "If I eat all of this, I definitely won't have room for cake."

Ruby Jean shrugged. "You only get one birthday a year. Eat your burger and have your cake too." She winked under her thick mascara. "And don't let that one steal a bite," she said, pointing a finger at Jack.

Jack's jaw dropped. "I would never try to steal a bite of Emma's birthday burger."

"Just a kiss, huh?" Ruby Jean winked again. "I know how lovebirds do." She laughed and then left them to their meals. The conversation fell quiet for a moment while everyone prepared to eat and took their first bites.

"So tell me again what brings the three of you together?" Edward asked. "Jack is helping you find a spot on the calendar, but that doesn't explain why you're seated at a restaurant with him."

Emma reached for her drink, appearing to have difficulty washing down her bite of burger. "Well, Dad, Jack and Sam were kind enough to invite me out tonight. It was this or cold cereal alone at my place."

"Oh, you're always welcome for dinner with us," Angel said. "I've been telling Eddie to invite you over for your birthday. At least we can celebrate tonight."

Edward looked at Jack, his blue eyes hard and calculating. Jack didn't blame him one bit for thinking poorly of him. He was holding a grudge over just that one night, but that one night could've put Emma's life in danger. It was stupid, foolish, irresponsible, and unforgivable.

"Why wouldn't Emma be with us tonight?" Sam asked. "I mean, she is Uncle Jack's girlfriend."

Jack didn't breathe for a long moment. He looked at Sam and then Emma, but he didn't look at Edward. No, that was the last face he wanted to look at right now.

* * *

Emma coughed. She reached for her soda again, trying to wash down her bite of food, but her throat was so tight it wouldn't budge.

Jack patted her back, which was probably the last thing that needed to happen right now. Her father looked murderous at the moment. He'd loved Jack once upon a time. What had changed between them?

"You okay?" Jack asked.

No. No, she was nowhere in the vicinity of okay. She nodded. "My food just went down the wrong pipe."

"So you two are dating?" Angel asked, her expression light and happy. Her eyes were even twinkling under the low-hanging lighting at their table. She was a hard woman to dislike, and Emma had really tried to do just that. She couldn't though. Angel was in fact angelic.

"Well, um..." Emma picked up her burger, needing something to do with her hands. Taking another bite right now was risky business; she might choke on it. "Jack asked me out tonight so I guess technically this is a date," she admitted, not wanting to go back on her deal with Jack. She looked at him for help.

He looked like he was walking to the edge of a cliff with a hurricane-force wind at his back. "Uh, well, Emma and I have been out a few times."

That was the truth. They'd met at the home improvement store and then had gone to her café and back to her house the other night. And he'd been to her house on her birthday to keep her from celebrating alone.

"It's a recent relationship," Emma added, looking between her father and Sam. "It's not really common knowledge yet."

"When I stopped in your café, you didn't say a word about Jack," her father said.

"I guess it didn't come up." Emma took a bite of her burger now just to give herself an excuse not to talk for a few seconds. She was never going to finish this thing, but she would probably need to eat her feelings with cake after this dinner was over.

"I see." Her father nodded the way he did when he disapproved of something. The way he used to when she had done something that disappointed him.

Well, she could straighten this out later when Sam wasn't around and let him in on the little arrangement. Not that she needed to explain anything. She was a grown woman. Why should she care about his opinion on who she dated? He certainly hadn't asked her opinion on dating her mother's former hospice nurse.

She sat a little straighter and scooted closer to Jack. Then she put on her best smile and looked between her father and Angel. "I guess the secret is out now."

Jack coughed beside her.

"Well, I couldn't be happier," Angel said. "You haven't dated anyone in a while, Emma."

That was true. "I've been busy with the café," Emma justified. "But there was the delivery guy who brought me supplies once a week."

"Oh yes, I remember him." Angel reached for her napkin and wiped a smear of ketchup off her lips. "I liked him, but he was a bit rude."

Emma nodded. She and the guy in question had gone to dinner at her dad and stepmom's house. And her date had eaten like a caveman and belched once without excusing himself. That had been the end of that. "He was," Emma agreed.

"Then there was the fireman," Angel said.

Jack groaned. "I'm glad she stopped seeing that guy," he muttered under his breath.

"Well, one day soon, you and Jack will have to come over to our house and have dinner with Eddie and me. Sam too, of course. We can all get to know each other a little better. Wouldn't that be wonderful?" Angel asked.

By the looks on everyone's faces at the table, Angel was the only one excited by the prospect.

"Maybe so. But I'll be busy planning my mom's event, assuming I can find a date to make it happen."

"I think blending with the Women's Wellness Fair is an amazing idea," Angel said, her voice still full of cheer.

Pressure built fast and suddenly inside of Emma just as if she were a bottle of soda and someone had shaken her up. She felt like she might explode in this one second if she didn't spew the words that she regretted before they'd even come out of her mouth. "Well, I didn't ask you, and you didn't even care enough about her to stay away from my dad."

"Emma Grace," her father said. "Apologize."

"You first," Emma said.

CHAPTER EIGHT

Sometimes things couldn't be taken back with a quick apology. Not that Emma had apologized yet. Instead she'd eaten her birthday burger, brooding and marinating in the guilt she felt every time she looked at Angel, who was no longer smiling. Her eyes were no longer twinkling either, thanks to Emma's little explosion.

Ruby Jean came with the check and laid it at the edge of the table. "Here you go. Unless I can get you some type of dessert." She eyed Emma's burger. "No birthday cake for you. Maybe next year, hon."

Emma shook her head. "I tried. It was too big." Add the heavy guilt to her full stomach and she might not be able to walk out of this diner tonight.

"Can I get you all something sweet? Maybe a slice of pie?" Ruby asked.

Everyone shook their head. There was no need to extend this awkward meal. Even Sam looked like this was some form of teenage torture. He hadn't even taken Ruby Jean up on her offer for free seconds.

"I'm paying." Her father handed his card to Ruby Jean.

"Dad, you don't have to—" Emma began to say, but he silenced her with a look. Once again, she saw the disappointment in his eyes, thick and heavy.

Her guilt deepened. She hadn't meant to snap at Angel, but this event for her mom wasn't any of Angel's business.

"Well, it was so nice catching up with you two," Angel said, sliding out of the booth. She wouldn't meet Emma's gaze. "We should do it again sometime. And my offer to have you all over for dinner still stands. I know you're busy, but if you change your mind."

"Thanks," Jack said. Then he offered his hand to Emma's dad to shake.

Her father stared at it, leaving Jack's hand hanging in midair for a long, tense second. Then he shook it, and Emma suspected her father squeezed the heck out of it in some kind of alpha handshake war. Emma scrutinized Jack's face as they gripped hands, thinking that he seemed to be suppressing a painful grimace.

"Good night, Dad." She slid out of the booth and gave him a big hug. It never mattered if they were fighting. She never avoided hugging her dad and giving him a kiss on the cheek, knowing that another opportunity wasn't promised.

"We'll talk later," he said, pulling away, warmness returning to his eyes.

She nodded. Then she faced Angel. "Good night, Angel." She mustered a smile but not a hug. Never a hug. And after all these years, Angel knew better than to try to initiate one.

Angel was pretty good at hugging with her eyes though. She was like a puppy, back in good spirits despite how

Emma had treated her. And that somehow made things worse. "My other offer stands too. Let me know if you need any help planning this event of yours. I want you to know that I loved your mom. I would never have done anything to hurt her. And neither would your dad. She was a special woman," she said before turning to leave.

Emma sighed deeply as she sat back down in the booth and watched her dad and Angel exit the restaurant. "That was..."

"Awful," Jack said, finishing her sentence and reading her mind.

"What was all that about?" Sam asked. His plate was completely clear.

Emma shrugged. "A dysfunctional family is a normal family," she told him.

Jack chuckled, looking a lot more relaxed now that her dad and Angel had left. "I guess we're normal, then, huh, Sam?"

Sam gave a half grin, his bangs falling in front of his eyes just a touch. "My mom has called me like ten times a day since you picked me up. She needed time away, but she won't leave me alone. I'd say that's dysfunctional. So yeah, normal."

"That's what mothers do, bud," Jack told him. "She wants to make sure you're okay and I'm not falling down on the job. So what do you think? Am I doing an okay job so far?"

Sam peered at his uncle through his bangs. "I guess. It's not your fault that your job is kind of boring."

Jack scoffed while Emma giggled beside him.

"You know, Sam, you could divide your time and help me at the café a little too. I need some part-time help.

The café is busier during the summer months, starting tomorrow. The Fourth of July is one of my busiest days of the summer."

Sam pushed his hair out of his eyes. "A job?"

"Yep. I'd put you on the payroll and everything. And you eat for free if you work at the café. An added bonus is that there are lots of girls that come in." What teen didn't feel better at the prospect of food and girls? "That is, if your uncle Jack can spare you for a couple days a week." Emma looked over at Jack.

"You sure?" he asked, surprise playing in his expression. And something else. Maybe gratitude.

Emma lifted a shoulder. "I have an event to coordinate, so extra help at the café will be a godsend."

Jack looked at Sam. "It's up to you, buddy. What do you think?"

Sam offered a full grin. "She's paying in money and food. That's a way better offer than what you gave me."

Jack's mouth fell open, and both Emma and Sam burst into laughter. "I pay in free rent and food."

"Except your fridge is always empty." Sam looked at Emma's half-eaten burger. "You're really not going to finish that thing?"

Emma slid the plate forward. "It's all yours. Ruby Jean likes you. She might even give you my slice of cake."

Jack chuckled beside her, and then, surprising her, he slid an arm behind her. She didn't mind. It was part of the act. They were just having fun, despite the previous hour with her dad and Angel.

Tomorrow, she'd dwell on that, and perhaps she'd make an attempt to apologize to Angel. Maybe she'd look into joining forces with the Women's Wellness Center for her event too. Emma hadn't realized that her mom had wanted to give back to the center. In that regard, it really was the perfect match.

* * *

Jack wanted to be enjoying the peace and quiet of doing his job solo today, but the park was extra busy with it being the Fourth of July. He also had too much on his mind. First, he was wondering how Sam was making out at his first day of work at the café with Emma.

Then he was thinking about Emma, and some of those thoughts needed to be reined in to a safe, nonromantic territory.

Lastly, he was watching his back just in case Emma's dad decided to come after him.

Edward St. James was a peaceful man, but the thought of a drunk dating his daughter might drive the senior St. James over the edge. Jack wasn't a drunk, but Edward didn't know that.

Jack's thoughts swung from topic to topic as he rode his ATV along the trails of Evergreen Park, slowing when he saw evidence of a recent campfire near Blue Sky Point, in the same place he'd seen evidence of a camper before. Jack stopped the vehicle and inspected his surroundings from where he sat. Who was making their home here these days?

"Hello?" Jack called out into the woods, his voice echoing just a touch. Most hikers stayed on the trails. There were warning signs posted about the dangers of stepping off. There were bears and all kinds of wildlife in this area, along with a variety of snakes, including rattlers. Now, being added to the list, there was a shady character who made illegal campfires out here.

Jack got off his ATV and walked around the charred earth, squatting low to look for any kind of clue or evidence. All he found was a penny and a toothpick. The toothpick wasn't the end of the world, but it was still litter.

Jack straightened and looked around again. "Hello out there? Care to come out and talk to me? It's illegal to camp out here, you know." He didn't think anyone could hear him, but if they could, that was a stupid thing to say. Telling the squatter that it was illegal was pretty much threatening jail time.

Well, good. Maybe the person would get a clue and go squat somewhere else.

After another ten minutes of futile searching, Jack hopped back onto his ATV and rode along the trails some more, helping hikers find their way and checking on some baby geese that had recently hatched near the Evergreen Park side of Silver Lake. He ended back at the ranger's office and returned some phone calls from his desk. One was from Mayor Brian Everson, who was having a function at the park this summer. Of course he was. Mayor Everson was always organizing something. The next event was for the Special Olympics, which Brian and his wife, Jessica, headed up.

Jack also needed to return a call to the Women's Wellness Center. Dr. Ashley Rivers wanted to review how many tables she'd have for her fair and where they'd be set up. Too bad Emma was still on the fence about combining events. Today would be a good time to swing the idea by Ashley, when she was still hammering out the final details.

"Knock-knock!" a woman called as she pushed open the ranger office's front door.

Jack stepped out of his office and saw Sophie Daniels walk in, dressed in springtime colors. She had her hair pulled back in a ponytail today. "Sophie," he said. "What brings you here?"

"Well," she said, stepping closer, "I was thinking that I would like to take up bird-watching." She looked at him expectantly.

Jack remembered what Granger had told him about Sophie and the Ladies' Day Out group. Apparently, they'd encouraged Sophie to make a play for him. Was that what this visit was? Was she interested in him romantically?

Sophie was a beautiful woman, no doubt. She was smart and sweet. And they were both single. Dating her should be a no-brainer for a bachelor like him. "You want to go on the trails today?"

"Oh no." She waved a hand. "Not today. Not in my good clothes." She gestured at her outfit, which included a T-shirt and a long flowing skirt.

"Well, there's really no need for lessons. I have brochures on the wall that help identify the birds around here. And the trails are labeled. Just wear good shoes, bring water, and stick to the paths. I can give you a map too if you want." He grabbed one from the rack on the wall. "Here you go."

"So you don't give . . . private lessons?"

He cocked his head. "Bird-watching lessons? No." He scratched the new growth of hair on the side of his jaw. He'd never had this request before. "Or at least, I don't usually."

"Maybe you'd make an exception for me?" she asked, a hopeful lilt in her Southern accent.

She was a nice woman, but she didn't light him up on the inside the way that Emma did. "Well, I guess you could let me know when you're ready. I might be able to go out with you."

One corner of her mouth curled. "Great. Then it's a date."

The D-word got his attention. Had he really just agreed to a date? No, he was out of practice, but he'd know if he'd just asked a woman out on a date. That usually warranted nervousness on his part, complete with sweaty palms and a racing heart. He didn't even give her a Hershey's Kiss, which was his go-to dating move. "It's a plan," he corrected, just to clear that D-word off the table.

"Definitely. Okay, well, I'm off to go finish errands and then get back to the boutique," Sophie said. "My mom is watching the shop right now. I can't leave her too long. She likes to give discounts to everyone she knows." Sophie's smile fell a notch. "And she knows everyone in town."

This made Jack chuckle. "You'll go out of business if you keep her behind the register."

"That's true." Sophie waved. "Next time I come, I'll have good shoes and athletic clothes." She rubbed her hands together. "I'll text you to make sure you're available. I have your number."

Jack wasn't sure what to say so he just nodded and gave a small wave, watching her leave. He did another internal check. Nope, he didn't feel anything. When Emma was around, on the other hand, he felt the spark between them ignite, turning into a hungry blaze inside his belly. When Emma was around, his world was brighter, sharper, kinder. With her, he felt everything.

Unable to help himself, he grabbed his cell phone and tapped in a text: I haven't checked on my girlfriend yet today. How are you?

* * *

When Emma finally got a chance to take a break from serving customers, she grabbed her phone and smiled down at the text from Jack. She was tempted to tap back a reply text, but she didn't want to look overeager. Instead, she shoved her phone back into her purse and looked out on the café. Despite being new on the job, Sam had carried a lot of the workload today. She'd hired him on a whim, but he was already working out perfectly. In fact, over the last hour, she'd noticed an influx of teenaged girls coming into the café.

Sam was just as cute as his uncle had been at that age. And Emma had been just as smitten with Jack as the girls currently sitting at the corner table were with Sam. Not that she'd ever let on. When Emma's friends had drooled over him, Emma had insisted that Jack was just her guy pal. Then she'd seethed when her friends had proceeded to flirt with him shamelessly.

Then again, the extra customers could be due to the fact that it was the Fourth of July. The holiday brought in an influx of family to the town, which increased business.

The door to the café opened, and Sophie Daniels walked in. Sophie had been one of Emma's friends who'd gone gaga over Jack back in the day. At least before she'd fallen head over heels with Chase Lewis, the town's veterinarian. Sophie was a bit of a flirt, but she was classy about it. She was beautiful, and most of the time the object of her attention returned her affection. And yet, she was still single. Emma had always wondered if it was because she'd never fully gotten over Chase, her first love.

"Hey, Sophie." Emma leaned against the café's counter. "Busy day at the boutique?"

"Oh yeah. I just got a new summer line out, and I can't keep it on the rack. My mom is covering for me right now, bless her. Women are loving these new clothes. You should come by before they're all gone."

Emma walked behind the counter, ready to prepare Sophie's order. "I'll have to do that. I need to brighten up my wardrobe. Your usual?"

Sophie laid her wallet on the counter and then dipped down to inspect what was in the bakery case. "Yes, along with a scone, please." She gave a sheepish look under her lashes. "They're calorie- and fat-free, right? And gluten-free, sugar-free, dairy-free, and free of everything else I'm supposed to avoid."

Emma laughed out loud. "Like you have anything to worry about."

"Oh, I do. My clothes are feeling tight these days."

"Well, I can't promise that the scones are free of all the things you listed, but I can promise they're delicious. I had one this morning," Emma admitted.

Sophie gave her a once-over. "And yet it looks like you might've lost a pound. If I didn't love you, I'd hate you."

Emma put a lid on Sophie's cup of coffee and slid it over. Then she dipped into the bakery case and grabbed a cherry vanilla almond scone and placed it into a small paper box. "Anything else?"

Sophie handed Emma her debit card. "Nope. Who's the new guy you have working here?"

Emma followed Sophie's gaze as she took the card. "Oh, that's Sam. He's Jack's nephew, here for the summer."

Sophie's eyes lit up at the mention of Jack. Or maybe it was Emma's imagination. "Really? Amanda's son?"

Emma zipped the card through the reader and handed it back to Sophie. "Amanda is Jack's only sibling, so yes." She could hear that edge coming through in her voice. It wasn't jealousy exactly. And she couldn't fault Sophie for being interested in Jack. He was single, and Emma had no claim on him. No real claim, that is.

"So is Amanda in town for the summer too?" Sophie asked, grabbing her coffee.

"No, just Sam. He'll be working for me part-time and with Jack at the park part-time. Although, if he keeps bringing in the teenaged girls, I'll have to fight Jack for him," Emma joked.

Sophie smiled brightly. "Just don't fight him too hard. We have a date planned soon, and I want him all in one piece."

"A date?" Emma asked, jealousy now in full effect.

"Well, it's not planned, but we've talked about hanging out. Who knows what will happen? Maybe my mom is wrong about me turning into an old maid after all." Sophie's eyes narrowed. "You're not jealous, are you?"

Emma's face burned, but she couldn't decide if it was fury or embarrassment. "No, of course not."

Sophie nodded. "I would be, if you were the one going out with Jack. So I guess that makes you a better woman than me. Anyway, I haven't seen you at the Ladies' Day Out festivities lately. What's been keeping you away?"

"Just working here at the café." Definitely not spending alone time with Jack. But if he wanted a pretend girlfriend, the least he could do was not make dates with other women in town.

Her face was burning because of anger, she decided. And a twinge of jealousy that she never intended to admit to anyone.

"I'm busy at the boutique," Sophie said, "but I still make time to go. We're all going to the Music in the Park tonight."

Evergreen was a state park, but Sweetwater Springs Park had vendors and a playground for kids. It also featured hiking trails and a natural hot spring to wade in. During the summer, the community flocked to the Sweetwater Springs Park for live music and picnics.

"It'll be extra special because it's the Fourth of July," Sophie added. "There'll be fireworks after the music. You don't want to miss that."

Right. When Emma was younger, she'd always pretended like the fireworks displays were a belated birthday gift just for her since the day typically landed in the same week.

Emma shrugged a shoulder. "I might do that," she told Sophie. It depended on how tired she was after she closed the café this afternoon. And whether she wanted to go out alone. Although she wouldn't be on her own for long. Once she arrived at the park, she'd be surrounded by friends and family.

"Well, I hope to see you there tonight." Sophie hitched a thumb behind her. "I better get back to the boutique. "Don't forget to come shopping before all the pretty things are taken."

"I'll come by soon," Emma promised as Sophie headed out. A few more customers strolled in after her. Before Emma could even blink, two hours had gone by and it was time to close.

She headed toward the door and started to turn the OPEN sign to CLOSED when Jack appeared on the other side of the glass. Her heart fluttered foolishly, and she felt an even more foolish smile lift her cheeks. "What are you doing here?" she asked as she opened the door.

"Well, I was hoping to get my sweet tooth fix, but it looks like I'm too late."

She cocked her head, her emotions still warring with jealousy and frustration about Sophie. She needed to tell him the café was closed, and he could come back when it reopens tomorrow. Her growing crush won out though. "Well, I can make an exception for my pretend boyfriend," she said.

"I'd owe you."

"In that case," she said, "come on in."

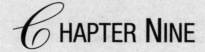

CHAPTER NINE

Jack heard the lock on the front door click as Emma turned the OPEN sign to CLOSED. "So I get private service? I must be special."

She turned. "You're special, all right."

He looked around the empty room. "Where's Sam?"

"We started cleaning early. He took off on his skateboard. I hope that's okay."

Jack folded his arms over his chest. "Yeah, I guess so. When I leave here, I can drive around and find him."

"You might find him with some girls. He's already been noticed," Emma said.

Jack pulled out a chair and sat down. "It's those handsome Hershey genetics," he teased.

Emma leaned against the counter. "Speaking of which, I hear you and Sophie are going on a date."

Jack's smile fell away. "You heard wrong. She came into my office earlier and asked about bird-watching lessons."

Emma crossed her arms over her chest. "You don't give bird-watching lessons."

"Not typically, no, but I know how to identify birds on the trails."

Emma pinned him with a look. "Just the two of you in the woods? Couldn't she just use one of your brochures?"

"If I'm not mistaken, I'd say you're a little jealous." He got up from the table and headed her way, noticing how she stiffened just slightly as he encroached on her space.

"No," she said. "I'm just stating the obvious. And if you and I are going to be a fake couple this summer, you can't date other women. That's the rule."

Jack stopped walking when he was a foot away from her. "I was worried that maybe you would have called off that arrangement since I didn't deliver on my end of the bargain."

"It's only been two days. I still have faith in you."

He looked down for a moment, wishing he wasn't going to have to let her down. No matter how hard he stared at that calendar, open spots weren't going to magically appear.

"I'm pretty sure your dad wasn't happy about you and me last night," he said instead.

Emma's lips parted, drawing his attention there. He willed his attraction back in its cage.

"I'll have to explain things to him once I get him alone."

"You're going to tell him the truth?" Jack asked.

"Well, yeah. I can't fool my dad."

"Seems to me he was pretty fooled last night," Jack pointed out. "You worried about what he'll think of you and me dating?"

Guilt flickered in her expression.

"I guess I don't blame you," he said. "You've always wanted his approval."

Emma straightened from the counter, which only worked to shift her closer to him. "I haven't always wanted my dad's approval."

"You're daddy's little girl. Not saying that's a bad thing."

But according to Emma's expression, it was one of the worst things Jack could say to her. "I've dated lots of guys that my dad didn't like. In fact, he hasn't liked any of my past boyfriends."

Jack smirked. "Neither have I, for the record." He enjoyed the way her lips turned into a subtle pout.

"What was wrong with Tim from the fire station?"

"Too cocky, if you ask me."

Emma tilted her head. "Okay, well, I'd have to agree with that. And he was never my boyfriend. We just went out a couple times."

"Did you kiss him?" Jack asked, unable to resist.

Her eyes jumped up to meet his. "What?"

"Well, he counts if you kissed him. Or, you know, did other stuff."

Emma's jaw dropped. "That's none of your business."

"I'm your boyfriend, so it kind of is."

"Fake boyfriend, so it's kind of not," she countered.

Jack put a hand over his heart as if that had hurt him deeply. "So you didn't kiss him? Or other stuff?" He grinned. "Good. You deserve better."

He wanted to step even closer, but his own words stopped him in his tracks. Those were her father's words too. She deserved better, and that wasn't him.

So he took a step backward, increasing the distance between them. Then his cell phone rang in his pocket. He tapped the screen and brought it to his ear. "Hello."

"Jack," his sister said. Her voice sounded threadbare and tired.

"Amanda." Jack connected gazes with Emma, and he held up a finger. She nodded and went around the counter to continue closing the café. "How are you?" he asked, returning to the chair he'd been seated in a few minutes earlier.

"I'm okay. They're feeding me three square meals and talking during everything in between."

Jack could only imagine what topics she was discussing in the addiction facility. Their family life had been rocky. There'd never been any physical abuse, but emotional abuse, yeah. Emotional neglect too. Their mom had tried to counter their father's negative influence, but she didn't leave their father until Jack and Amanda were grown.

"How's Sam?" Amanda asked.

Jack turned to look out the storefront window, wondering if he'd catch a glimpse of his nephew in passing. No sign of him. "He's doing okay. Don't worry about him. He's spending his days at the park with me or at the café with Emma, working part-time."

"Oh, that's nice," Amanda said. "I'll try to call his cell phone tomorrow when I can."

"He thinks you're having the time of your life with your boyfriend," Jack said, standing and walking off his restless energy. He stepped over to the glass door of the café to look out on Main Street for Sam again.

"I know. That's for the best right now. Tell him I love him," she added.

"Will do."

"And I love you too, Jack."

"Ditto."

They disconnected the call, and Jack stood at the door a few minutes longer, watching couples and families stroll along, seemingly without a care. Were they lying too? Or were they really that carefree? He didn't have anything to complain about. He had a good job, a nice home, and friends who had his back when he needed it. He got a little lonely sometimes, and those little urges to take a drink sometimes tapped his shoulder. He ignored those urges. Overall, life was good.

"All done," Emma said from a few feet behind him.

He turned to face her.

"How's Amanda?"

He gave a nod. "She seems to be doing okay. We could all benefit from some outside help sometimes."

Emma didn't look away as he stepped toward her. "Right. And some of us just avoid our issues altogether and pretend like they don't exist."

Jack kept walking until he was standing right in front of her once more. "Is that what you do?"

"Maybe." She hesitated. "After my mom died, I distracted myself and tried not to think about her. It hurt too much. And now I find myself forgetting her and trying to remember. Sounds crazy, doesn't it?"

Jack wanted so badly to reach out and touch her. Being around Emma was an exercise in willpower. "The good news is that we're all crazy. The bad news is—"

"We're all crazy," Emma said, finishing his sentence. A soft smile played on the corners of her lips.

"Good to know because I'm entertaining crazy thoughts right now," he said.

Her lips parted just a fraction. He saw her throat tighten as she swallowed. "Oh? What thoughts are those?"

This is where he needed to stop talking. "About kissing you," he said instead. "We're friends. Kissing isn't allowed."

She didn't turn around and run at his confession. She

also didn't laugh or criticize his words. So maybe it wasn't the worst idea.

"Then again, if we're going to pretend to be together, it might be easier if we crossed that line. We can call it research." He kept his gaze steady on hers. Was her heart beating as fast as his?

He never did satisfy his sweet tooth in coming here, and she was the sweetest thing he knew. Willpower shattered and weak, he leaned in slowly, holding her gaze and searching for any sign that she wanted him to stop.

Emma didn't flinch. She was so still that he wondered if she was even breathing.

As he dipped toward her, he reached for her hand and felt her fingers tighten around his. He saw her eyes close, and his did the same, preparing for something that he'd wanted forever.

"Uncle Jack?" a voice called from the back as a door slammed shut. "Uncle Jack?"

Emma yanked her hand away, and her eyes flew open. Jack didn't move for a second.

"Uncle Jack?" Sam entered the front of the café and looked between him and Emma. "Were you two kissing?"

"No," Jack said honestly. Regretfully. A second longer and they would've been though. But they hadn't, and now the moment was gone. "Everything okay?" Jack asked.

Sam nodded. "A bunch of kids are going out tonight to see the fireworks. Can I go too?"

"Fireworks. Right." He looked at Emma, who was avoiding eye contact. Somehow, he suspected, if he let Sam walk out of here right now, she'd turn Jack down if he asked her to join him on a picnic blanket in the park tonight. So now was his chance if he wanted to spend more time with her. And he did. He wasn't sure if that was right or wrong, but it's what he wanted more than anything in this moment. "What do you say, Em?"

She looked over at him. "Hmm?"

"Be my date to Music in the Park tonight? I don't want to watch the fireworks alone."

"Uncle Jack, she's your girlfriend," Sam said. "You don't have to keep asking her out."

Jack smiled. There were perks to having his nephew around. "She might be my girlfriend, but that doesn't mean she has to spend every second with me. Maybe she's tired of looking at my mug for today. I know I'm not tired of looking at her."

The color in Emma's cheeks deepened. She looked at Sam and back at Jack. "Okay, I guess." She nodded. "Fireworks and music in the park sound fun."

* * *

What was she thinking? She and Jack had almost kissed. In fact, they'd been so close to kissing that Emma had closed her eyes, taken a breath—ready to hold it for as long as the kiss lasted. Her entire body had flooded with endorphins just from the simple act of him reaching for her hand. Even now, an hour later, those endorphins were still firing in her body.

Emma finished making a third sandwich and slipped it into a Ziploc bag. She carried it to the picnic basket that she'd already filled with sliced fruit, bagged chips, and bottled water. Then she headed down the hall toward her bedroom to finish getting ready for Music in the Park, her mind whirling with thoughts and emotions.

This was Jack. She'd crossed the line with him once, and he'd failed her in a big way. She'd gone solo to her senior prom, which was embarrassing enough. Her friends all had dates so she'd spent an hour against the wall before shrinking into the shadows and out the door to go home.

Adding insult to injury, she'd gotten a flat tire on the road leading back to her house, and because she'd left her cell phone at home by accident, she'd had to walk the last mile to her front door while wearing heels. To add more misery to what was supposed to be one of the best nights of her high school life, one heel had broken, and she'd twisted her ankle. Instead of magical, it'd been one of the worst nights of her life, second only to the night her mom had slipped quietly from this world. Emma's world.

Emma changed into a pair of red capri pants and a T-shirt that read I'D RATHER BE IN SWEETWATER SPRINGS in dark blue print. She sold them at the café along with a few other novelty items.

Being stood up for her senior prom was good reason to never want anything romantic with Jack again. He didn't even have a great excuse for not showing up. On her long walk home that night, she'd wondered if he'd gotten into a car accident. Maybe he was in the hospital dying. Perhaps he'd hit his head and had amnesia. Or he was being held hostage at gunpoint at the florist shop where he would've likely stopped to get her flowers. What if he hadn't come because he was rescuing a woman trapped in a car that was dangling off a bridge somewhere?

Nope. Jack's excuse was that he fell asleep and forgot. She wanted to hate him more than anything. But she couldn't. Because he was Jack, her friend since childhood. The boy who'd walked her to school every day and fought off the mean girls. He was the boy who'd put his arm around her when she'd first learned about her mom's cancer and had stayed with her when she'd cried all night, riding his bike home in the darkness after she'd fallen asleep. He'd stayed during her mom's cancer treatments too. And he'd been there for Emma after her mom was gone.

Jack could do everything wrong, and she'd still adore him because of what he'd done right.

Emma looked at herself in the mirror, telling herself that it didn't matter if she looked attractive. Even that kiss wouldn't have been real. Jack had called it research. And tonight was part of the façade. A couple needed to be together on a holiday. Folks would be expecting them to share a blanket under the stars and fireworks.

She slipped her feet into a cute pair of strappy sandals and headed into the kitchen to get a glass of water. Jack and Sam were picking her up. Then Sam would go find his new friends at the park, leaving her and Jack alone. There was as much of a thrill in that prospect as there was trepidation. What if he reached for her hand again? What if he leaned over and really kissed her this time?

The doorbell rang, and Barnaby took off running. Emma headed to go answer.

"Hi," Jack said when she opened the door. He was wearing a pale blue polo shirt that made his dark hair appear even darker. She wanted to reach up and run her fingers through it to see if it felt as silky as it looked. Jack's tan also seemed darker, the way it always did in the summer months, making his blue eyes brighter.

"Hi." She remembered to breathe, settling the unrest in her body. "I, um, prepared some sandwiches and chips. A picnic of sorts. I have enough for Sam too, even though I doubt he'll join us."

"The boy can eat," Jack said. "If not, I'll eat his share." He winked, and she practically melted in a puddle at her doorstep.

"I'll get the basket of food, and we can go." She turned, forcing herself to rein in her hormones and emotions.

"Wait."

She turned to face him and then noticed him pull a hand from behind his back and offer her an arrangement of flowers.

"I almost forgot these," he said.

"What is that?"

"Wildflowers. I stopped into Halona's shop, and I guess it was my lucky day. She was arranging some of the older flowers to give away. She said they'd last about a week longer." Jack shrugged. "Anyway, she told me to use them to brighten someone's day."

"So you brought me old flowers, huh?" she teased as she reached for them.

Jack looked mortified. "No, well, I . . ."

"A pretend girlfriend doesn't get the new ones?" she continued.

"You're more than a pretend girlfriend, Emma," he said. "If I'd have thought you'd be okay with it, I'd have bought you a dozen roses. The red ones, not the yellow."

Her lips parted. She didn't quite know what to say as she cleared her throat and looked down at the wildflowers in her hands. "I love flowers from Halona's shop. Thank you. Although I'm sure your mom would've appreciated them too."

Jack nodded. "Maybe so. But choosing you was selfish on my part."

She looked up at him. "Oh?"

"I guess seeing you smile brightens my day, so it's a win-win."

Emma frowned. "We can't do this, Jack."

"Do what?"

She lowered the bouquet. "I'm not sure what we're doing, but we shouldn't be. Almost kissing. Flirting." Her heart was suddenly hammering in her chest. It felt like she couldn't breathe, not until she got everything that was on her mind out in the open. "If we're going to pretend we're dating, we need to set some boundaries. This is just for show. When there's no one else around, we should just be us."

He was watching her with a serious expression, the kind he got when he was thinking something over. "What exactly does acting like us entail?"

"You know. The way we've always been. At arm's length. No flirting or bringing each other flowers. No kissing as research." She pulled her gaze from his. No hand-holding or fantasies about running her hands through his hair and over his muscled chest. "That's the only way this will work. Neither of us wants a relationship."

"What makes you think I don't want a relationship?" he asked.

She shifted the arrangement of flowers to her other hand. "Because you never keep anything romantic going for very long. You flirt and go on a couple dates, and then lose interest."

"Only because it's never a good fit."

"Well, neither are we. Not romantically, at least. I'm too busy with my café and now planning this event. And considering your dating history, getting involved with you would never last. It would ruin our friendship, which I happen to value." They'd stopped being friends for a while after he'd stood her up, and she didn't want to lose him again.

He nodded. "I value what we have too."

"Then there's my dad...," she said, as if she needed any

more justification for why this fake relationship of theirs needed to remain that way.

"He hates me," Jack agreed. "I've received that message loud and clear."

"I wouldn't say he hates you. I'd say he strongly dislikes the idea of you and me together."

Jack looked away. "Well, then it's settled. We only need to pretend in the presence of others. When we're alone—"

"Which we should keep to a minimum," she cut in.

He met her eyes. "Right. When we're alone, we should just be us."

* * *

The sun was setting behind the distant forest. The rich orange colors in the sky were as vibrant as those in the wildflowers he had given Emma an hour earlier—before her whole spiel on why it was a bad idea for them to be a real couple.

She was right, of course. One hundred percent. About everything. Jack didn't date anyone for long. He always lost interest. He didn't have any issues with commitment; it was nothing like that. It was just that he didn't like to lead women on once he knew there was no long-term potential. It was a waste of energy and emotion, and it felt wrong.

"Sam seems to be fitting in well here in Sweetwater Springs," Emma commented as they sat on a picnic blanket in the park.

Jack followed her gaze to where Sam was lying back on a large beach towel with several other teens from the area. They were all dressed in various shades of red, white, and blue. All were laughing and seemed to enjoy the celebrations. "Yeah. I've tried to get Amanda to move back. The whole reason she moved away was for a job that she no longer has." That was only partly true. Amanda had also moved to get away from their father.

"Is she working right now? I mean, the treatment she's getting is probably expensive, and she has Sam to support."

Jack exhaled softly, running his hand through Barnaby's fur. The little dog had come along for the night and wedged himself between him and Emma. "Amanda has a job. She works from home. She tells me that her insurance is good, and her job is allowing the leave of absence for her health. I'll help her in any way I can, of course, but she's always been stubborn when it comes to asking for or accepting help." He pulled his gaze from Sam and his friends and looked at Emma. "I was surprised when she asked me to take Sam. That's a huge deal for her. That's how I knew something was wrong."

"Well, hopefully she's getting the help she needs. She's really lucky to have a brother like you," Emma said, reaching for the basket. "Hungry?"

Jack sat up. "Starving."

This made Emma laugh. "I hope I packed enough food, then."

They had to lean in close to one another while they spoke to be understood over the bluegrass music playing in the park. The genre of music changed from week to week, but bluegrass was one of Jack's favorites. The musicians were set to stay onstage until sundown, when the firework display would begin.

"I remember that playing music up there on that stage used to be a dream of yours. Do you still play?" Emma asked as she handed him a sandwich.

"Thanks." Jack shrugged. "I play a little bit on my porch at night. It keeps me and the fireflies company."

Emma handed him a bag of chips next. "That sounds nice."

"It is." And he'd invite her to join him if she hadn't established boundaries in their relationship earlier. "My dad used to play for the family at night. He taught me the harmonica first. After that, I got the guitar bug. Then the fiddle."

"You play it all. You should be up there on that stage," Emma commented.

"I'm fine right here. Better than fine." Was that considered flirting? He redirected his attention to the food, opening the baggie with the sandwich and reaching inside. "I guess my dad wasn't all bad."

His father had been his hero back then when he'd played nightly lullabies on the porch. Then Jack had gone through a stage where he loathed the very sight of his dad. He'd understood his father a little more when he'd battled his own demons.

"Is this pimento cheese?" he asked, inspecting the filling between the bread.

"It is. It's my secret recipe. You'll love it, I promise." She looked a little nervous as she watched him.

Jack had never been a fan of pimento, but he didn't want to disappoint Emma. He bit into his sandwich and chewed. "Mmm. That's good," he said honestly. "Is that bacon in there?"

She nodded. "Bacon makes everything better."

Jack looked at her. "A woman after my own heart."

Emma held his gaze for a moment and then turned away. She pulled a dog biscuit from the basket and gave it to Barnaby.

After they finished off their sandwiches, Jack leaned back on his elbows. He scanned the crowd as he listened to the music. Nearly everyone in town seemed to have come out to celebrate. His gaze landed on Edward and Angel St. James. They were pretty far away and hopefully wouldn't even see him and Emma tonight.

He also spotted Mitch Hargrove and his new wife, Kaitlyn, who owned the Sweetwater Bed and Breakfast. Tuck Locklear and Josie Kellum sat on a blanket next to them. And beside them were chief of police Alex Baker and his fiancée, Halona Locklear. So many couples in love. When would it be his turn?

"Jack?" Emma asked.

He looked over at her. "Yeah?"

"Tell me the truth. If I don't join with the Women's Wellness Fair, will I be able to do the event for my mom this summer?" Emma's hair fluttered around her face as a breeze seemed to dance with the music from the bluegrass band.

He blew out a breath as he resisted reaching up and swiping the locks away from her face. "Well, there's always a chance that one of the booked events will be canceled. But it's slim. You could plan your event on a weeknight evening, but the turnout won't be as good. If you want your event to be bigger and better, something you can really be proud of, and if you want it to happen this summer, then yeah. I think joining efforts with the Women's Wellness Center is your best bet."

Emma looked forward, seemingly lost in her decision.

"But they might not even agree. I haven't run it by Dr. Rivers yet."

She nodded her understanding.

"My turn to ask a question. Tell me the truth." He waited

for her to look at him again. "Why are you hesitating on combining events with the WWC?"

Emma looked shocked by the question. She shifted and began to fidget, her gaze bouncing around the field. Then he reached for her hand, giving it a gentle squeeze. "Is there a reason bringing up the WWC makes you nervous?"

CHAPTER TEN

*E*mma gulped in a breath, her heart beating out of its normal rhythm for multiple reasons. Her gaze moved to Jack's hand around hers. It was warm, also rough and calloused. It felt good to her frazzled nerves.

"I guess some part of me is terrified of the Women's Wellness Center right now," she admitted, looking away. She laughed softly at herself, but there wasn't any humor in this situation. "I feel foolish for even saying so." Jack's thumb traced over the back of her hand, distracting her in a pleasant way. "The WWC diagnosed my mom. They're the ones who gave her a death sentence."

"The Wellness Center also helped her," he pointed out.

Emma nodded. "I know. I guess some part of me has always feared that I'll be just like her. Everyone tells me I look like her. I act like her. Everyone says I'm the spitting image of her."

"You're afraid of getting sick like her?" he asked.

She could hear the surprise threading through his voice.

He wouldn't understand. No one would. She didn't have any sisters, but if she did, they'd likely get it. "Breast cancer can be hereditary. It runs in families." Just thinking about it made her heart start to race. Fear gripped her. "My grandmother had breast cancer. My mom got it too."

"But you're fine, right?" he asked. She heard the worry now. "I mean, everything is checking out okay?"

Emma usually kept her appointments, and she performed her own self-checks religiously. Except this year, she couldn't bring herself to go. There were too many what-ifs playing in her mind. Too many fears lining up for attack.

She knew there were just as many reasons to keep her appointment and track her health. Her only explanation was that she was a coward. But she wasn't about to tell Jack that. He'd laugh at her. Or lecture her. Or do one of any number of things. But he wouldn't understand.

She'd watched her mom grow sicker and never get better. Everyone's life had changed after the diagnosis, and in Emma's young mind, it had started at the Women's Wellness Center. "Yes. I'm fine." She nodded at Jack. "Of course I am."

His shoulders rounded as he exhaled, looking relieved. "Good," he said. "I think you need to change your way of thinking about the center. They helped your mom by diagnosing her," he said softly. "She was already sick, and they gave her a fighting chance."

Emma studied him as he spoke. For one, it was hard to hear over the music. Secondly, he was a handsome man. Every feature could be defined as strong. His strong jawline. Strong nose. The strong determination in his blue eyes. His neck and shoulders, chest and arms were thick and hard—also strong. She wanted to curl into him and just be held. "You're right. In my head, I know the center helps women. I appreciate all the services they provide, and I really like Dr. Rivers. She comes into the café all the time."

"She's young to have done so much," Jack agreed. "My mom sees her."

"Is she okay?" Emma asked.

"High blood pressure runs in the family. She's also a borderline diabetic. Dr. Rivers is watching her like a hawk, and so am I. If I see her with anything sweet, I nab it for myself."

Emma laughed. "Her knight in shining armor."

"I doubt that's the way she views it." He chuckled. Then his gaze dropped to their intertwined hands. "I'm not quite clear on the rules for this arrangement we have going."

There was only one rule that she hadn't dared mention. *Don't fall for Jack because...*

Her mind stuttered, searching and failing to remember the reasons why that one rule was so important. Don't fall for Jack because...because he was her friend. Because he'd broken her heart once, a long time ago. Because he'd never shown romantic interest in her again. Until now.

She looked from their hands back to him, her gaze sticking on his and holding. The rest of the people in the park seemed to disappear. *Poof.* It was just her with him, holding hands and staring deeply into each other's eyes. "It's okay," she said.

"Hey, you two." Sophie Daniels stepped up in front of them, her gaze moving from one to the other. Barnaby lifted his head to acknowledge Sophie, but for once, he didn't move or bark to announce her presence. "Looks like you're having a picnic. Together," she noted, her smile only faltering a little bit as she looked at their intertwined hands. Her eyes flashed disappointment for a brief second that Emma didn't miss.

"It's a good night for a picnic," Jack agreed, giving her an easy smile.

"Are you two on a..." Sophie whirled a finger, and then let it bounce in the air, pointing first at Emma and then at Jack. "I mean, you're obviously on a...date. Right?"

"Um, well, this wasn't exactly planned. Jack just invited me this afternoon. He didn't want me to miss out on the Fourth of July celebrations," Emma babbled. She carefully pulled her hand away from Jack's. "Would you like to join us, Sophie?"

"As a third wheel? No, thanks. You two look cute together," she said. "Really."

Guilt swirled in Emma's stomach. Sophie was so nice. Even though she'd been interested in Jack for herself, she was acting like this was no big deal.

"You really need to come down to my boutique," she reiterated to Emma. "Every woman needs a seasonal shopping spree every now and then. And my Independence Day sale will continue through Wednesday of next week. Just FYI."

"I'll definitely stop in."

Sophie gestured across the crowd. "I'm meeting a few friends here so I better go find them. It was nice seeing you two." She looked at Emma and gave her a reassuring smile that only worked to make Emma feel even guiltier. When Sophie walked away, Emma covered her face with one hand.

"What's wrong?" Jack asked, nudging her softly.

"She likes you, and now she's probably a little broken-hearted. And I knew she liked you, so it feels like I went behind my friend's back and started dating her crush."

"It's not like that. Sophie is great. She's beautiful, successful, sweet, smart..."

"Please don't let me stop you from going to sit with her," Emma said sarcastically.

The corners of his mouth curled softly, and he reached up to swipe a lock of hair that had blown across her cheek, sweeping it behind her ear. The movement sent shivers down her body. Then his hand returned to her cheek.

"Let me finish. Sophie is great, but I'm not interested in her. I never have been. And I'm pretty sure it's not me she really wants. She and my buddy Chase have unfinished business."

Emma remembered that Sophie and Chase had been an item in school. Then Sophie had been in a serious accident, and they'd stopped dating after that.

"I don't want to sit with Sophie," Jack added. "The only place I want to be tonight is right here with you. Is it breaking those rules of yours if I say that?"

She shook her head, her gaze still on his, just like a magnet trained on its point of attraction. "No, that's fine."

His hand was still lingering on her cheek, the sensation of his fingers on her skin making her body buzz. Barnaby, joining in the moment, lifted his head and lapped a tongue on Jack's cheek.

Jack laughed as he pulled away. "Wouldn't you rather kiss Emma? She's much more kissable than me." His gaze slid over to meet hers, and butterflies stormed her belly.

Then Jack propped himself on his elbows once more, and they continued listening to the music. Half an hour later, the band stopped playing and the park went quiet.

Emma felt breathless with anticipation, but not from waiting to see the explosive colors that would light up the mountain sky. She'd always found fireworks romantic. It was sitting next to Jack on a picnic blanket beneath the stars that already had her heart in her throat.

A high-pitched squeal penetrated the silence, making Emma jump. It was a solid second before a splash of red covered the sky. Jack reached for Emma's hand. She didn't look at him, but she didn't pull her hand away either. Instead, she leaned in toward him, absorbed in the moment. All her senses were bombarded by the experience, and she let herself get lost in it.

She wasn't sure how long the display went on, but it ended in a fitting finale with one firework following another in quick succession.

"I never wanted it to end," Jack finally said.

She looked at him now. "Me neither." The fireworks were still going off inside her chest though, and her heart was beating too fast.

Jack redirected his attention as Sam headed toward them.

"Jeremy is going to give me a ride home," Sam said. "We thought we'd go get something from the fudge shop first. Dawanda has some kind of red, white, and blue candy for the occasion. Is that okay?"

Jack nodded. "One hour. If you're not back, I'm getting in my truck and going looking for you."

Sam rolled his eyes. "An hour and a half?"

Jack hesitated. "Fine. But don't be late."

Emma stood and started packing up the basket and blanket as Sam and Jack haggled.

When Sam was gone, Jack sighed. "Caring for a teenager is harder than I thought."

Emma laughed softly. "I'm impressed at how good you are with him. You're a natural at being a parent."

"You think so?"

She nodded. "Not too strict, but you're not letting him walk all over you either. You're just right."

"Thanks. I guess I'm channeling my mom's discipline style this summer. That's how she was with me."

"And you turned out just fine," Emma commented, noticing how his jaw tensed. She was around a lot of people during her days at the café. She compared herself to a bartender of sorts. She people-watched, and many of her customers unloaded their worries and cares on her while seated at her tables.

Jack took the basket from her hand, shifting it to his opposite side. Then he offered his free hand for her to hold.

Emma hesitated for a moment. Were they pretending for the crowd? Or was this real? She couldn't tell. Even so, she took his hand because she wanted to.

They navigated through the crowd toward the parking lot. Then Jack opened the passenger door and waited for her to step inside with Barnaby hopping in at her feet. Jack shut the door behind her and got in on the driver's side. A moment later, he pulled onto the main road that led to her home on Pine Cone Lane.

"You don't talk about your dad much," Emma said, fidgeting with her hands. "How is he?"

Jack tensed some more. "He's okay. The divorce just made it easier for him to drink whenever he wants to. He stays sober long enough to work with the construction crew, so that's good." Jack looked over at her. "I think that makes him what you call a functional alcoholic."

Emma reached over to squeeze Jack's forearm. She knew Jack never drank, and she guessed it was because he'd seen what alcohol had done to his dad. His childhood couldn't have been easy, watching his dad passed out all the time. He'd had rough teenage years too, not just her.

He pulled into her driveway and parked. The darkness seemed to fold around them as the lights in the truck went out.

"I'd invite you in for a nightcap, but I know that's not your thing," she said.

"Plus, you said we can't be trusted to be alone together," he pointed out, his voice low.

"I don't think I said we can't trust ourselves." But yeah, that's exactly what she'd meant.

"So I'll just walk you to your door and leave it at that."

She protested. "You don't need to walk me to my door, Jack." But he was already pushing open his door and stepping out. Emma got out of the truck as well. Jack walked beside her up the porch steps and to the door. She pushed the house key inside the lock, opened the door, and let Barnaby inside. She didn't follow though. Instead, she closed the door again, leaving her and Jack alone. Barnaby barked his objections from inside. "Well, thank you for a wonderful evening," she told Jack.

"The pleasure was mine."

The way he was looking at her made her know they weren't just words. He was looking at her like a man who was about to lean in and kiss her. His gaze solidified the fact that going inside together would be the worst idea in the history of bad ideas.

She sucked in a deep breath, her mind trying to determine if she should step inside her house or walk forward and meet him halfway. What would one little kiss hurt? "Research," she whispered.

Jack raised one brow. "Hmm?"

She nibbled her lower lip, and his eyes lowered to watch.

"Well, we have a whole summer ahead of us, and I'm standing behind the idea that we should keep our boundaries. But maybe a kiss for research like you said…"

He leaned in, and one of his hands wrapped around her hip. Her body responded with a rush of need. Then he lowered his mouth, stopping just shy of hers. His gaze was pinned on her eyes, searching for permission.

She stepped toward him, her body pressing against his chest, and she went up on her toes just enough for their lips to collide. It was like a mini-explosion on her porch. Sparks times one million, lighting her up from the inside out. She didn't think, she just kissed. Somewhere in the distance, she heard fireworks going off. It sounded like they were right overhead. Maybe she and Jack were the ones setting them off with this kiss.

"Where did you learn to kiss like that?" Jack said in a breathless whisper when they finally pulled away. "Please don't say Tim, the firefighter," he said, making her laugh.

"No. That kiss was..." Her chest rose and fell in quick succession. "It was..."

"Perfect," he said, finishing her sentence for her.

She nodded, feeling awestruck by him suddenly. Who knew that Jack could kiss with such passion? Another question swam into her thoughts. Now that she knew it, how was she going to resist him?

* * *

Jack was searching for something to say and coming up speechless until Emma broke the silence.

"Well, thank you for taking me to the Music in the Park. Good night, Jack." She pushed her front door open and crossed the threshold.

"Good night, Emma."

She closed the door behind her, and Jack continued to stand there for a long moment. For what felt like his whole life, he'd been wanting to kiss Emma. He only wished he'd done it sooner.

He turned and headed back to his truck and reversed out of her driveway. He was consumed in his thoughts all the way to his cabin on Silver Lake. Technically, he wasn't on Silver Lake. There was a forest of trees between him and the water, but it was his land and he could hike back to it anytime he wanted.

He parked and headed up the steps, letting himself inside his home. It felt like he'd had about three cups of coffee tonight. There was no chance of going to bed and sleeping at this moment. Instead, he headed out onto the back porch and plopped into the wooden swing, replaying his time with Emma—especially that last part—on repeat.

The more he thought about her, the more he wondered if maybe it wouldn't be so bad to get romantically involved with her after all. The worst thing that could happen was that her father might kill him. Or he and Emma would end up hating each other when things went sour. Except if Emma hadn't hated him after he'd ruined her prom night, she probably wouldn't start now.

The best thing that could happen is they'd make each other happy.

He'd been envying his friends who'd found that with someone lately. Emma was his best friend. How amazing would it be to be with her, not just for the summer, but beyond that?

After an hour, Jack pulled out his phone and called Sam. No answer. The boy always had his phone on him so Jack suspected he was being ignored. On a sigh, he headed back inside and lay down on the couch, hoping to catch at least a few winks before he had to go to work. He needed to be awake during his shift to avoid driving off a cliff or stepping into a nest of rattlesnakes. He also needed to be awake and alert for the next time he ran into Emma. Maybe they'd do a little more research together and investigate this increasingly real thing between them.

* * *

Jack awoke on the couch just after one a.m. to the sound of Sam sneaking, not so quietly, into the house. "Stop right there," Jack said, his voice thick with sleep.

Sam froze.

"Are you seriously coming in this late? Where were you?"

Sam straightened and faced him in the dimly lit living room. "Just with friends. We weren't doing anything wrong. Just watching fireworks from the neighbors' houses."

"You didn't answer your phone when I called you, and you didn't come home when I told you to either. That's pretty wrong."

Sam shook his head. "This isn't home, and it's not like you were up waiting for me and worried sick." He gestured at the couch where Jack had just been startled awake.

"That's not the point." Jack sat up. "I need to be able to trust you. Was there alcohol involved?"

Sam's eyes widened. "I didn't drink."

"But did the other kids?"

Sam looked away. "What they do is none of my business."

"It's my business if you're hanging out with them," Jack growled.

"I don't think there was anything more than beers, okay? And only one guy was drinking. He offered me one, and I said no."

Jack nodded. "Good answer. You're too young." And it wasn't a good decision for anyone in the Hershey family.

"I'm sorry I was late, okay? Time got away from me," Sam said.

Jack hesitated, trying to figure out what he was supposed to do in a moment like this one. "Stick to curfew. Otherwise your summer isn't going to be all that fun. Got it?"

Sam nodded. "Got it."

"Good. Now go to bed," Jack said. "I'm going to do the same." Assuming he could once again rein in his thoughts about Emma.

Jack got himself a glass of water and retreated to his room, about to drift off to sleep once more when his cell phone chimed with an incoming text. Emma's name popped onscreen.

You awake?

He grabbed his cell and started texting. Yeah. You?

If I weren't, I wouldn't be texting you. I can't sleep.

This made him smile because he assumed her reasons were the same as his were earlier.

Oh yeah? Something on your mind? he texted, feeling a little cocky.

Yeah. I can't stop thinking about the WWC.

Jack's grin fell away. The WWC?

I really want to do this 5K, and if it's the path of least resistance, then I should take it.

His ego was a little bruised, but he was also thrilled.
Great. I'll contact Dr. Rivers tomorrow and see if she'll
consider the idea.

Thank you. Now I can sleep peacefully.

At least one of them would rest easy tonight.

* * *

The café was bustling the next morning. So much so that
Emma hadn't had time to think. When it finally started
to slow, she made herself a cup of coffee and headed to
the back to take a quiet break, collect her breath and her
thoughts, and do something she knew beyond a shadow of
a doubt that she shouldn't.

She opened her laptop and typed into the search bar:
Sweetwater Springs A-List. She'd told herself that she
wasn't going to stalk her reviews anymore. She could control her service, but not what a customer wrote online after
they'd left her business. So why waste time and energy
reading them?

The site loaded, and Emma took a breath. She reached
for her cup of coffee and took a large sip as if that
would give her liquid courage to continue looking. She
then searched the site for the Sweetwater Café. It loaded
quickly, and Emma stared wide-eyed at the screen. Her
heart did a free fall into her stomach.

Another bad review. Or actually, this one was mediocre.
She held her breath as she began to read.

The music coming through the sound system is too
loud and who can sit and enjoy their coffee with

that crap playing? I had to leave. The coffee was worth going back for though. Just make sure you get it to go.

Emma's eyes stung. She'd never been one to let criticism roll off her shoulders easily. She was a people pleaser to her core, and she dwelled on things like this—which was why she was supposed to be avoiding the site altogether.

"What are you doing?" Nina asked, walking into the back.

Emma looked up. "Why? Is it busy again?"

Nina shook her head. "No. I can handle it. But you look miserable. What's wrong?"

Emma sighed and turned her laptop around for Nina to see the screen. Nina took a moment to read the review and then started laughing. "For Pete's sake. You can't please everyone, Emma. You're not actually upset about this, are you?"

Emma looked up at Nina. "Maybe we should change the music."

"No, that's not the answer." Nina put her hands on her hips. "The only thing you need to change is your reaction to those bad reviews. It's not like she was saying the coffee was bad. That would be real criticism. Stop reading those."

Emma sipped from her coffee again. "You're right. I have better things to do, like plan the 5K, assuming that Jack can get the Women's Wellness Center to agree to combine events."

"I'm so happy that you're considering that suggestion. I don't know why you didn't jump at it in the first place."

Emma looked up at her employee and friend. If she told Nina that she didn't want to join with the WWC because she was suddenly scared of the clinic, so much so that she had canceled her annual checkup this year, she was pretty sure Nina would lecture her in the same way she just had about her response to the A-List review. Emma knew she was being silly, but that didn't change the fact that she was terrified of going to a doctor's appointment there and getting bad news. "I just needed some time to think it through, I guess."

Nina peeked into the café to make sure all the customers were happy and then stood in the doorway and continued talking to Emma. "So how is your fake relationship with Jack going?" she whispered. "I saw you two at the park last night. If I hadn't overheard about your arrangement, I would've been completely fooled. You two looked cozy on that blanket."

Emma felt her cheeks flush. She pulled her lower lip between her teeth and nibbled softly, trying to figure out how much she was going to divulge to Nina.

"Whoa. It is still fake, isn't it?" Nina asked. "Because the look on your face right now is telling a totally different story."

"Of course it's fake."

"Well, if you're just pretending for the sake of Jack's sister, who isn't even in town, why are you two having dates?"

"As you know, Sam is in town," Emma said. "And he needs to report back to his mother that everything is great here and that Jack and I are a happy couple."

The bell at the front of the store rang, and Emma got up from the table. She looked at Nina. "I'll get this."

"Thanks," Nina said.

Emma was hyper-tuned to the music as she headed to the front counter. Even though Nina had protested, maybe

Emma should consider changing the music to something softer in the café.

She smiled back at her customer, then suddenly realized who she was looking at. She was used to Ashley Rivers being dressed in a white doctor's coat with her hair pulled back. It was Saturday, however, and this morning, Ashley was dressed in jeans and a soft cotton top with her red hair down on her shoulders. She smiled back at Emma.

"Hi, Emma."

"Hi, Dr. Rivers."

"Ashley. I'm here as a customer, not a physician. I'm also here hoping we can take a moment to sit and discuss the Women's Wellness Fair that I'm putting on later this summer. I spoke to Jack this morning about combining our events and wanted to talk to you a little more. Do you have time?"

Emma looked around the café. Everyone was seated and seemingly content, and there wasn't a line of customers needing attention. Emma gestured behind her. "Sure. Let me see if Nina can cover the counter." Emma headed back to the break area and gave Nina a sheepish smile. "Can you cover the counter? Ashley Rivers is here and wants to discuss the event."

Nina pushed back from the table. "Of course."

"I'll make sure you get a break just as soon as I can."

Nina waved that idea off. "It's fine. Really. If I break for too long, I'm likely to fall asleep. I've stayed up reading way too much lately."

"Thank you. I'll just make a couple coffees for myself and Ashley and go grab a table," Emma said.

Nina tsked. "Nonsense. I'll get your drinks. You go sit and start talking. I can't wait to hear what you guys discuss."

"Thanks." Emma felt a flutter of nerves as she headed back toward Ashley.

"I saw that you have tables outside now," Ashley said. "Do you mind if we sit out there? I need a little sunshine and vitamin D."

"Perfect." Emma grabbed a notebook and pen off the counter and followed Ashley outside. They sat next to each other at one of the new tables that Emma had put out to appease her first bad reviewer. It offered the perfect mix of shade and sunshine and a nice view of Main Street.

"I have to say, I was surprised when Jack contacted me about your event. But I love the idea of doing a 5K in honor of your mom." Ashley pulled her sunglasses down off the top of her head and placed them over her eyes. Emma wished she'd brought her glasses out as well. The eyes were the window to the soul, and she didn't want Ashley getting too good a look at hers. Emma still felt guilty about canceling her appointment at the clinic.

Nina came outside holding two cups of coffee. "Here you are." She laid down two croissants as well. "You didn't ask for food, but these are on the house. I know the owner and I'm sure she'd approve." Nina winked at Emma and then turned to head back inside.

Ashley reached for her cup of coffee. "So what made you decide to do something for your mom after all this time?"

"Well, I was given a box of her things earlier this week. It was kind of a birthday present."

"Oh, happy belated birthday," Ashley said.

Emma nodded. "Thanks. In the box was a list of things my mom wanted to do before she died. Kind of a bucket list. One of those things was to organize a 5K. I thought I'd plan it for her. In her honor."

Ashley smiled. "Wow. I love that. You and your mom must have been close."

"We were. But lately, I feel like I'm slowly forgetting her," she confessed, not meeting Ashley's gaze.

"That's normal. My dad died when I was young."

Emma looked up. "I had no idea. I'm sorry to hear that."

Ashley shrugged. "I've had moments where I felt like I was forgetting him too. His voice, the way he smelled. Those memories slowly fade without you even realizing it. Then when you reach for them, they can feel so distant. It can be pretty disheartening."

"What do you do?" Emma asked, interested to hear that someone else was experiencing the same emotions she was.

Ashley's gaze moved to the people walking up and down Main Street. "I visit his gravesite for one. Somehow, I feel closer to him there. I know that's not true for everyone." She looked at Emma again. "I do some of the things we did together when I was growing up, like going to the movies. That was one of his favorite things to do. We'd grab a popcorn and take the back row. It never mattered what show was playing. We just enjoyed sitting there and getting lost in the magic." Ashley smiled easily. "That's what he'd call it, at least. I find that it's the little things that bring him back when I need him most."

"That's nice." Emma swallowed. "Mom and I loved to go shopping together. We'd try on a ton of clothes with the rule that we'd only pick out one outfit each. It kept things real and made it extra fun."

Ashley popped a piece of croissant into her mouth. "You should do that, then."

"Maybe so."

"It's a good excuse to go shopping, if nothing else," Ashley teased.

The conversation returned to the Women's Wellness Fair, and Ashley reviewed the agenda. Most of the activities she had planned were taking place in the morning. "A midmorning run along the trails and through the Evergreen Park side of Silver Lake would be a great addition. We can put up a banner with your mom's picture too. Or a poster telling her story. I think it's an important one. She was a fighter, and if we'd caught her cancer sooner, maybe we could've helped her more." Ashley gave Emma a meaningful look.

Emma looked down at her half-eaten croissant.

"People can learn from your mom's story. Maybe those who have been putting off health checkups and screenings will take your mom's story to heart and make an appointment."

Was Ashley talking about her now? Did she keep tabs on the schedule at the clinic and know that Emma had canceled her appointment earlier this week?

"I'm so thrilled about this fair and now your 5K as well. I really believe it could save a life."

Goose bumps popped over Emma's arms. "Save a life," she repeated. "That was one of the items on my mom's Life List too."

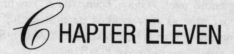

CHAPTER ELEVEN

*J*ack didn't mind silence. It was one of the reasons he loved his job. But Sam was with him today, and he was the kind of quiet that rang all kinds of warning bells in Jack's gut.

Was I too hard on him for coming in past curfew?

Rules were healthy, right? And if Sam got away with breaking one, he'd break them all. Right?

The whole morning had been filled with pushing paper and making phone calls, one of which was to Dr. Rivers about her upcoming event. He'd also given a brief lesson on how to identify poison ivy to a group of Boy Scouts.

Sam had been quiet through it all so Jack had suggested a hike, thinking his nephew was bored out of his mind. The hike was proving to be more of the same. "You okay?" Jack finally asked as they walked along one of the trails.

"Yeah," Sam said, his voice so low it was barely audible over the noisy wildlife surrounding them.

"You haven't said much today. Is this about last night?

Because if it is, I didn't even yell. I barely reprimanded you. If you ask me, you got off easy."

"I don't care about last night," Sam said. "You were right."

Jack glanced over. "Okay. Then what?" His breathing was heavier now as they walked up a steep hill in the woods, making him wish he'd taken the ATV out. But that wouldn't have been conducive to talking.

"Nothing," Sam said.

"You'd rather be working with Emma today?" Jack asked.

Sam laughed a little. "No. I mean, yesterday was cool, but I like it here too." He stopped walking and shoved his hands in his pockets. "It's just, Mom didn't call yesterday."

Jack folded his arms over his chest. "She was probably just busy, but I'm sure she misses you."

"Busy doing what?" Sam asked.

"You know," Jack said, as if that answered anything.

"No, I don't." Sam shifted back and forth on his sneakered feet. "She can never talk long when she calls, and she doesn't tell me anything about what she's doing. She just wants to hear about how I'm doing. And about you and Emma."

Jack straightened. "She asks about me and Emma?"

Sam looked down, letting his overgrown hair fall in his face. "She's kind of obsessed. I think she's really happy to see you two hooking up."

Jack frowned. "Hooking up" had a very different meaning in his mind, and he and Emma definitely weren't doing that.

"She said you were alone for a very long time, and she thought you'd always be alone. Mom says that seeing you and Emma together makes her think that things can change for the better." Sam swiped at his hair and faced Jack. "See?

If she was on vacation and having the time of her life, she wouldn't be wanting a change. She'd sound happier."

Jack nodded. He'd have a talk with Amanda about Sam's concerns. Maybe it was time to tell Sam the truth. There would only be more questions as time went on.

A hiker came up on the path, carrying a long stick. A ball cap sat on his head, and he smiled at the two of them as he approached. "Hi, Jack."

Jack recognized the man as Paris Montgomery, a graphic designer who'd recently moved to Sweetwater Springs from Florida. "Paris. Hey, man. How are you doing?"

"Never better." Paris introduced himself to Sam and then gestured behind him. "Looks like someone's been camping out in the park. Did you see that?"

Jack shook his head. "Not today." He'd been too distracted talking to Sam. "But I've seen evidence a few times lately."

"There's charred sticks and a half-eaten apple on the ground," Paris told him. "That apple could attract wildlife so I thought you should know."

"Thanks." Jack motioned for Sam to follow him, and they went to check out the situation while Paris continued forward on the path. Sure enough, there were charred sticks, a half-eaten apple, and a gum wrapper.

"What are you going to do?" Sam asked.

Jack shrugged. "I don't know who it is, so there's not a whole lot I can do."

"We can have a stakeout tonight," Sam suggested, his face lighting up with the idea.

"A stakeout? This person could be dangerous, Sam." Although that wasn't likely. The person was probably just homeless for some reason and possibly unaware they were even breaking the law by being here. "I can hang more signs that make the park hours more clear and that staying overnight is against the law."

Sam seemed to deflate and nodded.

Jack clapped a hand on his back. "Let's head back to the office. I need to make a report on this."

They started walking once more, both falling quiet on their hike back. At least Jack now understood a little bit of what was going through his nephew's mind. Amanda was withholding the truth to keep him from worrying, but that plan was backfiring. Keeping secrets and false pretenses always backfired, in one way or another.

* * *

A few days after her semi-date to the park with Jack, Emma took her time as she strolled down the sidewalks of Main Street. Nina was working the café this afternoon. Weekday afternoons were usually slow and usually only required one person to handle things. If it got busy, Nina knew she could call Emma back and she'd be there in a flash.

After meeting with Ashley a second time and solidifying the plans for the Women's Wellness Fair and the 5K, Emma had spent a little time making flyers for the event so that people could sign up for it online. She put up a couple flyers on the community posting areas as she strolled. Then she stopped inside Dawanda's Fudge Shop to talk to Dawanda about possibly sponsoring the event. Halona had already agreed that the Little Shop of Flowers would be a sponsor. Mayor Everson had too.

"Count me in," Dawanda said enthusiastically. "I love a good cause, especially one that will benefit the women in this town. And I loved your mom," she said, placing a hand over her heart.

"Did she come in here a lot?" Emma asked, wishing she could remember.

"For maple nut fudge." Dawanda nodded. "That was her favorite. I read her fortune in the cappuccino a couple times too."

Emma cocked her head. Dawanda was famous in town for her cappuccino readings where she claimed to see images in the frothy foam of her drinks and predict the future of her customers. "What did my mom's fortune say?" Emma asked. Surely it hadn't said that her mom would die young. Otherwise, she'd have gone to the doctor sooner.

Dawanda shook her head. "I saw a big heart and a full life."

"My mom died young," Emma pointed out. That didn't exactly imply a full life.

"A full life isn't measured by time." Dawanda dipped into the fudge cabinet and pulled out a square of maple nut fudge. She wrapped it in a napkin and slid it across the counter toward Emma. "On the house." She jabbed a finger in the air at Emma. "I still need to read your fortune in the foam."

Emma reached for the fudge. "Thank you. I'll have to get my fortune read another time," she lied. She wasn't sure she wanted to know what lay ahead. "Right now I'm going to Sophie's Boutique for a little retail therapy." She was hoping to take Ashley's advice and enjoy doing something that she and her mom had loved doing together.

"Ahh." Dawanda smiled brightly. "Retail therapy is nearly as good as fudge therapy."

Emma laughed. She bit into the maple nut fudge as she exited the store, sighing as the square melted in her mouth. Then she walked farther down Main Street and stepped inside Sophie's Boutique.

"Welcome to Sophie's—" Sophie's words cut off as Emma faced her.

She hadn't thought this through. She'd forgotten Sophie's disappointed look when she'd spotted Emma out with Jack at the music event on Friday night.

"Emma," Sophie said, a little thread of surprise in her otherwise cheerful voice, "what brings you here?"

"You told me I needed to come check out the summer line." Emma shrugged.

"But it's the middle of the day. You never leave the café."

"Nina and Sam are covering it, and the café isn't that busy right now."

Sophie nodded. "I see."

"Sophie, about the other night—" Emma cut herself off. She couldn't exactly tell Sophie her relationship with Jack was a hoax. Then again, they were only trying to fool Sam and his mom, who didn't even live in Sweetwater Springs. Sophie could keep a secret, and Emma didn't want to hurt their friendship over something so silly.

She stepped closer to Sophie, looking around the boutique to make sure no one else would overhear. The boutique was empty. "About the other night," she repeated.

"You don't need to explain."

"Yes, I do. And I have an explanation." Emma proceeded to tell Sophie all about how she'd somehow become Jack's fake girlfriend. For the sake of his sister, who was in a rehab facility. That wasn't Emma's secret to tell but Sophie was trustworthy. At least Emma hoped she was.

"Whoa. I had no idea. You and Jack looked so comfortable with each other. You looked real to me," Sophie said.

"He's my friend. I *am* comfortable with him." Emma headed over to the racks of new clothing now. "We've been good friends forever, since as long as I can remember. It's no big deal to hold his hand." Or kiss him. The kiss wasn't going to happen again. It'd been research, and now that they'd been there and done that, it was over.

"Well, I have to admit I was a little bummed when I saw you together at the park on Friday night," Sophie said. "Not that I have a huge thing for Jack. I don't. He's a nice guy, and he's cute and all. I was more disappointed that you would be dating him behind my back and let me blabber on about him in your café the other day, if you knew he was already taken."

"He's not taken," Emma reiterated, wondering at the jealousy crawling through her. Jack wasn't hers, and she didn't want him to be.

The conversation moved on to the fund-raiser for her mother, and Emma told Sophie all the details about that as well.

"Of course, I'd love for my boutique to be a sponsor," Sophie said. "You know, I'm meeting up with the Ladies' Day Out group this evening. I can bring flyers and get all of the LDO to sign up as well. And get them to spread the word. As you know, we're really good at spreading news."

Emma laughed. "Thank you."

"Maybe you should come with us and tell them the details yourself. I'm sure you could get a few more sponsors."

Emma used to hang out with the LDO all the time, but life had only gotten busier, and her feet usually ached after working at the café all day. "Where are you all going?" she asked, hoping the venue would sway her one way or the other.

"Kaitlyn has invited us to the Sweetwater Bed and Breakfast for a movie in the ballroom. Brenna McConnell is catering dinner for free, and I heard something about Dawanda bringing fudge and doing her cappuccino readings."

"I just dodged one of those on the walk here," Emma confessed.

"Well, I don't mind them," Sophie said. "It's all in fun, and I've heard that some of Dawanda's predictions have actually come true."

Emma had heard the same, which made the readings even more intimidating.

"Join us," Sophie said as she walked Emma to one of the fitting rooms. Emma had picked out a huge stack of clothes to try on as they'd talked. But in the spirit of remembering her mom, she'd only allow herself to purchase one outfit. Maybe something to wear out with the LDO tonight.

"Okay," Emma said. "I'll come."

* * *

Jack stared at the text on his phone.

> Two dollar drinks at the Tipsy Tavern. Come hang with us?

It was from Luke Marini, the local fire chief in Sweetwater Springs. Jack sometimes hung out with him and Granger Fields. He never drank though, and he never gave anyone a solid reason why. His friends probably assumed it was just because of his father. They didn't need to know that Jack had struggled with the same issues.

> Maybe next week, Jack texted back.

It had been a long day, and he wanted to make sure Sam was okay. His nephew had spent the day at the café. Jack collected his things and walked out his office door at five p.m. As he headed home, he answered a call from Amanda.

"Hey, Jack," she said. Her voice sounded rough and tired.

"You doing okay?" he asked.

"Oh yeah. Getting my head on straight is exhausting, that's all. How are you and Sam?"

"No problems here." She didn't need to know that Sam was suddenly asking questions about where she was. Amanda had already told Jack how she felt about telling her son the truth. But Sam was smart, and he was starting to see cracks in the story he'd been given. "He loves skateboarding."

"That he does," Amanda agreed on a laugh.

"It's better than some things he could be doing. Like those video games that kids are obsessed with."

"I've never bought him those games," Amanda said. "He's complained about that for years."

"You've given him everything he's ever needed."

Amanda scoffed. "He needed a dad. He needs his mom this summer."

"But he also needs you to be healthy. You're making sure he has that, and that's important," Jack told her.

"How are you and Emma?" Amanda asked.

Jack hedged, remembering their kiss on Friday night. They hadn't been out together since then, only texting a few times. He'd been in to the café with Sam to get drinks and a snack, but he and Emma hadn't been alone. "We're good," he finally said.

"And how are you?" she asked.

By the tone of her question, he knew she was asking if he'd taken a drink. Almost a decade sober and it still felt like the people who knew about his alcoholism were waiting for him to fall off the wagon. "Amanda, you don't have to worry about that with me," Jack said, feeling a little defensive. "I struggled with alcohol, got drunk too much and too often, but I got help. I'm done with that. It won't happen again."

"Jack, you've always thought you were invincible." Amanda sighed. "But you're human just like the rest of us. And it's nothing to be ashamed of. Everyone has their weaknesses. Everyone has something that they're afraid to face. No one is exempt, not even you."

Jack's jaw tightened. He wasn't sure why he was so irritated by her words. Why couldn't she just believe him when he said he was fine? "That therapist in there must be filling your head," he muttered, immediately regretting his words.

Amanda went quiet.

"I'm sorry," Jack finally said. "But I'm fine, okay? You'll be fine. Everyone's fine."

"Famous last words," Amanda said.

"Maybe for those who aren't in the Hershey family. But we've got each other," Jack said. "If you're in a bind, you can call me. And if I ever need a hand up, then I know I have you to call on."

"It's nice to have a brother like you. Thanks for helping me. I owe you."

"You don't owe me anything."

They chatted just a minute longer and then said goodbye. Jack released a pent-up breath. That phone conversation was an example of why he didn't tell his friends about his own struggles with alcohol. People expected alcoholics to fall off the wagon. He knew better than most what was at stake, and he intended to hold on tight and never let go.

CHAPTER TWELVE

Going out with the Ladies' Day Out group tonight was the best idea Emma had agreed to in a long while. She was having a fantastic time in the bed and breakfast's ballroom, which was set up with a large-screen TV for guests to watch old movies.

Brenna McConnell had brought enough food to feed the LDO for several days, and between all the women, they'd eaten it until there were hardly any leftovers. Now the women were on the last leg of a Julia Roberts classic, *Steel Magnolias*, and all the women were hugging boxes of Kleenex to their midsection, sniffling and, if they were anything like Emma, hoping just this one time the movie would end differently.

It didn't.

As the movie credits rolled, all the women fell back into easy chatter among themselves.

Kaitlyn flipped on the lights and started collecting everyone's trash in a large plastic bag.

"This was so much fun," Kaitlyn's best friend, Josie, said, seated on one side of Emma. On Emma's other side was Edna Baker, the chief of police's grandmother. Emma knew all the women in the room. They frequented the café and felt like family to her. Tonight, there was Kaitlyn, Josie, Sophie, Edna, Nina, Halona, Brenna, Dawanda, and Janice Murphy. Everyone was keeping a close eye on Janice to make sure she didn't get near the beverages that Brenna had brought. Janice had an uncontrolled inclination to spike drinks.

It was a small group tonight and not all the usual women could make it, but it was no less lively.

"Everyone, please make sure you go to Emma's website and sign up for her 5K walk/run event with the Women's Wellness Center this summer," Kaitlyn called out to the group.

All the women turned to look at Emma with interest.

"It's in honor of my mom," she told those who didn't know.

"Where can we sign up?" Josie asked, pulling her briefcase to her. She'd come straight here from work. She placed her ever-present laptop on her legs.

"Jenny's Wellness Walk for Women dot org," Emma rattled off. "There's a twenty-dollar entry fee, but you get a T-shirt and all the money benefits the Women's Wellness Center."

"That is so wonderful. My fudge shop is a sponsor. You other entrepreneurs need to think about doing so as well." Dawanda clapped her hands together and looked at Emma again. "Your mom would be so proud of you."

Emma's gaze fell to her lap. She wasn't so sure. There were some things her mom would be happy over. But Jenny St. James would likely be disappointed in Emma for cowering away from taking care of her own health right now.

"Don't worry. We will all be signing up," Edna told Emma, gazing over the group with a stern motherly look that told those around her they better agree. She was just as tough as her police chief grandson.

"I appreciate it." Emma offered a smile to her friends, hoping the subject would turn to someone else because she didn't necessarily like being the center of attention.

"So," Edna said, loud enough to gain everyone's attention, "tell us about your new beau, Emma."

Emma squirmed as everyone faced her once more. So much for not being the center of attention tonight.

"It's not what you think, everyone," Sophie told them before Emma could figure out what to say.

Emma felt her heart stop. She spun around to look at Sophie behind her, hoping to catch Sophie's eye and stop her from spilling what was supposed to be a secret. Sophie wasn't looking at her though.

"It's all pretend," Sophie told the ladies. "Jack is caring for his nephew this summer. He's worried about his sister, so Emma and Jack let Amanda believe that they were dating for some reason. I don't really get it, but it's just pretend."

Emma let her face fall into her hands. "Sophie," she said, "I told you not to tell anyone."

Sophie looked over. "You did? I thought you were only keeping it a secret from Sam so he wouldn't tell Amanda, who doesn't even live here."

Emma shook her head. "No, but Jack and Amanda's mom does. And his aunts and uncles. And word travels at light speed around here."

Edna put a hand on Emma's shoulder. "Oh, I was so

thrilled when I heard that you and Jack were the town's newest item. I'm sad to hear it isn't true."

"I'm sorry, Edna. But this secret stays in this room." Emma looked around. She could trust Kaitlyn and Josie to keep her secret. Brenna too. It was mainly Dawanda, Edna, and Janice that worried her. Between the three of them, they'd told her many a secret that she wasn't supposed to know.

"Jack has always been overprotective of his sister," Dawanda told the group. "He's such a sweetie. Handsome too. If I were you, I'd milk this pretend relationship for all it's worth," she told Emma. Then she pretended to zip her lips. "Don't worry about me. I won't tell a soul. I promise."

Emma exhaled. "Thank you. It's just a few weeks, and neither of us are interested in dating anyone or having a real relationship anyway. It's kind of fun having someone I can call to do things like Music in the Park with."

"That is the nice part of being half of a couple. You're never alone. That's also the downside," Kaitlyn said. "Especially when you own a bed and breakfast."

Everyone laughed.

Then Dawanda stood and got everyone's attention. "Notice the table set up in the back? I'm doing cappuccino readings tonight," she said, her eyes lighting up. "And since we're all focused on Emma's personal life right now, I suggest she come to the cup first."

Emma's mouth dropped open. "Oh, I don't know, Dawanda." But Dawanda grabbed her hand and pulled her toward the table, as all the women started insisting.

Emma followed Dawanda to the back of the room, searching for a way out of this. When she couldn't find one, she told herself that this was all in fun. No big deal. Relax.

She sat down at the table and watched Dawanda and Kaitlyn hurry around, gathering the needed supplies. A mug with a handle. Coffee. Steaming milk.

"I don't suggest you actually drink that," Janice said, standing near the table. "You'll never get to sleep tonight."

"She doesn't have to drink it," Dawanda offered. "But this is caffeine-free so she can if she wants to."

"Sounds like you thought of everything." Emma inhaled deeply, her nerves suddenly on edge. She didn't want to know what her future held. The future was a scary thing. What if hers was destined to be short and incomplete like her mom's and grandma's?

Dawanda slid the cup in front of Emma, turning the handle to point directly at Emma's chest, and then ceremoniously poured the steaming milk into the beverage's center. The crowd closed in to watch. The fudge shop owner leaned in over the cup, her blue eyes pinned to the white froth that moved slowly, forming shapeless blobs. At least they were shapeless if you asked Emma.

"Hmm," Dawanda hummed.

"What? What is it?" Emma asked, even though she really didn't want to know.

Dawanda concentrated, unblinking, her breaths shallow as she studied the foam. "I see a rose." She pointed at one of the circular blobs that did kind of look like a rose with a thin jagged line traveling down the cup. "A rose blooms in the spring and summer, but the petals fall away in the winter months. It's as beautiful as it is painful. You can look, but be careful grabbing that kind of flower."

Emma shook her head. What was that supposed to mean?

As if hearing her thoughts, Edna said, "What the heck does that mean, Dawanda?"

Dawanda straightened and blinked as if she were exiting a trance. Her gaze fell on Emma, the look in her eyes making Emma feel a knot of dread in the center of her chest. "Emma is blooming this summer, and it's going to be beautiful," she finally said.

But there was more that Dawanda wasn't saying. It would be short-lived, and winter was sure to come.

"What happens after summer?" Emma asked.

Dawanda reached for her hand and gave it a squeeze. "We all have seasons. The thing about roses is that they're resilient. They come back year after year, stronger and more vibrant every time."

"Can't get rid of them even if you wanted to," Janice agreed from the group, making a few women laugh.

Emma didn't feel like laughing though. Instead, something about her reading left her feeling unsettled.

* * *

Jack needed to go home and shower after a long, hot summer day in the park. He was overdue to visit his mom though. He hadn't seen her since he'd stopped by to get the box of Jenny St. James's things to give to Emma on her birthday last week.

Jack pulled into his mother's driveway and cut the engine. Since divorcing his father almost a decade ago, his mom had lived alone. She worked part-time as a dental assistant and spent the rest of her time tending to her garden. Sam would've gone stir-crazy staying with his grandmother this summer, even more so than he was with Jack.

"Mom?" Jack called, opening her front door and stepping inside. "It's Jack."

"In the kitchen," she answered back.

Jack headed in that direction, finding her sitting on a stool at the kitchen island. She set down the book she was reading and pulled off her reading glasses.

"I didn't know you were stopping by this afternoon."

Jack shrugged as he dipped to hug her. "Just checking on you."

She tsked. "No need. I'm fine, but it's always nice to see you. Where's Sam?"

"With friends. I'll have him stop in to say hello tomorrow."

His mom nodded. "Good. I'll bake him some cookies." She lifted a brow. "Yes, I know he's not a kid anymore, but I remember how much teenagers eat."

Jack chuckled and then noticed that his mom was wearing a nice pair of pants and new top. "You look like you're going somewhere. Hot date?" he asked, teasing, but he also wouldn't mind seeing his mom get back out there. She didn't need to be alone forever.

"Yes, in fact. I'm leaving in ten minutes. There's an AA group tonight."

Jack ran a hand through his hair. It'd been years since the divorce. He'd understood why she attended those meetings when she was still married to his father, but his mom had never stopped attending. She was as loyal to attending the AA meetings as she was her weekly Bible study. "I see."

"No, I don't think you do," she said, standing and walking to the cabinet. She pulled out a glass and carried it to the counter. "Sweet tea?" she asked.

"You know me. Can't turn down liquid sugar."

This made her laugh. "Sometimes I can help someone at the group with my story. Sometimes the group still helps me." She poured Jack a glass of tea and handed it over. "I spoke to Amanda today, by the way."

"So did I." He took a sip of his tea.

"She sounds good. I'm glad."

"Me too," Jack said.

"And you look good," his mother said.

"I feel as good as I look." He winked at his mom, making her laugh again. After all she'd been through in life, she still loved and laughed easily.

"Come with me to the meeting tonight," she said, her expression turning serious.

Jack started backing up. If he'd known it was her AA meeting night, he wouldn't have stopped by. This wasn't the first time she'd asked him to go. He'd gone with her before. When he'd first stopped drinking, he'd also attended a group outside of town. "I don't think so, Mom. I'm tired and sweaty," he said.

"It's only an hour. And it'll be good right now. Amanda is seeking treatment, and whether you realize it or not, that could bring up issues for you. Or memories of your dad. I know it does for me." His mom's gaze dropped, her happy demeanor turning crestfallen for a moment.

Ah, geez. He couldn't say no now. "Okay, Mom. I'll go with you."

She looked up and smiled. "Oh, I'm so happy." Then she patted his chest. "You are a good son. But you really are sweaty. You have spare clothes in the guest room. Go change into those," she said, making Jack laugh.

He took another sip of his tea and then set his glass down. "Fine. I'll be right back," he told her, heading toward the back bedroom. He changed, splashed some cold water on his face, and then headed back into the kitchen. "I'll drive."

* * *

For the next hour and a half, Jack listened to people of various backgrounds share their stories, some of which sounded similar to his own. He could relate to everyone in the room. He'd been the son, the brother, and the alcoholic himself. He didn't say a word as he sat with his mom. He just listened. When it was over, he stood and walked out to the parking lot.

"Sometimes it's good to know that you're not alone," his mother said on the ride back.

Jack glanced over. "You have me, Mom. You're not alone."

She patted his shoulder. "I know that. But I was talking about you not being alone," she said. "You were always that kid who took care of himself. And who took care of everyone around him. It's good for you to know that you're not alone."

Jack stared at the road ahead. Her words sucker punched him in the gut. She was right. He was the guy who carried his own burdens. Why shouldn't he? "Okay," he finally said.

"I'll cook dinner before we go next time. Would that be nice?" his mom asked.

Jack shook his head. "Is that your not-so-subtle way of asking me to attend another AA meeting with you?"

She laughed easily. "I guess it is."

Jack pulled up to a stop sign and turned onto her road. "Have you ever known me to turn down one of your home-cooked meals?"

"No, I haven't," she said.

He nodded. "I'm not going to start now. I'll be there."

* * *

Early the next week, Emma scrolled over the website she'd designed for the first annual event. One hundred fourteen people had already signed up for Jenny's Wellness Walk for Women. Given that the website had just gone up and was already doing this well, she was thrilled. That meant she'd already raised over a thousand dollars for the WWC minus costs.

She admired the site a little more. It was simple with a mission statement on the home page, a picture of her mom, and a paragraph detailing her mom's story. Then there was a sign-up page and a link to donate to the cause without signing up. If she could get at least a couple of hundred people to sign up, that would be a great first year.

Her cell phone buzzed on the nightstand. Emma eyed Barnaby sound asleep in his bed before glancing at the clock. Almost midnight. Who would be texting her at this hour?

She picked up the phone to check the screen, and her body received a little jolt when she saw Jack's name. They'd been a pretend couple for just under two weeks now, which so far had amounted to Jack coming into the café every morning, offering her a Hershey Kiss, and winking at her on his way out. It was likely all show for his nephew, but sometimes Jack did those things when Sam wasn't even around. There was also that very real kiss on the Fourth of July.

Emma tapped her phone's screen and opened a text from Jack.

Is Sam with you?

Emma found the text concerning. No. Why would Sam be with me?

She waited anxiously, watching the dots bounce along her screen as Jack texted back.

He's not here, and it's an hour past his curfew.

Emma sat up in bed, clutching her phone and watching more dots bounce.

He's not answering my calls either.

Where was he tonight? Emma texted back.

With friends. That's all I know, which makes me an awful caregiver.

I know a couple of his friends. They've been to the café to see him, she texted. But it's late.

She waited for her phone to buzz with another incoming text, but instead her phone began to ring.

"What do I do?" Jack asked as soon as she connected the call. "Do I go look for him? Wait here for when he comes home? I can't call everyone I know and wake them up. Can I?"

Emma wasn't sure what to tell him. "Sam is probably fine. And if he wasn't, someone would contact you and let you know."

"If he's fine, he won't be once he gets home," Jack threatened.

Emma knew he wasn't serious. She'd never known Jack to be aggressive in any way. He was just scared and with good reason.

"So this is what it feels like to be a parent, huh?" he muttered. "Absolutely terrifying. Remind me to never do it for real."

She and Jack were pretend so his future and hers weren't intertwined. Not that she allowed herself to envision a future with a family of her own either. "I'll call Sam. He's not answering for you, but he might for me."

"Yeah. That's a good idea. Okay," Jack agreed.

"I'll do it now. Talk to you in a minute." Emma said goodbye and then pulled up Sam's contact. She tapped the number, praying that Sam would answer.

"Hello," Sam's voice answered on the fifth ring.

"Sam." Relief poured through her. "Where are you? Your uncle is worried sick."

There was a hesitation on the other end of the line.

"Sam?"

"I don't like being lied to," Sam said. "You guys have been lying to me all along."

Emma's heart flew into her throat. "What?"

"You and Uncle Jack aren't telling me the truth," Sam reiterated. "And I don't want anything to do with liars."

CHAPTER THIRTEEN

*E*mma blinked, her hand aching from clutching the cell phone so tightly. "Wait a minute. What do you mean we're liars?"

Emma never should have told anyone that her relationship with Jack was a farce. Telling one person was like telling the entire town, and now Sam was upset.

"You and Uncle Jack aren't telling me the whole story. Or any of the story. My mom isn't on vacation this summer with her boyfriend."

Her phone buzzed with a second caller, probably Jack, wanting to know if she'd been able to reach Sam. "Your mom?" she repeated, processing what Sam was talking about.

"I went on her Facebook page and her Instagram. If she was on vacation, why wouldn't she be posting pictures? My mom loves to post pictures. She's always on her phone."

Emma shook her head. This kid was too smart for his

own good. "Maybe she's just busy. Or having a screen-free summer."

"Yeah, right. Like every adult, she pays more attention to her screen than she does to the people around her."

"That's not true. Your uncle Jack isn't that way. Neither am I." And from her point of view, it was teenagers who couldn't be separated from their electronic devices. When they came into the café, that's mostly what the younger generation did. Instead of pulling out a book or engaging with a person nearby, they stared at their screens.

"Where's my mom for real? I went to Reginald's social media, and he's posting all kinds of pictures, but none of them are with her. In fact, he's with some other lady. Not my mom. What's going on?" Sam demanded. "Why am I being lied to?"

Emma didn't know how to answer. "This is something you need to discuss with Jack, not me. I know he's been trying to call you, and he's worried about you right now. Call him and ask him these questions. Or better yet, go back to his place and do it in person."

There was a beat of silence on the other end of the line. "I want you to be there," Sam said.

"Me? Why do you want me there?" Emma asked.

"I don't know. He'll get mad because I didn't make curfew and...I just need someone to make him listen to me. In case he doesn't."

"He will. Of course he will."

Sam grunted. "I'm not going back unless you agree to be there."

Emma didn't really have a choice. "Okay. I'll pick you up. How about that? Where are you?"

"I'm at the parking lot behind your café. It's good skateboarding turf."

Emma stood and started looking for a pair of jeans and a T-shirt to pull on. "I'll be there in ten minutes. Don't leave."

She disconnected the call and dialed Jack.

"Hi," she said as she dressed. "I just spoke to Sam. I'm going to pick him up and take him home."

"I can do that," Jack said.

Emma grabbed a brush with her other hand. "He asked me to. He wants me to be there to moderate your conversation tonight."

"What does that mean?"

"He has a lot of questions about what's really going on with his mom, Jack. I think you need to tell him the truth because he knows she isn't on vacation with her boyfriend."

Jack groaned.

"I told him I'd be there in ten minutes so I better go. I'll see you soon."

"Yeah," Jack said. "I'll be here. Emma?"

"Mm-hmm?"

"Thanks."

"Of course. This is what fake girlfriends are for, right?"

They disconnected, and she quickly pulled her hair back into a low-hanging ponytail. Then she grabbed her keys and headed to her car in the driveway. Five minutes later, she turned into the lot behind the café.

Sam was seated on one of the curb stops, holding his skateboard. He stood and headed over when he saw her. Then he climbed into the passenger seat.

"Ready?" she asked.

"Yep." He stared out the passenger window.

She'd expected that he'd pepper her with more questions as she drove him back to Jack's, but he seemed to be saving them for his uncle. She hoped Jack came clean with the teen. It was no fun to be lied to.

Guilt settled in her gut. That's what she and Jack were doing though. Just another lie, this one for Amanda's sake. Amanda was the one who didn't want Sam to know she was struggling with addiction. She wanted to spare him and make sure he had a good summer, which was a noble effort, but Sam wasn't having any fun right now.

Emma pulled into Jack's driveway, parked, and got out. The quarter moon offered only a sliver of light as they headed up his porch steps. His motion detector light flicked on when they reached the top step and Jack opened the door.

His mouth was set in a grim line. "You can't just skip curfew," he said in a gruff tone of voice as soon as they crossed the threshold. "We've already had this discussion. I thought you understood."

Sam folded his arms over his chest, mirroring Jack's posture. "Well, you can't just tell me lies."

"Who's lying to you?" Jack asked.

Emma held up a hand. "Okay, you guys. Take the tone down a notch or nothing will get resolved tonight."

Jack looked at her and took a breath.

"Maybe we should sit on the couch and talk civilly," she suggested.

The guys hesitated and then took her advice, leaving a space for her to sit between them. She was glad that Sam had invited her over. Otherwise, she thought Jack would be too upset over Sam staying out late and worrying him. And Sam would be too defensive to get the answers he needed.

"Sam, tell Jack what you told me." Emma gave a soft nod at the teenager.

Sam still had his arms tightly crossed. "I've been on my mom's social media. She's not on vacation. And her boyfriend isn't her boyfriend anymore. He's living it up with some other chick. It's all over his Instagram page."

Jack looked like a deer in the headlights. He probably didn't know that Amanda and her boyfriend had broken up. Maybe Amanda didn't even know.

"Okay." Jack looked at his hands, which had fallen into his lap. "Maybe your mom isn't with her boyfriend anymore. Maybe they broke up, I'm not sure. It's none of my business though, and it's not yours either."

Sam huffed. "You see?" he said to Emma. "He's going to feed me more lies."

Emma held up a hand to him and then looked at Jack. "Jack...," she pressed.

He met her gaze and gave his head a slight shake. "It doesn't matter what Amanda's Facebook or Instagram page is showing or not showing. She's Sam's mom, and she needs some time to herself. She wants you here, Sam," he said, looking at his nephew. "And while you're here, you follow my rules and you come home when I tell you to. Otherwise, you don't go out at all."

Emma gulped a breath. The tension in the room was palpable.

"So you're just going to lie all summer?" Sam shook his head. "Fine. I'll follow your rules, but I don't trust liars." He stood. "If it's okay with you, I'm going to bed now."

"That's probably best," Jack said, "because you're working with me tomorrow, and we have a lot to do."

"Whatever." Sam walked past them without another word and headed down the hall.

Jack ran a hand through his hair, and for a moment, he looked like he wanted to pull it out.

Emma reached out and touched his arm, gaining his attention. "You could've told him the truth."

"It's not mine to tell," Jack said. "Amanda doesn't want him to know."

"Maybe you should talk to her, then," Emma suggested. "Sam already knows she's not with her boyfriend. Or ex, it sounds like."

Jack nodded. "I'll ask Amanda again. But she might not even be aware of the ex part. Learning that could set her back."

"So many secrets."

Jack looked at her, his gaze dropping momentarily to her hand still on his forearm. "It's late."

She nodded. "Yeah." They held each other's gaze for a long moment. She didn't know what he was thinking, but that kiss they'd shared was at the forefront of her mind, where it'd been since it'd happened. "I better head back home." She said the words, he nodded, but neither of them moved. "Or . . ."

Jack's brow lifted subtly. "Or you could stay a bit longer. I can make us a sweet tea or lemonade, and we could sit on the porch. We could talk."

Talk. That sounded innocent enough. But that was yet another lie she was feeding herself.

* * *

The view from Jack's back porch looked out on a thin forest of pines. Through the tangle of limbs and tree trunks, slivers of Silver Lake were visible, reflecting the quarter moon overhead.

"It's so beautiful here." Emma sighed as she sat in the deck chair beside him.

Jack thought so too. That's why he sat out here so often. It was serene. Calm. Peaceful. Some nights he told himself that sitting out here by himself and enjoying nature was something that would never happen if he settled down. His married friends seemed to have active and full lives. The ones with children seemed loaded with activity and noise. At least that's what he told himself to stay contented in the moment.

Now his mind was telling him something completely different. How nice would it be to share this view with someone every night? To share the details of the day, his hopes and fears, his successes and letdowns. To have kids who ran barefoot beyond the deck, chasing fireflies and wishing on falling stars?

How would it be to retreat to bed with someone at night instead of alone?

Jack looked down at the glass of lemonade in his hands. One kiss did not lead to him and Emma sleeping together. As friends, that was a line they could never uncross.

"Most men keep beer in the fridge," Emma said suddenly. "Most that I know, at least."

Jack looked over at her. "Do you open these men's refrigerators regularly?" he asked.

She laughed softly and shook her head, a tendril of hair slipping off her shoulder to rest along the back of her chair. "No, I guess not. Most men have at least one drink when they go out. You never do. Why is that?"

Jack felt slightly taken aback by her question. He shrugged as if the answer were simple, but it wasn't. "I don't want to, I guess."

"Because of your dad?" she asked.

Jack started to nod but stopped short. His mom was right tonight after the AA meeting. He was that kid who tried to do things on his own, and he'd grown into an adult who did the same. He was tired, and like Emma had said, there were too many secrets this summer. Telling Emma the truth might push her away, but if it did, maybe that's what needed to happen.

"No, because of me." Jack looked over and met her eyes. "I struggled in college and barely made it through my forestry degree. I'm not one of those guys who can stop with just one drink. Not easily, at least. It's something I've learned about myself. One drink leads to two. Two leads to more."

Emma's mouth fell open. "I've never seen you drunk."

"Then you've never seen me drink. I don't blame it on my dad," Jack said. "In fact, he's the reason I know that's not a road I want to go down. I've watched him lose what matters most because of his drinking. We learn from our parents' mistakes, right?"

He sipped from his lemonade. While he was baring his soul, he might as well tell her the full story. "I drove drunk to your house the night of your senior prom. I'm not sure how I navigated the roads and made it there alive, but I'm mortified and ashamed that I did that. Your father answered the door."

"What?" Emma stiffened in her chair. "You stood me up that night."

Jack frowned. "Not exactly. Your dad put me back in the truck, and he took the driver's seat and drove me to my mom's place. He lectured me the entire way, but I was too out of it to hear much of what he said. I know he told me to stay away from you, and I don't blame him. What would've happened had you gotten into my truck that night with me behind the wheel? I could've hurt you, Emma. I could've hurt anyone else on that road. I'll always regret that."

"Jack...," she whispered. "I had no idea. But it's been a long time since you were in college."

Jack nodded. "That's the thing that makes it a problem for me. It's been a long time, but I still want a drink. I still think about it. It's not something that'll just go away."

"I guess that's why they call alcoholism a disease."

"In a way, my dad did me a favor by being who he is. Now I know I don't want to be like him and that's motivation enough to keep my willpower. The memory of what I could've done to you is good motivation too." He was surprised at Emma's reaction. Or lack of reaction. She didn't seem overly surprised or upset. "I'm sorry I ruined your prom, Em."

"You've apologized a million times already."

"Yeah, but now you know the real reason why. It wasn't because I overslept or forgot about you. I never forgot about you, Emma."

"Prom night is an awful memory for me, but I survived it. It's you I'm worried about."

"No need for that. I haven't had a drink in years, and I don't plan to. That's why you don't see my fridge stocked. I know my weaknesses." Alcohol was one. Emma was the other. He'd done well to stay away from the first, but lately it was becoming an impossible feat to distance himself from the woman beside him, no matter what he'd promised her father.

A tiny strand of her hair blew in the night breeze, clinging to her cheek. Jack lifted a hand and slid it away, his fingers trailing longer than they needed to. He searched her expression, trying to decipher how she felt about his touch. About him.

She smiled back at him, a clear signal that she didn't mind.

He leaned toward her, and she didn't pull away. Another clear signal that she was okay with him being so close. He leaned some more, and this time she leaned toward him as well. A kiss was just a kiss, but this impending one felt like so much more. He'd just confessed all of his secrets and she hadn't let it push her away. Instead, it had drawn her closer, and while he had iron willpower when it came to alcohol, he no longer had any willpower when it came to Emma.

* * *

Emma was spending far too many nights staring up at the ceiling these days. And listening to the soft snore of her dog, who could apparently sleep through anything.

She blinked into the darkness of her bedroom an hour later, after excusing herself from Jack's home and driving back. He'd argued with her that it was too late to drive. That she could sleep on the couch or he could drive her home and get her car for her in the morning. Those were noble offers, but she'd refused and driven back, texting him when she'd safely arrived and locked herself inside. Sweetwater Springs had a few instances of crime over the last couple years, but overall, it was one of the safest places to be, in Emma's experience.

Burrowing deeper under her covers as if it were a cold night instead of summer, her thoughts returned to Jack and what he'd told her. She'd often wondered about his aversion to alcohol, but she'd never considered that he was a recovering alcoholic. When he'd told her his story, she'd seen shame and guilt warring in his eyes. He didn't need to feel those things though. All she saw was a man who'd overcome something that had taken many good people down. He was strong, a fighter, and should feel proud of who he was.

She, on the other hand, wasn't proud of herself right now. Emma closed her eyes, willing sleep to come, but now that she was alone in the quiet of her room, her thoughts began blaring. Another day had gone by without scheduling her annual checkup. She'd promised herself that she would today, but she hadn't.

Emma slipped her hand under her tank top and brought it up past her navel. She hadn't even done the self-checks that she was usually so religious about. What was wrong with her? She closed her eyes and moved her fingers over the soft mound of her left breast, moving in a circular motion the way she'd been taught.

She didn't breathe as she palpated. Finding nothing, she moved to her right breast. Her hands were shaking uncontrollably now. How could she even do this accurately? She palpated again, making tiny circles that started at the center of her breast and moved to the widest area. When she was done, she gasped and realized that tears were streaming down her cheeks.

Everything had checked out. No lumps. She swiped her hands over her cheeks, collecting her tears. Then she cried herself to sleep. They weren't happy tears. Or sad. They were just overdue, like a lot of things in her life.

* * *

When Emma's alarm clock went off just hours later, she opened her eyes and flinched. Her eyes felt raw, and she just wanted to close them again and return to sleep. Not that she'd gotten much rest.

On a yawn, she sat up and went through her morning

routine on autopilot, preparing coffee, freshening Barnaby's water and food bowls, showering, dressing, and taking a moment to watch the morning news. Once she'd gotten an update on the latest happenings in town from local newscaster Serena Gibbs, Emma headed out the door to her car.

She jumped straight into serving customers and making beverages when she arrived at the café.

"You look tired," Nina said as she and Emma handled orders from the initial customers.

Emma felt that way too. "Gee, thanks. You look beautiful as always."

Nina laughed. "Liar, but I'll take a compliment where I can get one. And even when you're tired, you're still beautiful," she amended.

This made Emma smile. "Liar," she shot back, and couldn't help but think about Sam and how he'd been so upset last night. Her mind had too much weighing on it—Sam, Jack, and the upcoming event. There was also her annual checkup that she still hadn't rescheduled at the Women's Wellness Center. At least she'd finally gathered her nerve to do a self-check. *Baby steps.*

She needed a way to turn her mind off completely. Otherwise, she'd never get to sleep tonight. She took the next order and started working on it, waiting for Nina to head back in her direction to do the same. "Remember when you wanted to take me out for my birthday a couple of weeks ago?"

"Yep," Nina said as she prepared a mocha latte. "It was after the fact because you never told me it was your birthday on the actual day. I haven't even gotten you a present yet."

"Well, you can buy me a drink tonight," Emma said. "I need a night out. I need fun."

Nina glanced over, worry playing in the soft crease between her brown eyes. "You okay?"

Emma nodded. "Yeah. Of course. I'm just in more of a celebratory mood this week."

"Okay then. I'm free tonight after the café closes. I'll meet you at the tavern."

"Sounds perfect." Emma carried the beverage she'd just prepared to her waiting customer. Tonight, she would drink her cares away and laugh until her worries floated into oblivion. Then tomorrow she would call the WWC.

CHAPTER FOURTEEN

It was lunchtime, and Sam had barely spoken a word to Jack all morning. In the night, Jack had realized just how unfair the whole situation was for Sam, but there wasn't much he could do about it.

"Let's do one more patrol around the park and then grab some sandwiches from the diner. Sound good?"

Sam shrugged. "Sure."

"You know," Jack said as they walked out to the ATVs, "when I was your age, I would've loved a summer job like this one. Most kids wind up working at a fast-food place, but you've got connections. Having a job where you can get out into the sunshine and fresh air is a great deal."

"Most of my friends back home don't have to work the summer," Sam pointed out. "They're hanging out, skateboarding, and going to concerts."

Jack pushed out the doors of the office building and slid his sunglasses over his eyes. "Lucky them. We have concerts every Friday night. Don't forget that."

Sam scoffed. "No names I recognize."

"Music is music. You need to make the best out of what you're given, buddy. Even if you don't like the cards you're dealt."

Sam climbed onto the ATV that Jack was letting him use under his supervision. Judging by Sam's stance, this conversation was over. Jack climbed onto his own ATV, and they headed down the trails of Evergreen Park, the wind whipping against his face and through his hair. As they approached Blue Sky Point, Jack slowed and gestured for Sam to do the same. There was a hiker in the woods that set off alarm bells in his gut. She leaned against a tree, looking out toward the distant mountains. She didn't even seem to notice them ride up.

Jack looked over at Sam, who seemed to be on the same page as him. Was this woman the illegal camper?

She wore a pair of jean shorts and a T-shirt along with socks and tennis shoes. Her dark brown hair was pulled back in a messy bun. Her skin was deeply tanned, and as he drew closer, gesturing for Sam to stay back, he thought maybe she was injured. She flinched as she shifted, keeping weight distributed on only one leg.

"Ma'am?" Jack said, wanting to make his presence known.

She didn't acknowledge him.

He noticed now that she had earbuds in. They were attached to a small radio hooked to the pocket of her shorts. Jack hadn't seen a little radio like that in a long time. Most people used their cell phones to listen to music these days.

Once he got in line of her peripheral vision, she startled and whirled to look at him. For a moment, she put weight on her opposite leg. Then she flinched and quickly leaned against the tree to shift her weight off it again.

Jack held up a hand. "It's okay. I'm the park ranger here. Are you hurt?" he asked.

Her wide eyes stared back at him.

"Can I help you?" he asked. "You seem like you might have hurt your leg."

She shook her head, throwing off her balance just slightly.

Jack sighed. "Your leg is hurt." He gestured at his ATV. "I can give you a ride out of the park and arrange for you to get medical attention."

"No," she said. "I don't want to go to the hospital."

That sent out all kinds of warning signals in Jack's gut. "Are you in trouble?" he asked.

She shook her head. "No."

Well, he couldn't make her seek help if she didn't want to. "You can't camp at the park," he told her. "It's illegal."

She sucked in a tiny gasp. "Oh. I didn't know. I'm...I'm sorry. Please don't call the police."

Jack noticed the duffel bag nearby. She wasn't camping for the sake of camping. "You don't have anywhere else to stay?"

She didn't answer.

Hurt and homeless it was.

"I won't call the authorities, but I will give you a ride out. You can't walk on that leg, and you can't stay here. My nephew and I were just about to get lunch. I'll take you too if you want."

She eyed him suspiciously.

"Just friends. My treat." He scratched the bottom of his chin. "Except I know most of my friends' names." He jutted out his hand. "I'm Jack Hershey, like the candy."

This made her smile. Reluctantly, she put out her hand as well. "I'm, um, Diana."

He noticed that she didn't include a last name in her

introduction. "Can you walk to the ATV, Diana, or do you need help?"

"I can walk," she said. "But I can't walk and carry my bag. And I'm not leaving my bag," she said quickly.

"Don't worry about it. I'll get it." Jack jogged over and looped the strap over his shoulder as she watched him closely, almost as if she was worried that he might steal her belongings. He didn't blame her. If everything she owned was in this one bag, it must be very important to her. He led her back to the vehicle and hesitated. "You'll have to ride with me. Do you need help climbing on?"

She shook her head. "I can do it."

"It's just a short drive. I'll go slow to minimize the bumps on that leg." He climbed on first and waited for her to climb behind him, readying himself to catch her if her balance became compromised.

Once she was on the back, Jack looked at Sam and nodded an okay to crank the engine and head back to the office. He'd expected that when he took the illegal camper out of his park, it would be to meet chief of police Alex Baker. After looking into Diana's eyes—if that was even her real name—he realized that she hadn't intended any harm. Instead, she seemed to be in need of help.

* * *

Emma loved a good jolt of caffeine first thing in the morning. She loved it so much that she'd built her whole career around that buzz of caffeine. But she also loved drinks of a different variety every now and then.

As she sat with Nina at the Tipsy Tavern, she thought that maybe she should do this more often. This was a good stress reliever. Just as much as the alcohol felt good buzzing through her veins, it also felt good to laugh. The kind of laughter that squeezed tears out of the corners of your eyes and made your belly ache a little. That's the kind that she and Nina had been having for the last hour.

"So...," Nina said. She was just as tipsy as Emma, if not more so. "Which guy in here would be the one?"

Emma shook her head while grinning. "Which one?"

"You know...the one you'd pick to go home with. If you could choose any guy, no strings."

Emma laughed softly. "No, that's not me."

"What's not you?" Nina asked, taking a sip of her lime margarita.

"There's nothing wrong with casual hookups, but it's not what I do." She felt her cheeks burning at just the discussion. "I mean, I never have before."

"You've never had a one-nighter?" Nina asked in mock shock. Or maybe it was real.

Emma narrowed her eyes. "I'm guessing by your reaction that you have."

"Of course I have. I'm twenty-seven years old, and I've never been in any serious relationships. Without the one-night stands, I'd still be a virgin."

Emma and Nina started laughing hysterically again.

"I'm not a virgin, but it's been so long that I might as well be," Emma confessed.

Nina giggled softly. "So, which guy? Just for the sake of pretending."

Emma groaned and looked around the room. "It's a definite no to all the guys in here that I already know because that would be weird. And I know every guy in here," she clarified, returning her gaze to Nina. "So none."

"Aw, you're no fun at all."

"But you have to admit meaningless sex with guys you

know could be awkward the next day when you're serving them coffee."

Nina shrugged, and if Emma wasn't mistaken, her cheeks were now turning red.

"Wait. You know exactly what I'm talking about. You've done the casual thing with a guy in here and seen him the next day at the café. Who?"

Nina shook her head, her body shaking as she giggled. "Sorry, I don't kiss and tell."

"Now you're the one who's no fun." Emma harrumphed. She looked around the tavern again, this time her breath catching.

"Aha. So Jack is the one," Nina said with a wide grin. "I knew it."

"No, I know him too, and that would definitely be awkward."

"Not really. He's already your boyfriend," Nina pointed out.

"Fake boyfriend and that whole scenario is just silly. I'm not sure why I ever agreed to it."

"I know why. Because you've always been into him and this was a safe way to test the waters. If it turns out to be a disaster, you could throw your hands up and chalk it up to the fact that it was never real anyway. And if it's amazing, you can ease into it and pretend like you knew it was meant to be all along. It's genius actually."

Emma blinked across the table at her friend. Was that true? Is that what she and Jack were doing?

Nina flagged the waitress as she walked by. "I think we're going to need another round."

"And some for us too," Sophie said as she pulled out a chair with Brenna. "Do you ladies mind if we join you?" she asked.

"No, of course not," Emma said.

"I saw your boyfriend over there." Sophie winked.

Emma regretted telling anyone about her arrangement with Jack.

"I suppose I won't ask him to dance," Sophie added. "I don't want to cause any sort of scandal."

Emma shook her head and drained the last of her drink as she anxiously awaited another.

Nina knocked her elbow against Emma's. "But *you* should ask him to dance. Seeing that you two are an item these days. What could it hurt?"

Nina was right. This pretend relationship was a safety net for going after something Emma had always secretly wanted. She scooted back from the table. "I think I'll take your advice and go have that dance."

Her world shifted and realigned every few steps, telling her that she should return to the table with her friends after this dance and have that last drink she'd ordered. Tomorrow morning's headache was going to be a doozy. But she'd worry about that when she got there. Right now, she was stepping up to Jack's table and pulling him out onto the dance floor. If he'd let her.

And she'd worry about what happened after that when she got there too.

* * *

Jack knew in an instant that Emma had been drinking. She was adorably flushed and swaying just a touch. He was here tonight waiting for Luke and Granger. They'd called and asked to meet up tonight after work. From a quick scan, he knew they hadn't walked in yet. He'd somehow missed the fact that Emma had.

"Fancy meeting you here," he said.

"I'm here with Nina. And now Sophie and Brenna too."

He glanced back, seeing the table of women now. They were all watching Emma and him with interest. He lifted a hand and waved before turning back to Emma. "And you left their company for me?"

"You are my boyfriend after all." Emma tilted her head in a flirtatious way that left her hair falling across her cheek. "And as such, I came over to ask you to dance."

Jack leaned back in his chair. "I don't dance."

Emma stuck her lower lip out. "I'm not buying it."

"It's true."

She reached for his hand anyway. "You would've danced with me at my prom, if you'd have taken me. You owe me at least one dance. Probably an entire night's worth."

Jack felt his own mouth spread into a wide grin. "Collecting on debts, huh?"

She gave a soft tug. "Something like that. Now come on."

Relenting, he stood and let her pull him into the corner where other couples were swaying to the music. He put his arms around her and gathered her close. He wasn't much of a dancer, but he was willing to give Emma whatever she wanted.

"I'm sorry that I've been drinking. I hope it doesn't bother you." She looked up into his eyes. "I didn't realize you'd be here tonight. Otherwise, I wouldn't have—"

Jack shook his head. "If I was bothered by being around people drinking, I wouldn't have come to a bar. Don't worry about me."

She kept her eyes locked on his. "Okay... Where's Sam?"

"Hanging out with a couple friends."

"Oh, that's nice."

"I think he's doing well here," Jack said. "He was a little quiet this morning until we had an issue at the park. Then he perked up a bit."

"What kind of issue?" Emma asked, seeming to melt into his arms. He enjoyed the feel of her there, her skin sliding over his softly as she swayed.

"The illegal camper I was looking for turned up with a sprained ankle. I also discovered that she's camping in Evergreen because she's temporarily homeless."

Emma gasped softly. "Oh my goodness. Why?"

Jack shrugged. "Sam and I took her to the urgent care and then to get something to eat, but she didn't offer much. She was laid off from work and couldn't afford to pay rent. So she's been camping at the park."

"But she can't do that, right?"

"No. We gave her a ride to the women's shelter," Jack said. "Trisha, the director there, is well connected. She might be able to help her find a job."

"Wow." The song ended, but Emma didn't pull away. If anything, she leaned closer. Jack slid a lock of hair out of her face, trailing his finger along her skin as he looked at her. "I'm sorry I missed prom."

"You don't have to—"

"I'm not apologizing to you this time," he cut in. "I'm sorry for myself. Dancing all night with you would've been one of the most amazing nights of my life, and I missed it. Who knows where things would've led between us after that night if I'd have been there?"

Emma's lips separated.

"Maybe we would've ended up, you know..." He trailed off, not saying what he was thinking. Maybe he'd already said too much.

"Jack..."

He looked away, scanning the other couples on the dance floor. They were all laughing and smiling, and here he was being serious. "Yeah, I know. We're friends, and nothing would've happened between us anyway. I'm talking crazy. Forget I said—"

Before he could finish his sentence, Emma went up on her toes and pressed her lips to his. His grasp tightened around her waist, holding her there as he deepened the kiss. Even though they'd kissed twice before, she tasted forbidden, like his best friend and alcohol. The first kiss had been under pretenses. The second, they were still holding back. This kiss, however, was a no-holds-barred kind of kiss, and more real than anything he'd ever experienced.

Step away, Jack.

Instead, Jack inched forward and kissed her some more, blocking out all the reasons that had kept him away so long. He swore he'd never lose his self-control in a bar again, but here he was, losing it with Emma.

CHAPTER FIFTEEN

Emma was drunk, but not so much that she wasn't completely in control of what was happening right now with Jack. Nina was so right. She was in a rare situation this summer where she could throw caution to the wind and have a get-out-of-jail-free card if things went south.

Jack pulled away and looked at her, concern etched in his brow. "Sorry."

"I'm not," she said.

"I don't want to take advantage of you when...you're like this."

She tilted her head. "Maybe I'm the one taking advantage of you, Jack Hershey."

"I don't mind one bit." The corner of his mouth kicked up. "So you're leaving here with Nina and the other women at your table?"

Emma lifted a shoulder. "I don't know. You're my boyfriend. It only makes sense that I'd leave with you. Nina can get a ride home with Brenna or Sophie."

"Or," Jack countered, "I can give you all a ride home when you're ready to leave."

"What about your night with Granger and Luke? Won't they be upset if you bail on them?"

"Nah. Ladies come first. That's the code."

"I thought the code was in favor of the guys."

"Depends on the guys, I guess," Jack said, his breath tickling her ear as they continued to slow dance. "I'm not that kind of guy."

She looked up and practically melted in his arms. "It was so much easier when I thought you just didn't want me."

"Is that what you thought?" he asked, pulling back to meet her gaze.

"Well...You stood me up, and then you never gave me any reason to believe you were interested in being more than friends."

"I wasn't in a good place, Emma. Your dad was right. I didn't deserve you."

"What?" Emma asked. "Did he say that?"

Jack looked away. "I had to pull myself together, and I did. Although some days I don't feel that way. Your dad still hates the idea of us. I can tell."

"Who cares?" she asked.

"I do." He looked at her again.

"Because you're a good guy. And you deserve to be happy."

"So do you," Jack said.

His fingers curled into her waist as he held her. The sensation and the vibration of the music in the air made her body buzz. A dance wasn't enough. She wanted Jack—all of him.

"Maybe, once you drive me home, I'll invite you inside for a sweet tea?"

He gave a slight nod. "Sounds nice."

"Yeah," she whispered, "it does."

"So how much longer until your friends will be ready to go home?" Jack asked.

"An hour maybe."

He nodded. "That gives me just enough time with the guys. And an excuse not to drink tonight if I'm your DD."

Emma felt her face contort into a frown. "I had no idea that you had to go through this every time you went out."

"It's no big deal." Jack shrugged. "Really."

"Then why don't you just let your friends in on what's going on with you?"

"I guess it's like when you tell someone you're sick. Everyone starts treating you that way. If I tell people I struggle with alcohol, they'll stop asking me to hang out here at the tavern. Stop asking me to come by and watch the game with them because there'll be beer. That's not what I want."

"I think you're selling your friends short. But I'm glad you told me. I promise I won't treat you any differently."

"Thanks." The music stopped, and he stepped back. "So we have one hour. Then I'll give you and your friends a ride."

Emma nodded. "If you're sure you don't mind."

"I don't," he reiterated. "Just come tap my shoulder when you're ready to leave."

He headed in one direction, and she headed back to the table where the ladies were waiting for her, wishing that she could fast-forward the next hour. She loved her friends, but she wanted to spend more time with Jack, alone.

* * *

When Jack sat down at the table with the guys, they stopped talking and looked at him.

"We had a bet that you were going to ditch us in favor of Emma," Granger finally said.

Jack chuckled, noticing the drink in front of him. One of the guys must have ordered it for him when he was dancing with Emma. "Who bet who?" Jack asked.

"I bet Luke his next drink that you would come back and ditch us," Granger said.

Luke shrugged, sitting next to Jack. "I bet that you wouldn't. Emma's with the ladies, and you're with the guys."

"Looks like I win," Jack said. "I'm not leaving just yet. But I did agree to be the DD for Emma and her friends in about an hour. So you both lost and you owe *me* a drink."

Granger and Luke gave each other a look that told Jack they'd discussed something privately about him.

"Except you don't drink, right?"

Jack nodded, willing his body to stay relaxed. "No, I don't," he said. Maybe Emma was right, and he was selling his friends short by thinking they'd treat him differently. "I'm a recovering alcoholic."

Luke frowned at him. "What? Since when?"

"Since college," Jack said. "I haven't touched a drink in almost ten years, and I won't."

"I'm sorry for inviting you here," Granger said. "This is the last place you should be."

Jack shook his head. "If you stop inviting me here, we're going to have words. I like the tavern. I like hanging out with you guys for some odd reason." He smiled at his friends. "I get to drink Coke and watch you two make fools of yourselves. It's a great pastime."

Granger and Luke stared back at him. Maybe he'd made a mistake in telling them.

A waitress stepped up to the table. "Need anything, guys?"

Jack raised his index fingers. "Yes, matter of fact. These two made a bet and lost, and they owe me a drink. But since I'm the DD, can I get another soda?"

"Sure thing," she said.

"And these two need another beer," he added. "I'm buying."

"You got it." The waitress walked away, and Jack looked at his friends as if to prove a point. They could still drink with him. *Please don't treat me differently.*

"How's the tree farm?" Luke asked, looking over at Granger.

Granger lowered his gaze to his drink. "Well, let's see. The fire in the spring wiped out half my lot. It's an abnormally hot summer, which isn't helping the surviving trees or the new ones we planted." He looked up. "Which means this Christmas is looking bleak for sales." He lifted his drink to his mouth, didn't give Jack so much as a cursory glance, and took a healthy gulp.

"Anything we can do to help?" Jack asked.

"The Sweetwater Springs Fire Department loves a good cause," Luke added. "Just say the word."

Granger shrugged. "Thanks, but unless you have some kind of miracle liquid to pour on the new trees and make them grow into full-grown spruces by the holidays, I don't think so."

"Fresh out of miracles," Luke said with a frown. "I used my miracle quota when I got Brenna to fall in love with me."

The guys laughed as the waitress placed their fresh drinks in front of them.

"We'll figure it out," Granger said. "I'm just glad no one was injured in that fire." He looked over at Luke as did Jack. They both knew about Luke's burn injuries from childhood.

"I can drink to that." Jack held up his glass.

"To surviving," Granger said, which had a different meaning for them all. He tapped his glass to Jack's and so did Luke, a serious beat passing between them.

"To surviving," Jack and Luke repeated in unison before bringing their glasses to their mouths and drinking.

Then the conversation returned to normal, which was exactly what Jack wanted.

* * *

Emma's body was buzzing, and it had nothing to do with the drinks she'd had at the tavern.

Jack pulled into her driveway after dropping off her friends and cut the lights.

"So that sweet tea I offered you earlier still stands. Want to come inside?" Her heart was beating erratically. She wasn't thirsty in the least.

Jack looked at her for a long second. "I'm not sure going inside your house right now is the best idea. You've been drinking, Em."

"Not since our dance over an hour ago," she pointed out. "And not enough to where I don't know what I'm saying and doing right now."

Jack pinned her with an assessing look. "To be clear, what are you saying and doing?"

She laid a palm on his forearm, the touch of his skin igniting a spark of heat that zipped straight through her body. "I'm saying, if we want to kiss, we should. If we want to hang out with one another, we can. If we want to do more..." She didn't complete that sentence, but she was pretty sure Jack could fill in the blanks. "There's nothing stopping us, Jack."

"Except each other. That's always been the case," he said in a low voice. "One of us has always held back. We've taken turns doing that. So what's changed?" he asked.

"Nothing, I guess." She shrugged a shoulder. "And everything."

He reached up and trailed a finger down the side of her cheek, looking at her in a way she'd never been looked at before. Like a man who adored her. "I don't want to mess things up with you, Emma. But I want more. I want the freedom to kiss you any time I want. To hold your hand. To touch you."

Emma's mouth was suddenly dry.

"I want to go inside your house and have that tea with you." His gaze didn't waver. "I want more than tea."

Her breath hitched, and her heart skipped a beat. "I want more than tea too."

He leaned in and brushed his lips over hers, kissing her sweetly at first. The kiss evolved and deepened until their hands were running over each other as they sat in the front seat of the truck. His hand traveled along her back, moving down to the hem of her shirt and slipping underneath to caress her bare skin. She nearly moaned at the pleasure of skin-to-skin contact, even though what they were doing was innocent enough. Then his hand circled around to the front of her body, his fingers trailing from her navel upward to the band of her bra.

"Just say the word and I'll slow down."

That's the option that Emma's mind was rooting for. Her heart, however, was ready to jump all in with Jack. No more resisting. No more pretending. She'd resisted and pretended long enough.

"You're not going too fast," she told him. "But maybe we should move this inside. I can make that tea, and we can talk." She scrutinized his expression, and he didn't seem disappointed in the least. He was still looking at her like she was the most beautiful woman he'd ever seen. And that made her want to pull him into her bedroom and rip his clothes off. "Or we could just go inside and skip the tea," she said, leaning forward and pressing a kiss to his mouth.

"I'm following your lead tonight." Jack reached for the handle of his door and pushed it open. Then he ran around and opened the passenger door for her. "Lead the way, Emma."

Emma didn't allow herself time to think once they were inside. As soon as Jack closed the front door behind him, she stepped into his arms as if she'd been waiting her entire life to do so. And maybe she had.

They'd already kissed, but never with the green light to keep going. If she wanted to have sex with Jack tonight, it was almost a sure thing. And it'd been so long since she'd been with anyone. Her body was screaming yes. Her heart was screaming yes. Her mind would probably have a few reservations, which was why her mind wasn't allowed to offer an opinion tonight.

Jack groaned as he pulled away. "You feel so good, Em."

Barnaby barked at their feet, making Emma laugh. She looked down at her furry friend and then bent to scoop him up. "Sorry, pal, but you don't get to stay inside this time." She carried Barnaby quickly to the back door and placed him on the porch. "I'll open this in a little bit," she promised. Then she closed the door again and sealed off his doggie door, which was the equivalent of hanging a DO NOT DISTURB sign for dogs. Hurrying back to Jack, she hoped he hadn't changed his mind.

He quickly stepped toward her, getting back to where they'd left off. His hand moved down her back and tugged at the hem of her top, lifting it over her head as they moved into the dining room and then stumbled down the hallway toward her bedroom.

An unspoken question filled the silence as they finally took a breath and looked at each other in the shadowed darkness of the room. Was this really going to happen?

Emma kissed him first, giving an unspoken answer. Yes.

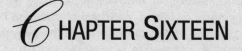CHAPTER SIXTEEN

*J*ack shifted to look at a sleeping Emma, snuggled against him. Her breathing had slowed half an hour ago, and her body had seemed to melt into his.

As he lay here, his mind was running at lightning speed, jumping from the woman in his arms to what had just happened to what might happen next.

Next, they might wake up as a real girlfriend and boy-friend. Next, Emma might freak out and want to slow things way down. Next, he might freak out. Not because he had any regrets. He didn't.

A soft moan escaped Emma's mouth. He stroked her hair off her face, gazing down on her as she slept. She looked so peaceful in this moment. Was she dreaming of him? He wanted nothing more than to stay, but instead he slowly slid out of her embrace and out of bed. He was responsible for a fifteen-year-old this summer, and he needed to be at home.

He quietly dressed and headed down the hall toward

the kitchen. He bumped into the table and then stumbled over a stack of books on the floor as he looked for a pen and paper, shocked that Barnaby didn't come barking after him. Emma had let her little dog back inside the house between getting a glass of water and returning to bed for cuddling. Barnaby had simply huffed at the two and then curled up on his large pillow beneath the window.

Aha! Jack located a pen and notepad and carried it to the counter where there was a thin sliver of moonlight shining from her kitchen window. He started to write.

Dear Emma,

I'm sorry I had to leave without saying goodbye, but I didn't want to wake you. Sam shouldn't be left alone overnight. I'll call you in the morning.

He debated whether to write *Love, Jack*. There was too much implied in that word. *Later, Jack*? *Sincerely, Jack*?

In the end, he just wrote his name. Then he grabbed his keys and quietly let himself out, locking the front door behind him.

Ten minutes later, he walked into his own home, headed down the hall, and fell into bed.

"Uncle Jack?"

Jack's eyes popped open. "What are you doing up?" he asked, seeing Sam's shadow in the doorway.

"I was waiting for you," Sam said.

Good thing Jack had decided to come back. "Everything okay?"

Sam fidgeted with his hands. "I want to talk about Mom."

"Now?"

When Sam didn't immediately answer, Jack sighed.

Then he sat up and got out of bed. "All right. We can talk. How about I make some tea?" He hadn't gotten any at Emma's after all.

"Old people drink tea at midnight," Sam said. "I'm fifteen."

"Old enough to know better than to insinuate your favorite uncle is old." Jack clapped a hand on Sam's back as they walked toward the kitchen. "You don't have to tell your friends you liked it." He pointed at the kitchen table. "Sit. It'll only take a minute." And in that time, he needed to make a choice about what to tell Sam.

He'd told his friends about his struggle with alcohol tonight. He and Emma had also decided to stop pretending.

The water bubbling in the kettle was the only sound for a minute.

"Are you going to tell me the truth this time?" Sam finally asked.

Jack glanced over his shoulder as he poured hot water from the kettle over the tea bags in the mugs. "Yes." A moment later, he sat down and looked at his nephew. Sam was in that weird age between a child and a man. A child needed to be protected, but a man learned to handle things as they came.

"Your mom isn't on a vacation this summer," Jack said.

"Duh. Where is she?"

Jack didn't want to break his sister's trust, but there really was no other option. "She's sick, but she's going to be okay. She's in a facility that's helping her work on her issues so she can be a better mom to you."

Sam frowned. "What kind of facility?"

"It's a place for addiction rehabilitation. I'm not going to get into the details," Jack told Sam. "All you need to know is she's going to get better and come home.

Everything will be fine." Jack reached a hand out to lay on Sam's shoulder. "Your mom wasn't trying to keep things from you. A parent just wants to do what's best for their child. Your mom didn't want you to worry about her. She wanted you to enjoy a carefree summer. There are so few in childhood, and they go so fast."

Sam nodded. "I get it."

"Good. So then how about you try to do that for her? I know your preference isn't to be here in a new town, away from your usual crowd. But it's not so bad, right? You're making friends and finding new hangouts."

"It's actually kind of fun here," Sam admitted. He grew quiet for a second. Then he looked up at Jack again. "Can I go visit my mom? Just to see that she's okay?"

Jack sucked in a breath. He'd need to tell Amanda that Sam knew the truth for that to happen. "Let me talk to your mom first, okay?"

Sam nodded. Then he stood, having never even touched his tea. "I'm going to bed. I'll see you in the morning."

"You're working at the café tomorrow, aren't you?" Jack asked.

Sam nodded. He looked at Jack thoughtfully again. "Is my mom the only thing that you were keeping from me? Is there anything else?"

There was Emma, but that seemed irrelevant now. "Nothing else," Jack said. "Good night." He stood to go to bed as well, leaving his barely touched tea on the table. He'd go to bed, but he doubted he'd get good sleep. Tomorrow he'd call Amanda and let her know that Sam knew where she was. He'd also find Emma and see if things had changed between them. Sex always changed things, one way or another. Hopefully he hadn't made a mistake...or two...tonight.

* * *

Emma stirred in bed and rolled over, opening her eyes to the empty side of the bed next to her. The memories of what had happened hours before bubbled up in her mind, reminding her that she hadn't gone to bed alone. No, Jack had been with her, holding her in his arms.

Where was he now?

She got up and slid her feet into a pair of slippers. Then she shuffled down the hall, her body feeling slightly off-kilter because she'd done some drinking before she'd taken Jack back to her home and bed. Now she felt dehydrated in addition to being confused. There was no evidence of another person in her house. She walked into the kitchen and glanced around, noticing a handwritten note in plain view.

She stepped over and picked it up, reading it quickly.

He was gone. An ache pinged in her chest, but she understood why he'd needed to go. Hopefully Sam was the only reason he'd slipped away. As far as she was concerned, last night was amazing.

Instead of letting her mind jump to conclusions, she hurried about her morning routine, took a few minutes to play with Barnaby, and then headed to open the café.

"What happened after Jack dropped me off last night?" Nina asked at some point in the morning.

Emma turned to face her employee after serving the last customer in line. Sam was working in the back, unboxing supplies that had just arrived yesterday. "Not much. We may have decided to stop pretending to be a couple though."

Nina's large smile dropped into an immediate frown. "What? No. I thought you two had actual sparks. I thought maybe you might turn into something real."

Emma grinned. "I said we decided to stop pretending. I didn't say we weren't going to see each other anymore."

Nina's brows dove toward her nose. "I'm confused. So you're going to keep seeing each other? But for real this time?"

Emma shrugged. Unless Jack had changed his mind after leaving her bed. She didn't peg him as the love 'em and love 'em type. He wasn't the kind of guy to have long or serious relationships either, which worried her a little. She didn't want to lose him in her life. "Jack and I are just taking things as they come," she told Nina.

"But you're hoping that things work out between you two?" Nina asked.

Right now, Emma was just hoping not to screw up a relationship with one of the most important people in her life. "I'm hoping for the best. Whatever that is."

"Well, I'm glad about this change of events. And I'm glad to see you smiling instead of sulking over a couple bad reviews."

Emma shook her head. "I'm staying away from that website from now on. I can't please everyone, and I have enough things to deal with. I can't afford to spend a night sulking over an anonymous reviewer who thinks my coffee tastes stale."

Nina gasped. "Someone wrote that online?"

Emma pressed a hand to her heart. Just thinking about the comment made her heartbeat speed up anxiously.

"Our coffee is fresh. Always, no exceptions. Who wrote that review?"

Emma shrugged and took a breath. "I don't know, but I'm staying off the A-List. Constructive criticism is fine and adding the tables outside has been great. But the big race is two weeks away and there's too much to do to sulk over a bad review." She held up a finger. "Which reminds me, I still need to have the T-shirts made. Paris Montgomery is designing the graphic for the shirts. I need to contact him today and see how that's coming along."

Nina prepared herself a cup of coffee during the lull of customers at the counter. "How many people have signed up so far?"

"Just over two hundred, which is way more than I ever could have imagined."

"That's twenty dollars a person to register, right?"

Emma nodded.

"Whoa. That's quite a chunk of change for the Women's Wellness Center."

Pride bloomed inside of Emma. The donation would be in her mother's memory, and that felt amazing. "Not to mention that some people just made donations through the website instead of registering. Donations alone have contributed over a thousand dollars."

Nina's eyes widened over her cup of coffee as she sipped. She lowered her cup back down. "But you have to pay a fee for the park, right?"

"Since we're joining with another event, there's no fee. I got a lot of sponsors at the Ladies' Day Out event the other night, which should pay for the T-shirts. I just need to follow up with a few of the ladies." Emma grabbed a notepad on the counter and wrote that down as a reminder to herself. "See? Too much to do to worry about a couple of bad reviews."

Nina took another sip of her coffee. "This is not stale brew. Can I reply to that review and tell that person to get their taste buds checked?"

"Don't you dare," Emma said on a laugh.

Nina narrowed her eyes. "You're glowing a little bit this

morning. And you never did answer my question about what happened after Jack dropped me off. You said you decided to see each other for real but you didn't say what happened."

Emma took a breath. "Jack and I may have...um..."

Nina clapped both hands over her mouth and looked around the café. There was only one customer at the moment. "You two slept together?"

Emma laughed despite the awkwardness. "This stays between us. But yes." She squealed softly.

"Of course," Nina said, lowering her hands down by her side. "This is huge. Since the time I've known you, you have never slept with a guy."

Emma had known Nina for three years now. "Maybe I have and just haven't shared it with you."

Nina gave her a look. "Have you?"

"No," Emma admitted. "It's been a long time since a guy has even gotten to second base."

"And you're not the kind of woman to sleep with someone unless there are real feelings involved...unless it was because you were drunk. Oh no. Did you sleep together because you were drunk?" She suddenly looking horrified.

Emma shook her head. "No, I knew exactly what I was doing."

"And?" Nina asked, drinking more of her coffee. "How was it?"

Emma felt her cheeks burning hot. She looked around to make sure that Sam wasn't within earshot. He didn't need to know the details of her and Jack's relationship. "Amazing. And that's all I'm saying on the matter."

Nina ignored Emma's attempt to cut the topic off. "And when is it happening again?"

Emma shook her head. "I don't know."

She pulled her cell phone out and checked the screen. No messages from Jack yet at almost ten a.m. She knew he was an early riser. Maybe he'd awoken with regrets. Maybe she and Jack weren't happening again.

* * *

Jack stepped out of his truck. After driving for two hours to see his sister, his legs were stiff. He stretched and then twisted at his waist a couple times before sliding his sunglasses over his eyes and heading toward the Whispering Pines Addiction Management Facility. He'd spoken to Amanda on the phone, but he hadn't seen her since he'd come to get Sam.

She was doing well, but what he had come to tell her might send her on a backslide. She didn't want Sam to know about her struggles, and even though Jack had promised to keep her secrets safe, he'd told them anyway. Some at least.

Jack didn't really feel like he had much of a choice. Sam knew something was up, and it was also the right thing to do. Knowing your family history helped you make better choices in life. Jack had made better choices than his father. Amanda was making better choices too. Jack was proud of her for knowing when to ask for help. Hopefully she wouldn't be disappointed in him right now.

He stepped inside the air-conditioned building and spoke to the receptionist. "I'm here to see Amanda Hershey. I'm Jack Hershey, her brother."

The receptionist nodded with a smile and then picked up the phone, speaking to someone on the other end of the line. After hanging up, she pointed at the double doors down the hall. "They'll buzz you in, sir. Have a nice visit."

"Thanks."

As he stood in front of the doors, his heart sped up and irrational fears of getting locked inside swirled through his mind. Maybe someone would decide he was a ticking time bomb and lock him in a room and throw away the key.

The door opened, and Jack forced his feet forward. He found Amanda sitting at a table in a small community room inside the facility. She glanced up at him with a bright smile that touched her eyes. She looked so much better than when he'd last seen her.

"Hey, Jack," she said. "I didn't know you were coming to see me today."

Jack sat down across from her. "I'm sorry. I should've brought you something, huh? A candy bar or a magazine."

Amanda laughed. "This isn't prison. I have access to those things if I want them. And just seeing you is treat enough. How's Sam?" she asked, cutting to the chase. She was a mother, and that was her top priority.

"Good. He's working with Emma at the café today."

Amanda's smile grew even bigger. "That's great. He's getting a lot of job experience this summer. That's good for him."

Jack nodded in agreement. "I think so too. And he's a really hard worker once you pry him from his phone."

"Oh, I know all about competing with the screen."

"He's made friends, and I think he's happy..." Jack hesitated, wondering if it was best to just jump in on what he came here to say.

"You look happy too," Amanda said before he could say anything more. "Things must be going pretty well between you and Emma."

Jack nodded. "Amanda, Emma and I have always been

friends. She was only with me that night in the truck as a friend, and I let you believe we were dating because it seemed to offer you some kind of hope for yourself."

Amanda's smile fell. "What?"

"Then we pretended for Sam so he wouldn't tell you." Jack ran a hand through his hair, knocking the sunglasses off the top of his head. He bent to pick them up, realizing that his hands were shaking. He took a deep breath as he straightened and looked at Amanda. "But while we were pretending, this thing between us became real. So I guess I should thank you because Emma and I are actually dating now."

"You lied to me?" Amanda asked, her expression unreadable.

"Kind of. Yeah, I'm sorry."

She exhaled softly. "You lied to me because you wanted to protect me just like you've always done. My overprotective brother."

"You're not mad?" he asked, relief flooding through him.

"No. I think it's funny actually. You didn't have to fake a relationship for my sake. That's kind of…"

"Silly?" Jack asked before nodding. "Yeah, I know. It seemed like a good idea at the time."

"You mean, an excuse to be close to Emma seemed like a good idea," Amanda corrected. "And now you're dating her for real. Wow. That's great, Jack."

He sucked in another deep breath. One confession down, one more to go. "Amanda, there's something else."

She met his gaze and seemed to wait.

"Sam has been asking a lot of questions. He's quite the investigator."

"What kind of questions?" she asked.

"About you. He searched your boyfriend's social media

and saw that you weren't with him." Jack left out the detail about the other woman in case Amanda didn't know. "He knows you two aren't on a vacation together."

Amanda's expression pinched. "What?"

"He's acted out just a little bit, and he's demanded answers from me a couple times."

"What did you say?" Amanda asked, looking increasingly worried.

Jack massaged a hand over his face. "I didn't have much of a choice, Amanda."

"What do you mean?" she snapped. "You told him where I was? You promised, Jack."

Jack held up a hand. "Slow down. I only told him you were at an addiction facility working on some things that would help you."

"Jack." Amanda shot up from her seat. "I trusted you. I didn't want Sam to know that his mom was here. I didn't want him to worry about me—"

"He was already worrying about you, Amanda. He was already angry that he'd been lied to. He needed the truth."

"Then you should have told me first so I could tell him." Amanda put her hands on her hips.

Jack paused, giving the conversation some breathing room. They both needed to take a moment. "I told him as little as I could. I told Sam that the rest will have to come from you, when you're ready. I'm sorry, Amanda. I really am." But he also didn't think he'd do things any differently if given a chance. Sam needed answers last night. He couldn't wait.

Tears brimmed in Amanda's eyes as she stood there in front of Jack. "I just...I never wanted my son to see me this way."

Jack stood and walked over to her. "To see you which

way? Strong? Determined? Completely kickass? Because that's the way I see you."

Amanda shook her head and covered her face with her hands. Jack reached out and pulled her into a hug, willing to take the risk that she might use the right hook he'd taught her and completely take him out. She didn't.

After several minutes, she stepped back and swiped at her tears. "Well, I guess I better tell him everything."

"When you're ready," Jack said. "He knows enough right now. And he's happy, Amanda. He just wants you to be happy too."

Amanda looked up at Jack. "Working on it."

"Take your time," Jack reiterated. "He can stay with me as long as you need him to."

"I do feel better knowing you have Emma by your side. Two is better than one, and you've always been a better version of yourself when she is around. More patient. More relaxed. She's good for you, Jack."

Jack thought so too. He probably should've contacted Emma by now. He'd wanted to first thing this morning and then again as he drove up to see Amanda. But fear had stopped him every time his finger hovered over Emma's contact. They'd crossed a line last night that couldn't be uncrossed. He wouldn't change a thing even if he could, but how was Emma feeling today?

At the end of his visit, Jack walked out of the facility. His fears about being locked inside were ridiculous. Hopefully the same was true about his fear of Emma having second thoughts about last night. And about him.

CHAPTER SEVENTEEN

The morning-after was officially over. It was now noon, and Emma hadn't heard a word from Jack.

She tried not to dwell on that as she pulled up the website for Jenny's Wellness Walk for Women. It was up to two hundred fifteen participants today. That was far more than she'd ever thought possible for its first year.

Her cell phone rang, and she grabbed it quickly, hoping it was Jack. Instead, Paris Montgomery's name popped on her screen. "Hi, Paris," she answered.

"Hey, Emma. I have the graphic ready. I just shot you an email with the design to see what you think."

"Thank you so much. I know it was kind of last-minute. I really can't believe how easily this event has come together."

"That's how you know it's meant to be," he said with a small chuckle.

"I guess so." She and Jack had come together so easily too. At least, that's how it had felt from her vantage point. But now he was MIA on her.

Emma pulled up her email and clicked on the message from Paris, waiting anxiously for the graphic to load. Then a picture of two sneakers showed up, the laces undone. An apple lay beside them, and they were encircled by the words 1ST ANNUAL JENNY'S WELLNESS WALK FOR WOMEN. It was simple, but Emma loved it. "It's perfect," she told Paris.

"Yeah? You think so?"

"Yes. One hundred percent. Can you send this to the Print Shop so they can get started on T-shirt production?"

"Sure thing," Paris said. "Lacy and I plan to walk, you know? We signed up last night."

"That's awesome. Thank you so much for all your hard work and support on this," Emma said. It would be so nice to see friends and family joining this event, as well as all the strangers who'd registered to help the cause and support women's health.

After saying goodbye, Emma went back to work with Nina and Sam. Sam was unusually quiet today, but he was a teen and they were prone to brooding moods that swung with the wind, right?

"Want a coffee?" Emma asked him. "I can make you one."

He looked up from cleaning one of the café tables. "Sure. Thanks."

"You okay, Sam?" she asked.

He nodded. "Uncle Jack went to see my mom today," he told her. "I'm guessing you know where she's really at." He looked around the café where customers were seated.

Jack hadn't told her he was planning to visit Amanda today. She wondered if this was planned or if something had happened. And, last she knew, Sam didn't know that his mom was staying in an addiction facility. This wasn't the time or place to discuss these things, so Emma just nodded.

"I guess I just wish I could have gone with him." Sam finished cleaning off the table and walked back behind the counter with Emma while she started preparing him a coffee.

"A mom just wants her child to be happy and healthy, you know?" Emma said.

"You're not a mom," Sam pointed out.

"No, but I had a mom, and I know that's what she always wanted."

And if her mom were alive, she'd be going nuts to know that Emma was ignoring her health because of her. She was celebrating women's health but being a hypocrite by neglecting to stay current with her own routine checkups and screenings.

"Well, moms should know that's all their kids want for them too. It goes both ways."

Emma smiled at Sam. "You are wise beyond your years, you know that?" She poured some creamer into his coffee and slid it down the counter toward him. "Here you go. Loaded with sugar. The solution to all that ails you."

If only that were true.

"Thanks." Sam took it and looked around the café. "It's slow. Do you care if I go sit outside at one of those tables with this?"

"Of course not. Nina and I can handle things. Take your time." Emma exhaled as she watched Sam head out. So Jack was visiting Amanda today. Was that why she hadn't yet heard from him? Emma was missing some important facts about what happened after Jack left her home last night. Hopefully when Jack returned, he'd fill in the holes.

Emma took the washcloth that Sam had left on the front counter and carried it to the back where dirty washcloths were kept for cleaning. As she did, her mind went back to her conversation with Sam. A mother wanted her child to be happy and healthy. If she really wanted to honor her mom's memory, that's what she needed to work on. Without giving herself time to think, she pulled out her cell phone, took a breath, and tapped the contact for the Women's Wellness Center. When the receptionist connected the call, Emma asked to make an appointment.

"I just had a cancellation for this Friday if you want to come in then."

If Emma gave herself time to think, she might end up with another excuse. "Do you have anything today by chance?"

"Let me see."

There was a long silence on the other end of the line as the receptionist checked. "You're in luck. If you can be here this afternoon, Dr. Rivers can fit you in. Does that work for you?"

Emma would make it work. For her mom.

* * *

After driving two hours each way and visiting his sister, Jack was more exhausted on his day off than when he'd worked a full day. He pulled into the downtown parking lot and got out of his truck, then walked toward the Sweetwater Café. He'd thought about texting Emma several times today, but one didn't follow up one of the most amazing nights of his life with a text.

Jack needed to look Emma in the eye and see for himself how she felt about what had happened between them.

Was she happy? Did she have regrets? Was it one of the most amazing nights of her life too?

Jack breathed in deeply, pulling the fresh mountain air

into his lungs and hoping for its calming effect. That's one of the reasons he'd fallen in love with hiking in the foothills and down the trails of Evergreen Park. The exercise and increased elevation forced him to take deep breaths, and the physical effect on his body was the best medicine on earth. Nature's prescription for stress.

Jack walked into the café and noticed Sam and Nina working behind the counter.

Sam looked slightly worried when he saw him. "Hey, Uncle Jack. How's Mom?" he asked when Jack approached the counter.

"She's doing amazing. I'll fill you in when you get off shift," he promised. "Maybe we can go to Joe's Pizzeria. What do you say?"

Sam nodded. "Yeah. Sounds good."

"Hey, Jack," Nina said brightly. "Emma isn't here, if you're looking for her."

"Oh?" he asked. "Do you know where I can find her?"

"She left about fifteen minutes ago. She said she had an appointment, but I don't know with who or where or why." Nina shrugged.

Jack didn't remember Emma discussing any appointments with him, but it could be for anything. It might even be related to the event she was planning. He looked over at Nina, noticing the look she was giving him—like she knew all his secrets. Had Emma told her about last night?

He shifted uncomfortably and took a step backward. "When do you get off shift?" he asked Sam.

"He can leave now," Nina said. "The café isn't that busy, and I'm used to covering it on my own. Go ahead," she told Sam. "When pizza calls, you have to answer. What can I say? Pizza makes me cheesy," she added with a wink.

Sam grinned.

"Want us to bring you a slice back?" Jack asked.

Nina folded her arms across her chest. "So you have an excuse to stop back in and see Emma if she returns? Sure. That'd be great."

Jack shook his head. "I was offering for you," he clarified, but the added benefit was that he'd have a reason to see Emma. "It might be a couple of hours. We have a stop to make first."

"Where?" Sam asked, coming around the counter to join him.

"I thought we'd go check on our illegal camper at the shelter. Maybe she needs a slice of pizza too." And honestly, Jack wanted to make sure Diana was still there. She hadn't seemed keen on staying at the shelter, but she couldn't keep camping out at the park. "See you later, Nina."

"I'll let Emma know you stopped in," she called back.

"Thanks." Jack and Sam stepped onto the sidewalk and silently weaved between people. They didn't talk until they were in his truck and driving toward the women's shelter across town.

"So?" Sam prompted. "You told Mom I know where she really is. Does that mean I can go see her now?"

Jack needed a good gulp of that fresh mountain air in his lungs right about now. "She's in a rehab facility because she needs to get clean. She needs space from her daily life, to give her a chance to regroup and figure out some things. She loves you, buddy, but I think we need to give her some time. I know you wouldn't intentionally set her back, but the more she can focus while she's there, the faster she'll be ready to leave."

From the corner of Jack's eye, he saw Sam lower his head. He fidgeted with his hands in his lap. "She's okay though?"

"Yeah. Better than okay," Jack said, and he believed that to be true. "And I need you around here so..."

Sam returned to looking out the window. "Do you think Diana is still at the shelter?"

"I don't know where else she would've gone," Jack said, which he knew didn't answer Sam's question at all. "I guess we'll see."

A few minutes later, they parked and walked inside the women's shelter. Jack spotted Trisha, the director, and headed her way.

"How's Diana?" he asked, shaking Trisha's hand.

Trisha smiled. "Good. She's gone to a few job interviews today, as a matter of fact."

"Yeah?" Jack asked. "That's awesome."

"Yeah, I sat down with her and helped her look for a few that might work. She's just one of those people who had a turn of bad luck, but I'm positive we can help her get back on her feet."

"Thank you," Jack said.

"I should be thanking you. You gave her the first helping hand. I just took it from there."

Relieved to hear about Diana doing so well, Jack turned back to Sam. "Hungry?"

Sam nodded. "Always."

This made Jack chuckle. "Let's go eat, then."

* * *

Emma was checked in and sitting in the waiting room at the Women's Wellness Center. She could still leave. Feigning a stomach bug would be the perfect excuse to get out of here.

Instead, she forced herself to stay seated. *I'm doing this.*

The waiting room door opened, and a nurse looked at her chart. "Emma?"

Emma felt wobbly as she stood and headed toward the nurse. "That's me."

"Right this way." The nurse led her down a long hall of closed doors. Emma guessed that each had a woman inside, taking care of her health. In Emma's book, that made those women smart and courageous. She was feeling short on courage right about now but followed the nurse into the last room on the left anyway.

Panic gripped her as the nurse shut the door.

"Have a seat, Emma. Let's talk for a moment."

She asked Emma a series of questions for the medical chart and jotted them on her form. Then the nurse stood and handed Emma a paper gown. "Put this on and Dr. Rivers will be in shortly."

Emma clutched the paper gown, noticing the trembling of her hands. Hopefully the nurse didn't see it. "Thank you." She waited to move until the nurse closed the door behind her and left Emma alone. The room seemed small, closing in around her. She sat down with the paper gown and took several long, deep breaths.

It was just an annual checkup. No big deal.

"Emma?" Someone knocked on the door, and Emma jumped.

Dr. Rivers stepped inside and closed the door behind her, her gaze dropping to the untouched paper gown that Emma had yet to put on.

"Sorry. I haven't had a chance to change yet," Emma said. She was sitting with the gown in her lap, which she guessed made it obvious that she hadn't made any effort toward doing so either.

"Are you okay?" Dr. Rivers asked.

Emma wanted to say yes, but she felt about as flimsy as the gown she was supposed to be wearing. "No." Her whole body started shaking.

Dr. Rivers sat down in the chair in front of her. "You've put this checkup off this year. Sometimes you just have to push through things."

"Rip off the Band-Aid," Emma agreed.

"I get it. You're worried because of your family history. You're about the same age your mom was when she got sick."

Emma sucked in a breath. She didn't correct Dr. Rivers by pointing out it was actually the same age her mom had been when she'd died. "Something like that."

Dr. Rivers reached for her hand. "Okay. Worst-case scenario. What if you do turn out like your mom?"

Emma's mouth dropped open. "Then I die, I guess. Worst case."

Dr. Rivers nodded. "Or fight."

"My mom fought," Emma pointed out. Her mom had fought against her illness, and everyone around her had rallied.

"She did, but there are new treatments now. And catching any kind of illness early can be key in a prognosis."

Emma shrugged. "You said worst-case scenario. That's death."

Dr. Rivers smiled softly. "You're right. That's death. And if it's the worst case, it's going to happen either way, right? But let's say the next-to-worst case. That would call for a fight, and you can't fight if you don't know what you're up against." Dr. Rivers shrugged. "But best-case scenario, you're completely healthy and worried for nothing. Then you can stop worrying."

Emma sucked in a breath, followed by another. After

a moment, she nodded. "Okay. Well, let's do this and see which it is."

Dr. Rivers nodded. "Emma, since you're here, I'd like to order some extra tests if you're willing. Genetic tests can tell you if you have the genetic mutation linked to breast cancer. I suspect that, even if you get a clean bill of health today, you'll still worry. This genetic test would give us more information. If you have the mutation, we can discuss measures to improve your odds of preventing a life-threatening cancer."

"Genetic testing?" Emma repeated. That sounded like a little much. She had never even considered doing something like that.

"With more information comes peace of mind. At least as far as I'm concerned. Genetic testing is something I've been able to add to our services here at the clinic. I don't recommend it for everyone, but with your family history, I think it's a good idea."

Emma felt like the world was spinning way too fast. Her world. Dr. Rivers was right. Even with a clean bill of health, Emma would still live with some level of fear. She didn't want that. "Peace of mind sounds good," Emma finally said, gathering as much courage as she could muster.

"Is that a yes?" Dr. Rivers asked.

Emma nodded. "Yes."

CHAPTER EIGHTEEN

An hour later, Emma walked out of the Women's Wellness Center and got into her car. She sat there for a long moment and collected her thoughts. She didn't want to think too much. In fact, she'd prefer not to think about what she had just done at all.

She grabbed her cell phone and dialed the café.

"Sweetwater Café," Nina answered a couple rings later. If she were busy, there'd have been more rings. This was a good sign.

"It's Emma. Are you busy over there?"

"Not especially. Jack stopped by, and I told Sam to go with him. It's just me, and even so, I have time to play Words with Friends on my phone."

"Not something you should probably confess to your employer," Emma pointed out.

"I can play while cleaning. Don't worry."

Emma laughed, which was good medicine. "Mind if I just go home, then?"

"Of course not. I'm fine here. Jack dropped off a couple slices of pizza for me a few minutes ago, so I have everything a girl could want...except a handsome single cowboy who wants to ride off into the sunset with me."

"A cowboy, huh?" Emma asked.

"That's my preference. Although, there aren't too many in the mountains."

"You said you saw Jack? How was he?" Emma asked.

"He was bummed that he missed you here. I told him you had an appointment. What kind of appointment did you go to anyway?" Nina asked.

So much for not thinking about it. "I met with Dr. Rivers."

"Right. This event you're planning is a lot of work," Nina said.

Emma didn't tell her that she and Dr. Rivers hadn't discussed the event. It was bad enough she had to wait for all the results to come back. She didn't want someone else waiting anxiously with her or asking for updates. This felt too personal.

Dr. Rivers said the genetic testing could take one to two weeks. From now until then, Emma intended to distract herself in any way she could. She hoped that she could do that with Jack, but it'd been a full day and she hadn't heard anything from him. "Thanks for watching the café tonight. I'll see you in the morning."

"Sure thing. Bye."

When Emma arrived home, she closed the door behind her, not intending to open it back up until the next morning. She walked into her kitchen with Barnaby at her heels and poured herself a glass of water, her eye catching on the note that Jack had left her at some point during the night. It promised that he'd call her sometime this morning. But he hadn't.

He had stopped by the café this afternoon though. Was it just for Sam or was he looking for her too?

Her questions were interrupted by the doorbell ringing. Barnaby set off running.

Emma set her glass down and hurried to stand behind the door, taking a moment to catch her breath. Then she peeked out the peephole, seeing Jack's distorted figure on the other side.

She opened the door and smiled at him, unable to even pretend that she wasn't happy to see him. She'd thought she wanted to be alone right now, but she suddenly needed him. "Hi."

"Hey." He held an extra-large pizza box in his hand. "I come bearing pizza."

"Well, then you can certainly come in. But I only want you for the food," she said.

Jack chuckled. "Warning. I dropped off a couple slices to Nina at the café, and Sam took a couple. So this is only half of an extra-large pie, but I think that'll suffice for the two of us." He headed toward her kitchen and slid the box onto the counter. Then he reached into his pocket and pulled out some silver-foiled chocolates. "I also came with Hershey's Kisses to sweeten the deal if you were miffed at not hearing from me all day." He dropped five Kisses beside the pizza box, all tip-side up, waving their white flags in the air just like her heart was doing.

"The only kisses I want are yours," she said, stepping up to him until he was pressed against the counter. Then she went up on her tiptoes, bringing her lips to linger just a breath away from his. He was here, bearing treats, so he must not regret last night. She met his eyes and searched for anything less than desire.

"About last night," he said. "I guess we should discuss it."

Emma swallowed. "If you really want to."

"I loved every minute of it."

She grinned. "That makes two of us."

His gaze dropped from her eyes to her mouth and back. "I'm done talking now. And if it's okay, I'm going to kiss you." His hand slid around her waist.

She was done with words too. Instead, she leaned forward and kissed him first. She'd been waiting for this all day. Waiting to melt into his arms and let go of everything but him.

"I'm sorry this isn't how we woke up this morning," he said once she'd finally pulled away.

"Me too."

Emma glanced back at the pizza box on the counter, the aroma wafting under her nose and making her mouth water. "As much as I love kissing, I'm starving."

"That makes two of us."

She was about to offer him wine because that would cap things off perfectly but then stopped herself. "I have sweet tea in the fridge."

"Sounds perfect."

Even though taking things slow would be the sensible thing, perfect would be having a repeat of last night. And while Hershey's Kisses were nice, Jack Hershey was what she hoped to have for dessert.

* * *

Jack had been a little worried that Emma would slam the door in his face when he'd come over tonight. Instead, she'd acted like it was no big deal that he hadn't contacted her during the day. Maybe he hadn't started the day with

Emma, but he was ending it with her. And there was no place he'd rather be.

"So what kind of appointment did you have this afternoon?"

Emma's smile disappeared, which got his attention and made him think it wasn't a simple hair appointment. She shrugged a shoulder and looked away.

"What's wrong?" he asked. "Are you okay?"

She nodded. "Yeah. It was nothing."

"We're done with secrets and lies this summer, remember? Everything is out in the open now. My sister knows about you and me. Sam knows that she's getting help for her addiction. No more keeping things from the ones we care about."

Emma met his eyes again, and he saw an emotion there that got his attention. "I, um, went to the Women's Wellness Center."

Jack didn't think this had anything to do with the 5K event for her mom. "Oh?"

"Just for a routine checkup." She swiped a lock of hair away from her face, anchoring it behind her ear. "I canceled my last appointment. I've been avoiding it."

"Why?"

Emma's chin quivered. "My mom's illness happened so fast. I guess I've been just...terrified of going. One day she was healthy, or so we thought. Then she went to an appointment and suddenly she was preparing me and my dad for her leaving us."

Jack scooted his chair right up to Emma and took her hand. "Are you...okay?"

He could feel Emma trembling. "Dr. Rivers said everything checked out great. There's no reason for concern. It was just a matter of me making myself go there. If I'm going to be a part of an event encouraging women to take care of themselves, I need to do the same. And if I want to honor my mom's memory, this is what she would've wanted."

This was a big deal for Emma, and he'd had no idea she was even struggling with it. "Hey," he said, gaining her attention, "she'd be really proud of you."

Emma nodded. "Thanks."

She said she was okay, but she looked completely drained, so he added, "I'm really proud of you too. For everything you've accomplished this summer. You're kind of like Superwoman."

She giggled weakly. "Hardly."

"You could've told me, you know? I'd have gone to support you. And stayed in the waiting room, of course."

Emma laughed softly. "You would have gone and waited for me at the Women's Wellness Center?"

He felt his face burning. "I mean, yeah. For you I would. I'd pretty much do anything for you, Em."

She stared at him, and he wondered what was going through her mind. "We just started dating. That's a pretty strong thing to say to someone you've only gone to bed with once."

He reached up and stroked her cheek. "But I've known you most of my life. And I've liked you more than just a friend way before this summer. Maybe we just agreed to a label, but my heart has been yours for a long time. Last night only deepened the feelings I already had for you."

Her lips parted. "Wow. I'm not sure what to say. I want to ask you to stay with me tonight, but I know you can't."

"Sam will be home in a couple hours," Jack agreed. "But I can stay awhile, and I want to hold you." *And never let go.* He didn't tell her that last part. He also didn't go into detail about the feelings he had for her. They went well beyond like or lust and bordered on something he'd never felt for any woman.

She was the one who'd gotten away. She was the one who'd kept him firmly in his bachelorhood all this time. She was the one, the only one, he wanted.

He pushed back from the table, stood, and reached for her hand. "I'm here for whatever you need from me tonight." It'd been an emotional afternoon for her. If all she wanted was to be held, that's all he'd do.

When she stood and met his eyes, however, the desire was obvious, darkening her brown-green eyes. Then, confirming his suspicion, she reached for him. "I want to feel your arms wrapped around me tonight."

* * *

Two hours later, Jack arrived home. Sam was already there and in bed. *Good.* Jack was exhausted and didn't feel like waiting up or searching all over town for his nephew.

He went straight back to his bedroom and changed clothes before plopping onto his bed and closing his eyes. It didn't even take five seconds before he was dreaming of a younger version of himself, dressed in a tux for the first time.

"You look like money," his roommate Danny said, walking into the room of their little apartment in college. "You must like this girl." He shoved a beer into Jack's hand and popped the top of his own.

Jack looked down at the can. Felt the coolness against his fingers. He was more nervous than he'd been even on his first day of college. Taking Emma to her prom tonight might open a lot of proverbial cans that he maybe wasn't

prepared for. "*I've known Emma forever,*" *he told Danny,
lifting the beer to his mouth and taking a sip. Something
about the taste soothed those nerves.*

"*I've heard you talk about her,*" *Danny pointed out.*
"*Are you guys going to ditch the prom and do something
more afterward?*"

Jack felt his whole body tense.

"*Hey, just saying. On my junior prom night, my date
and I had fun in the back seat of my Corolla. For senior
prom, I booked a motel room.*"

"*So romantic,*" *Jack said sarcastically.* "*Emma isn't
like that.*"

"*Like what?*"

"*She's special. I don't want to mess things up with her.*"

"*Now you're sounding romantic,*" *Danny pointed out.*

*Jack took another sip, realizing the can was half-empty.
How had that happened? He really was nervous about
tonight. This was a date, and being away at college had
only served to make him miss Emma more.*

*Suddenly the beer can was empty, and he was drinking
another. He couldn't seem to stop himself. His body and
mind were relaxing, drifting off to some distant place.*

"*You no longer look like money,*" *Danny said with a
laugh that seemed to reverberate in Jack's head.* "*You look
like sh—*"

Jack held up a hand. "*Stop right there. You're just
jealous. I'm going to prom with a beautiful woman, and
you're sulking over being dumped by your girlfriend.*"

Danny frowned. "*Wrong. I'm going to sit here and
finish off the rest of the beers. I passed sulking after the
third one.*"

Jack looked at his watch. "*I have to go. It's an hour's
drive to get to Emma.*" *The world shifted on its axis as*

Jack stood. How many drinks had he had? He couldn't remember. But he'd been drinking awhile, spacing them out. At least he'd thought he had.

Once his world had righted, he reached for his keys. Some small voice inside his head told him he should put them right back down. A larger voice, his roommate's, called behind him, "Go get that girl and make her fall in love with you tonight."

Jack turned, his body swaying with the quick movement. He was definitely drunk, but probably not over the legal limit. He was a big guy, which meant he could drink more than the average Joe. "Don't wait up."

* * *

Emma could hear her automatic coffee maker brewing a pot for her down the hall. She stared at the empty side of her bed. No Jack. At least she'd watched him go this time. He'd kissed her forehead and then her lips, telling her that he would let himself out.

Wouldn't it have been nice to wake up with him this morning though? It'd been so long since she'd woken with a man in her bed that she might not have known what to do.

After several long moments, she got up, went to the bathroom, and then made her way toward the coffee as Barnaby trotted leisurely behind her. As she reached the kitchen, she flipped on the lights and jumped when there was a knock on her front door.

Who would be knocking at four a.m.? She stood frozen in her kitchen for a moment, only moving when the knock came again. She looked down at Barnaby, who obviously wasn't fully awake yet either. "Now's the time to be that guard dog you think you are," she said quietly. Then she headed over to stare out the peephole, sucking in a breath when she saw Jack.

"What are you doing here?" she asked after she opened the door.

"This." He stepped toward her and kissed her until she melted against him.

"No, really. What's going on?" she asked once they came up for air. She stepped back, allowing him to come inside, and then closed the door behind him.

"Sam is taking your place at the café this morning. I wanted to wake up with you."

Emma felt her heart skip a happy beat.

"I waited to knock until I saw your light come on. I wanted to catch you before you brushed your hair."

Or her teeth. Emma slid a tongue over her teeth to do her own sort of cleaning.

"I thought if we can't have the real thing, we could pretend...It worked before," he said, charming every bone in her body.

She was still in her cotton shorts and T-shirt. Her hair was probably a sight to behold. She looked at Jack, who looked like he'd just rolled out of bed as well. "Now what?"

"Now we go back to bed and wake up together. We can take as long as we want. You don't have anywhere to be, and neither do I."

Emma smiled. "That sounds heavenly."

Jack stepped toward her, locking his arms around her, engulfing her in his embrace. Then they headed down the hall and climbed into bed, disappearing under the sheets with tangling limbs. Emma wouldn't mind waking up this way every morning. Forever.

* * *

At noon, Emma did the walk of shame into her café. Nina lifted a brow at her as Emma headed into the back room to put her bag away. She slipped an apron over her clothes and headed back out front.

"How was the morning?" Emma asked.

"I should ask you that," Nina said.

"Thanks for opening."

"Not a problem. Jack texted me last night before bed and said Sam would help."

Emma shook her head and smiled. Had he planned this before they'd even made it to the bedroom last night?

"I wouldn't have pegged Jack as such a romantic," Nina said.

Emma grabbed a cloth and started wiping down the front counter. "Oh, he's very romantic."

When Nina didn't come back with a witty comment, Emma looked over and met her dumbfounded expression. "If I didn't know better, I'd say you were falling for him. Like, really falling for him."

Emma paused. She'd resisted any feelings for Jack since he'd stood her up at her prom. They'd stepped safely back into the friend zone. But things had changed between them now.

She wanted a relationship. She wanted to fall in love and get married and have kids. There was nothing standing in the way.

Emma straightened. "I guess I am."

Nina clapped a hand over her mouth. Then she flung open her arms and wrapped Emma in a huge hug. "I'm so happy for you. This is the best news."

"Yeah." Emma laughed as she pulled back.

"Does Jack feel the same way?" Nina asked.

"I . . . I don't know. It's too soon. I mean . . ." Emma shook her head. "We haven't talked about our feelings really."

"Well, actions speak louder than words. That's what my mom always said, and it's true. And his actions last night and this morning are of a man completely head over heels in love."

CHAPTER NINETEEN

A week later, Jack bumped along the trails at Evergreen Park with a trash collection bag and a long-handled reacher.

Park events were a great way to pull the community together, but it usually left a lot of work to be done the next morning. *Who knew the Save the Bears event last night would create such a mess?* There were maintenance workers who handled trash pickup, of course, but Jack tried to give them a hand when possible.

He stopped to grab empty cans, tossed out by event goers who'd decided to go for a walk in the woods. What those lovers had done in the woods he didn't want to know.

Once the area was clean, he moved to another. He came to a clearing in the woods near Blue Sky Point where he'd found Diana. He wondered how her interviews had gone. He hoped someone had given her a shot. Everyone deserved a second chance. Even him. He and Emma were dating now, and this time he was going to do right by her.

During the past week, they'd spent every possible second they could together. It wasn't easy with a fifteen-year-old shadowing him, but they'd made it work.

Jack pointed the ATV back toward his office. He had a full bag of trash that he dropped in the dumpster behind the building before going inside for a cool drink. When he walked inside, Amanda was waiting for him.

Jack wiped the sweat off his brow. "What are you doing here?"

She shrugged and got up to hug him.

He held up his hands. "Oh no. You don't want to do that. I'm gross."

"You've always been gross," she said, hugging him anyway. "I'm out."

"You didn't tell me you were leaving the facility so soon."

"Well, I checked myself in, and I can check myself out. I'm feeling a lot better, and I miss Sam."

Jack inspected his sister outwardly. She looked much better than she had when she'd first gone into treatment. "Sam is working at the café this morning. He's got two jobs this summer."

"I think I'll wait to let him know I'm here until his shift is over." Amanda smiled. "Maybe I'll take him out to dinner."

Jack nodded. "I recommend somewhere with a buffet because your son can eat."

This made Amanda laugh. "Oh, I know."

It was good to see his sister happy. "You work from home so there's no reason to run off anytime soon. Why don't you stay with me on the lake for the rest of the summer?" he asked.

"What?" Her smile dropped.

Jack shrugged. "I have room. Stay with me. Sam is just

getting settled in here, and I think he's got himself a girl-friend." At least Jack suspected that's why Sam's mood had been so chipper lately. Emma had mentioned a teenage girl who was frequenting the café when Sam was on shift.

"My Sam?" Amanda asked with a little surprise. "Wow. I guess he's growing up." Amanda shook her head. "If I stayed awhile, we'd probably drive one another batty like we did as kids."

"Doubt it. Just consider it."

"I will, but don't get your hopes up."

Jack nodded. "Too late." He gestured toward the refrigerator in the far corner of the room. "I'm going to grab a water. Want one?" he asked.

"That'd be great. Thanks."

He brought two bottles back and sat on a chair across from her. The cool AC felt good on his skin after being outside in the hot sun for the last couple hours. "So you're doing better, huh?"

Amanda twisted the cap off her bottled water. "A lot."

"You never did tell me all the details. I mean, did something happen to put you in a tailspin?"

She sipped for a long moment. "It was just a slow descent. Sometimes it happens so slowly that you don't even know it's happening."

Jack nodded.

"I tried to get better on my own. I wanted to be there for Sam. He needs me."

"He's pretty grown these days," Jack countered.

"He is. One day he'll leave to live his own life, and then I'll really be alone."

"You're never alone. You know that. You can always call me. Or Mom...Probably not Dad," he said, knowing it would get her to laugh.

"Yeah, Dad is about the last person I'd call for help."

"If you won't commit for the rest of the summer," Jack said, "just commit to staying until next weekend. Emma has organized a 5K event in her mom's memory for next Saturday. She's doing it alongside the Women's Wellness Fair in Evergreen Park. It'll be a great day, and I know Sam would want to go. He's helped out a lot."

Amanda peeled the label off her water bottle. "Yeah, okay. I can handle a week with you. Is it too late for me to sign up to walk in the event?"

Jack smiled. "I happen to be dating the event coordinator. I can get you in, if it is."

Amanda laughed. "You're dating her for real this time, right? Not just pretending for some goofball reason."

"I take offense to that," he joked.

"Are you walking or running?" she asked.

"Walking."

"I remember Emma's mom," Amanda said. "We were just kids, but I still think about her. You and I went through a lot growing up, but we never lost a parent. I can't imagine how hard that must have been for Emma."

Jack nodded. He hadn't realized just how hard it'd been on Emma. She'd been avoiding seeing a doctor because she was terrified of ending up like her mom. He was glad she'd finally gone and gotten her clean bill of health. Now she could live her life fully. "Emma is strong," he told Amanda. "Courageous. She inspires me to do better."

"Oh. Wow."

Jack looked at his sister. "What?"

"How long have you been in love with her?"

He scratched the side of his face where a beard was already trying to fill in even though he'd shaved three hours earlier. "I'm not."

Amanda tilted her head. "I thought you were done pretending with me."

Jack started peeling the label of his water bottle too. "Since college. Maybe before that." Amanda already knew about the night he'd driven drunk to take Emma to her prom. It was one of his most shameful moments. "Her dad still thinks I'm scum of the earth."

"That night was over ten years ago. People change. You've changed."

Jack nodded. "Maybe so, but Emma is still his little girl. I'm pretty sure he hates the fact that we're dating. There's no way he'll ever let things get further than that."

Amanda's mouth popped open. "You mean marriage? Oh my goodness, my brother wants to get married."

Jack waved a hand. "No. I mean, yes, one day, but not now. Emma and I just started dating. And the point was that her dad isn't thrilled."

"So change his mind," Amanda said with a broad smile. "You said you admired how courageous Emma is. Follow in her footsteps and be brave."

"Brave how?" Jack asked, not understanding.

"Invite Emma's family over for dinner," she suggested.

Just the suggestion sent fear coursing through Jack's body. "Be brave," he repeated to Amanda's steady smile. He looked at her for a long moment. "Emma isn't the only one I admire for her courage. I admire the heck out of you too."

"Aww." She tilted her head. "Thanks."

"The women in my life rock." He nodded to himself. "And I'm going to follow their lead and win Emma's dad's approval."

* * *

The coffee was weak.

Emma drew back and sucked in an audible breath. "What?" she said as she looked at her iPad.

Nina glanced over her shoulder at her from the café's counter, tossing her a questioning look. She used a pair of tongs to place a pastry on a napkin and offered it to Mayor Everson, who scrunched his brows at Emma as well.

"Everything okay, Emma?" he asked.

Emma lifted a hand to her forehead and turned away from the tablet's screen. Then she walked over to say hello to Brian. "Yes, fine. I should just stay far away from the A-List website, but I can't seem to help myself. I got a review that said the coffee was weak."

Brian tsked. "That's an opinion, and it depends on the coffee drinker. I've always loved your coffee, which is why I'm here so often. You don't seem to be suffering for business so I'd say a lot of others agree with me."

Emma placed her hands on her hips. "Who writes these reviews anyway?"

Brian shrugged. "I learned a long time ago that some people will love what you're doing and some won't. It's just part of the territory."

"I for one love you," Nina told him. "And your wife is amazing too."

Brian smiled. "I think so."

"Is Jessica going to join the race?" Emma asked him.

"Oh yeah. We both are," he said. "She'll be walking, and I've got wheels and two strong arms. I think a day to focus on the women in this community and their health is a wonderful idea. And, as you know, Jess and I are all about worthwhile causes. I'm also spreading the word to everyone I come in contact with."

"So it's you. The registrations have far surpassed what I had hoped for. At last check, I think there were almost five hundred people signed up."

"That's a lot of T-shirts," Nina commented.

Brian took the coffee and his pastry. "Speaking of Jessica, I'm meeting her for a little midmorning date. We thought we'd nab one of the new tables you placed outside and enjoy the weather."

"Please do," Emma said.

She watched the mayor head toward the door, where another patron opened it for him. She'd put the table outside because of a negative review, and it had proved to be a good idea. She turned back to Nina. "Maybe we should add a new coffee drink that has an extra shot of espresso for those who want something stronger."

Nina gave her an are-you-serious? look. "You're a people pleaser to a fault."

Emma didn't take offense. "What's wrong with that?"

"Nothing, but that's totally what you are. I think the new drink will be a hit. We just need a really good name for it. What do you think?"

"Double Stuff?" Emma suggested.

"Like the Oreo?"

Emma frowned. "Caffeine Overload?"

Nina grimaced. "We can keep thinking on it. It's a great idea, but you don't need to check the A-List and get yourself upset in order to think up new ways to improve the café. You're the boss so I can't tell you what to do, but you should stop reading that site."

"I know." An idea came to Emma, and she straightened. "Maybe you can check the site for me. If there's a negative review, you can read it, and if there's a way to address the feedback, then you can tell me."

Nina slid her a look. The café was slow right now so she was leaning against the counter looking relaxed. Emma was slightly jealous. She was juggling so many balls right now between the café and the event.

There was also the genetic testing that was hanging over her like a storm cloud. She hadn't told anyone she'd taken the test. Hopefully it would be negative, and she could put her fears to rest once and for all.

Nina pointed a finger. "Okay, I'll screen the site for you if you promise to stay away from it yourself. I'll check it once a week and let you know only if there's something legit that needs to be addressed."

Emma nodded. "I'm okay with that."

"Good. And since you're agreeing to things, it's slow in here. You need to go out and clear your head. Maybe even think up a name for the new drink."

Emma pulled off her apron. "A walk sounds great, actually. But why do I feel like you just want to get rid of me?"

Nina chuckled. "Your stress is stressing me out. I'm just trying to help you find a more relaxed vibe, that's all."

"Vibe!" Emma said, pulling her bag over her shoulder and turning toward Nina. "We could call the new drink Vibe."

Nina seemed to consider the name. "I'd like a Vibe, please," she said, pretending to be a customer. "It has a good ring to it. Very hip."

Emma smiled. "See? I don't even need a walk."

"Oh, but you do. Your vibe is still stressed." Nina gave Emma a soft push to start walking around the counter. "I'll call you if things get crazy here."

Emma waved. "I'll be back soon."

She had to admit that a walk to clear her head was a good

idea. As she walked, her cell phone vibrated in her pocket. She pulled it out and smiled at the sight of Jack's name. She had it so bad for this guy. She opened his text.

Dinner tonight? Tammy's Log Cabin around 7?

She didn't even have to think about it. Yes.
She watched dots bounce along the screen as she waited for his response.

It's gonna sound weird, but can you invite your dad and stepmom?

Emma stopped walking and felt her face scrunch. Why?

It's too late to ask permission to date you, but if we're going to do this for real, I want your dad to like me.

She grinned. I'll ask them. I'm sure they'd love to.

Thanks. TTYL.

Emma switched contacts and typed out a quick text to her dad, inviting him to dinner. He was usually slow to respond so she slid her phone back into her pocket and strolled for a while longer, window-shopping along Main Street. She didn't consider going inside any of the stores until she came to stand in front of Dawanda's Fudge Shop.

Dawanda looked up from behind the counter as Emma pushed through the door. "Emma!" she called excitedly. Dawanda wasn't one who would ever need a Vibe coffee. She was already as lively as her red, spiky hair. "Did you come for another piece of maple nut fudge?"

"No, thank you."

"Another cappuccino reading, then?" Dawanda asked hopefully.

"I just had one, Dawanda. You saw a rose, remember?"

Dawanda nodded. "Blooming beautifully this summer. That prediction is already coming true. All I've heard about lately is you and Jack. You're causing such a buzz around town. And this event of yours too."

Emma glanced around the fudge shop to make sure she wasn't taking up too much of Dawanda's time. There weren't any other customers so she went ahead and asked the questions that were weighing on her mind since the LDO get-together at the B&B. "Explain my fortune to me. You said the rose blooms and then the petals fall off."

Dawanda pulled out a chair along the wall, gesturing for Emma to do the same. She waited to talk until Emma took a seat. "We all have periods of blooming and then dying back. Blooming and dying back. That's the rhythm of life."

"So that fortune could've been told to anyone?" Emma asked. "It wasn't specific to me?"

Dawanda straightened. "No. That fortune was definitely yours. But you shouldn't worry about what I saw. Dying back just means that you're getting rid of the old stuff to make room for the new. We all need that pruning season to get rid of our junk."

Dawanda was starting to sound like a therapist more than a fudge store owner now. "The thing to focus on, Emma, is the moment that you're in. And the cappuccino says you're in a season of bloom. Enjoy it."

* * *

Jack was driving five miles an hour under the speed limit to get to Tammy's Log Cabin. He'd had a surge of determination when he'd planned this dinner with Emma and her family, but now he was wishing he was home with Amanda and Sam.

Emma reached for his hand and gave it a squeeze as he drove. "My dad's harmless."

Jack nodded. "I don't think he's going to take me outside and take a swing at me. That's not it."

She giggled in the passenger seat. "I should hope not. Maybe he's still upset about something that happened a decade ago, but once he gets to know you more, he'll see that there's no reason to worry about you and me being together."

Jack looked over. "Wow. I really like the sound of that. You and me together."

She smiled back at him. "Eyes on the road, Hershey. If you get us in a wreck tonight, it might take longer to win over my dad."

Jack returned to facing forward. "I don't know Angel that well. Is she easy to win over?"

Emma sighed. "Angel loves everyone. And she participates in every charity event in town, so if you're interested in hearing about one of those or volunteering to help, you'll earn brownie points."

Jack turned onto Main Street and followed it down to the restaurant. "She's not helping with Jenny's Wellness Walk for Women, is she?" From the corner of Jack's eye, he saw Emma turn to look out the side window.

"I don't really need any extra help. I've got it covered."

Jack nodded. "I see."

"What?" Emma looked in his direction again.

"It's okay that you don't want her helping you on this

event. I mean, it's to honor your mom and she's your stepmom. It might feel kind of weird."

Emma grew quiet.

He reached for her hand. "I'm sure she understands."

"I don't even understand," Emma said. "If it were anyone other than her that my dad married. My dad waited a year to search out Angel, but still." Emma shook her head. "It's my problem, not theirs, and I'm working on it."

"You don't need to justify how you feel to me." Jack parked and sucked in a deep breath. Then he blew it out and looked over. "If your dad still hates me after tonight, is that the end of us?"

Emma's lips parted. "Do you seriously think I'd stop seeing you based on my dad's opinion?"

"I'm hoping not." Jack leaned in and kissed her, drawing courage from the feel of her lips against his.

"But he's going to love you just as much as I do," she said.

Had she just said what he thought he'd heard?

Emma's eyes widened. "I didn't mean it that way," she said quickly. "I don't love you."

"You don't?" Jack's heart was on a rocky ten-second roller coaster.

Emma shook her head. Then her brows scrunched as she stared back at him in the truck. "This is not the time for this kind of conversation."

"Yeah, you're probably right. We can save it for later." Because he was 100 percent in love with her. That was becoming more obvious by the second, and he wanted to tell her so. But first, he needed to handle this situation with her dad. He wanted Mr. St. James to approve of them dating, and he'd do just about anything for that approval.

Jack pushed his door open and walked around to open Emma's door for her. Then they headed inside, where Edward and Angel were already seated and waiting. Angel offered a wide smile when she saw them coming. Jack didn't miss Edward's slight frown in his direction. Then Edward's gaze slid to his daughter, and his eyes seemed to light up.

This just might be the longest dinner of Jack's life.

Jack reached out and shook Angel's and then Edward's hand, trying not to flinch at the death grip Emma's father offered him. Then he and Emma took their seats across the table from the older couple.

The conversation flowed easily as Emma talked about the café and business. "We're creating a new drink with double espresso. I'm thinking about calling it the Vibe."

"Your coffee is already the strongest in town," Angel said.

"Just the way I like it," Edward agreed.

"Thank you." Emma fidgeted with a napkin in front of her. "I got some feedback this week that said my coffee was weak so I'm trying to accommodate those customers who want something even stronger."

Edward tsked. "You've always cared too much about what others think. Your mother was the same way. You get that from her."

Jack noticed the way Emma looked down for a moment, as if collecting herself. She didn't like to be compared to her mom, and now he understood a little bit why. If she shared the good qualities, she probably shared the bad too. And the bad scared her.

"I don't know how you do it," Angel said. "Being a businesswoman is so much work. I really admire how much time and thought you put into your café."

Emma looked up, but her enthusiasm had noticeably drained. "It's no big deal."

"Oh, but it is," Angel insisted. "You wake up early, and you give your best service. Everyone I know loves the Sweetwater Café. You've created a place where people enjoy gathering. It's just amazing to me."

Jack felt a little jolt of sympathy for Angel. He could tell that she was trying hard with Emma, and he could relate. He wanted Edward to like him just as much as Angel was trying to get her stepdaughter to like her.

A waitress approached to take their order.

Jack looked up, taking a moment for his mind to process who she was. Judging by the look on her face, she recognized him immediately. "Diana?"

The woman was cleaned up with her hair neatly pulled back in a low-hanging ponytail. She smiled hesitantly. "Hi, Jack."

Jack looked around the table. He didn't really want to invade Diana's privacy by telling them that he'd met her because she'd been illegally camping out in his park. Or that he'd taken her to the women's shelter. That might embarrass her. "Good to see you," he said instead. "This is Emma, my, uh…" He met Emma's eyes, unsure of what to call her. "My girlfriend," he finally said, making Emma grin.

Edward was frowning when Jack gestured across the table.

"And Emma's dad, Edward. And this is Angel," Jack introduced.

Diana nodded at them all. "Well, Jack here is my hero. He helped me pick myself up when I was down."

Jack waved a hand. "I don't know about being a hero."

"I do. You and Sam both," Diana said. "And Tammy."

"I didn't know you got a job here," Jack said.

"It's just a few nights a week. I'm still looking for something with more hours. But I'm thankful to be here tonight, and to have you all at one of my tables." Diana pulled out a notepad and pen. "Speaking of being your waitress, what can I get you?"

She took their drink orders, and since they were all prepared to order tonight's house special, she took their full order. "I'll be back with your teas in just a minute," she said, walking away.

"She seemed nice," Angel said once Diana had left. "I don't think I've seen her around town before."

Jack shrugged. "I think she's new in town. I met her at the park a week back. She seemed to be struggling so I'm glad she's found work here," he said, deciding that was more than enough information for the group.

An awkward silence fell over the table.

"So," Angel began, "Emma, how is the event coming along?"

"Good." Emma nodded.

"Well, Edward and I are all signed up. We can't wait. If you need help with anything, just let me know. I'd be more than happy to lend a hand, you know."

"I think everything is pretty much covered," Emma said.

Jack noticed Angel's demeanor deflate just a touch. His turn. "Mr. St. James, how's real estate these days?"

Edward gave him a long, hard stare before responding. "The market is good. I sold three houses this week."

"Wow. Congratulations," Jack said. "That's a good week."

"I've had better," Edward said. "And how is your work?" he asked.

"The summer months keep me busy. All of the events are great to bring people to the park, but the more people that flow in, the more I need to patrol and monitor what's going on. I've already had a few injured hikers this season and a bit of illegal activity."

As if on cue, Diana stepped back up to the table with four drinks. "Your food will be out shortly," she promised.

"Diana?" Edward said, stopping her before she walked away. "I don't get together with my family too often so this is kind of special." His gaze slid to Jack for a steely moment and then back to Diana. "I'd like to order a bottle of wine. Whatever you recommend to complement our meal," he said. "Wine and four glasses, please."

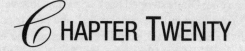

CHAPTER TWENTY

$\mathcal{E}$mma had barely tasted a bite of her filet mignon. She was too preoccupied with the tension around the dinner table. There was also the tall bottle of red wine at the table's center. A wineglass sat in front of all four diners, although hers and Jack's hadn't been touched since her father had poured a deep serving.

She really wanted a sip to take the edge off, but if Jack wasn't drinking, which she understood, then neither was she. She was mortified actually that her father would order the wine. It was almost as if he was daring Jack to drink. Or not drink. She wasn't sure what her father wanted, but he was definitely testing Jack.

Jack was proving something tonight too. And Emma knew that Angel was doing the same. Ever since she'd come into Emma's father's life, Angel had been trying to prove that she belonged. And Emma, despite knowing that it was wrong, was trying to prove that she didn't.

Emma took another bite of her beef, tasting nothing.

"Why aren't you drinking your wine?" Angel finally asked Emma. "It's your favorite, if I remember correctly."

"I'm just...I guess I'm not in the mood."

"Are you sick?" Angel asked. Then her eyes widened. "Are you...?"

Emma's heart soared up into her throat. "No. No, I'm not..." Was her stepmom really asking if she was pregnant at the dinner table in front of her dad? As if to prove another point, Emma reached for her glass and took a healthy gulp. "See?" The wine tasted good. Bitter and sweet. She took another sip, this time because she wanted it.

Her father looked at Jack. "Your turn," he said.

"I'll pass, sir." Jack stabbed at a piece of beef. He popped it into his mouth and chewed, looking back up at Emma's dad, the two of them having a stare-down.

"Come on, Jack," Edward said, "you must enjoy having a glass of wine at dinner."

"Dad," Emma cut in, "he said he didn't want any. Leave him alone."

Her father ignored her and continued to watch Jack. "It's a good wine. Not even a taste?"

Jack set his fork down. Then he reached for his wineglass, wrapping his fingers around it. His grip seemed to increase, until Emma wondered if the glass might shatter. Then Jack lifted the glass off the table and brought it to his mouth, where he held it just under his nose. He breathed in deeply. "It smells good, sir. I've always loved the smell of a good wine. But I don't want to taste it." He set the glass back down. "I gave up wine and beer and every other form of alcohol. I don't need it."

Emma looked at her dad. She knew when he was deep in thought. She could practically see the wheels turning in his mind. Why was he challenging Jack this way? If her father knew that Jack struggled with alcohol once upon a time, why would he rub it in Jack's face? It wasn't like him. Her father was a good guy.

Her father lifted his own glass to his mouth and took a healthy gulp. "Suit yourself, Jack. A good dinner certainly doesn't have to be accompanied by a glass of wine."

"No, sir," Jack agreed. "My filet is perfect on its own."

Her father nodded, his posture softening. "Glad to hear it."

Emma looked between the men. She shared a glance with Angel, who looked equally as worried. "My food is wonderful too," Emma finally said.

"It's delicious," Angel chimed in as they all continued to eat.

"So, Jack, how are your parents?" her father asked then.

"Mom is doing well. She's enjoying working in her garden."

"You have your nephew staying with you right now, don't you?" her father asked.

Jack nodded. "Sam."

"Where's his mother?"

Emma saw Jack stop and take in a full breath.

"Well, sir, she was at a treatment facility for addiction. But she's doing much better now, and she's actually staying with me." Jack popped another piece of meat in his mouth.

"Dad," Emma said, "why are you grilling Jack? It was his idea to have dinner with you and Angel tonight. Jack is a great guy, Dad. We're dating, whether you approve of him or not. You didn't ask my permission when you started dating Angel, did you?" As soon as those words left Emma's mouth, she regretted them. It made it sound like she wouldn't have approved of Angel if her father had asked.

Angel looked down at the food on her plate. She wasn't as tough as Jack. She didn't have any rebuttals. She just reached for her glass of wine with a shaky hand and took a sip.

"I didn't mean…," Emma began, waiting for Angel to look up. She didn't.

"It's my job to protect you," her father said after a long moment.

Emma shook her head. "I don't need protecting from Jack, Dad."

Jack laid a hand on her thigh under the table. "And I don't need you to defend me. Your dad has good reason to be wary of me. I understand."

"His reasons are old," Emma said. "You don't deserve this."

"I do." Jack looked across the table. "I'll keep trying to prove myself to you, but I won't stop dating your daughter, sir. Like she said, she chooses who she wants in her life."

"So I just have to deal with it?" her father asked.

"Pretty much," Emma said, even though her father was asking Jack. She turned to Jack. "I'm actually not feeling too well. I think it was the wine. Can you take me home?" She pushed back from the table without waiting for anyone to respond, grabbed her bag, and headed to the front of the table. "It was so nice to see you both. Angel?"

Angel looked up.

Emma wanted to apologize for hurting her stepmom's feelings. She hadn't meant to insult Angel. "It's always so nice to visit with you. We should do this again soon, just you and me." It was enough of a peace offering to make Angel smile, but it wasn't an apology.

"We should," Angel agreed.

Jack stood and stepped over to stand next to Emma.

"We'll stop by and pay on the way out." He offered his hand to her father. "Good night, sir."

Emma mentally willed her father to take Jack's hand and shake it.

It took a long drawn-out moment, which seemed to be happening a lot at this dinner. Then he took Jack's hand, and they shook. "Good night."

Emma waited until they were out of the restaurant before she leaned into Jack. "I'm so sorry about that. I don't know what got into my dad tonight."

Jack stopped walking and turned toward her, reaching for both of her hands. "I do. He's just looking out for you. Because he loves you. I one hundred percent understand that."

She blinked, wondering if he meant it the way it'd sounded.

* * *

Edward St. James made it clear that he didn't want his daughter seeing Jack.

That wasn't the reason Jack had declined to go inside with Emma when he'd driven her home though. He just needed some space to think. When he'd come home, he'd been careful not to wake Sam and Amanda, and he'd come out on his porch to stare out at the woods and the slivers of Silver Lake in between.

He understood Edward's reasons, but Jack wasn't like his dad. He'd made mistakes, but they didn't define him.

"Hey." The back door opened, and Amanda walked out, wearing sweat shorts and a T-shirt. Her hair was pulled back in a messy ponytail that told Jack she'd just woken up.

"Did I wake you?" he asked.

"No. I mean, yes, but it's not your fault. I heard the front door open and close, and when I didn't hear you creak down the hall, I figured you were out here thinking." She sat in the chair beside him and looked over. "I'm guessing tonight didn't go well."

"That's an understatement. It went about as bad as it possibly could go."

"Oh no. Mr. St. James used to like you. Wasn't he the one who suggested you take Emma to her senior prom in the first place?"

Jack chuckled dryly. "Yeah, well, he learned his lesson there, I guess."

"My point is he saw the good in you before. He'll see it again. And there's a lot of good."

"I tried to show him tonight. I really did. He refused to even give me a chance." Jack looked over at Amanda. "He bought an expensive bottle of wine and practically demanded that I drink with him."

Amanda's jaw dropped in a dramatic fashion. "What? That's...that's just wrong. Knowing you have an issue with alcohol and then rubbing it in your face like that. Please tell me you didn't..."

"No." Jack shook his head and returned his attention to the trees. "I don't need to drink to feel good."

Amanda reached for his hand. "You have it all figured out. I'm proud of you and also a little jealous."

"You're figuring things out too," he said.

"Trying." She looked out on the backyard with him. "It's beautiful here."

Jack nodded. "It is."

"I could've just come here for the summer to clear my head and get it back on straight."

Jack smiled. "I think you did the right thing. Is your head on straight now?" he asked.

"Pretty much." She grinned over at him. "Thanks for taking care of Sam for the last few weeks."

"No problem."

"You know, one of the things I learned in counseling is that you can steer your life in the right direction, but you have to know that waves are going to toss you all about. Or something like that." She furrowed her brow and looked at Jack. "It was a boating analogy of some type. My therapist said to know the people and things that will keep you afloat if you fall out of the boat. Your life preservers, he called them. You're one of my preservers, Jack. And Sam and Mom. I need to get back to church too."

Jack looked over. "That's good advice."

"Okay, then tell me. Who or what is your life preserver?"

He scratched the side of his face as he thought. He enjoyed hanging out with Granger and Luke lately. Then there was his family, small as it was. "You're on the list. You'd save me, right?"

"After all these years saving me? Of course."

"Good to know." Emma came to mind too. She'd always been his friend and more. If he lost her, he wasn't sure any of his available lifelines would keep him afloat. But he wasn't going to lose Emma, no matter what her father thought of him. Now that he'd found her, he was going to hold on to her.

"Whoa. I don't know what thought just crossed your mind, but it was pretty serious," Amanda said on a laugh. "I'm guessing it was about that girlfriend of yours."

Jack didn't feel the need to respond, which was its own sort of answer.

"I've always wanted a sister," Amanda said. "Emma would make a good one."

Jack looked over, feigning offense. "A brother isn't good enough for you?"

Amanda chuckled softly, the sound drifting off toward the woods and the water. She still had her hand on his, and she brought her opposite hand to cover it as well. "You're more than enough, but you'll never get your hair and nails done with me or go dress shopping on Main Street."

Jack furrowed his brow. "No, I won't. And if I did, I think your dreams of Emma being your new sister would be over."

Amanda laughed some more. It was good to see and hear her so happy. Then she squealed softly. "Uh-oh. I think that was a raindrop...There's another."

They both lifted their faces to the sky to check just as a heavy downpour broke over them.

Amanda let out a quiet shriek. Then they both jumped up and dashed for the back door, already drenched by the time they got inside.

"You look like you just fell in a pool," Amanda whispered to him.

"I'll grab us a couple towels." He headed back to the bathroom, grabbed two, and came back to dry off.

"I think that was my cue to go to bed," Amanda told him when she was done. She hung the wet towel on the back of a chair to dry out.

Jack nodded. "Good night."

"Night." He watched as she tiptoed down the hall.

Jack wasn't the least bit tired, especially after that unexpected shower. He listened for a second as it came down on his metal roof. The sound was its own form of music. He wished he was with Emma tonight, enjoying the sound together and making love as it stormed all around them.

For a moment, he considered getting in his truck and driving down there, knocking on her door, and doing just that. He chose the side of self-control, just like he did with the glass of wine tonight and every other time he was faced with an opportunity to drink.

And tonight, self-control meant retreating to his own bed. Another day, it might be seeking out Edward St. James and telling him that he would never hurt Emma, ever again. That he would protect her, respect her, and adore her. He had no other choice than to do those things because he loved her.

* * *

On Friday, the eve before the big event, Emma didn't need coffee or her most recent addiction to seeing Jack to get her through the day. She was running on pure adrenaline. Nina and Sam were operating the café today, and Emma was completing a to-do list. At the top of that list was picking up the T-shirts from the printing company.

She stepped into the store and headed straight to the counter, where a balding middle-aged man greeted her. "Hi. I'm Emma St. James, here to pick up an order of T-shirts."

He nodded, put a receipt in front of her, and X'ed the bottom signature line. "Sign here, and I'll help load the boxes in your car. That's a lot of T-shirts," he observed.

"Yes. Much more than I'd expected to order." She couldn't contain her smile as she said it. She was so proud of herself that she was practically giddy. She'd pulled this off. She was celebrating her mom's life by influencing the lives of so many women in the community. This was a great way to begin her thirtieth year. "Hopefully next year my order will be even bigger," she told the man, sliding the signed receipt back toward him.

They filled her entire car with boxes of T-shirts, and then Emma headed off. She had one more important stop to make. She needed to go see Angel. She felt awful about the way she'd behaved the other night, and it was time they sat down and talked.

Angel worked as a nurse in a walk-in clinic in town. Emma thought she'd just stop by and leave a message for Angel to call her. She could text but she was in the area. She parked and went inside the small building with few cars in the parking lot. The receptionist looked up and smiled.

"You're Angel's stepdaughter," she said immediately.

Emma slowed her walk. "Yes. I'm, um, Emma."

The woman nodded. "She has a framed picture of you and your dad in her area. She talks about you a lot. And she brings us coffees from your café all the time. Love the brew. Best in town," the woman said.

Emma nodded. "Thanks. I just wanted to leave Angel a note. Do you mind if I borrow a pen and Post-it?"

The receptionist didn't listen. "Angel!" she called behind her. "Hey, Angel, your stepdaughter is here."

Emma should've just sent a text.

Angel appeared a moment later, a look of confusion and surprise on her face. "Is Eddie okay?" she asked immediately.

Because why else would Emma pay her an unexpected visit? "He's fine. I was just going to leave you a message to call me. I was hoping we could talk sometime soon. Just you and me."

Angel nodded and started peeling off her white nurse's coat. "It's not busy. There's a picnic table outside." She started leading the way.

This was why Emma didn't usually act on her impulses, which is what stopping here had been. She hadn't planned out what she'd say to Angel. She didn't know how or what she wanted to discuss.

Angel sat at a picnic table outside and Emma plopped down in front of her.

"I'm sorry," Emma said. "I guess that's what I really wanted to say. About the other night. I didn't mean to hurt your feelings."

Angel reached for her hand.

Emma considered yanking her hand away, but she wasn't a kid. She'd been a budding teenager when she'd first met Angel, and she was still acting that way toward her.

"When I first met your mom, as her nurse, one of the things that impressed me most was how much she loved her family. You and Edward. Your mom and dad had one of the best relationships I had ever seen." Angel blew out a shaky breath. "I came from a broken home and a broken marriage."

"So you were jealous of my parents?" Emma asked. It was an honest question with no attitude behind it. She really wanted to know.

"No," Angel said, pulling her hand back now. "Yes. I was inspired by watching them together. Your mom was my patient, and I loved her. I grew closer to her than I ever have with a patient, and when she was gone, I missed her." Angel looked down at her hands on the table for a moment. "She told me that she had recently been working on her marriage to your dad. She said she wanted to fall in love with him all over again, and I think they did."

Emma remembered the checked item on her mom's list. *Fall in love with my husband all over again.*

"She sent me out to get little trinkets for him. I played matchmaker in a way." Angel looked at Emma. "I never had any feelings for your father during that time. We barely even talked. When your mom was in the room, Edward only had eyes for her. You need to know that."

Emma rolled her lips together as emotion surfaced. This conversation was way overdue. But maybe she wouldn't have listened until now. Maybe she wouldn't have believed Angel if she'd tried to explain this to her before. "I believe you," Emma said.

Angel smiled. "After your mom died, I never saw your dad until about a year later. He was sitting alone, and I felt like he needed someone to talk to. So we talked, and it felt good to both of us so we decided to do it again..." She squinted under the shelter of the umbrella. "You don't get to choose who you fall in love with. He was Jenny's Edward. But he became my Eddie."

Hearing Angel call her dad Eddie had always scraped on her nerves, but now, in this context, it made sense. "I'm sorry, Angel," Emma said, reaching out for her stepmother's hand this time. "I'm really sorry."

Angel shook her head. "No need to be. I was a hospice nurse. I know all the stages of grief. You were angry."

"I stayed angry too long, and you didn't deserve it."

"One thing I learned in hospice is that there are no rules for how people deal with the bad stuff. They just do and feel what they need to in order to get through it. That's all any of us are doing."

Emma nodded. "I'm glad my dad has you in his life. I'm glad he's not alone." She hated to think about Angel being lonely once upon a time. "I'm glad you have him too."

"And now we have each other," Angel added, her eyes squinting warmly, hugging Emma across the table like she'd done for years. This warranted a real hug though.

Emma stood and wrapped her arms around Angel's neck. She felt Angel tense initially and then relax. When she pulled away, Angel looked at her.

"I knew about your mom's Life List. I never left her side toward the end. I've thought about that list over the years. When I heard about the race you were planning, I knew you'd found it."

Emma's lips parted. "Deb Hershey sent it my way."

"Your mom's best friend." Angel nodded. "The 5K was the one thing on the list she never got to do."

"Well," Emma hedged, "she didn't save a life. And she wanted to leave something special behind when she died."

Angel pushed back from the table and stood, meeting Emma at eye level. "It depends on what you consider saving a life. I was a different person back then. I was bitter about all the things that had gone wrong in my own life, and I was lonely. I thought it would always be that way. But while I helped your mom die, she helped me learn to live. She saved my life, Emma. I'm not the same person because of her."

Emma's eyes burned. She didn't want to cry.

"And she did leave something wonderful behind when she passed," Angel said quietly, laying a hand on Emma's shoulder. "That one's obvious. She left you."

Emma couldn't help it. Tears started streaming down her cheeks. Angel started crying too. "We probably look a mess out here," Emma finally said, sniffling and wishing she had some Kleenex on hand.

"It's okay. These are happy tears. At least for me."

Emma swiped her hand under her eyes. "Me too. But you need to get back to work."

"And so do you," Angel agreed. "I'll see you soon. You and Jack should stop in and visit with me and Eddie."

Emma nodded. "We will. I look forward to it," she said, meaning it for the first time.

They hugged one more time, and then Emma returned to her car in the parking lot. There was a voicemail from Dr. Rivers waiting for her on her phone. Nervous prickles ran up her spine, which was silly. She didn't need to be anxious. Dr. Rivers was probably calling about the event and wanting to review some detail. Emma tapped her screen and listened to the message.

"Emma, this is Dr. Rivers. I need to make an appointment with you to review the results of your genetic testing. Please call the office at your earliest convenience."

Emma played the message again, listening for any hint of whether this was good news or not, but Ashley's tone was nothing short of professional. There was no hint of anything positive or negative.

It was fine, of course. Emma's other tests had come back fine, and if it was serious, Ashley would have said so. Wouldn't she?

Emma gathered her courage and called the office back, but it had already closed. It was Friday, and the message said it wouldn't reopen until early Monday morning. She had Ashley's cell phone number but calling would seem desperate, and Emma wasn't desperate. She could wait until Monday. This weekend, she needed to focus on the event anyway and make sure everything went off without a hitch.

Jack's truck was in her driveway when she got home. He was sitting on her front porch steps, waiting for her.

"What are you doing here?" she asked as she stepped out of her car.

He grinned. "That's some greeting."

"Sorry," she said. "I'm just surprised." Did they have plans and she forgot?

"It's Friday night," he said. "Everyone's bringing their special someone to Music in the Park. I was hoping you'd be my date again tonight. Unless you feel like you need to rest up for tomorrow. The day starts early, but I promise not to keep you out too late."

Emma headed toward him. The closer she got, the more she thought it might be even better to tug him inside and stay there for the next few hours.

He chuckled under his breath and wrapped his arms around her waist. "We could just make a quick appearance and come back here. In which case, I promise not to keep you up too late," he said, brushing his lips over hers.

"I like the sound of that." She smiled up at him. "Let me just change inside."

He followed her in and shut the door behind him. Barnaby trotted over and propped his paws on Jack's shin. He dutifully rubbed behind the dog's ears. "I'm not picking you up tonight, pal, because I can do without your sloppy kisses. It's your owner's kisses I'm interested in," he said.

Emma laughed. "Make yourself comfortable. I won't be long."

When she got into her room, she closed the door and stood behind it. She didn't want to think about the message from Dr. Rivers tonight, or even this weekend. When Jack was around, her head was in the clouds, and it was hard to think of anything other than him.

She slipped into a sundress and slid on some sandals.

Then she headed back down the hall, stopping short when she saw Jack holding a bottle of wine in one hand and a glass in the other. "Jack? What are you doing?"

He turned toward her, his expression dissolving from a smile to a grim line. "What does it look like I'm doing?"

$\mathcal{C}$HAPTER TWENTY-ONE

$\mathcal{J}$ack wasn't a defensive guy, but the way Emma had just looked at him made all his defenses go up. "This is for you," he said. "My glass has the apple cider from Merry Mountain Farms in it."

Emma looked from the wine bottle to the second glass that Jack was lifting up now. "Oh. I'm sorry. I just..."

"Thought that I'd break my sober streak for a glass of wine?" Jack shook his head. "No. I never liked wine that much. I liked beer and hard alcohol, but I'm never indulging in either of those again." He poured wine into the empty glass and handed it to her. "I thought we should make a toast."

Emma took the glass and then he reached for his glass of juice. "To what?" she asked.

"To a lot of things. But mostly to how amazing you are. The event is tomorrow, and it's going to touch a lot of lives. You decided to do something, and you did it, whereas a lot of people just talk about doing things."

"Thank you, Jack." She looked away shyly.

It was hard to stay mad at her. He didn't blame her for her assumption. That was the downside to telling people about his struggle with alcohol. If he'd never told her, she wouldn't have thought anything about him pouring wine into a glass. But then he would've had to make an excuse not to drink the wine himself. The old DD excuse could only work so long.

"To you," he said, lifting his glass and waiting for her to tap hers against it.

She did, and then she added. "To you as well."

Jack gave her a questioning eyebrow lift. "Me?"

"You're equally amazing. You stepped up for your sister and took your nephew in this summer. You helped me. You're like a small town superhero."

He grinned. "Except I can't fly. Superheroes should fly."

She tapped her glass to his, and they both took a sip of their drinks to complete the toast.

Jack set his glass down and took Emma's from her hand to put it safely on the counter. Then he pulled her close, looping his arms around her waist. "Correction. Maybe I can't fly like Superman, but I feel like I'm flying when I'm with you."

She tilted her head. "Aww."

Jack contained his grin. "Not trying to get mushy on you. Just trying to tell you how I feel."

"And how is that?" she asked.

"Flying and falling at the same time." He watched her pupils grow large. "Or the falling feels like flying. I guess I'm trying to tell you that I'm falling for you, Emma. I've been falling for a long time, and I don't ever want to hit bottom."

She blinked up at him, her lips slightly parted. Judging by her expression, he'd done a miserable job of telling her he was falling in love with her. Maybe she hadn't even gotten the message.

"And I'm going to win your dad's trust. He'll be there tomorrow, and I'm going to be his running partner."

Emma went wide-eyed. "You told me you don't run."

"Correction. I don't like to run but I can."

"You don't have to do that," Emma argued. "I'm not even sure how that would prove anything to my dad."

"We're men, Emma. This is how we prove ourselves."

She leaned into him some more. "Well, you don't need to prove yourself to me. I already know how wonderful you are." She went up on her tiptoes and kissed him, driving him crazy with just this simple touch. He'd never liked wine, but he loved the bittersweet taste on her tongue.

"I've changed my mind about going to see the music. No one will miss us if we stay here," he said.

"Great minds think alike," she said in a soft voice. Then she kissed him again, and this time their hands explored each other's bodies. They kissed and touched all the way to her bedroom, closing the door and barring one nosy dog.

Jack was once again flying and falling, hard and fast, slow and easy. Three little words hung on his lips. But his timing with Emma had always been off, and if he was going to tell her he loved her, he wanted the timing to be perfect.

* * *

Somewhere around eleven p.m., Jack woke in Emma's bed. Emma stirred beside him. He really didn't want to leave, but tomorrow was only a few hours away, and he had responsibilities at home.

He kissed her forehead and then her mouth. "Sorry to

wake you, but I should head home just in case Amanda or Sam need me. I plan to get to the event early and make sure everything is in order for your big day."

She smiled sleepily. "Thank you. You're amazing."

"No, that's you. See you tomorrow, Em." He stared at her face for a moment, wanting to say more. Then he peeled himself away and headed out, locking her door behind him.

When he got back to his place, he let himself inside and headed straight to bed. He didn't sleep a wink though. He loved Emma. He was sure of it. And he wanted to tell her, but not until he was sure she felt the same way. And not until he'd smoothed over his relationship with her father.

A knock on his bedroom door startled him. "Uncle Jack?"

Jack lifted his head to see Sam peek his face into the doorway. He gave a cursory glance at the clock on his nightstand. "It's late, buddy. You need something?"

Sam headed into the room. "Yeah, kind of. I know you just got home so I didn't think I'd wake you."

"You didn't." Jack sat up in bed.

Sam sat on the edge of the bed, his body slumped. "It's just, well, Mom was acting weird tonight. Like really happy and chatty."

"Okay. That's good, right?" Jack asked.

Sam shrugged. "It felt forced. Like she was trying to prove to me that she was okay, and I still don't think she is."

"Well, you don't become all better overnight, bud. It takes time. And yeah, she might be trying a little harder than normal to prove herself to you but can you blame her?"

Sam looked up. "What do you mean?"

"She's your mom, and she had to leave you for the last month. I'm sure she feels guilty about that."

"She doesn't need to feel bad," Sam said.

"No, she doesn't. But that's just the way moms are. They try to carry everything on their shoulders so you don't have to." Which reminded Jack he needed to call his mom and thank her. It had been a while since he'd called her just because.

Sam fidgeted with his hands in his lap. "I know it's a lot to ask, Uncle Jack, but I don't want to go back home. Like you said, it's a lot for a mom to do it all on her own, and it's a lot for a son to watch his mom try to do it all. This summer has been great. I mean, you made me work and all, but I had a good time and I made some friends."

"I'm glad," Jack said.

"So can we stay?" Sam asked, looking up. "Me and Mom. With you?"

Jack furrowed his brow. "You're staying tonight and maybe tomorrow night after the event. How long are you talking?"

"Longer than that," Sam said. "She probably can't afford to find a place for us here. She can barely afford the house we're at in Whispering Pines. But this is a big house, and we wouldn't cause too much trouble. You wouldn't even know we were here," Sam pleaded.

Jack wasn't sure how to answer. Amanda hadn't been open to staying for the rest of the summer, much less long-term. "Buddy, I don't mind you staying, of course, but I doubt your mom wants to give up everything and move back here. She couldn't wait to leave when she was your age."

Sam suddenly looked defeated. "Family is supposed to help each other. It's just me and my mom in Whispering Pines, and she's acting like everything is perfect, but it's not. She needs you and Grandma, and I need to be a kid. At least for another year."

Jack laid a hand on Sam's back. "It's late, and I can't make any promises tonight. But I'll see what I can do. Okay?"

Sam hesitated, his eyes still pleading as he looked at Jack. Sam feared Amanda returning to her old ways. And apparently, Sam had seen what was going on around him. Jack remembered watching his own father spiral on a similar path. A kid had to grow up fast around that.

"Better get to bed," Jack advised. "I'll need your help with the event tomorrow. You're handing out water bottles to the walkers and runners."

"What will you be doing?" Sam asked.

"I'm running." He was going to match Emma's father step for step, each one with something to prove. Maybe he and Amanda would always feel like they had something to prove after where they'd come from. You couldn't change your past, he knew that. But he could do his best to make sure the future was better. For himself, and for Amanda and Sam.

* * *

Emma awoke with a start, her heart thumping in her chest. She felt disoriented for a split second, knowing that she needed to hustle but grasping at the reason why.

The event. Today.

She glanced back at the clock on her nightstand and leaped out of bed, startling Barnaby with her commotion. She should've awoken half an hour ago. Had she slept through her alarm? She needed to dress and get over to Evergreen Park before everyone else.

Jack.

Emma looked at the empty side of her bed. One of these nights, Jack would stay until morning. Maybe this one.

Focus, Emma. The event.

She changed into a pair of running shorts and one of the T-shirts that the rest of the registered walkers and runners would get once they arrived. Then she pulled her hair back into a ponytail and brushed her teeth. She slowed down when she grabbed the bandana off her dresser, carrying it back to the long mirror.

The bandana was her mother's. Her mom had worn it when she was going through chemotherapy so long ago and was losing her hair. It was colorful and vibrant, just like Jenny St. James herself.

Emma tied the bandana over her ponytail. This bandana didn't represent sickness. It represented strength. "I love you, Mom," Emma said out loud. Then she turned and started quickly buzzing around again, jogging out of the house ten minutes later to drive to the park.

Excitement and nerves bubbled through her. In a couple hours, it would all be over and then she could relax, but until then, she needed to hustle.

Emma stopped at the café on the way to the park. Nina was already opening and working the counter.

Nina smiled as Emma headed in. "Dressed for success. You look great. Love the do."

"Thanks. I need a coffee," Emma said, walking around the counter to prepare herself one. "And I wanted to make sure you were okay this morning."

"I'm fine. Enjoy your big day and don't worry about me. The part-time help has been called in, remember? I'll have a second body working the counter in about an hour."

Emma nodded. "Good." She poured some cream into her coffee and took a sip. "Mmm. I need this so much."

"Jack's already been in here," Nina commented.

Emma snapped to attention. "Really?"

Nina laughed. "You are so obvious, you know that?"

Emma shook her head. "So we like each other."

"Like or love?" Nina asked.

Emma held up a hand. "I'm in a hurry, remember?" She lifted her coffee. "I'll drink this on the way. Wish me luck."

"Good luck. Don't break a leg out there," Nina called, making Emma laugh as she headed outside and back to her car. A short drive later, she pulled into the parking lot for Evergreen Park and cut the engine. The sun was just creeping over the mountain skyline, promising a beautiful day.

There were other cars in the parking lot, and she spotted Jack's truck on the far side. Emma assumed the other cars belonged to people manning the tables for the Woman's Wellness Fair. She recognized one as Dr. Rivers's vehicle.

Emma froze as her nerves began to fray, these unrelated to the event. Her genetic testing results were in, and all the what-ifs circled around in Emma's mind. She pushed them away and kept walking.

"Good morning, beautiful," Jack said, walking toward her.

She stopped briefly and inspected him before he dipped to kiss her. "What are you wearing?"

Jack looked down. "I'm running today, remember?"

Her mouth fell open. "I thought you were joking about running with my dad."

"No. I'm running for women's wellness, of course. And for you."

"And he'll approve of you based on your athletic skills?" she asked on a laugh.

"Something like that. This is my running attire." Jack gestured down at his sweatpants and T-shirt.

"It's the beginning of August. You'll burn up in that, Jack."

"I'll be fine."

"Well, let's trade that shirt of yours for one of the event shirts. I have the boxes in my trunk. Will you help me carry them to the registration table?"

"Sure."

They dropped the boxes under the registration table, and Emma pulled out the registration forms for last-minute walkers and runners. She'd already met her goal for this event. It was already a success in her mind but the more the merrier.

"I missed you when I woke up this morning," she told Jack, once she'd gotten her table all set up.

"I know. I missed you too."

"Is Amanda coming today?" Emma asked.

"She is. I'm hoping she'll visit all the tables too. She needs to take care of herself. For her own sake and Sam's." He looked down at his feet for a moment, and Emma could tell he was worried about his sister. "I need to go. Granger and Luke are headed over to volunteer this morning. Mitch and Alex are working the event in their professional duties as police officers."

Emma smiled. "Well, their respective significant others, Kaitlyn and Halona, will be here running with me. Josie and Brenna too."

"We have some pretty supportive friends, huh?" Jack asked.

"The best." Emma went up on her tiptoes and gave Jack another lingering kiss. "Okay, no more kissing until tonight. We need to focus."

"Hard to focus on anything else when you're around," Jack said.

"Good luck with my dad. Even though I still don't understand how running along with him will help."

Jack shrugged and kissed her again. "See you later. I love you." He turned and jogged away, leaving Emma standing at her registration booth, speechless. Had she just heard him say what she thought she did?

* * *

Jack was already sweating bullets, and he hadn't even started running yet. He hadn't meant to tell Emma he loved her. The words had just slipped out as natural as breathing—and now he was finding it hard to take in a full breath.

"You look like you've just seen a ghost," Granger said, stepping up to him. "You okay, man?"

Jack nodded. He wasn't about to tell the guys he'd just told Emma he loved her for the first time and then turned and ran. He hadn't even looked at her after the words had come out. He'd just left, processing what had just happened as he jogged away. *What an idiot.*

"Jack?" Granger said again. "You sure? You need water or something?"

"Nah. I'm good. You two are patrolling the event on bikes," he told Granger and Luke, "and making sure that no one overheats or needs medical attention."

Luke turned to Jack. "The Sweetwater Springs Fire Department is on standby to help in case of any emergencies." Luke had been promoted to fire chief earlier this year and was doing a fantastic job from what Jack had heard.

"Thanks," Jack said, trying not to think about his last words to Emma. He'd wanted to do something special to tell her, not just blurt it out.

"And you're running?" Luke asked with a clear look of concern lining his brow.

"Yeah."

"You don't run regularly," Luke pointed out. "You sure you're up for it?"

"I'm in great shape. I go rock climbing and paddling all the time. I walk around this park all day, every day."

"So walk today," Luke suggested.

Jack shook his head. Emma's dad was jogging, and Jack intended to be his running partner. "Don't worry about me. I'm fine."

"Well, we'll just make sure to check on you a little more often," Granger said. "To make sure you don't pass out on the trail and eat those famous last words."

"I love your confidence in me," Jack said sarcastically. "There are walkies in the office for you two to communicate with each other on the trails."

"Roger that," Luke said.

Jack left the guys and headed toward the water table that Sam was manning. The fire department had donated and set up the bottles.

"Hey," Sam said.

"Hey. Thanks for working this event today. It means a lot."

Sam nodded. "No problem. Mom's here, you know. In case you want to talk to her or something."

Jack chuckled. "Yeah, okay. Probably not until later. I'm running. Water me when I pass by?"

Sam smiled. "Sure thing, Uncle Jack. So...you are going to talk to Mom though?"

Jack nodded. "I will." Sometime between winning over Edward St. James and telling Emma that he loved her in the right way. Assuming he hadn't scared her off and she hadn't decided to run this morning and keep on running even after the event was over.

CHAPTER TWENTY-TWO

Jack saw Edward St. James in the crowd that was collecting at the starting lineup and headed in that direction.

"Good morning," he said as he drew closer.

Edward gave him a cursory glance and nodded. "Morning, Jack. I was wondering if you'd be here."

"I'm here every day, even on my days off, it seems." He rubbed his hands together. "I wouldn't miss running in this event that Emma has pulled together. She's worked hard these past weeks. It's a lot to pull off in such a short amount of time."

"And I hear you pulled some strings to help make that happen. Thank you."

"It was nothing. The Women's Wellness Fair seemed like a perfect fit for what Emma wanted to do, and Emma's event is raising money for their cause. Win-win."

"So it seems." Edward kept his gaze forward. "I jog every day. This run will be nothing for me. Do you jog, Jack?"

Jack hesitated. "I have before. I've been a bit busy lately with work and . . ." His words trailed off.

"And with my daughter."

Jack's palms were sweating. He cleared his throat. "Emma and I haven't really talked about formal titles or anything." No, he'd just jumped the gun by saying he loved her instead. "But I think a lot of your daughter. I always have."

Edward gave him a wary look. "You weren't thinking too much when you showed up to my house drunk."

Jack sighed. "Are you ever going to forgive me for that?"

Edward didn't even blink before answering. "If you were a father of a young woman, would you forgive the stupid kid who could've gotten her killed?"

Jack cleared his throat but didn't answer.

"No, I didn't think so," Edward said.

What was Jack supposed to say? It was all true.

Emma stepped up in front of the crowd, and everyone quieted at the sound of her voice through a megaphone.

Just seeing her made Jack's world right. He had to get Edward to change his mind about him. And he would. Before this day was over.

* * *

Emma looked out on the crowd. She saw Jack standing next to her father, the tension thick between them. Jack was trying so hard to win her dad's approval. It was sweet, really. The actions of a man in love. With her.

Her knees had buckled a little when he'd said those three little words. He hadn't even given her time to respond before he'd turned and left. She wasn't sure how she would've responded. She was falling for him too. The L-word was appropriate even if it seemed so soon in their relationship, half the time of which they'd spent supposedly pretending.

She continued looking around and saw Jack's sister Amanda standing with a few other women in town, presumably ones she'd known from growing up here. Emma watched Jack's sister for a moment. Amanda looked pale under the summer sun, but she'd spent more time indoors this past month than working on her tan. Emma suddenly worried that perhaps Amanda wasn't up for a run today. Maybe she should be at Jack's place resting. He was the overprotective one though. If he wasn't worried, Emma shouldn't be concerned either.

She continued looking out on the crowd. The LDO group was here in full effect, which didn't surprise Emma in the least. They were a great group of women who loved a good cause. Her stepmom, Angel, stood alone. She planned on walking instead of running, which Emma guessed was why she wasn't with Emma's dad.

Guilt curled its way into Emma's belly. She and her father were Angel's family. But Emma hadn't made a huge effort to be close to Angel. She'd thought a lot about her chat with Angel. They'd made amends, and it was time for them to start acting like a family.

"Thank you all for being here today," she said. "It really means the world to me to have your support for this event that I put together to honor my mom, Jenny St. James. A lot of you knew her. You were her friends and family. If you didn't know her, it's because her cancer took her away from this world too soon." Emma took a moment, willing her racing heart to slow down. "I promise you that you would've loved her though. No one met Jenny St. James and didn't love her. She was just that kind of person. This race is in honor of who she was in life. It's also to raise money for the Women's Wellness Center so that they can continue helping women in the community. Women like my mom."

Emma cleared her throat and pushed down the emotion bubbling up inside her. "Anyway, I'm not one to give a big speech. I just want you all to know that I appreciate you being here. Thank you. I know if my mom were here, she'd thank you as well. Now let's run or walk or do whatever we need to do to reach the finish line. But that won't be the end by any means because I'm planning to keep this event going year after year and make it bigger and better each time."

One person clapped and then another, and then the whole crowd was clapping and cheering. Emma smiled and swiped at a tear that rolled down her cheek as her emotions got the best of her. Then she stepped up beside her friends, wishing Nina could be here as well.

"Hey, Emma. Great speech," Josie said. "I took notes. I'll be doing a write-up on this event in *Carolina Home* magazine next week."

"That would be great. Thank you." Emma again glanced back at Angel alone in the crowd and frowned. "Ladies, thanks for being here. I'll join you later. I need to go say hello to someone. My stepmom is over there all alone," she pointed out. "I should walk with her."

The women followed her gaze.

"Bring her over here with all of us," Kaitlyn suggested. "This event is about women banding together and supporting one another, right? You could join her, and she wouldn't be alone, but if you bring her over here, she'll have all of us."

Emma smiled. "I have the best friends in the world. Be right back." She cut through the crowd and stopped in front of Angel. "Hi, Angel."

Angel looked up with surprise. "Oh. Hi, Emma. What are you doing back here?"

"Grabbing you. You should be up there with me and my friends."

"Oh no. I'm okay. You don't want me intruding," Angel objected.

Emma grabbed her hand anyway. "You are my friend too. And my family. Let's go before the event kicks off." She tugged, and Angel started following. A few steps in, she saw Diana, who had been their waitress the other night at Tammy's Log Cabin. Jack had mentioned that Diana had been camping out at the park illegally for a little bit this summer. Emma grabbed her hand as well. "Diana, it's so good to see you."

Diana furrowed her brow. "Jack's girlfriend, right? Emma?"

Emma nodded. "Right. Come follow me up to the front. I'll introduce you to my friends, and we can walk together."

When they reached her small group of close friends, they waited for the flare gun that she'd handed to Alice Hampton, an older woman who was working the event. Alice raised the gun with a shaky arm, looked at Emma, and pulled the trigger.

The crowd of women, men, children, and even some dogs took off down the trail. A surge of pride shot through Emma as she looked around at them all. She'd done it. This was happening. "This one's for you, Mom," she whispered.

Her gaze caught on Jack, who jogged ahead with her father. She was tempted to be nervous for him, but he could handle himself. And she knew her father. He'd always given a hard time to the guys she'd dated, but he was a reasonable man. He'd come around once he realized what she already knew—that Jack was good for Emma.

"How do you feel about jogging?" Angel asked.

"Great. I probably can't do all three miles," Emma said, so if you need to go ahead of me, I won't be offended."

Angel laughed. "Let's go, then."

Emma picked up her pace, realizing she was a lot like her father too. She'd given Angel a hard time but she finally was coming around. Hopefully it wouldn't take her dad nearly as long as it'd taken Emma.

"Hey, Emma." Ashley Rivers jogged up beside her and kept pace with her.

"Hi." Emma was already slightly out of breath from the jog, but her breath became even shallower. "I didn't think you were running."

"Well, I already set up my table so I registered at the last minute. Then I'll freshen up and finish out the day at the health fair. Will I see you over there?"

"Of course."

"Great," Ashley said. "You got my message?"

Emma nodded, sliding her gaze over at Angel, who wasn't listening. "I did. I called the office back, but it was already closed."

"Sorry about that. We definitely need to make time to talk early next week. Find me after the race, and we'll arrange a time to meet."

"Okay."

"Great. See you later." Ashley picked up her pace and jogged ahead, leaving Emma behind.

* * *

Jack liked to think he was in shape. He was an outdoorsy guy who walked, fished, boated. You name it, he did it.

But running was a sport you had to keep doing to stay

conditioned. He was one mile in, the heat of the sun was beating down on him, and his legs felt like they were made of lead. Edward hadn't said a word to him since they'd started moving down the path, and Jack didn't think he could talk if he wanted to.

Emma was right. This was silly. Running alongside Edward wasn't going to fix anything. Why was he torturing himself? He was about to start walking when Edward surprised him by talking.

"I always liked you before that night, you know. I was impressed at how you'd turned out despite your old man."

Jack glanced over, reenergized by the adrenaline flowing through him.

"Your dad is a good guy too when he isn't drunk."

Good guys didn't choose alcohol over their family. Jack would've said so if he thought he could run and talk at the same time.

"That night when you showed up, I was angry at you but more than anything, I was sad. I thought, what a waste of all your potential, throwing it all away for something as silly as alcohol. But I've never seen you drink again, and I've been watching you."

"I stopped drinking not long after that," Jack said, breathless as he jogged. "I'll never drink again."

"You could've killed my only daughter," Edward said. "I want to hold that against you and never let go. But more than anything, I also want to see Emma happy. You seem to do that for her."

They ran a few silent beats before Edward continued. "If you hurt Emma, I won't forgive you next time."

Did that mean Edward was forgiving him now? "I would never intentionally hurt Emma."

Edward glanced over. "Good. Now stop jogging before

you drop dead out here, and I have to do CPR on you. See you at the finish line."

"Not arguing with you on that one." Jack stopped jogging and leaned forward over his knees for a moment. If he weren't tired, he might do a little victory dance out here in front of everyone. He had Edward's approval. There were no hurdles being together with Emma, assuming he hadn't scared her off by telling her he loved her.

He wanted to tell her again. A dozen more times. But first he needed to cool down. He straightened and spotted the water stand up ahead with Sam handing out bottles to passersby. Jack started walking in that direction.

"Got one for me?" he asked.

Sam tossed it, and Jack caught it like a football. He twisted the cap and drank half the bottle before taking a breath.

"I'm going to take up jogging so I'll be ready for next year."

Sam grinned. "I haven't seen Mom or Emma go by yet. I'm looking for them."

Jack nodded and drank some more water, noticing how Sam reacted when a teenage girl ran by. "She's pretty. Does she know you exist?" Jack asked.

Sam shrugged. "I don't know. I've talked to her a little bit."

"Wanna know my secret with the ladies?"

Sam looked at him again. "What?"

"Our last name is Hershey, bro. Use it to your advantage. I always carry some Hershey's Kisses with me. I used to leave one behind every time I saw Emma. I still do it sometimes. It makes an impression."

Sam handed a bottle to another walker. "Maybe I'll try it."

"You should." Jack winked. "Got to go. Keep up the good work." He started walking, feeling lighter than he had when the event had started. He didn't mind passing on his secrets to his nephew because he didn't need those tricks anymore. All he needed was Emma.

* * *

The event had been over for half an hour, and Emma hadn't been able to find Jack anywhere. Everyone she'd asked said they hadn't seen him.

"Hey, Dad," she finally said, reaching for her father's arm. "How was the run?"

"Great. Perfect weather, and I could've run another three miles."

She shook her head. "You've always had more energy than most twenty-year-olds. Hey, wasn't Jack with you?" she asked.

"For half the run. I left him in my dust for the other half."

Emma drew a hand to her forehead. "Dad, you didn't. He's trying so hard to get you to like him."

"I know," her father said.

"So give him a chance, okay? For me?"

Her father smiled. "I already am giving him a chance. And I gave him my blessing to date you, not that he ever needed it. Guys don't ask for that anymore, do they? It's a bit old-fashioned, which makes me like him even more."

Emma expelled a breath. "So you forgave him?"

"And I trust him. I trust you too. If you think he's the one for you, then who am I to stand it the way?"

"You're my father." Emma wrapped her arms around him in a huge hug. When she pulled away, she looked up. "That still doesn't explain where Jack is."

Her father shrugged and then smiled as Angel walked up to them. "There's my lovely bride. How was the run?"

"Amazing. Emma and I ran together the whole way," Angel said proudly.

Emma felt a surge of pride that intertwined with her guilt. She should've made more effort to get close to Angel earlier than now. But it was better late than never. "We should all get together for dinner again soon. You two and me and Jack. If I ever find him," she added.

"Great idea. We'd love to," her dad said.

"Well, enjoy the booths and tables set up," Emma said. "There's lots of great information out there, not just for women but for men too. And there's food," she added. Emma hugged him one more time and then, surprising herself, she hugged Angel too.

After saying goodbye, she headed off to visit the tables and booths, hoping she'd find Jack somewhere along the way. When she called him, it kept going straight to voicemail, which made her wonder if his phone ran out of charge or if he'd turned it off for some reason.

Music played softly in the air as she stopped at the first table. This one was a free blood pressure check. The nurse occupying this booth gave out handouts on heart health. The next booth was about healthy eating. A nutritionist gave out pamphlets on which foods to eat. She also had a few dishes to try and the recipes to take home if you liked them.

Emma kept walking. Eventually she stopped at a covered table where Ashley was sitting. Ashley was still dressed in her running clothes from earlier. She smiled up at Emma. "Emma, the race was fantastic. Don't you think?"

Emma nodded. "It really was. And this Women's Wellness Fair seems to be a success too. It looks like the whole town is here."

"And then some," Ashley agreed.

Ashley's table was set up with a checklist of things that

women needed to do for themselves, categorized by age. Things that Emma had been neglecting, out of fear. She'd done her checkup though, and everything was fine. She was worrying for nothing.

"Emma?" Ashley said, her smile wilting. She looked around at the crowd briefly and back at Emma. "Please make sure you come in on Monday. We need to discuss your genetic testing."

Emma didn't want to ask. She didn't want to know. If she waited until Monday, she'd probably end up canceling the appointment. "I'm positive for the mutation, aren't I?"

Ashley hesitated. "It would be better if we discussed this in my office when I can show the results in print."

Emma shook her head. "Waiting for news is torture. I'll come by on Monday, but can you please tell me so I know what I'm walking into? Please. Do I have the gene mutation?"

Ashley frowned, and then she looked around. There were no other people at her table right now. "I'm afraid so," she said. "But I don't want you to worry yourself over this too much. There are a lot of options for what you can do next. Come see me on Monday, and we'll talk more in depth."

Emma nodded as her knees threatened to collapse. She needed to be alone. "Thank you, Ashley. I'll see you Monday."

Emma left the booth as other people headed toward it. Then she changed directions and headed toward the parking lot, hoping this time that she didn't run into Jack. He was the very last person she wanted to face right now.

CHAPTER TWENTY-THREE

Jack saw a lot of familiar faces in the crowd as the race died down and participants went to explore the educational booths set up by the Women's Center. He was looking for one face in particular. Emma's. He hadn't seen her since she'd kicked the race off.

She'd done what she'd set out to do this summer. Emma had pulled an event together in honor of her mother. If he wasn't in love with her before, he was now. And he admired the heck out of her.

As he looked around, he saw Amanda sitting on a nearby bench that lined one of the trails in the park. She was holding a bottle of water in one hand and an apple in another. He headed over.

"You okay?" he asked.

Amanda looked up, squinting at the sun behind him. "Better than okay. I just walked three miles. I should probably be tired, but I feel amazing. And hopeful."

Jack sat down beside her. "Yeah? I just feel tired,"

he teased. But he also felt hopeful as he looked at his sister.

She shoved her elbow into his side. "Liar. You walk this park all day every day. This was probably nothing for a big lug like you."

"But I don't run it." He shrugged. "I think I'll start though. Maybe I'll begin training for next year's race."

Amanda grinned at him. "I bet you're proud of Emma for pulling this off."

He nodded. "I am. I'm proud of you too," he added, lowering his voice and giving her a serious look. He could see the wear of the last few weeks on her face, but she also looked clearheaded and happy.

"You know what? I'm kind of proud of myself too." She unscrewed the top from her water bottle and took a sip. "Maybe I'll take up running too and train to keep up with you for next year's 5K."

"It'll probably be me keeping up with you." He winked. Then he looked down at her hand. "You going to eat that apple?"

"Eventually. They're handing them out at one of the tables."

"You've already been around?" he asked.

"Not all of them. I'm just taking a small break." She took another sip of water and then screwed the lid back on.

"Well, after you've visited all the tables, let me know. I'll drive you home."

She narrowed her eyes. "And by home, you mean your place?"

"My home is your home. I really mean that." Jack supposed now was as good a time as any to discuss what Sam had asked him last night. "Amanda, I want you and Sam to stay in Sweetwater Springs. My house is more than big enough, and you don't need to do everything on your own. Being a single parent is tough. I got a taste of that this summer watching Sam."

"Sorry," she said.

He reached for her hand and gave it a squeeze. "Don't be. I love spending time with Sam. I just realized that raising a teenager isn't easy. Especially when you're going through stuff. You should be here with family and friends to support you. Move back to Sweetwater Springs. Stay with me as long as you need. I'm sure Mom would love to have you and Sam closer too."

Amanda turned her gaze to the crowd in the distance. "I don't know, Jack. That's a lot for me to ask of you. You just started dating Emma. I don't want to intrude—"

"You won't. Emma has her own place. I can go there if I want to be alone with her." He tugged her hand until she looked at him again. "I know you wanted a fresh slate when you moved away from Sweetwater Springs and that you never intended to move back home."

Amanda choked out a laugh. "I took the things I was running from with me, it seems."

"That's what happens. Sam wants to stay too. He likes it here. And he has a job. Two actually," Jack said with a growing smile. "He's a big help around the park. I need him. I think we all need each other."

Amanda narrowed her eyes. "Are you just saying all this because you need a running buddy to train for next year's event?"

Jack chuckled. "That would be an added perk. So what do you say?"

Amanda hesitated. "I work from home so I can do my job anywhere, I guess." She shook her head. "I can't live with you forever though. We'd probably drive each other insane."

"It'd be just like the old days," Jack said with a small chuckle, waiting and hoping she'd agree.

"But a little while might be okay," Amanda finally said.

Jack grinned at her. "I'm taking that as a yes."

* * *

It'd taken a short hike to get to Blue Sky Point. Emma remembered coming here with her mom once upon a time. It was like looking down on Sweetwater Springs from heaven, her mom used to say.

This is what the angels must see.

Emma could hear her mom's voice so clearly in her head. Being here was better than sitting at her mom's grave, which had never made her feel close to her. Emma had been holding back tears, but now they streamed freely down her cheeks. She futilely wiped them away, but they kept falling.

Ashley hadn't said she was sick, but the genetic mutation meant she could get sick, right? Just like her mom and grandmother. The mutation was a dark cloud hanging overhead, threatening her future.

Emma choked on a sob, suddenly flooded with images of her sick mother. She tried to remember her mom as healthy and vibrant, but now all she could think of was the other version. She didn't want to become like that version. And the last thing she wanted was to leave her family and friends all broken by her absence. She couldn't spare her father pain if she got sick.

But Jack. She could spare him. There was no way she could continue down the path they were on when she knew how this story, her story, would end. Jack had told her he loved her today. And she was falling in love with him too. She couldn't leave Jack the way her mom had left them. The way her grandmother had left her mom's family.

Emma wiped at another tear, struggling to breathe, and not because of the high elevation. She had to give Jack up. There was no other choice. His childhood had been less than perfect. He'd been through so much, and loving her and losing her could send him spiraling down a path he'd worked so hard to avoid.

He was resisting his genetics in the same way she'd always resisted hers. Except she didn't really get a choice. Jack did. She knew to her core that the right thing to do was to end things between them, sooner rather than later, so that he could get on with his life. And so she could figure out what to do in order to keep living hers.

Her phone dinged. Emma glanced at the screen, surprised that she even had reception here. It was a text from Nina.

Where are you?

Emma blew out a breath and started typing. Blue Sky Point.

What for?

She and Nina were close, but she didn't think her friend would understand. It doesn't matter. Is everything okay?

The dots on the screen started bouncing as Nina typed her reply. Not really.

Emma stood and started heading down the trail. What's going on?

Our weekend employee called in sick. Big surprise, Nina

typed. It's busy here and I can't make the coffees fast enough.

Great. Just great. That old saying "When it rains, it pours" was definitely true. As if to prove that point, the sky rumbled, promising afternoon showers ahead.

I'll be there asap, Emma texted as she headed away from Blue Sky Point with more thunder on her heels.

* * *

Twenty minutes later, Emma walked into the Sweetwater Café and headed straight behind the counter where Nina seemed to be extra busy this afternoon.

"I got here as fast as I could," Emma said, pulling on an apron.

"I had no idea it'd be this busy today. It's never this busy, even on the weekends. It must have something to do with your event," Nina said.

Emma nodded. "Looks like it's time to hire someone new for the weekend schedule."

"And fire the current employee. What's her name again?" Nina tapped a finger to her chin as she pretended to think. "She's only shown up once or twice in the last several months. I'm not even sure I'd recognize her."

"Yeah, she's overdue to be let go." They'd only managed to do without her because Sam had been here to help this summer.

Emma headed to the counter, took the next customer's order, and started preparing the drink. When she turned to carry it to the register, she anxiously looked out on the growing line and saw a familiar face. "Diana!" she said as her next customer approached.

Diana stepped up to the counter. "It's a busy day, huh?"

"I have more work than I can handle," Emma said. She couldn't even offer her usual customer service smile. "What can I get you?"

"Maybe I should be asking you that question. Want a hand?" Diana asked.

Emma straightened. "Really?"

"I've worked at a coffee shop before," Diana said. "I can help out, and I don't mind."

Diana had been a great server at Tammy's Log Cabin. And desperate times demanded forgoing the résumé right now.

A smile swept over Emma's face. "Absolutely."

"Great." Diana headed behind the counter.

A few minutes later, Sam arrived and started cleaning the tables as customers came and went.

They worked steadily until the crowd died down and everyone had their caffeinated drink of choice. Diana learned quickly and had amazing people skills. She was exactly the kind of employee that Emma needed at the café.

"Want me to stay a little longer just in case?" Diana asked, turning to Emma after serving the last customer.

Emma knew Diana meant for the rest of the afternoon, but Emma wanted more. "Yes, actually. You're hired."

Diana blinked and then shook her head. "I'm sorry?"

"I mean, if you want another job. If you don't, I'll be disappointed but I'll survive." Emma grimaced. "I might not survive many more days like this though."

Diana nodded excitedly. "Of course I want the job."

"Great. Can you work tonight?"

"I'll stay until close," Diana said. "Thank you so much, Emma."

"I should be the one thanking you. You were a big help to us this afternoon. The line would still be out the door if you hadn't stepped in."

"Just a matter of being in the right place at the right time." Diana went to greet the next person in line.

Nina stepped up beside Emma. "Well, that worked out perfectly. It was almost like fate."

Emma side-eyed her. She'd had enough talk of fate and fortunes with Dawanda and her cappuccino reading.

"Oh, come on." Nina leaned a hip against the counter. "You have to believe in fate after the way you and Jack got together this summer."

Emma didn't want to talk about Jack right now either. Or think about him.

"Anyway, I know you're tired after today. I've got Diana to help me close tonight," Nina said.

Emma nodded. "Thank you."

"And there's something else." Nina wasn't smiling anymore. She gave Emma a hesitant look. "You told me to tell you if another bad review popped up on the A-List site."

Emma didn't like the way this conversation was going.

"But maybe you shouldn't look," Nina suggested.

Emma's heart dropped in her belly. "That bad, huh?" She started toward the back room where her laptop was waiting for her. Then she sat down and quickly pulled up the A-List site, clicking on the Sweetwater Café. She scrolled down, seeing a two-star rating and review:

The two women who run that counter chat constantly as they work. It makes me wonder if they're spitting into my coffee as they laugh over the cups.

Emma gasped. "Spit into the coffee?"

"I told you that you might prefer not to read it," Nina said. "And now that you've read it, it can't be unread."

"I would never spit into the coffee. Is this the same

reviewer? Am I being trolled?" Emma felt like strangling the reviewer through her computer screen. "If people read this, they'll never come to my café. This is awful. I can't even fix this complaint unless we start wearing masks as we work."

Nina frowned. "Sorry, but I'm not wearing a mask. Besides, you can't please this person. They'd just complain about something else. Some people are just so unhappy that they want to spread it around," Nina said. "It's sad, really."

It was sad, and Nina was right. They couldn't wear masks. Emma was done catering to a few bad reviews that were possibly all coming from the same person. "I'm not going to stop laughing with you up there either. Life is too short not to laugh whenever possible." She pressed a hand to her heart as emotion surfaced. "My mom used to say that."

Nina tilted her head as she looked at Emma. "Smart lady."

"She was," Emma agreed.

Nina nudged her softly. "I was talking about you."

Now Emma's eyes were burning. Today was one big roller-coaster ride. "You know, I think I should create my own Life List. Just like my mom did. Number one on the list, laugh even more."

Nina grinned. "I like the sound of that."

Also on the list, keep the 5K she'd started in her mom's name going. Never miss another annual checkup—her health was too important. Be her own best friend just like her mom had put on her list. Emma could start by not letting a little criticism take her down.

They were both alerted by the bell on the door, signaling a new customer up front. Emma's Spidey sense went off. "I'm not here," she told Nina quickly. "Whoever it is, tell him I'm not here."

"Him, huh?" Nina grinned. "Okay. I'll lie to Jack for you, but you have some explaining to do once he's gone."

Emma smiled gratefully and stayed in the back while Nina walked up front.

Her mom was right. Life could be short, especially for the women in the St. James family. And the men who loved these women were left picking up the pieces after they were gone. Emma wasn't going to let that be Jack.

* * *

Jack's mood lifted as he walked into the Sweetwater Café. It'd been several hours since he'd seen Emma. Since he'd told her he loved her.

Nina offered a wobbly smile. "Hi, Jack. How was the run?"

"I'll be sore for a week, at least. It was a good reminder that I should get back to daily jogging."

"Yeah, I take a run every morning when I wake up. On the mornings that I have to be here, I'm out and running before the sun is even up yet."

"Is that safe?" Jack asked, looking past Nina for Emma, who he didn't see anywhere. He'd have sworn this was where she'd be right now.

"It's safe when you have a hundred-fifty-pound guard dog running alongside you," Nina said on a laugh. "And when my new puppy gets bigger, I'll have two. Wanna coffee?"

"No, actually, I was looking for Emma. Is she here?" he asked.

"Nope, haven't seen her. I'm not sure where she is," Nina said as she stood on the other side of the counter from him. She shifted back and forth on her feet, no longer making eye contact. Instead, she was looking past him at the tables in the café, all of which were occupied. It was a busy afternoon here.

"I see. Well, she's not answering her phone either," Jack said. "I'm starting to get a little worried about her."

"She's probably wiped out after the event. I'm sure she's fine. Her phone's probably just turned off. She's probably resting somewhere." Nina spoke quickly, her sentences jumbling together as if she'd drank one too many caffeinated beverages. She also wore an exaggerated smile, which made Jack wonder if she was hiding something.

"Uncle Jack, can I catch a ride with you?"

Jack looked at Sam. "I don't know, bud. It's pretty busy in here."

"It's okay. I can spare him," Nina said. "Our newest employee, Diana, has offered to stay tonight."

"Diana? That's great to hear," Jack said.

"It is." Nina looked at Sam. "So you are free to go be a teenager."

Jack turned to his nephew. "All right then. I'll drive you back to the house."

Sam grabbed his skateboard from under the counter and hurried to catch up to Jack as he headed to the door.

"Did you talk to Mom?" Sam wanted to know as soon as they were on the sidewalk.

"I did." Jack clicked his key fob as they reached the parking lot, and his truck honked in response.

They climbed in, and Jack pulled onto Main Street.

"And?" Sam asked, his voice a little shaky on the end.

"And she said staying in Sweetwater Springs awhile sounded like a good idea. If you still want to stay, that is."

"Yeah. Yeah, I really do."

"Anything to do with that girl I saw you watching at the event?" Jack asked, teasing him.

Sam flushed a little. "I just like it here, that's all. And the girls are prettier in Sweetwater Springs."

"Yeah?" Jack asked on a chuckle. "I always thought so too. It's a good place to grow up."

"I'm practically grown already," Sam claimed.

"Yeah, but you're still a kid too. Enjoy it while you can. Being a grown-up isn't easy," Jack warned.

"Neither is being a teenager," Sam said.

Jack looked over and laughed. "Well, everything is easier when you have your family around. I'm glad you and your mom are going to stay. Whatever comes, we can tackle it together."

Sam frowned a touch. "Are you and Emma fighting?"

Jack looked over at him. "No, why?"

"Well, she was in the back room when we were just there. I overheard her talking to Nina. She didn't want to see you for some reason."

"She was there?" Jack asked.

Sam nodded. "I'm not sure why, but she didn't seem happy to see you." Sam frowned. "What'd you do, Uncle Jack?"

Jack focused on the road. "I don't know," he told his nephew, even though he had a sneaking suspicion. Last time he'd seen Emma, he'd accidentally told her he loved her. And now she was avoiding him. That spoke volumes. When you told a woman you loved her and she suddenly disappeared, that could only mean one thing: She didn't love him back.

$\mathcal{C}$HAPTER TWENTY-FOUR

$\mathcal{E}$mma stared at the text on her phone later that night.

Can we talk?

She didn't know what to say. It was time to break up with him. What choice did she have? If she told him the truth, he'd just minimize her fears, but they were big and they were real. She had a dead grandmother and mother to prove it.

I'm tired, she texted back. Let's talk tomorrow.

And maybe by then she'd have figured out what to say to him to end things.

I'm not leaving until we speak face to face and I know you're okay. I guess I'll just sleep in my truck tonight.

Emma sat up in bed. Was he in her driveway? She hurried to the window, careful not to wake her sleeping dog, and peeked out. Jack must have seen her because he flashed the truck lights at her.

Emma stepped back from the window, her heart suddenly racing. She wasn't ready to face him tonight. All she wanted to do was step into his arms and beg him to tell her again that he loved her. She wanted to say those words back.

Her phone buzzed with an incoming text. She looked at the screen. Then the phone started ringing in her hand. Seeing no other way, she tapped the screen and accepted the call.

"Hi, Jack," she said, hearing the shakiness of her own voice.

"What's going on, Emma? It's pretty obvious that you're avoiding me. Why? What'd I do?"

"Jack . . . I . . ." She closed her eyes, holding back her tears. "I just realized that we were moving too fast. And I really don't think it's going to work between us."

"Emma? Tell me the truth."

"I am. You and I aren't working out. Not for me."

There was a long silence. So long that Emma almost wondered if he'd hung up.

"If you're going to break up with me, open the door, look me in the eye, and tell me. That's the least you can do for a friend."

Emma turned and walked to the door. She paused behind it, steeling her emotions. When she opened it, Jack was standing on her porch. All she wanted to do was step into his arms and let him hold her. Instead, she reminded herself of how hard life had been for her father after her mother died. She reached for her mom's bandana that she'd tied around her ponytail for the event. *Where is it? Did it fall off?*

"Emma?" Jack's eyes were pools of sadness. "Is this because I told you I loved you earlier?" he asked. "Because if it is, I take it back, Emma. If that's what I need to do to make you stay. I take it all back." His jaw clenched. "I don't love you."

Emma felt her eyes sting against the tears she was holding back. "What?"

He shook his head and reached for her hand. "Whatever lie you need me to tell you, I will, because I don't want you to say goodbye. You are the best thing in my life."

Emma shook her head. "Jack..." She was done people pleasing, done pretending. Jack deserved to know why they couldn't be together. "The truth is, when I had my appointment the other day, I took a test."

"What kind of test?" he asked.

She noticed how his eyes widened and realized what kind of conclusion he might jump to. She wasn't pregnant.

Emma blew out a breath. "I took a test to see if I carried the genetic mutation for breast cancer. It predicts my chances of getting sick like my mom and grandma." She pulled her hand away. "I have the mutation."

Jack stared at her. "Okay. So? Are you telling me you're just going to resign yourself to the same fate they had?"

"No." Emma folded her arms across her chest. "No. I'm going to fight, of course. I'm going to live."

"Seems to me you're going to hide. Breaking up with me is not living, Emma. Shutting yourself off from people just because of some crazy gene that may or may not even result in cancer is just..."

Emma lifted her chin. "Just what? Say it."

"Well, it's not something I would do," he said. "Why would you do that to yourself? You're healthy now."

"Maybe, but if I'm going to get an illness, I want to

know about it. I want to do everything I can to prevent it or catch it early. Maybe if my mom had gotten that chance, she would still be here."

"Yeah, well if she was, she wouldn't be turning her back on the people who love her. I remember your mom, Em. Friends and family were everything to her. Your mom was amazing. She wouldn't deny those friends and family out of fear. She wasn't a coward. She was strong."

Emma's mouth dropped open. "A coward? Is that what you think I'm being by breaking up with you?"

"No, I think you're trying to play the hero by breaking up with me and telling yourself that you're saving me by keeping me from this distant possibility that you'll die someday. Guess what, Emma? We all die. Everyone." His voice softened. "But not everyone loves."

He reached for her hand again but she pulled it away. "I need some time alone. I'm overwhelmed right now, and you're just making it worse."

"Emma?" His voice softened.

She held up a hand. "I mean it, Jack. I want you to leave. Now."

* * *

For the last hour, Jack had been driving around aimlessly with his thoughts. He slowed at his house but didn't pull in. Amanda and Sam were in there, and he didn't want to grace them with his bad mood. Heck, Amanda might change her mind about staying if she saw him right now.

Instead, he kept driving, finally pulling in at the Tipsy Tavern. It was Saturday night so the bar was crowded. Music accosted him as he walked in. He wouldn't be able to hear himself think, which was exactly what he wanted right now.

His thoughts were muddled and dark, just like the gathering clouds in the sky above. A summer storm was brewing.

He headed straight for the bar and sat down, nodding at Skip, the bar's owner.

"Hey, Jack. How are you?" Skip asked.

"Good. I haven't seen you working the bar here in a while." Jack regretted his decision to sit at the bar now. He liked Skip, but he wasn't in a social mood at the moment.

"Yeah, well. A couple of employees called in, and I'm not too good to pour drinks and shine glasses. What'll you have?"

Jack stiffened. His gaze moved beyond Skip to the selection of drinks behind him. The regular bartender knew that Jack took a Coke on the rocks. Nonalcoholic. One of those bottles behind Skip would definitely take the edge off though. It would make all his feelings disappear. Temporary relief for what ailed him. "I, uh…I'm not sure," Jack said.

Skip's smile slid away. "How about what's on tap?"

Jack knew his answer should be no. No, he didn't want anything alcoholic. A simple Coke would do. The feeling alcohol provided was only temporary. It wouldn't help anything. Jack was strong, and he'd been sober too long to fall off the wagon now.

He lifted his gaze to the wall of alcohol again and then looked at Skip. "Nah, man. I'll just have a Coke with ice."

"You sure?" Skip's brow furrowed.

"I'm sure." The woman Jack loved had just broken up

with him. If he could resist drinking tonight, then he could stay sober for the rest of his life.

Jack watched Skip prepare him a soda and slide it in front of him. "Do you, uh, do that whole bartender thing where I spill my guts and you tell me how to fix my life?"

Skip laughed as if that was the funniest thing he'd heard all day. "That's only what happens in the movies. But go ahead. I'll do my best."

Jack nodded, folding his arms on the counter in front of him, his fingers curled around his glass. "There's this woman…"

"Every story starts with a woman," Skip said, leaning against the counter.

"I think I've fallen in love with her this summer. I know I have." Jack took a sip of his Coke, enjoying the zing on his tongue. "She broke up with me tonight because of some crazy fear she has. She thinks she's doing me a favor, I guess. Saving me from a bunch of anguish if something were to happen to her."

Skip reached for a glass and started polishing it. "I see."

Jack slumped. He could see too. He understood Emma's reasoning even if it didn't make a lick of sense. "So what do I do?"

Skip looked thoughtful as he continued polishing. "She loves you. If she didn't, she wouldn't be so hell-bent on sparing you. When you love someone, you don't want to be the reason for their pain."

Jack held out his hands. "I'm in pain right now, and she's the reason."

"Touché," Skip said. "My advice: If you love her, you gotta fight for her."

Jack shrugged. "How do I do that?"

Skip shook his head. "No idea. I've never heard a

problem quite like yours. It's one that an apology, chocolate, or jewelry won't fix."

Jack laughed dryly. His pocketful of Hershey's Kisses
wouldn't make a dent in this problem. "No, neither of
those things will fix this. The only thing that will fix this is
changing her genetics."

Skip frowned as he put one glass down and reached for
another. "Are you talking about Emma?"

Jack looked up. "Yeah. But there's a bartender confidentiality rule, right?"

"Your secrets are safe with me, buddy. And I guess
hers are too."

Jack sat up. "What's that supposed to mean? Has she
been sitting here talking to you?"

Skip lifted his gaze from the second glass he was polishing. "Why do you think that stool was empty when you
walked in? She left right before you got here, buddy."

"What did she say?" Jack asked.

"Bartender confidentiality, remember? She was pretty
heartbroken too though."

"Where she'd go? Do you know?" Jack asked.

"I guess she was going home. I hope so at least because I
think the storm that's coming is going to be a nasty one."

Jack pushed back from the bar and stood. He laid some
cash down to cover his soda.

"What are you going to say to her?" Skip asked.

"I have no idea," Jack said, turning to walk out of the
bar. All he knew was that he was going to find Emma
and say something. The last time he'd seen her, he'd said
all the wrong things. This time he hoped he said something right.

* * *

Emma had searched her entire house for her mom's bandana. It wasn't there. Then she'd searched the café and ended up at the tavern, hoping to forget her troubles. Instead, she'd figured out where her bandana must have fallen off.

Blue Sky Point.

After the event, she'd hiked up there to think. If this was where she'd lost the bandana, she needed to find it soon. Otherwise it would be ruined by the rain and mud. Or worse, it would blow off the cliff and she'd never see it again.

It was just a silly bandana, but it meant something to her. Her mom had worn it with grace and courage. Emma needed to get it back.

She aimed the flashlight on the path and kept walking, climbing higher and higher into elevation. Everyone who lived in the mountains knew not to hike at nighttime for a million justifiable reasons. For one, there was wildlife out here. Two, it was easy to get lost if you strayed off the path.

But Emma knew how to deal with wildlife. She had a flashlight and a knife in her side satchel. She also knew to stay on the path. She'd just get her mom's bandana and turn back, making it home ahead of the storm.

At least that was the plan.

Thunder rumbled overhead, and Emma picked up her pace, moving faster. Her breaths were labored as she climbed higher. When she was almost there, her cell phone rang. Once again she was surprised that she had reception out here.

She pulled out her phone and checked the ID. When she saw Jack's name, she considered not answering, but in her haste, she'd forgotten to tell anyone where she was. And in the unlikely case that something did happen out here, someone should know where to locate her.

"Hi, Jack."

"Emma. Where are you?"

"What makes you think I'm not at home?" she asked, already suspecting his answer.

"Because I'm parked in your driveway and you're not. Are you okay?"

"I'm fine. Just taking a nice, long hike," she said sarcastically.

"What?"

"I'm going up to Blue Sky Point. I left something important up there earlier today. I don't want the storm to ruin it."

"Emma, it's dark, and the sky is about to break open. It's not safe—"

"Which is why I don't have time to argue with you. I need to hurry. But please don't be at my house when I get home, Jack. I'm not up for any more lectures tonight on how silly you think I am, or stupid, or whatever else you think about my train of thought."

"Emma," Jack said, "you shouldn't be going to Blue Sky Point alone right now. That's crazy."

"See? You're already lecturing me. Save it, Jack. I'll be fine on my own."

"Damn it, Emma. You don't have to do everything on your own. You could've called me. I could've come with you if you insisted on going. I can be with you for it all, come what may."

"We're not talking about my hike right now. And I'm not talking about anything else. I'll text you when I get back to my car, Jack. Now go home."

She disconnected the call and stopped for a moment

to gain control of her breath and her emotions. A light sprinkle began to fall as she stood there.

Crap. She needed to keep moving. More thunder rumbled and then Emma's flashlight flickered and cut off.

"No. No, no, no." She hit it against her palm, but the light didn't come back on. This was bad. She reached for her phone in her pocket and turned on the flashlight app. The battery was only at 30 percent, and using the app would drain the rest of it fast. Hopefully it would be enough to get her to Blue Sky Point, find her mom's bandana, and get back to her car.

Hopefully.

CHAPTER TWENTY-FIVE

Jack would grant Emma's plea to leave her alone. But not until he found her and made sure she was safe.

Jack reversed out of Emma's driveway and sped toward Blue Sky Point. He made what would've been a fifteen-minute drive in ten minutes despite the rain, which had started to come down harder by the minute. By the time he pulled up beside Emma's car, the rain was falling fast enough to make her car just a blur of red paint.

Jack pulled his rain jacket out of the back seat, slipped it on, and grabbed a bag that he kept under his middle console. Inside he kept a flashlight, a knife, and a few first aid items. Jack knew this trail like the back of his hand, the same way he knew all the trails in Evergreen Park. He'd taken it many times, and it climbed to the highest peak in the park.

She must've come up here right after the event. After he'd professed his love for her. Somewhere in between she'd found out she had some genetic predisposition to get sick like her mother.

Jack headed up the path, lighting the way with his flashlight even though it did little to clear his vision because of the rain. The soil was wet and he didn't want the wheels of an ATV to tear up the ground. Hopefully Emma was already on her way down the path, and he wouldn't have to walk far.

After about ten minutes of walking, when he was over halfway up, he began to worry. He'd spoken to her at least half an hour ago. They should've crossed paths as she headed back down. With the rain coming down as hard as it was, she wouldn't waste any time. Something felt wrong.

"Emma?" he called out in the rain. "Emma, where are you?" He slipped on the wet ground as he took a step higher, and his flashlight went flying into the darkness. Jack cursed softly under his breath. He could see the light somewhere off the path. He needed it, and Emma needed him.

He stepped off the path, swiping back bushes and tree branches. Then he bent to grab the flashlight and drew his hand back quickly when something snapped his flesh. Or more accurately, bit him. He knew a snake bite when he felt it. He also knew that this kind of rain filled up the snakes' dens, forcing them out, searching for higher ground. He should've been more cautious sticking his hand into the brush.

Jack grabbed his flashlight and shined it on the ground all around him, hoping to get a glimpse of the snake, but it was long gone. He stood and yanked off his T-shirt. He tied it above the bite site, hoping to keep the venom from traveling through his body.

Then he started heading back toward the trail, feeling light-headed already. He stopped walking to keep himself steady. Falling face-first on the path in the middle of the driving rain might not turn out well. And he needed to get to the hospital. Right after he located Emma.

Jack pulled out his cell phone, shielding it under his raincoat, and tapped on Emma's contact. She didn't answer. Then he tapped on Granger Fields's contact. He lived close by on Merry Mountain Farms. He'd be able to get here quick.

Granger answered almost immediately. "Hey, Jack. What's up?"

"Granger," Jack said weakly. He'd been bitten by a snake before, and it hadn't affected him this fast. That wasn't a good sign for what kind of snake had bitten him. "I'm on the trail to Blue Sky Point, and I've been bitten by a snake."

"What?" Granger said. "Are you okay?"

Jack couldn't worry about himself right now. "Emma's up here too. I'm looking for her. I need your help, buddy."

"On my way," Granger said. "And I'm calling nine-one-one."

"Thanks. Might want to hurry," Jack said. As he reached the trail, he began calling Emma's name again. This time, she called back to him from somewhere in the distance.

* * *

Emma had never been so glad to hear Jack's voice in her life. She'd also never been so glad for someone not to listen to what she'd said. The downpour had come just as she'd located her mom's bandana in the dirt. At that same time, as fate would have it, her cell phone battery had died. She was stuck on this cliff, huddled under a large bush, which was providing some shelter. Even so, she was cold and wet, and a little terrified of the wildlife that she knew was up here.

"Jack!" she called out again, wondering what was taking him so long. He'd sounded close when she'd heard him call to her. Where was he?

"Emma?" he said after a moment.

She blinked past the rain and saw him standing on the path. She dashed out of the bush and wrapped her arms around him. "I'm so glad you're here!"

"Thought you didn't need me," he said slowly. He sounded out of breath, and she wondered if he'd jogged up here. Knowing him, he probably had. Such an alpha male, and she was thankful for that today.

"I need your flashlight," she said, pulling back to look at him. "And you, I guess." She wanted to kiss him, but she'd just broken up with him, and she'd meant it. Watching someone you love suffer wasn't easy, and if that was a possibility in her future, she didn't want Jack to have to deal with it. "It's pouring. Let's get off this mountain."

"Good idea," Jack said as a slow smile slid across his mouth. Then his eyes rolled back, and his body dropped under her hold on him. She tried to catch him, but he fell as the rain beat down on them.

"Jack!" Emma dropped to her knees in the mud. She leaned over him and looked at his face. He was out. "Jack! Wake up!" She tried to lift him up, but he was too heavy. Removing her own jacket, she shielded them both as she slapped at his cheek. "Jack, what's wrong with you?"

When he didn't answer, she searched for his phone. Where was it?

She yanked on Jack again and then bent down to talk to him. "I'm going for help. I don't want to leave you but I'll be quick. I'll be right back."

"Promise?" he asked, opening his eyes just a touch.

"Jack! Are you okay? What's going on?"

"It's nothing," he said.

"Stop it. What happened? What's wrong?"

"Just a little snake bite," he said, half groaning.

Emma gasped. "What? We need to get you to a hospital, Jack. You look awful."

"You look beautiful." He opened his eyes all the way. "I've always thought so. I've always loved you, Emma, long before today."

"Jack, it's not the time to talk about this. You're hurt. You could be..." She trailed off, not wanting to go there. Bite injuries could be serious.

"I could die? Yeah, if you'd have known the summer would end like this, you probably wouldn't have dated me, huh?"

Emma was starting to shiver uncontrollably as the rain fell harder. "That's not fair and you know it. I'm going to get you help. Stay there." She pointed a finger at him.

"You are not leaving me, Emma St. James." He sat up slowly.

"You're afraid of being alone with the wildlife?" she asked.

Jack laughed. "I can handle myself. I'm afraid of what might happen to you. Whether you like it or not, I'm in love with you and I don't plan on leaving your side. No matter what."

Emma wrapped her arms around him to help him stand. "Jack, we're not going to—"

"Technically, I'm a dying man right now." He looked over. "And having you stay with me is my dying wish. So you have to grant it."

"This isn't funny, Jack," Emma huffed, wanting to hate him right now but loving him instead.

"I'm not joking. I'm pretty sure the snake that bit me was venomous. We probably need to get off this mountain."

Emma gasped. "I'm so sorry you followed me up here. This is all my fault. If something happens to you, I'll never—"

"Nothing is going to happen to me," Jack said. "We're going down this trail together. And then you're going to make sure I get help. I trust you, Emma."

Emma wished she had as much faith in herself. She started walking faster, nearly dragging Jack along. After a few steps in, she heard the sound of motors growing louder as utility vehicles traveled up the trail.

"I called Granger, and he called nine-one-one," Jack said. His voice was barely audible. Then his knees gave way, and he fell to the ground once more. Emma watched helplessly as the guys who'd come to their rescue lifted Jack up and put him on a stretcher to load him onto an emergency vehicle. She got in beside him, and the vehicle turned back down the path.

All Emma could think as they rode in the pouring rain was that she didn't want to lose Jack. She needed him; she loved him. And he loved her. If he died tonight, she wouldn't regret a single second except all the wasted time she'd spent this afternoon pushing him away.

But he wasn't going to die tonight. Jack was as stubborn as he was tough. He'd pull through, and when he did, she was either going to strangle him or kiss him for scaring her like this.

* * *

Jack could hear the steady *beep, beep, beep* on the monitors around him. That's how he knew he was still alive. His eyes weren't opening though, probably a result of whatever anecdote the doctors had given him.

Beep, beep, beep.

Sniffle.

He struggled to figure out who was crying at his side. Maybe Amanda or his mom. Hopefully Emma. Not because he wanted her to be upset but more because he wanted hers to be the first face he saw when he woke up. He also wanted hers to be the last face he saw when he fell asleep at night. When had he turned into such a sappy, lovestruck guy?

He cracked an eye open and glanced over, his heart giving a little kick when he saw Emma at his bedside. "You look awful," he said, his voice coming out broken and dry from the night's events.

She gasped and met his gaze. "You're awake. How do you feel?" she asked in quick succession.

He lifted a hand and ran his fingers through his hair. "Like a rattlesnake bit me."

"That's exactly right. Not once but twice." She narrowed her eyes. "I'm surprised you're even breathing. You're pretty tough, Jack Hershey."

"Tougher than you give me credit for, right?" He reached for her hand, and she let him take it. "Thanks for sticking by my side tonight."

"You're welcome. And I didn't really have a choice, you know. Thanks for coming to my rescue. I guess we're even."

Jack frowned. He didn't really feel any pain so he guessed he was on some pretty good medicine right now. "You're the one who saved me. I didn't do anything for you."

"You came for me even when I told you not to. That's enough." She looked down at their intertwined hands, appearing to be thinking over what to say next. "I don't want to be afraid of the future, Jack. When I turned thirty, I decided I wasn't going to live under this umbrella of fear that I would turn out like my mom and grandma. I wanted to have goals and dreams. I wanted to fall in love."

"Liar. I don't think you had any intentions of falling in love with me. But you did," he said quietly.

"Another thing you didn't give me a choice in." She offered him a small smile, and he thought he'd never seen her more beautiful.

"Emma, I could have died tonight. No one is promised another day, much less another hour. All we have is the moment we're in. And I, for one, want to spend every second I'm given with you. Even if it's chasing you up a mountain in the pouring rain."

"And getting bitten by rattlesnakes?" she asked as a tear slid down her cheek.

"If that's what it takes to be at your side." He searched her eyes, hoping for a sign that he was getting through to her.

Emma swiped at another tear that slipped down her cheek. Then she leaned over and kissed him softly. "I want to spend every moment with you too."

"Does this mean you're going to stop pushing me away and let me love you?" he asked.

Her face hovered only an inch from his. "Only if you let me love you back."

He grimaced teasingly. "Hmm. I don't know. That's a tall demand."

She laughed for a moment. Then she grew serious. "I have an appointment with Dr. Rivers on Monday. We're going to discuss the results of the genetic testing and what I can do about them." Emma shrugged. "If I decide to do anything. Just because I have the genetic mutation doesn't mean I'll get sick."

"You couldn't have realized that before you broke up with me and made me follow you up a mountain and into a storm?"

She sniffled as she laughed. "What fun would that be?"

"Not as much." Jack squeezed her hand, holding her gaze. "I'll go with you. If you want me to."

She hesitated for a moment and then nodded once. "I'd like that."

"We're in this together, okay? For all the good stuff and the bad. All the birthdays and every moment in between."

"This sounds serious," Emma said.

"Oh, it is. Very serious. One of these days, if I get out of this hospital bed, I might even drop to one knee and ask you to marry me." He'd only just told her he loved her today. It was probably too soon to talk about marriage. But he didn't think Emma was going to push him away or run anymore.

"And one of these days," she whispered as she leaned toward him for another kiss, "I'm going to say yes."

*E*PILOGUE

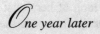

One year later

*T*he sun came up just like any other day but today was special. Emma had spent her entire thirtieth year chasing new ideas and dreams and letting go of old fears. She had the gene mutation linked to breast cancer but she had taken her control back by creating a plan with Dr. Rivers to have more frequent screenings at the clinic in addition to her own self-checks. She was doing her part to stay healthy by exercising, eating well, and being in love, which was maybe the best medicine on earth.

There was a lot to celebrate on her thirty-first birthday.

Emma continued to climb up the path, higher and higher until she reached Blue Sky Point. She had Barnaby at her heels, and Jack would be joining her in a little bit. She'd wanted to come here alone first. The land flattened out, and Emma stepped toward the guardrail to look out on the town of Sweetwater Springs, remembering her mom's awestruck words: *This is what the angels must see.*

Emma wasn't sure if there were angels looking down but she hoped her mom somehow knew that she was doing okay. "I have another event planned this summer, Mom. It's going to be bigger and better than the last and make a difference in people's lives. It made a difference in mine."

Emma wasn't afraid anymore. Knowledge was power, and so was love. With Jack at her side, she was fearless.

"Dad and Angel are throwing me a birthday celebration later. Jack and I are going. I wanted to come say hi to you first though. And I wanted to thank you for being my mom."

Emma pulled the bandana from the loop of her waistband and held it up, watching the fabric flutter in the growing breeze. "I'm returning this to you. I don't need it to remember you. I have every memory I need in my heart." She released the bandana and watched it take flight, feeling free herself.

Jack would probably have something to say about this as the park ranger here, but this felt like the right thing to do. And it was her birthday after all.

She inhaled deeply. "Also, Mom, I'm pretty sure Jack is coming up here with a ring and he's going to ask me to spend my life with him. And I'm going to say yes." Her heart fluttered in anticipation. Jack told her he was meeting her here this morning and bringing a gift. He'd been secretive for the last couple of weeks but they weren't secrets like last summer's.

Emma watched the bandana rise with the wind again. "I know you and Jack's mom always dreamed out loud of Jack and me getting married one day. That's become my dream too. He's my best friend and the man of my dreams." And she couldn't wait to spend the rest of her birthdays with him.

The ground crunched behind her, and Barnaby took off downhill, barking like the ferocious guard dog he thought he was. Emma turned to see Jack coming off the path toward her. Her heart did a silly little dance.

"You didn't let me serenade you last year," he led with, "so I'm definitely going to sing happy birthday to you this year."

She laughed as he stepped in front of her.

"Happy birthday, Emma," he said softly, staring deeply into her eyes. "I have something for you." Then he reached into his front pocket and pulled out a Hershey's Kiss, its white flag raised high.

She took it and breathed a laugh, wondering if she'd gotten it all wrong. Maybe he wasn't proposing up here this morning. "I should've known I'd be getting one of these today."

The corner of his mouth curled. "If I have it my way, I'll be bringing you these for the rest of my life."

Her gaze jumped back up to meet his. Then, even though she'd been expecting it, she gasped as he dropped to one knee.

He held up his hand. "Don't worry. I haven't been bitten by a snake," he teased.

Always teasing. Always making her laugh.

"I told you I was going to ask you to marry me one of these days," he said, holding her gaze.

Emma nodded. "And I told you I was going to say yes."

He smiled back at her, and then he reached into the pocket of his jeans, pulling out a small red velvet box. Her gaze dropped to it, and she stopped breathing for a moment. "Yes," she finally said.

"I haven't asked the question yet." He grinned as he clutched the box. Then he dodged a sloppy kiss from Barnaby, who propped himself up on his leg.

"My answer will always be yes to you. I love you, Jack. I want to spend our lives together. You make me a better person. You make me stronger."

"No. You were always the strongest woman I know." He reached for her hand. "You've stolen half my lines, so I only have one thing left to say. To ask really."

Emma held her breath.

"Emma, will you marry me?" He opened the box and revealed a round diamond that caught the light of the sun, reflecting a beautiful rainbow of colors.

Emma held out her left hand. "Yes," she said, trembling as he slid the ring onto her finger. Then he stood and kissed her softly. When he came up for air, he had a song on his lips.

"Happy birthday to you," he sang. "Happy birthday to you."

She giggled softly.

"Happy birthday, dear Emma. Happy birthday to you... and many more."

She grinned back at him. "You're going to serenade me on my birthday for the rest of our lives too, aren't you?"

"Forever," he agreed. Then he kissed her again, slow and easy like the breeze that lifted around them. "And I for one can't wait."

PERFECT PICNIC PIMENTO CHEESE SANDWICH

A pimento cheese sandwich is perfect for picnicking with your special someone. Hungry for seconds? Pack an extra container of your homemade pimento spread to dip chips in later as the sun goes down behind the mountains and the fireflies come out!

Ingredients:

- Pimento cheese spread (see homemade recipe below)
- Sourdough bread
- Avocado slices (optional)
- Bacon slices (optional)
- Bread and butter pickle spears (optional)

HOMEMADE PIMENTO CHEESE SPREAD:

- 2 cups of shredded sharp cheddar cheese
- 8 ounces of cream cheese, softened
- ½ cup Duke's, Hellmann's, or another high-quality mayonnaise
- ¼ teaspoon of garlic powder
- ¼ teaspoon of smoked paprika
- ¼ teaspoon of onion powder
- 1 (4 ounce) jar of diced pimento, drained

1. Place all ingredients into a large bowl. Use a hand mixer to thoroughly combine them. Season to taste with salt and black pepper.

2. Once the ingredients are mixed, spread a thick layer (to your preference) on a slice of sourdough bread.

3. Add bacon and/or avocado slices as desired. (Bacon makes everything taste better!) Bread and butter pickle spears go great on the sandwich or as a crunchy side.

4. Top off your sandwich with a second slice of bread and load up your picnic basket and favorite blanket. You might want to pack more than one sandwich for each picnicker because these are sure to be a hit!

About the Author

Annie Rains is a *USA Today* bestselling contemporary romance author who writes small-town love stories set in fictional places in her home state of North Carolina. When Annie isn't writing, she's living out her own happily ever after with her husband and three children.

Learn more at:
    www.AnnieRains.com/
    Twitter: @AnnieRainsBooks
    Facebook.com/AnnieRainsBooks
    Instagram: @AnnieRainsBooks

A Fairytale Bride

HOPE RAMSAY

Melissa Portman is fighting a losing battle when it comes to saving her grandmother's bookstore—and selling the historic building may be her only option. Yet when a handsome stranger wanders in one day, she wonders if her very own fairy tale is just beginning...

Please turn the page for a bonus story from *USA Today* bestselling author Hope Ramsay.

FOREVER

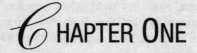

CHAPTER ONE

*J*efferson Talbert-Lyndon turned up his jacket collar and hunkered down in an easy chair by the front window of Bean There Done That, the trendy coffee shop in downtown Shenandoah Falls, Virginia.

He fired up his tablet, connected to the coffee shop's Internet, and scanned the headlines from the *Washington Post* and several cable news networks. Things had not improved since he'd left New York a week ago.

Jeff was still being pilloried by the president's political party for a series of articles he'd written for *New York, New York* about Joanna Tyrell-Durand, the nominee for the Supreme Court, and her husband's and brother's illegal lobbying on behalf of various oil and gas interests.

Jeff's stories had relied on information from Val Charonneau, a well-known climate-change advocate and one of Jeff's longtime friends. But it turned out Val's source of information, which included printouts of several damning e-mails, was the unreliable Helena Tyrell, the nominee's soon-to-be-ex sister-in-law.

So what had appeared to be a career-making scoop had turned into the blunder of the century, featuring a philandering husband and a vengeful wife. The embarrassment reached critical mass last week when Brendan Tyrell filed a defamation suit against *New York, New York,* and on the same day, Jeff's father, Thomas Lyndon, the US ambassador to Japan, issued a statement saying that Jeff was a lifelong screwup who had no business trying to be a journalist.

Jeff had resigned from the magazine the next day and headed out here to the wilderness of the Blue Ridge Mountains in order to escape the carnage he'd unloosed on himself and his career.

He turned his tablet off. He needed to move on. But toward what?

If he wasn't a journalist and a writer, then who was he? The man his mother wanted him to become? The CEO of the Talbert Foundation?

He couldn't think of anything he wanted to do less than managing his family's money.

He returned his gaze to the picturesque town beyond the window. Despite the chilly spring rain, the town reminded him of a Norman Rockwell painting. The wrought-iron light posts lining Liberty Avenue were hung with American flags, in honor of the upcoming Memorial Day celebrations. Several of the storefronts were draped in red, white, and blue bunting.

His eye was drawn to the store across the street—a used bookshop called Secondhand Prose—which wasn't draped or decorated. Instead, like independent bookshops everywhere, this one had flyers for upcoming community events and a large orange "Help Wanted" sign taped to its front windows. The store reminded him of his favorite bookshop in Park Slope. He found himself smiling.

Until his gaze snapped to the dark-haired woman dressed in a blue raincoat and carrying a blue umbrella, standing at the corner in front of the shop.

What the hell was Aunt Pam doing in downtown Shenandoah Falls on a rainy Friday morning? Her husband, Mark Lyndon, was a US senator. Didn't they live in DC most of the time?

Oh, wait, the Senate had probably adjourned yesterday because of the holiday. Crap. He'd lost track of time up in his cabin. This was bad.

Aunt Pam was the only member of the Lyndon family, besides his father, who would recognize him on sight. Pam was the only family member who had remained a friend after his mom and dad's messy divorce. Although Jeff had a bunch of Lyndon cousins, he'd never met most of them. He'd visited the family compound at Charlotte's Grove only once in his life, when he was fourteen. That year Dad had been posted in Washington instead of someplace foreign.

Aunt Pam crossed the street and swept into the coffee shop as only Aunt Pam could—like she owned the place.

Jeff leaned his elbow on the table and planted his face in his hand. He stroked the patchy, one-week's growth of scruff on his face. He didn't have a lot of faith in his disguise.

He needed to get out of here. If Pam knew he was hiding out in Dad's fishing cabin, she'd tell Mom, and Mom would come running. Even worse, Pam would invite him to stay at Charlotte's Grove. Jeff couldn't think of anything more excruciating, especially after what Dad had done to him last week. Jeff might have Lyndon in his hyphenated name, but he'd never, ever been a member of Dad's family.

Jeff waited until Pam's attention was focused on the barista behind the counter. It was now or never.

He stood and scooted out the front door, then loped across Liberty Avenue, but had to wait for the traffic on Church Street before he could cross. The rain pelted him as he waited for the light to change.

Pam must have ordered black coffee because she came out of the coffee shop when he was halfway across Church Street.

He needed to hide. Now. He headed for the used bookstore, collar up, head down. A little jingle bell rang as he pushed through the front door.

Jeff loved the way old bookstores smelled, and this bookshop had a lot of old books on its shelves that gave the place the aroma of bookbinder's glue and dry paper.

Jeff turned toward the window, intent on Pam's whereabouts, and discovered a cat tree, complete with a cat, sitting in the front window. The cat was gray and regarded Jeff with a pair of cool, amber eyes.

"Hello," he said in his most cat-friendly voice as he ducked down and glanced through the dusty window. Where was Pam going?

The cat arched its back and hissed.

"Shhh," he hissed back at the cat. Oh, good. Pam had gone into the real estate office across the way.

The cat growled.

"Sorry," Jeff said as he backed away.

He ought to leave the store, but the thought of going back to the solitary cabin on a rainy day left him slightly depressed. Besides, the only good reading material up there was a complete set of Hardy Boys mysteries, and he'd already been so desperate for entertainment that he'd plowed through all of them.

He had planned to download some reading material at the coffee shop, but Pam had put the kibosh on that. And now the coffee shop was officially off-limits. Maybe he should rethink. Maybe he should hunt down Val and wring his neck.

Or maybe he should just buy a couple of books.

He spent the next twenty minutes browsing the store. He selected four books on various aspects of American history, a couple of John Grisham novels that he found in a box in a dusty corner, and a clothbound edition of *Walden* that was shelved with a bunch of philosophy.

He'd been thinking a lot about Henry David Thoreau. Thoreau had spent years living alone and off the grid. Maybe the long-dead author had some tips for surviving cabin life.

Jeff headed for the checkout, where he stumbled over a second cat—a long-haired calico—intent on winding itself around his ankles. This one was like a puffball with legs. Jeff put his books on the counter and scooped the animal into his arms.

It settled, purring like the engine of his vintage Porsche 911—the car he'd reluctantly left in Brooklyn. He'd "borrowed" Mom's Land Rover from its garage at the house on the Hudson. He'd left a note so Mom wouldn't worry, but she would worry anyway.

He stood there a moment, stroking the cat, waiting for someone to arrive at the checkout, when he realized that he'd been browsing for almost half an hour without seeing another soul.

"Hello?" he called.

Crickets. The silence was almost deafening.

"Is anyone here?" He shouted a little louder this time.

Footsteps sounded from the back of the store, and

a moment later a girl appeared, heading slowly in his direction with her face buried in a paperback. Dark, horn-rimmed glasses perched on her nose. Thick, curly chestnut hair tumbled around her narrow face like an untamed mane. She wore a T-shirt with a vintage book illustration of Cinderella under a faded orange plaid flannel shirt and rust-colored skintight jeans that showed her slender figure.

She looked up with a puckish smile. "Hello," she said. "I heard you the first time. But I was at a particularly good part of the story." She closed the book, marking the place with her finger.

He had to return the smile. "What are you reading?" he asked.

The girl's pale cheeks colored. "Oh, just a paperback," she said in an I-just-got-caught-with-my-hand-in-the-cookie-jar voice. She hid the book behind her back.

Then, with catlike grace of her own, she climbed over the box of books that blocked her path to the cash register and quickly transferred the secret novel to a shelf under the counter where he couldn't see it.

"I'm sorry about the mess," she said in a rush, her face growing pinker still. "The books are from a large estate sale, and I haven't gotten around to cataloging and shelving them all."

No doubt because she'd been spending her time reading paperback novels. What had she been reading? Mystery, suspense, *Fifty Shades of Grey*? He warmed at the thought.

Her eyes were the dark blue color of a fall sky, and the moment their gazes connected, he revised his estimation of her. She wasn't just some girl in colorful clothing. She was older than he'd first thought, and behind those smart-girl glasses, she was stunningly beautiful.

Awareness jolted him right behind his navel.

He had all day with nothing to do. A crazy, halfway desperate idea popped into his head. "I saw the sign in the window," he said as he gazed at the disorder around the checkout. "Guess you need some help, huh?"

She tilted her chin up a fraction. One eyebrow arched. "Do you know someone who loves books and is willing to work for nothing?" She had a low, sexy voice that did something strange and hot to his insides, while it erased his better judgment.

He rested his hip against the counter and, forgetting all about his recent troubles, he said, "How about me?"

* * *

Melissa Portman almost laughed in the man's face. He was most definitely not the teenager Grammy had been searching for when she'd put the "Help Wanted" sign in the window three months ago.

He was a grown man, probably her age or a little older, in his late twenties or early thirties. He wore clothes that branded him as someone who came from way, way out of town: a brown tweed jacket with elbow patches, a striped button-down shirt, and a pair of skinny jeans that showed off his muscular thighs. All in all, he gave the impression of a hot college professor.

He also had dark, soulful brown eyes, too-long black hair that curled over his forehead like a sensitive poet's, and a well-groomed scruff of beard that Melissa found way too attractive for her own good. To top it all off, he held Hugo in his arms like a man who knew something about cats. In fact, just watching his long fingers stroke the cat was vaguely erotic.

No question about it. He was delicious eye candy. And she wasn't stupid enough to believe that he needed a job. The guy was flirting.

Wow, that hadn't happened in, like, forever.

She arched her eyebrow the way Grammy used to when faced with the utterly absurd and said, "You want to work here? Really?" She invested her voice with just the right tone of skepticism.

His mouth quirked and exposed adorable laugh lines that peeked through his *GQ*-style stubble. "Really," he said. "I appreciate literature."

His voice was low, deep, and had just the right hint of tease in it—like he might be calling her out for the book she'd hidden beneath the counter. Had he seen the title? She hoped not.

"Seriously," he said, "I'm interested in the job."

"It's minimum wage," she said.

"How much is that? I'm new around here."

No kidding. "Seven twenty-five an hour." She managed to say this with a straight face.

The professor's eyebrows lowered. "That's not very much, is it?"

Obviously Mr. Professor had been spending all his time in ivory towers or something. "Right," she said, nodding. "And that's why we only hire high school students. You're a little old for that."

He continued to stroke Hugo as he gazed at her out of those impossibly hot brown eyes. "I know, but I need the work. I recently lost my job."

Something in the set of his broad shoulders suggested that he was telling the truth, even if he was flirting at the same time. A momentary pang of sympathy swelled inside Melissa. She was in the same boat. She'd given up a good job with the Fairfax County Public Schools in order to take care of Grammy, and now she'd be out a full-time teaching job until next September. She didn't know how she'd pay her bills.

Unless she sold the historic building that housed Secondhand Prose. The Lyndons were willing to pay a fortune for it—enough to pay all of Melissa's bills, cover the property taxes, and give her something left over to invest. But selling out to the Lyndons was the last thing Melissa wanted to do. In her heart of hearts, she wanted to keep Secondhand Prose's doors open, which was just silly, wishful thinking.

"I could be very helpful," Mr. Professor said, breaking through Melissa's financial worries. "I'm good at organizing things, and I have other experience and qualifications that could be valuable to you."

She eyed the cat and then his handsome face. "Aside from charming killer cats?"

His mouth twitched again. "I'm an avid reader."

She rolled her eyes. "Aren't we all? But really, there is no job."

"But the sign. And you're clearly short—"

"The sign has been there for a while. My grandmother put it up before she died. I'm sorry, but there's no job available here."

"Oh. I'm so sorry about your grandmother."

For an uncomfortable moment, their gazes caught, and the kindness and concern in his eyes surprised her. "Grammy was pretty old," Melissa said, her voice barely hiding the sorrow that had hollowed out her insides. "So let me ring these books up for you, okay?"

Melissa picked up the books he'd laid on the counter while Mr. Hottie Professor continued to lean his hip into the counter, his mere presence disturbing the atmosphere and making Melissa adolescently self-conscious.

"That'll be twenty-five dollars for the books," she said in her best customer-service voice. She expected him to hand over a credit card, but instead the guy pulled out a money clip that held a big wad of bills. He sure wasn't a professor, not carrying cash like that. He had to thumb through several hundred-dollar bills to find a five and a twenty. So who was he? She was suddenly dying to know.

He put Hugo down, but the damn cat continued to circle his legs. "Nice cat," he said.

"His name is Hugo—well, his full name is Victor Hugo— and he's not friendly."

"Could have fooled me."

The cat meowed as if he knew they were talking about him. What was Hugo up to? He never made friends with strangers.

She handed the guy his bag. "So, where are you staying?" she asked, hoping she might prolong this conversation and get his name, e-mail address, or even his profile on Match.com.

He took his bag and broke eye contact. "I love your store. Next time I'm going to make friends with the cat in the window."

"Ha. I don't think so. Dickens is half wild."

"I already figured that out. Have a nice day."

And with that the guy turned and strolled down the aisle toward the door, looking amazingly like the hero in the romance novel she'd been reading when he'd first arrived.

CHAPTER TWO

At six o'clock Melissa locked up the store and headed down Liberty Avenue with *The Lonesome Cowboy* tucked into her purse. She took her usual spot at the lunch counter and ordered the meat loaf blue-plate special and a glass of iced tea.

She'd been there for about ten minutes when Gracie Teague, the diner's owner and chief waitress, leaned over the counter, casting a shadow on page 183 of Melissa's book. "So what's it tonight, English aristocrats or down-home cowboys?" she asked.

"Cowboys," Melissa said, blinking up from the page. Gracie and Mom had been best friends in high school; maybe that's why Gracie had nominated herself as Melissa's keeper. Even before Grammy died, Gracie had been a fixture in Melissa's life. Their relationship started that summer when Mom and Dad had dropped Melissa off with Grammy while they'd pursued their lifetime dream of buying a sailboat and sailing from the Caribbean up the East Coast.

Even as an eight-year-old Melissa had loved books, but an eight-year-old wasn't patient enough to spend a whole day in a bookstore. So she'd come down to the diner and hung out with Gracie. Then the news had come that Mom and Dad had perished in a storm. The death of her parents had changed Melissa's life forever while simultaneously cementing her relationship with Gracie.

Gracie had attended Melissa's high school graduation. Gracie had made her prom dress. Gracie had driven Melissa down to Charlottesville to help her set up her freshman dorm room at the University of Virginia. Gracie had fed her ice cream when she'd broken up with Chris. And in the last three weeks, since Grammy had died, Gracie had provided the blue-plate special free of charge.

Gracie also made no bones about the fact that she intended to dance at Melissa's wedding—someday soon.

She gazed down at Melissa's book and shook her head. "Girl, it's Friday night, and here you are perched on your stool like you have been every night since Harriet died. You need to stop with the books and go find yourself a real man."

"I don't think so. I tried that once, and you know how it turned out. Besides, book boyfriends are much easier, and you don't have to clean up after them."

Gracie snorted. "You wouldn't clean up after anyone anyway."

Melissa nodded. "That's probably true. I love my dust bunnies. They're way sweeter than Grammy's cats."

"Exactly my point. You're too young to settle into the role of crazy cat-lady spinster. You should sell out, hon, and go somewhere exotic where rich, handsome bachelors hang out in droves."

Melissa gave Gracie one of Grammy's evil-eyed looks. "I could say the same for you."

"I don't have cats, and I don't want to sell out."

"So?"

"I guess you have a point," Gracie said as she scanned the diner, which had exactly one other customer this evening.

Several chain restaurants had opened up at the new strip mall down near the highway interchange. The new competition had siphoned off a lot of Gracie's evening business. Just like the online book retailers had siphoned off a lot of Secondhand Prose's business.

"I think I need to change my menu," Gracie continued on a long, sorrowful sigh.

"I like your menu just the way it is. People will get tired of the chain restaurants. I'm sure of it."

Gracie could give a look as well as she could take one. "Melissa, you are so stuck in your rut you can't even see the road in front of you anymore."

Melissa shrugged this off and turned back to her book.

Gracie freshened her tea, rang up the other customer, and returned to the lunch counter, where she sat down with a copy of *People* magazine. They sat together reading for a few minutes before Gracie asked, "Do you think he got her pregnant?"

"Huh?" Melissa looked up from her book, which just happened to have a plot line involving a secret baby. She was momentarily confused. "Who got pregnant?"

"Mia Paquet."

"Mia Paquet's pregnant? That's good news, if it makes her retire from reality television."

"Don't be superior, Melissa. A lot of people liked her in that show about Vegas pole dancers."

"So someone knocked her up?" Melissa glanced at Gracie's magazine. A big color photo of Mia Paquet and her cleavage dominated the page. A small black-and-white inset showed the reality star on the arm of some ridiculously cute guy wearing a tux and a bad-boy smile.

"Not just someone," Gracie said. "Daniel Lyndon."

"Oh, for crying out loud. Which Lyndon is he?"

"One of Charles's boys. Dropped out of college and seems to be intent on blowing his trust fund out in California."

"Give it a rest, Gracie. The Lyndons are not the saints and martyrs you seem to think they are."

"Danny is just young and misguided. He'll come around."

"If he got Mia Paquet pregnant, I certainly hope he marries her."

"I do, too. But you know how things go in Hollywood."

"Whatever." Melissa went back to reading.

"I'm much more worried about David," Gracie said, smoothing back her outrageously bright red hair.

When Gracie got on the subject of the Lyndons, she was like a pit bull with a bone. Melissa put her finger down at her place in the book and looked up again.

"He's not moving on with his life, bless his heart. He needs to find love again," Gracie continued.

Melissa closed her book. If she wanted to finish *The Lonesome Cowboy,* she would have to leave the diner. "Okay, I can see how David needs to move on, but please don't put me on your list of possible mates for him, okay? I mean, I feel for the guy. I knew Shelly a little bit. She used to come in the store all the time with Willow Petersen and buy romances by the dozens."

"See?" Gracie said. "You and David's late wife are a lot alike."

"No, we weren't. She was all about being a nice wife and fitting in with the Lyndon family's plans for David's political career. Can you see me doing that? Ever?"

"You could learn..."

"Gracie, please. I don't like Pam Lyndon, and I'm not interested in her son."

"Only because your grandmother carried a grudge. You know it's time to lay that to rest with her, don't you?"

"I guess."

"And you could do worse than hooking up with a Lyndon. If David isn't the one for you, he's got four or five cousins. They're all handsome as the devil."

Melissa ground her teeth. "Gracie, stop. I don't want anything to do with any of the Lyndons. Period. End of subject."

But of course it wasn't the end of the subject, because the way things were shaping up, she would be selling the Lyndons the one thing she held most dear.

CHAPTER THREE

$\mathcal{M}$r. Hottie Professor made Melissa's Tuesday when he returned to Secondhand Prose. He walked through the door and almost bowled Melissa over in the front aisle, where she was shelving a few books on military history. In fact, she would have toppled right over if the guy hadn't snagged her shoulders and steadied her.

"Oh, hi," she said, taking a step back and shrugging off his touch, which had sent an electric shock down her backbone that woke up her girl parts. They had been dead to her for such a long time that she hardly even remembered she had them.

And now suddenly there they were, awake and aware and...well...aroused.

Whoa, wait one sec. She was not about to let her hormones take a dive into insanity. This guy was more than merely handsome. He was like Chris—an intellectual. And Chris was just the latest in a long line of attractive, brainy boyfriends, all of whom had broken her heart.

Mr. Professor looked utterly tempting today in his skinny jeans, oxford cloth button-down, and a blue tweed sweater. The guy definitely had the urban casual vibe going for him—the kind that took a sizable clothing budget to achieve.

"Hi," she said. "How did you enjoy the Thoreau?"

"To be honest, it sucked."

"You didn't like *Walden*, really?" She blurted the words in surprise. He looked exactly like the type of guy who would not only enjoy Thoreau, but make a big deal of discussing it.

"No, I didn't. It doesn't work as a manual for living off the grid in the twenty-first century. And Thoreau is kind of preachy. I mean, it's depressing to discover that I'm living a life of quiet desperation caused by the weight of my personal possessions."

"Only if you're the type of person who values material things."

"I know. And that's why I'm here. I have a plan to improve myself."

"You do?" she asked. Was he flirting or trying to have a book discussion, or maybe both?

"Yes. I came to volunteer," he said.

"Volunteer?"

"Yeah. You need help, and I'm here to lend a hand."

"Doing what?" Several things came to mind, none of them involving books, unless he might consider reading poetry to her. Robert Browning would be perfect. She took another step back.

"I'm here to do whatever it is you need me to do. And I don't need the seven twenty-five an hour. According to Thoreau, working for nothing is more enlightening than working for peanuts."

He took another step forward, invading her space with impunity. He plucked the books from her hand.

"Ah," he said, studying their spines, "these are military history, so they get shelved here, right?"

She found herself nodding.

"By title or author?"

"Author."

He turned and started shelving the books.

"Look, you can't just—"

"What? Give you some help?" He finished shelving the books and turned back toward her.

"Um, I can't pay you."

"I know. And I have a plan for that, too. See, I've been trying to follow in Thoreau's footsteps—staying in a cabin that's way off the grid—but I've discovered that I can't survive without Internet. So I thought maybe we could work out an arrangement, you know? I'll give you a few hours a day doing whatever, and in return you can let me set up my laptop somewhere and borrow your Internet."

Something didn't add up. The guys who lived in those remote cabins usually wore camo vests or fishing shirts, not urban-hip tweed sweaters. She cleared her throat and tried to sound tough and decisive. "Uh, thanks, but I told you I don't need help."

"Then why do you keep the 'Help Wanted' poster on the front door?"

She shrugged, and they stood staring at each other for a long moment.

"Look," he finally said on a long breath, his eyes going even more soulful, "the truth is I'm a writer and—"

"Wait a sec. You're a writer?" Now she understood the tweeds and the bulky sweaters and the Byronic hair and her fatal attraction. She loved writers. They were, in her opinion, practically gods. And here stood a particularly handsome specimen, right in the middle of her bookstore.

He nodded. "Yeah, I am a writer, and I—"

"Oh my God. What's your name?"

* * *

Damn. What now? If the bookshop girl stayed abreast of current events, she'd recognize his name, and he damn sure didn't want to have a discussion of his failings as a journalist. He also didn't want her blabbing her mouth around town. He just wanted something to occupy his time while he considered what he was going to do with the rest of his life. He'd discovered that brooding about the future, while spending endless days utterly alone in a cabin, was murder on his psyche.

He would have to lie.

"I'm not famous," he said. "I'm not even published."

"Oh," Melissa said in a disappointed tone.

He stuck out his hand. "I'm Jeff Talbert. Author in the making." This was only a half-truth. Like every journalist worth his salt, Jeff was sure he had a novel in him somewhere. He'd been talking about writing a book for years, but he'd done nothing about actually starting it.

He studied her face, waiting to see if she bought any of this, especially the abridged version of his Jefferson Talbert-Lyndon byline. She seemed to take him utterly at face value.

She took his hand, her palm warm and soft. "I'm Melissa Portman," she said. "I inherited this store from my grandmother."

"And I'm here to help you shelve books in return for borrowing your Internet. Oh, and I also intend to make friends with your demon cat."

Melissa let go of a long breath. "I've told you, I don't need help. And forget about Dickens. He doesn't like people."

"I find that hard to believe."

She cocked her head, and Jeff swore her cheeks colored. She looked a lot like the vintage book illustration of Snow White on her pink T-shirt—pale skin, a round face with rosy cheeks, and a dark cloud of hair pulled away from her face with a plaid hairband. Her skinny jeans were green and hugged her curves, and she wasn't wearing any socks with her red Converse low-top lace-ups.

She eyed him from behind her black glasses, one eyebrow arched. "I'm not kidding. Dickens is a crazy cat. Don't try to pet him. You'll draw back a bloody nub."

"Okay. I'll stay away from the cats." He took another step forward in the narrow aisle, forcing her to retreat again. "I'll just head over to the checkout and start sorting the piles of books over there."

"I told you already, I don't need or want your help," Melissa said, crossing her arms over her Snow White T-shirt. She looked bad-ass, in a colorfully hip way.

He ignored her and simply took another step forward and then eased his way around her, brushing against her in the process. She smelled great, like a field of wildflowers.

He headed for the checkout, where he picked up the book on top of one lopsided pile—a hardback edition of *Robinson Crusoe*. "This is fiction," he said, laying the book aside and picking up the next one, a reference book on how to knit. "This goes in the how-to, reference area."

He laid that one down to start another subpile, then glanced over his shoulder. The adorable Melissa Portman still had her arms crossed, only now there was a big rumple across her brow. He wanted to erase those lines.

"How am I doing so far?" he asked.

"I don't need your help."

"Of course you do." He turned away and sorted several more books, while Melissa's gaze burned a hole in his back between his shoulder blades.

The standoff lasted several minutes until Dickens, the demon cat, jumped down from his throne in the window and padded toward Jeff, his amber eyes dilated, his tail erect, ears perked. The body language seemed friendly enough, but Jeff could only see the cat out of the corner of his eye.

Jeff had had plenty of experience with feral cats in his day, so he avoided direct eye contact. He'd learned just about everything anyone ever needed to know about wild cats during his visits to Grandmother Talbert—a woman lovingly referred to as the Crazy Cat Lady on the Hudson.

So he braced for the cat to pounce, with claws extended.

But the attack never came. Instead Dickens gave a friendly sounding meow and then pussyfooted up against Jeff and gave him a little head butt that was a cat's classic request for attention.

He squatted down slowly and let Dickens get a good sniff of him before he carefully and gently rubbed his hands from the cat's head to his tail. The animal arched its hind end up to press against his touch.

Dickens's eyes closed to slits, and he started to purr as Jeff settled in to scratch him liberally behind his ears. When Jeff took his hand away, the cat moved forward and leaned his forehead against Jeff's knee.

He picked Dickens up and settled him in his arms. Then he turned toward Melissa. "See, I told you I would make friends with your cat."

Melissa's eyes had grown wide behind her glasses. "I'm seeing it, but I don't believe it," she said. "What are you, some kind of cat whisperer?"

CHAPTER FOUR

When Dickens came down from his tree and allowed Jeff to pick him up, Melissa had no choice, really, but to let Jeff stay and volunteer.

She relented for Dickens's sake. Since Grammy's death, Dickens had occupied the cat tree in the window almost twenty-four-seven, allowing no one to touch him, hardly eating, and leaving his perch only for litter-box calls.

She told herself that letting Jeff volunteer was about the cat, but having Jeff shelve the books that Grammy had purchased before she died gave Melissa a big dose of hope in a situation that was utterly hopeless. Having someone else around the store eased the loneliness that had settled into the deepest recesses of her heart.

Still, it was a fantasy, this idea of fixing up the store. She needed to end the charade. Tomorrow she would make an appointment with Walter Braden, the Realtor in town who handled commercial real estate sales. He'd already called a few times to let her know that the Lyndons were anxious to make an offer on the building Grammy had owned for sixty years.

But Melissa's resolve disappeared on Wednesday morning, when Jeff showed up on her doorstep bright and early bearing gifts: a new, expensive-looking coffeemaker for the back room, a bag of cat treats for Hugo, and a cat-nip mouse for Dickens, who came down from his tree and played with it for a solid hour.

"So what's on today's agenda?" Jeff asked after he'd set up the coffeemaker and brewed the first pot of the day. Why the man didn't just get his coffee across the street was a mystery. But once she took her first sip of coffee from his new machine, she had to admit that the guy knew how to brew a good cup of coffee. Obviously Jeff was a master at winning lonely cat ladies over.

Plus she had a weakness for guys who wore tweed jackets...and formfitting white T-shirts and jeans, which was Wednesday's outfit.

Yup, he was as yummy as the coffee.

"Let's get the boxes behind the counter cleaned up and shelved," she said, casting aside her resolution about calling Walter Braden.

They went to work hauling books around the store while she attempted to give him the third degree. But he was slippery. Their conversations always left something to be desired.

"Where are you staying?" she asked.

"Up on the ridge." No specific address. And the Blue Ridge ran right through the middle of the state. Saying you were living in the Blue Ridge Mountains wasn't very informative.

"Where are you from?" she asked as they tidied up the history section.

"New York." Of course he was from New York. She could hear it in his accent.

"State? City?"

"Both." He was a master of the one-syllable response.

"Where did you learn to handle cats?" she asked as they reorganized the fiction department.

"My grandmother. She was a cat lady."

Two sentences. She was on a roll. "Mine too."

"I figured."

And that was the end of that conversation, unless she wanted to tell him all about Grammy, and at the moment conversations about Grammy tended to become overly emotional. She wasn't ready for Jeff to see her cry. And besides, she really ought to be calling Walter about selling the place. Tomorrow.

But on Thursday she forgot all about calling Walter. She'd had trouble sleeping that night, and she was all prepared with a bunch of book-related questions. Jeff seemed to know his literature.

So as they started dusting every inch of the store, she asked him if he'd ever read any Jack Kerouac. It was just the first question on her list of sneaky ones designed to see if he was a literature snob, like Chris.

He gave her a look from the measureless dark of his eyes. "Is that a trick question?"

Damn, he was onto her. "How could a simple question about a book be a trick question? Have you read *On the Road*?"

"Have you?"

"Of course I have."

"Did you read it because you thought it was hip?"

She blinked at him because the truth was she had read it because Chris had told her she needed to read it in order to be well rounded. She had not particularly enjoyed the book.

Jeff smiled before she could respond. "Don't worry. I won't tell the in crowd that you didn't much like it. The problem with reading Kerouac today is that everyone thinks he's cool, when the truth is, he was just the writer guy, you know, the dude with the journal keeping notes on the crazy stuff his friends did."

"I'm not worried about what people think," she said. "So, are you like him? I mean, are you the writer guy who keeps a journal and chronicles the crazy stuff your friends do?"

His smile faded. "No. Not really. But I have a question for you."

"Okay." She wasn't sure she wanted to be on the receiving end of any questions.

"What were you reading that day when I came in the store the first time?"

Oh, crap. She wasn't about to tell him she'd been reading a romance novel. How pathetic would that be? So she thought fast and lied. *"Oliver Twist."*

His mouth turned up adorably. He didn't believe her. "Good book. I wholeheartedly believe that we should all ask for more."

And that was the end of her attempt at using book talk to discover his secrets. It was, however, the beginning of several long conversations about the classics, where she discovered that Jeff Talbert had actually read *Jane Eyre.* He'd hated every minute of it, but he'd read it in high school.

He'd also read *The Call of the Wild* and *The Last of the Mohicans.* Those books he'd liked. She wasn't surprised.

All that book talk was tantalizing. So when Thursday

came to a close, she took a leap and asked, "So, uh, you want to go down to the Jaybird for a drink or something?"

He gave her a soulful brown-eyed look and shook his head. "No. Maybe some other time." And then he left the store, but not before he glanced out the window as if checking to see who might be out there on the sidewalk, watching.

* * *

He should stop. Now. Going to Secondhand Prose on a daily basis was a dumb idea. Even though the store wasn't exactly the type of place Pam would frequent, he still risked being seen. He'd learned from the grapevine that Aunt Pam didn't spend much time with Uncle Mark in DC. She stayed at Charlotte's Grove and managed things. What things she managed were not precisely clear, but it wasn't unusual for Aunt Pam to be seen on Liberty Avenue shopping or visiting with merchants.

Maybe he should book a flight to the Bahamas or something.

He jettisoned the idea. For some reason, helping Melissa clean and organize her grandmother's bookstore had become the thing he wanted to do right now. It filled his days. It gave him purpose.

And maybe he was accomplishing something important—pulling Melissa out of her funk. She may not have shed a tear or said a word, but Melissa was grieving for her Grammy. Working to clean and organize the place seemed to have given her a purpose, too.

She obviously loved that store and wanted to keep it open. But she didn't have enough customers. That kept him up at night, worrying. And worrying about how to save Secondhand Prose seemed way more productive than worrying about his lost career in journalism.

So, despite his better judgment, he returned to the shop on Friday with a bag filled with color-coded adhesive tags.

"We're going to change your pricing system," he announced as he came through the door and gave Dickens a long head scratch.

"Why would we do that?" Melissa asked.

She must have been anticipating his arrival this morning, since she was standing in the history section at the front of the store, but she didn't seem to be shelving books or doing anything at all, except waiting for him. Today she greeted him wearing a bright yellow *Hansel and Gretel* T-shirt with red jeans.

He warmed at his first sight of her. What was she going to do today? Yesterday's book discussions had been way more fun than Wednesday's third degree. Last night she'd even asked him out for a drink. Saying no had been hard, but he needed to figure out where the Jaybird Café was located and whether Aunt Pam was a regular customer.

Scoping the place out was on his to-do list. But until he could fully define safe, Pam-free zones, he was sticking to his plan of mostly hiding out at Dad's cabin or here at the bookstore, where no one ever shopped.

"Change is good for the soul," he said, knowing full well that Secondhand Prose didn't really need a change in its pricing system. It basically needed a total makeover and an influx of lots of cash. Not to mention advertising and new merchandise. But she would probably get all freaked out if he said any of that. And besides, saying stuff like that might be offensive. After all, the bookshop had been owned and managed by Melissa's grandmother, and

Melissa hadn't said one thing to suggest that she wanted to change things around here.

In fact, Melissa was resistant to change. Which was to be expected. So small steps were called for.

"I've got colored adhesive tags. I figure we could group books and price them accordingly. Like all hardbound books at one price and all mass-market paperbacks at another."

"Uh, well, we sort of do that already."

"Yeah, but you have to handwrite a price sticker for every book in the store. Wouldn't it be easier to post signs with the color codes and then just put colored dots on each book?"

She nodded. "I guess, but it's a lot of work to do that for books that already have prices on them."

He shrugged. "I know, but I don't have anything better to do."

So he got to work, and before noon came around, Melissa was helping him while they had a lively discussion of *The Catcher in the Rye*, *The Color Purple*, and Ayn Rand's political philosophy.

When Friday came to a close, he didn't want to leave, but he didn't dare ask her out for a drink. So he reluctantly headed back up the ridge, but before he was out of cell phone range, his phone vibrated. It was his father, calling all the way from Japan.

He pulled the Land Rover over to the side of the road and punched the talk button on his phone. "Hello, Dad," he said.

"Where the hell are you?"

Jeff said nothing.

"Don't pull the silent treatment on me. Your mother is about to call the police and proclaim that you've been kidnapped."

He sighed. "I told her I was going away for a while. She knows I haven't been kidnapped."

"That's debatable. She's hysterical."

"You know, she wouldn't be hysterical if you hadn't allowed the White House to issue that statement in which you said I had no business being a journalist. I think that ticked her off. It sure ticked me off."

"Well, that's too bad. Because it's the truth. Go home, Jeff. Go manage your mother's money. She has so much of it, I doubt that I you could screw things up the way you've screwed up the Durand nomination. But whatever you do, stay out of journalism and stay out of politics. Because you sure didn't inherit any of the Lyndon smarts when it comes to those things."

That was it. He'd had enough. "Ambassador Lyndon," he said in a tight voice, "I'm happy to comply with your request that I take myself out of the family. Tomorrow I'll be calling my lawyers and starting the formal process of removing your last name from mine." He pressed the disconnect button and sat there for several minutes breathing hard while his fury subsided. He hated his father. The feeling was clearly mutual.

He probably ought to move out of Dad's cabin. But what the heck. The guy was in Japan, and Jeff had the key. Besides, leaving Shenandoah Falls was the last thing he wanted to do right now.

* * *

On Saturday Melissa found herself anticipating Jeff's arrival, and the moment the front door opened with a jingle, she and Dickens had almost the same reaction. The cat sat up and meowed plaintively until Jeff stopped and gave him a good scratch behind the ears and told him what a beautiful feline he was. Melissa got hot and bothered just watching him stroke the cat.

Hugo wasn't about to let Dickens get all the attention. He waddled out from his lair in the back and demanded equal time. Jeff lavished praise on him, too, allowing Melissa to appreciate Jeff's manly but gentle hands, with their long, patrician fingers.

Once Jeff satisfied the cats, he turned and strolled past her toward the back room and the coffeemaker. "Can I interest you in a cup of hazelnut coffee light on the cream, heavy on the sugar?"

He pulled a package of coffee and a coffee grinder from the sack he was carrying. "I stopped at the store on the way in."

Wow. He'd been listening when she'd said that hazelnut coffee was her favorite. Boy, he was kind of terrific, wasn't he?

He disappeared into the back room and emerged several minutes later with a mug of coffee, made exactly the way she liked it. She was ready to melt right in front of him. Where had this guy come from and why was he here?

"So what's it going to be today?" he asked.

The coffee warmed her hand. The spark in his brown eyes warmed up every other part of her. "I don't know, Jeff," she said. "I told you I didn't need help. Why don't you tell me what I need?"

He grinned. "How about I fix the ladder?" He gestured to the floor-to-ceiling shelves along the northwest wall. "Then you could use the upper bookshelves again."

"I can't even remember the last time we had access to those shelves. I'm pretty sure the ladder is long gone."

"Actually, I found it in the back room when I was tidying up."

She was tempted to tell him to forget the ladder. She could use someone to tidy up the small apartment above the bookstore where she was living. But she held her tongue. She didn't want him to know what a slob she was. Her inability to keep things neat and tidy had been a serious bone of contention between her and Chris. "It's missing some pieces, I think," she said instead.

"Is it? Let's figure out what it needs and get it working again." He strolled past her, leaving his yummy scent— soap, coffee, and cedar—behind.

She settled into a comfy chair behind the checkout and watched him work. Today he was channeling his inner lumbersexual. His beard was impeccably groomed, and he wore a plaid flannel shirt and a chest-hugging black T-shirt. He'd left his skinny black jeans behind this morning and instead he wore a pair of faded blue ones that were almost threadbare in the seat and the knees.

Yummy.

He'd been impressive with his colored dots, but when he pulled out the old toolbox from the back room, along with the pieces of the broken library ladder, the show definitely took an erotic turn. What was it about a man in a flannel shirt and faded jeans using a screwdriver?

It took him two trips to the hardware store for parts, but by noon he had the ladder rolling along the rails the way it had when Melissa was eight years old and had first come to live with Grammy.

He was using the ladder to reorganize the books in the children's area, near the back of the store, when the front door opened, jingling the bell. Pamela Lyndon—who Grammy always referred to as the Duchess of Charlotte's

Grove—came gliding into the store wearing a designer dress in her signature shade of pale blue.

The duchess got about two steps into the bookshop before Dickens arched his back, fluffed out his fur, and yowled at her in a way that could only be called bloodcurdling.

Several things happened in quick succession after this.

First the duchess said, "Goodness!" and retreated a step, clutching her purse in front of her like a shield. "Shoo, kitty," she said in a totally ineffective voice.

Second Jeff, who was up on the ladder shelving fiction on the highest shelf, turned toward the cat and said several X-rated words. He must have thrown his weight to one side, because the ladder's rail (which he apparently hadn't checked earlier in the day) detached from the bookshelf. The ladder unexpectedly pivoted and slammed Jeff into the back wall of the store.

And that's when the unthinkable happened.

A long time ago, when the store had been more successful, Grammy had put up a bunch of coat hooks on the back wall, where she'd hung merchandise for kids. The coat hooks were empty at the moment. But when Jeff slammed against the wall, somehow his slightly threadbare jeans got snagged, so when the ladder pivoted again, Jeff didn't pivot with it. Instead, he was left behind, hanging there on the wall for a moment, suspended by the seat of his pants.

That didn't last very long. There was an audible *riiiiippp* as his jeans split. Jeff came down, dumped unceremoniously onto Melissa's favorite beanbag chair. His pants stayed put, snarled in the coat hook, his legs still caught in them.

"Good God," the duchess said.

Which was totally an understatement, because Jeff had started his day without underwear.

Melissa was momentarily stunned by the view, which

probably explained why she was a little late in coming to Jeff's aid. But that was okay because the beanbag chair had cushioned his fall. He shucked off his shoes, disentangled his legs, and covered his private parts with those manly hands of his.

Even so, the view was stirring. Especially when he stood up and streaked into the back room, slamming the door behind his incredibly hot backside.

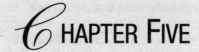

CHAPTER FIVE

amn.

It was bad losing his pants. Although he still wasn't sure exactly how that had happened. One moment he'd been up on the ladder, and the next he'd been stuck to the wall and then falling.

A flush of embarrassment heated his body from head to toe. This was his penance for not doing his laundry. Although he had to admit he didn't mind Melissa seeing his junk, and in the nanosecond before he covered himself, she'd certainly been looking. With interest.

Being half naked in Melissa's presence didn't suck. Not so much with Aunt Pam though.

Why the hell was Pam here? Of all the places in Shenandoah Falls, this was the last place he'd ever expected his aunt to visit. Had she recognized him?

He eased the door open a crack, just large enough to see the checkout counter where Pam and Melissa were talking.

"So, Melissa," Pam said in her Tennessee drawl, "I see you've been making improvements. I'm so glad. Maybe my visit is well timed." She cleared her throat, then glanced toward the scene of his disrobing. "Who was that man?"

He tensed. Pam would figure it out if Melissa said his name.

"Just the new helper," Melissa said, thank God.

"Uh-huh." Pam paused for a long moment as she swept her gaze over the store's interior before turning back toward Melissa. "Darlin', I know your grandmother had a blind spot about some things. But we both know her determination never to mortgage this property was old-fashioned."

"She had her reasons," Melissa said, crossing her arms over the *Sleeping Beauty* T-shirt she was wearing today.

"Well, yes, I suppose she did. But look, we need your help. The Town Council and the Liberty Avenue Property Owners Association have agreed to move forward with a request for a block grant to revitalize the historic structures downtown. That means we need every property owner between Lord Fairfax Highway and Sixth Street to agree to a special assessment that will provide the matching funds for the project."

"Every property owner? That means the Lyndon Companies and me, right? And when you say a special assessment, you mean a special tax, don't you?" Melissa sounded downright belligerent. Her body language said it all. She didn't like Aunt Pam.

Pam spoke again. "It's true that the Lyndon Companies owns more buildings than anyone else, but there are a total of five additional landowners, including yourself. And an assessment is not a tax."

"Oh, okay, how is it different?"

"To begin with, it's voluntary. But those who chip in

will get matching funds to renovate their storefronts. By participating, you'll save a lot of money on the storefront renovations needed to get this building listed on the historic register. And, darlin', this building is worthy of that honor."

"I would love to see this building on the historic register, Mrs. Lyndon. But I can't afford your assessment without a mortgage. And if I mortgage the place, I'll probably have to close the store and find a more lucrative tenant."

"Darlin', that doesn't sound terrible to me. You could make money on this building. And while I know this is a difficult time for you, I really need your support. The deadline to submit our application is June fifteenth. That's just three weeks away. We'll have a better chance of winning this grant if we have unanimous participation."

"I need to think about it," Melissa said.

Aunt Pam leaned over the checkout, her body language aggressive. "In a few days you'll be officially in arrears on your property taxes. At that time the county will start proceedings to foreclose on this property, and Lyndon Properties is ready, willing, and able to buy this building. We'd prefer to pay full price if you're willing to sell. But you could finance this, Melissa, and make a lot of money. Rick Sharp down at the bank is ready to help you with the financing, and I know Walter Braden would help you find a well-paying commercial tenant."

"I need to think about it," Melissa repeated as she uncrossed her arms and stood toe to toe with Pam, staring her down.

Pam stepped back. "All right. I understand. But you don't have much time left, you hear?" She turned and headed toward the door. Dickens hissed at her on her way out.

* * *

Melissa was shaking when the bell above the door finally jangled and Pam Lyndon left the store. The time had come to make a decision. And, unfortunately, the decision would require her to close Secondhand Prose. Forever.

Her eyes filled with tears as she studied Dickens. "Maybe Jeff will take you," she whispered, then blew out a long breath. She stood there for a moment, collecting herself and wiping her cheeks.

When she'd regained control, she headed toward the back of the store to examine the damaged pants; then she headed toward the back room.

"Hey, are you okay in there?" she asked through the door.

"I'm good," Jeff replied. His voice eased her jangled nerves and soothed her aching heart. Just the sound of him calmed her down.

"I just checked your jeans. They're beyond repair."

Silence greeted her from the other side of the door, and her momentary melancholy was replaced by something else. It might be fun to open the door and have a good look at him. It would definitely distract her from her problems.

"Guess I picked the wrong day to go commando, huh?" he finally said. "Truth is, I need to do some laundry."

"Do you do laundry?"

"What does that mean?"

"Oh, nothing. It's just that your wardrobe is always so..."

"What?"

"I don't know. Together. I figured you took everything to the dry cleaner's."

"Well, yeah, I do."

"There's a good dry cleaner on South Third Street. Just sayin'."

"Thanks. But that doesn't exactly solve my current problem. Got any ideas?"

Melissa had a few, but they were all bad ones. The best thing would be to get him some pants so her libido would go back to sleep.

"Okay, look, hang loose..." She paused a moment because these words brought an image to her mind that was X-rated. "Uh...um, maybe that was the wrong choice of words. Just wait there for a minute, and I'll get you a pair of pants."

She checked the size of the shredded jeans and then headed down the street to the Haggle Shop, the local consignment store, where she scoured the rack for a pair of jeans with a thirty-four-inch waist and a thirty-six inseam.

The Haggle Shop had lots of cool vintage stuff, but you never knew what you'd find there, and the selection of guys' pants in a thirty-six inseam was limited to four pairs of ugly beige khakis and one pair of cool argyle golf pants in kelly green and pastel yellow.

* * *

The pants were loud. And fun. Wearing them was like being invited into Melissa's slightly weird, totally unique world of fashion. He opened the door to find her standing there with a naughty gleam in her too-blue eyes.

"I like the pants," he said. "I'm thinking I need more color in my life." He took a step forward. This time she didn't retreat, and he caught a whiff of her scent: a mountain meadow.

"Look, Melissa, I overheard what that woman said." He touched her shoulder, and she pressed herself in to his hand. Just like a cat hunting for a good scratch.

"I've been trying to tell you that the bookstore is a lost cause," she said. "I have to put it up for sale.

I'm scheduling an appointment with Walter from Braden Realty on Monday." Melissa's voice was full of defeat.

His heart stumbled. "Won't that play right into that woman's hand?" His words came out in a rush.

"Maybe. But it's got to be done. Jeff, I'm sorry. I've been sitting here for a few weeks, unable to make a decision. That's why I left the 'Help Wanted' sign on the door. And then you arrived, and I got all caught up in the ridiculous fantasy that maybe I could keep the store going. But I can't. Taxes are due, and I have to mortgage the place to pay them. But I can't make mortgage payments by selling used books. There just isn't enough income in it." Her voice wobbled as she spoke, and then her eyes filled with tears.

He took her big black glasses off her face and pulled her into his arms. "It's okay. Just let it out. I'm thinking maybe you haven't even let yourself cry for your grandmother."

She didn't cry. But she leaned against him like Hugo did when he wanted attention. Jeff stroked the back of her head, her curly hair gliding under his palms, igniting a deep yearning. He had to admit the truth. It wasn't so much the bookstore that had him coming here every day as it was Melissa. He wanted to protect her. He wanted to be the comic book hero who swoops in and saves the world and gets the hot girl at the same time.

And why the hell not? He didn't need any superpowers to fix this problem. Money would do the trick, and if Jeff had anything, it was money—a gigantic and bothersome trust fund that made people think he didn't have any ambition or drive. A mother with so much money she needed someone to manage it all. Money was a big pain in the neck for Jeff, but it could solve all of Melissa's problems.

He could fix this for her and thwart Aunt Pam's plans

at the same time. He just needed one day to make the arrangements.

Like changing his name, it would be the ultimate statement of rebellion.

* * *

Oh God. She was in Jeff's arms, and it felt like heaven, leaning up against his hard, male body. A girl could get used to leaning on a guy like Jeff. He was steady. Dependable. Sweet. Considerate. And he dressed well.

Also, his lips were warm and soft where they rested against her forehead. She wanted him to do something naughty with those lips.

She tilted her head, hoping he would get the message that she wanted to be kissed. He was all blurry since she wasn't wearing her glasses, so she couldn't read his expression. Was he just being kind? That would be so frustrating.

She wanted more from him than help with the store. The store was irrelevant. It had to be closed and the building had to be sold.

And just like that she made the decision she'd been putting off. She would sell out, and she would stop waiting around for life to begin.

Today was the first day of the rest of her life, and she was going to seize control of it. Jeff Talbert might not be a forever love, but he was a nice guy and she was alone in the world. Besides, she'd been living like a nun for too long.

"So," she said, letting her voice drop into the husky range. "The store is closed tomorrow. You want to do something fun? I could take you up to the falls. It's a fun hike. Or are you opposed to long walks in the woods?"

"Are you asking me out on a date?"

"Uh, yeah, I guess."

"You guess? You don't know?"

Damn. The man was impossible.

"Yes, I'm asking you out on a date. Tomorrow."

She must have frowned at him or something because he started stroking her forehead with his thumb. The touch was comforting and arousing all at once. The cats loved it when he rubbed his thumb over their foreheads. Now she understood. She didn't purr, but her body definitely started to rev itself up for more. In fact, she closed her eyes and made a little moan of pleasure.

That obviously did it for him. He stopped stroking her, settled his hands on her hips, and pulled her in tight against his chest and thighs and all his other hard manly parts. His lips went back to her temple, but this time he kissed his way down the side of her face, over her cheek to the corner of her mouth. She moved into the kiss and opened up for him.

When their tongues finally met, she threw her arms around his neck and pulled him into the kiss. He was a virtuoso at this dance of tongues, doling out something sweet, carnal, mysterious, and addictive.

But when one of his hands left her hip and moved up toward her breast, she inadvertently stiffened. It happened like a reflex. She might fantasize about no-strings sex, but she was abysmally bad at actually having it. Her underlying caution always reared its head.

Damn.

And wouldn't you know it? Jeff was such a gentleman that he backed away a little. "Not okay?" he asked.

What was she supposed to do now? It was all so awkward. So she said nothing, even though she really wanted him to go back to kissing her and maybe even touching her.

Instead he relaxed his grip and put her in a safer zone without actually letting her go. "So," he said in a rough voice, "I'd love to take a hike with you up to the falls."

Oh, good. She'd have a second chance to get this right. "Great," she said.

"Cool," he replied. "Why don't we meet at Gracie's Diner for brunch or something?"

No, no, no. She backed out of his embrace. "Uh, no, not Gracie's. Let's meet at the Old Laurel Chapel. In the parking lot. At nine o'clock."

"The Old Laurel Chapel?"

"It's off Morgan Avenue, just north of State Road 606. There's a little gravel parking lot there and access to the Appalachian Trail, which connects to the trail that leads to the falls."

"What about brunch?"

"I'll pack a picnic."

There was a beat of silence before he said, "Are you ashamed to be seen in public with me?"

"Oh, no, that's not it. You see Gracie is…" Her shoulders tensed and her voice stumbled.

"Gracie's what?"

"A busybody." And so much more. Gracie would grill Jeff because she saw it as her purpose in life to find Melissa the right husband, and Jeff was probably not that guy even if his kisses were amazing. He was probably just a guy passing through, looking for some fun.

"Oh, I see. Good thinking. I don't want any gossip," he said. Which seemed odd for a guy from out of town. But she let it slide.

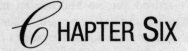

CHAPTER SIX

*M*elissa hardly slept a wink. She kept replaying the kiss in her mind, not to mention that moment when Jeff had scooted, butt-naked, into the back room. Hot. So hot.

She gave up trying to sleep at six a.m., when she got up and took a frigid shower, threw on some clothes, and headed to the Food Lion for the picnic stuff and a box of condoms.

Buying them was like burning the bridges to her past. Deciding to have a little fun with Jeff had become an important part of letting go of the store and moving on with her life.

A few hours later, with a backpack full of sandwiches and other goodies, she pulled off Morgan Avenue into the patchy gravel lot by the Old Laurel Chapel.

The stone ruin hadn't seen a congregation in more than a hundred years, and it had been sadly neglected during that time. Its roof had all but fallen in, leaving behind four stone walls with empty vaulted windows. Today the mountain laurel surrounding the building was in full, glorious bloom, edging the cemetery and dotting the woods with its pale pink blossoms.

Jeff hadn't arrived yet, so Melissa left her car and strolled through the ancient graveyard, where many of the headstones bore the surname of Lyndon or McNeil—families who had helped to found Shenandoah Falls almost three centuries ago.

The sound of tires crunching on gravel had her raising her head in time to see Jeff pull a late-model Land Rover into the lot. With a car like that, he wasn't hurting for money. But what did he do for a living besides being an unpublished author? Where did he come from? Why was he here?

Maybe she'd learn the answers today. Or maybe not. She'd decided that it didn't matter. Today was about not grieving, and not worrying, and just having a little bit of fun.

"Hey," she called, and waved. "I'm over here."

He locked his car and strolled toward her, wearing a pair of jeans and a black body-hugging T-shirt that showed off his shoulders and the wide, muscular expanse of his chest.

"Sorry I'm late," he said. "I had a few phone calls I needed to make. One of them took a while."

"Business?" she asked in a leading tone.

"No, just a personal call. Family stuff." He turned away from her to inspect the church. "Wow. That looks like it's been here three hundred years."

"So, you have a family?" she asked, ignoring his comments about the chapel.

"Yeah. A mother in New York. She's kind of over-bearing and overprotective."

"Ah."

She wanted him to elaborate. Instead, he turned his gaze on her and then pulled her into a hot, sexy kiss that fogged her glasses and her brain. She wrapped her hands around the back of his head, running her fingers through his too-long hair, and tried to eat him up.

The kiss might have led to other things, but they were interrupted by a little girl who came skipping out of the woods like Little Red Riding Hood with a wicker basket on her arm. She wasn't wearing a red cloak, but her hair was certainly red. And tangled.

The child skidded to a noisy stop before she said, "Oh!"

Jeff and Melissa jumped apart like guilty teenagers caught in the act.

"Hello," the girl said.

Melissa adjusted her glasses. Oh, great. Nothing like being caught in the clinches by a Lyndon. The girl was Natalie, David Lyndon's daughter. A moment later Natalie's grandmother, Poppy Marchand, appeared at the forest's edge. Poppy was in her sixties, and Laurel Chapel was on the grounds of Eagle Hill Manor, which Poppy owned. Technically, Melissa and Jeff were trespassing.

Poppy eyed Melissa and then shifted her gaze to Jeff, where it remained for a long moment. "Hello," she said.

"Uh, hi, Mrs. Marchand. Good morning," Melissa said in a rush. "We're taking the shortcut to the Appalachian Trail. Is it okay to leave our cars in the lot?" She pointed with her thumb over her shoulder.

"You hiking up to the falls?" Poppy asked.

"Yeah."

"Nice day for it. The laurel is lovely this time of year. It's no problem about the cars. No one ever comes up here anymore." Poppy paused for a moment as she continued to study Jeff. "Do I know you? Have you visited Eagle Hill Manor before?"

"No. I'm sure we've never met."

Poppy nodded. "I guess not. But you look very familiar for some reason."

Natalie tugged at Poppy's hand. "C'mon, Grammy, let's go." She pulled Poppy toward the old church. "Let's play princess, 'kay?"

"Y'all have a nice hike," Poppy said as the girl pulled her up the steps and into the ruined chapel.

"Let's go," Melissa said, pulling Jeff in the opposite direction. "There's a short path here that connects with the Appalachian Trail. We'll walk that for a couple of miles and then take the turnoff for the falls."

They found the main trail without much trouble, and Jeff took the lead as the ground began to rise. About half a mile before they reached the turnoff for the falls, they came to a break in the forest's cover that provided a view up a rise to a grand Georgian-style brick mansion. The house stood atop the hill, with the Blue Ridge Mountains at its back and its grand portico facing the Shenandoah Valley.

Jeff stopped in his tracks and stared at the house for a long, silent moment.

Melissa played tour guide. "That's Charlotte's Grove," she said. "The house you see was built after the Revolution. But the original cabin—"

"Save the history lesson. I know all about Charlotte's Grove."

"You do?"

"That's where the Lyndons live. The people who want to buy your store." There was no mistaking the enmity in his voice.

The big concrete bunker she'd built around her heart

cracked a little bit. Jeff Talbert was on her side. She had an ally. "Yeah, they are. But the store has to be sold, you know."

He turned on her, his dark eyes suddenly intense. "No, it doesn't."

She laughed. "Jeff, it does. And I've finally made up my mind about it. So let's not talk about the store. Let's just have a fun day in the woods, okay?"

* * *

The sky got into Melissa's blue eyes somehow, and for a moment Jeff lost himself in that deep, limitless color. Looking into her eyes was almost like free-falling. He took her shoulders and drew her forward for another hard, needy kiss on her soft, open lips.

She tasted like the outdoors. Like springtime. He should have planned this better. He should have brought a couple of blankets. Maybe some condoms. She was sending up all kinds of signals that he was receiving loud and clear.

No. Just. No.

Not here, within sight of Charlotte's Grove. And not with her wearing that T-shirt with a truly gruesome illustration of innocent Little Red Riding Hood and a menacing wolf. Where did she get these T-shirts anyway? From the Brothers Grimm Department Store?

He broke the kiss. He owed her the truth about his background or he was no better than that ogling wolf on her T-shirt. He ought to say something right now, but that would ruin everything he'd put in motion yesterday afternoon. He needed one more day before he told her the truth. Once his plans were fully in place, he could tell her about his father, and she'd know right away whose side he was on.

She gazed up at him as wide-eyed as ever, even behind those glasses of hers, so innocent, so beautiful. She'd certainly found a place in his heart.

"Okay, you've got it. Today we'll pretend the Lyndons don't exist," he said.

"That sounds like the perfect plan," she said.

He gave her a quick kiss on the cheek and headed up the trail at a brisk pace, even though the path began to ascend steeply. By the time they arrived at the turnoff for the falls trail, Melissa was wheezing behind him. He turned. "I'm sorry. You should have told me to slow down."

"No, it's okay. I'm out of shape," she said on a puff of air. "This is what happens when you spend too much time in a beanbag chair reading genre fiction."

He laughed. "So you admit that you read genre fiction?"

She shrugged. "Yeah."

"So, what were you reading that day when I first came into the store and bought the Thoreau?"

She eyed him warily. "I'm not telling."

"Afraid to lose your credentials as a discerning reader?"

She laughed. "You're funny." She pointed to the trail that led off to the right. "C'mon. Let's go, but maybe a little slower. The falls are only two more miles."

The trail went up sharply for more than a mile, while the rushing sound of a fast-moving stream met their ears. Then, abruptly, the path narrowed and headed downhill through lichen-covered rocks to a patch of sandy beach at the edge of a fast-moving freestone creek—Liberty Run.

Upstream, the run cascaded down a twenty-five-foot fall, sending water droplets into the air and filling the forest with its powerful roar. Eons of flowing water had cut a plunge pool at the base of the waterfall surrounded by tumbled rocks of various sizes.

They stood for a moment, under a canopy of red oaks and yellow poplars, interspersed with the occasional hemlock. It was green here. Green rocks, green canopy. Even the run had a brown-green tinge to it, created by the tannins in the water.

"It's magical here, isn't it?" he said.

"Magical?" Melissa stepped up onto the first stone of a rocky staircase that led to the top of the falls. She didn't climb all the way. Instead she sat down and started taking off her hiking shoes.

"Look around. Can't you imagine wood elves living here? Or maybe fairies?" he asked.

She cocked her head. "Have you been reading Tolkien on the sly?"

He laughed. "No. I haven't. I don't even like fantasy. It's just that this place seems enchanted somehow."

"Well, I've been up here to the falls at least a hundred times, and it's usually just like this. No fairies or elves. But you will encounter snakes and bugs. I can also attest that the falls are ghost-free. I know this because I spent one cold, wet night up here hoping to see Elakala's ghost."

"Who's Elakala?"

"She's supposed to have been an Iroquois princess whose father insisted that she marry the wealthy son of a rival chieftain. But Elakala loved a poor brave who didn't have much in the way of worldly goods. So on her wedding day she sneaked away and threw herself off the falls." Melissa gazed up at the cascades. "I find it hard to believe that she could actually accomplish that feat, to tell you the truth, since the water doesn't drop straight down. Some have speculated that she drowned herself in the plunge pool, which is also unlikely.

"Of course, you know how these Native American legends go. Every waterfall has a similar legend, and wherever there's a story of tragic death, there's also a ghost. And the legend grows bigger every time some foolish boy dives into the pool and comes up with a Native American relic."

"People dive for relics? Really?"

She stood up and scrunched her toes in the sand by the river's edge. "You'd be surprised by some of the stuff people have brought up from the bottom of the pool. Mostly junk, but every once in a while you find something cool."

"Oh." He took off the backpack and set it down on one of the rocks by the pool.

"To tell you the truth, teenage boys dive in the pool because it has the reputation of being dangerous. And also boys will be boys," she said, rolling her eyes in a way that was clearly a challenge.

"And that means... ?"

"Every girl who grew up here in Jefferson County knows a boy who tried to impress her by diving into the pool, looking for Native American relics. It's a macho thing."

"Are you daring me to dive in the pool?"

"No. I wouldn't do any such thing," she said. He didn't believe her for one minute. Like every female, she gave off two messages at the same time. One with her words and another one with her gaze and her body.

Oh, yeah, her body. He hadn't forgotten about the feel of her hips beneath his hands or the pleasure of standing that close to her. Yeah, he had designs on her body, but he wanted her admiration, too.

Just then a purely adolescent idea popped into his brain.

He didn't stop to think it through. He simply shucked his shoes, pulled his T-shirt over his head, and dropped trou. He streaked across the sandy beach and took a deep breath.

"Oh my God, no, Jeff. The water is—"

He didn't hear the rest of her admonition before the water closed over his head. Holy God, it was freezing cold. But then again, it was only May. The summer hadn't yet warmed the water, which was also dark and murky.

He frog kicked down, fighting the stream's current, until he reached the rocky riverbed. The pool wasn't all that deep—maybe eight or nine feet—but he was totally blind. He felt along the bottom, encountering mostly round river rocks and scree. But one of the stones had an oddly flat shape. He palmed it, and with lungs burning, he pushed off the bottom.

* * *

Melissa stood by the water's edge with her heart pounding in her ears. Her racing pulse had more to do with the magnificent sight of Jeff's naked bod than her fear for his safety, although this time of year the water was pretty cold. Good thing she'd brought a blanket and some beach towels. Not to mention the box of condoms.

Which just might come in handy after all.

She was pondering what came next when his head popped up above the water. He wore a big grin, like he'd proved something to someone. Such a guy.

"Guess you just discovered that it's probably too cold to go diving for relics this time of year." These were not exactly the first words her heart wanted to say. But they were what came out when she let her brain take over.

"I found something," he said as he swam toward her.

"You found something?" Her heart, already beating hard, began to race now in anticipation of him reaching the shallow water. Full-frontal nudity worked for her. Although she had to remind herself not to be disappointed. The water was probably no more than fifty-five degrees.

He stood up, water sluicing down his chest and abs and...other parts. He held out his treasure in his open palm, but Melissa's gaze was locked on his family jewels.

He seemed unaffected by her intimate study. "It's an arrowhead. Who knew?"

"What?" Her brain was starting to work again, sort of.

He raised his head and seemed to notice for the first time that she was totally ogling him.

"Enjoying the view?" He gave her a wolfish, predatory grin.

"Yes, I am, as a matter of fact."

He took a step forward. She stepped back. "Uh, look, um, you're all wet. And..."

Oh, bad move on her part, because he lunged and caught her in his cold, wet embrace. An embrace that immediately kindled an undeniable heat inside her.

"I could throw you in," he whispered in her ear, setting off hot, freezing shivers.

"Uh, please don't. I didn't bring a change of clothes."

"Oh, well, we can make sure your clothes don't get wet."

That was probably a challenge, but she wasn't getting naked to go swimming. She had other ideas in mind. So she wrapped her arms more tightly around his neck, pressed her mouth against his, and gave him a hungry kiss. Taking charge of it this time made her feel powerful, especially when Jeff let out a small, inarticulate growl and then kissed his way down her throat to a spot right by her earlobe that more or less set her on fire.

She tilted her head and let him have access to the sensitive flesh, groaning out loud while she snaked her hands up through his wet hair and pulled him closer, losing her glasses in the process.

Who knew where they fell? She didn't care as the world went out of focus, especially, a moment later, when Jeff snaked his hand under her T-shirt and cupped her breast. Blood pounded in her ears in a rhythm that echoed the rush of the stream at their feet.

"You're beautiful," he whispered wetly against her neck, and she drank him up like it was happy hour at the Jaybird Café and Music Hall and the margaritas were half price. She let him touch her, and she touched him right back, running her hands over the muscles of his chest and then down his spine, cupping his hard backside. And suddenly standing there was not nearly enough. She wanted to feel the weight of him. On her. In her.

"There's a blanket in the backpack," she whispered against the stubble on his chin. She was kissing her way down his neck when she spoke.

"You brought a blanket? Why?"

"We needed a place to sit. You know, for the picnic." She murmured the words across his collarbone. She was planning to take her mouth even lower, but he tilted her head up. His face was almost in focus even without her glasses. But it didn't matter because she closed her eyes while she was kissing him. Plus he smelled really good. She buried her nose in his skin and took a deep breath.

"You're a genius." His words rumbled in his chest. "Don't go anywhere. I'll be back."

He took his body and his fabulous smell away for a moment, leaving her standing there blind and almost deaf and totally dumb.

"Uh, wait," he said from across the beach. "You brought more than a blanket."

She didn't even blush when he started laughing. "I think we're going to be here for a while."

Thank goodness he returned a moment later, spreading the blanket on the sand and tossing himself and the box of condoms down onto it. Then he leaned back on his elbows, the condoms right beside him.

Even all blurry, a naked Jeff made her burn. So hot that she needed to take off her clothes. Now.

She pulled her T-shirt over her head and shucked out of her jeans with a little flourish, turned on by the fact that he was watching her every move. When she finally joined him on the blanket, he grabbed her by the shoulders and tilted her back. "You're killing me," he said in a gruff voice right before he covered her body with his own.

Finally they were skin to skin, chest to breast, sex to sex, heart to heart.

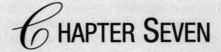

CHAPTER SEVEN

*G*ood God. She had actually carried through with her crazy plan to have sex with Jeff Talbert. In public, no less. She had wanted to be brave, but she'd never truly believed she could be *that* brave.

But why not? Jeff was delicious and erotic. And...well...lots of things that her heart shouldn't be thinking right now. Hearts had no business doing the thinking anyway. Brains were much better for that sort of thing.

She wanted more, but he hadn't invited her back to his cabin. She hadn't invited him up to the apartment above the bookstore either. But that was only because the apartment needed a total spring cleaning.

Knowing Jeff, he'd take one look at it and feel the need to reorganize before they could get naked. So she spent Sunday afternoon scrubbing her bathroom, straightening the living room, hosing down the kitchen, and putting fresh sheets on the bed.

Her mind was preoccupied reliving those moments by

the plunge pool. But as evening approached, it wandered
and became fixated on her phone. She expected him to call.
She wanted him to call. In fact, she was stupidly hoping he
would call so she could invite him over for a pizza or something else, with the emphasis on the something else.

Maybe she should call him? She was being brave, after
all. She was taking charge. She was about to do just that
when the doorbell at the back entrance to the apartment
rang, sending her heart racing. She sprang to the door,
threw it open...

And found her BFFs, Courtney Wallace and Arwen
Jacobs, standing there looking concerned and positively
grave.

"Uh, hi," Melissa said.

"Hi," Courtney answered, peeking around Melissa's
shoulder at the freshly dusted surfaces in her living room.
"Expecting company?"

"Uh, no. Come on in."

"No," Courtney said. "We're making an intervention."

"And taking you to the Jaybird for drinks and dinner,"
Arwen added.

"And we want to know who the hell this new guy
is. Gracie called us both this afternoon. Apparently the
Liberty Avenue Merchants Association has taken note that
you've hired someone to redo Secondhand Prose. They've
informed Gracie of this because, you know, Gracie is their
fearless leader," Courtney said.

"And this afternoon Poppy Marchand came into the
diner and told Gracie that she'd seen you this morning up
at the Old Laurel Chapel, holding hands with someone,"
said Arwen.

Melissa's face began to burn.

Courtney turned toward Arwen. "Note the red face.

The clean apartment. The fact that she's wearing a pair of common, ordinary blue jeans and a shirt that doesn't have one of those fairytale illustrations all over it. This is serious."

Arwen nodded. "Who is he?"

The answer to that question was so complex Melissa didn't even know where to start. So she changed the subject. "You know," she said, grabbing her purse from the hook beside the door, "margaritas sound great. Let's go."

Ten minutes later they strolled into the Jaybird Café and Music Hall, located in an old warehouse on the south side of town. Juni Petersen, whose family owned the Jaybird, had reserved a corner table in the back for Melissa and her friends, proving that Juni was also in on this intervention— a big problem, because if Juni knew about Jeff, then everyone would know about him by tomorrow morning.

The margaritas were also waiting for them when they arrived.

Melissa sank into a hard-backed chair and snagged her drink. She took a healthy swallow, the salt and sweet bursting on her tongue, just as Courtney said, "All right, we want all the details. Pippa Custis apparently told Gracie that your new assistant is 'the bomb.' "

Melissa put down her drink. "The bomb, really?"

"Well, you know, Pippa is sixty, and she's trying to be cool. She thinks he's cute."

"Is he?" Arwen asked.

"C'mon, guys, he's just a guy." Melissa turned away. "Who's singing tonight?"

"Earth to Melissa, it's Sunday, remember? Karaoke night."

"Oh, uh, yeah." Melissa's insides broiled. A girl in her situation—having just gotten all sweaty with a guy she didn't know that well—needed time for reflection, not the third degree from her friends. How much of what had happened today was plain garden-variety lust? And how much was something else?

Her heart said there was something else there, but her heart was so notoriously wrong about stuff like this. She probably shouldn't have done what she did today. It was foolish. Reckless even.

Oh, but it had felt like heaven.

"Oh my God, she's got a dreamy look on her face," Arwen said.

Courtney touched Melissa's hand where it rested on the table. "We're concerned about you. We all know about the financial mess your grandmother left you. So when it gets around town that you've hired some guy no one knows to help you fix up the store, it's natural for us to worry. Who is this guy? Where is he from? What kind of business plan have you come up with to deal with the mess Harriet left you?"

Melissa picked up her drink and drained it in several long gulps, but chugging her drink didn't make her friends disappear.

Oh hell. She wasn't going to be able to keep this secret. But she needed more fortification before she spilled the beans. She waggled her glass at Rory Ahearn, the bartender, indicating another round for all.

"Coming right up, luv," he said in his sexy Irish accent.

"You're stalling," Courtney said.

"Okay, it all started last week, with Hugo."

"Hugo? The cat?" Arwen's big brown eyes widened.

"Is there anyone else in my life named Hugo?" Melissa said.

"What does the cat have to do with this guy you've hired?" Courtney demanded.

"Last Friday a guy walked into the store, picked up Hugo, and bought a copy of *Walden*."

"No way," they said in unison.

"Yes way. He held Hugo for a long while, and the cat actually purred."

Juni Petersen overheard this because she was delivering their drinks. "Someone made friends with Hugo? Really?" she asked.

"Uh, yeah." Melissa snatched up her drink and took a big gulp.

"Who?" Juni asked.

"A guy. And it's not just Hugo. Dickens likes him, too."

There was a moment of silence around the table. Dickens didn't like anyone. It was a well-known fact.

"Oh," Juni said, "that's a sign for sure." She cocked her head and gave Melissa a goofy stare.

Meanwhile Courtney and Arwen nodded like a couple of bobblehead dolls. It was totally annoying the way her friends believed the stuff Juni said. Juni was into crystals and manifesting and reading people's auras.

"Okay, Melissa, stop beating around the bush," Courtney said. "We need a name."

"His name is Jeff Talbert."

"And..." Courtney pressed, as if she were cross-examining Melissa.

"And what?" Melissa said.

"And what else do you know about him?"

"Not much." Except he knew how to kiss, and he knew how to touch, and for a little while he'd made her believe there was a way to salvage the bookstore.

"And you hired him anyway?" Courtney asked. "What is he? A librarian? A contractor? An interior designer? What?"

Oh, crap. She searched for a handy lie and came up empty. "I didn't hire him," she finally admitted.

"You didn't?" Juni and her BFFs said more or less in unison.

She chugged down her second margarita. The tequila was starting to make her face feel a little numb. "He's a writer. Well, he's an unpublished writer who doesn't seem to do much writing. But, anyway, he just sort of volunteered to help. For free. But he's good at sorting books and color-coding price tags. Plus, he's widely read."

"He *volunteered?*" Arwen said this in a voice loud enough so that half a dozen other Jaybird patrons turned and stared.

Courtney leaned forward with real concern on her face. "Are you out of your mind? Don't you realize this guy could be a serial murderer, or a rapist, or something? You don't know anything about this guy."

Melissa didn't know if Jeff was a serial murderer, but he sure wasn't a rapist. That was good, wasn't it?

Arwen pulled her iPhone from her purse. "Let's just Google his name and see what comes up, okay?" Her thumbs got busy in an impressive way.

"Hmm, interesting. There are at least three Jeffrey Talberts who are professors, but they're—"

"No way. That's totally awesome." Melissa got all warm and gooey inside as she grabbed Arwen's phone. "Lemme see."

The letdown was kind of momentous when the first photo—of Professor Jeffrey Talbert—was a balding guy in his late fifties. The next photo wasn't much better. Melissa's pulse kicked up as she continued to scroll through half a dozen Jeffrey Talberts, none of whom was younger than forty-five.

And then, finally, there he was. Only she almost didn't recognize him. The photo was a professional studio head shot, and Jeff was wearing a dark, conservative suit jacket and a red tie. His face was clean-shaven, and his hair was a whole lot shorter.

"That's him," she said with a wistful sigh as she pointed to his photo.

Arwen snatched her phone away. Her thumbs got busy again, and then suddenly she said, "Oh my God, I can't believe it."

"What? Is he really a professor, because he dresses like—"

"No, honey, unfortunately not." She tilted her phone so both Melissa and Courtney could see the screen. This time it was a photo of Jeff wearing a tuxedo with a blond bombshell on his arm. Jealousy pricked Melissa from the inside. Oh boy, she was an idiot.

"His full legal name is Jefferson Talbert-Lyndon. That should strike a familiar chord since the *New York Times*, the *Washington Post*, the *Wall Street Journal*, and every cable news network known to man have been dragging him through the mud for the last three weeks. Honey, he's a journalist. And he's also Nina Talbert's sole heir. When she kicks the bucket, he gets her billions."

"What? Did you say Lyndon?" Melissa was confused. The margaritas had fogged her brain.

"Lemme see that," Courtney said, grabbing the phone out of Arwen's hand. "Oh my God. Melissa, he *is* a Lyndon."

"What?" Melissa's brain was having trouble processing her friends' words.

"He's that guy on the news. You know, the one who wrote that article that everyone is screaming about. About the Supreme Court."

Melissa shook her head. She had no idea what Courtney was talking about. She'd been hiding out in the store these last few weeks, reading genre fiction and letting the world pass her by. She wasn't up on current events.

"Honey, the Lyndon family is in a snit about him," Arwen said. "He's Pam Lyndon's nephew, and my boss at Lyndon, Lyndon & Kopp is his uncle. You didn't know this? He didn't tell you?"

"Well, at least he's not a serial killer," Courtney said brightly. "We can be thankful for that, even if he is a lying douche bag."

"A filthy rich and unbelievably cute douche bag," Arwen added.

How could this be? The duchess had been in the store yesterday and hadn't acknowledged Jeff at all. Why? Surely she'd recognized him, even if he hadn't been wearing pants.

And why hadn't he been honest about Pam? She'd told him everything. Trusted him. And he'd been lying from the start.

Melissa sank her head to the table and *thunk*ed it a couple of times before the swearing started. The profanity didn't last all that long, because her vocabulary of bad words was limited, and also by the time she started to repeat herself, her throat had closed up, her eyes had overflowed, and talking had become impossible.

CHAPTER EIGHT

*S*econdhand Prose wasn't open on Mondays, but Jeff found himself standing on the sidewalk staring through the windows. Dickens was keeping watch on his cat tree as always, but the place was dark.

He pounded on the door because he desperately needed to talk to Melissa and she'd been ignoring his phone messages and texts. He was just about to channel Stanley Kowalski, the character in *A Streetcar Named Desire* who stood outside the window and yelled his wife's name for all to hear, when a diminutive, fiftysomething woman wearing a big, brown tweed sweater tapped him on the shoulder and said, "You know, if you would just read the sign on the door, you'd realize the store isn't open today."

"I know that," he said as civilly as he could manage, considering his current state of mind. Why the hell was Melissa avoiding him? Yesterday had been amazing. Had he screwed up somehow? *Damn*.

"Good. I'm glad you can read," the woman said with a nod. "And since the store is closed, it doesn't make any sense to be pounding on the door. You're disturbing my beginning knitters class." She waved in the direction of the adjacent storefront with the sign over the door that said EWE AND ME FINE YARNS AND KNITTING SUPPLIES. The women of the aforementioned knitting class were gathered around the yarn shop's window, trying to watch their instructor do battle with him.

"Do you know where I can find Melissa Portman?" he asked.

"I know who you are," the woman said. "And so does Melissa."

It was like the woman had just dumped a bucket of ice water over his head. "What?"

"You're Jefferson Talbert-Lyndon. And I heard at the Merchants Association meeting this morning that you lied to Melissa about your name and background. And everyone wants to know why."

The woman shook her finger in his direction as she continued. "Shame on you, lying to a nice girl like Melissa. What were you up to? Softening her up so that Pam Lyndon could buy her out on the cheap?"

The scorn in the woman's voice shamed him. "No. You have it all wrong."

"I don't believe you."

The knitting instructor gave him a cold stare that he was all too familiar with. He'd seen that look in his editor's eyes at the moment when George had lost faith in him, when the tide of public opinion had turned against him.

If the merchants were gossiping like this, then it wouldn't be long before his father's family heard all about it. And then things would get much, much worse.

He needed to do something fast if he ever wanted to regain Melissa's trust.

And not just talk. Talk was cheap, and apologies at this point would fall flat.

And not just writing a check. He'd already done that, and Melissa would be finding out about it soon. But paying her taxes had been easy, too. All it took was money—and not even a lot of it. For him, money might as well grow on trees. He had more than he'd ever be able to spend in several lifetimes. Money could buy a lot, but it couldn't buy trust and it couldn't buy love.

If he wanted Melissa in his life—and he did—he would have to earn back her trust. And then he might be lucky enough to earn her love, too.

* * *

Fifteen minutes later a maid ushered Jeff into Charlotte's Grove and left him waiting in a sitting room right off the main foyer. He'd visited Charlotte's Grove only once in his life, and his memories of the place were vague—just a sense of formality that left him cold. He'd expected the historic house to be filled with museum-quality Georgian furniture, but the room he was led to seemed surprisingly contemporary, with a couch and two well-used wing chairs.

"Oh my God, Jeff, I'm so glad you turned up." Aunt Pam entered the room from the hallway dressed for a day in the garden, in a pair of slacks and a long-sleeve cotton T-shirt that was slightly dirty. Her hair was pulled back in a haphazard ponytail, and she wasn't wearing makeup.

She hurried across the wide-plank wood floor and gave Jeff a fierce, motherly hug. She smelled of the garden. Like roses or lavender or something.

"I've called your mother," she said as she let him go. "She's so relieved. Honestly, Jeff, you should have called her. Where on earth have you been? And when did you grow a beard?"

Jeff steeled his resolve. He'd seen Aunt Pam in action; she certainly hadn't been this sweet to Melissa on Saturday. He took a step back. "I've been staying at Dad's fishing cabin, and I grew a beard so you wouldn't recognize me."

"But—"

"Look, Aunt Pam, I'm not here to reconnect with the family. I'm here to issue an ultimatum."

"What on earth...? About what?" A little V of puzzlement formed on her forehead.

"About Melissa Portman and Secondhand Prose."

The frown morphed into an expression of utter astonishment. "What in the...? Oh my goodness, you're the man who fell off the ladder." She chuckled. "I'm afraid I wasn't looking at your face that day."

His humiliation was utterly complete. But he wasn't going to let it get the best of him. It was well past time to go on the offensive.

"Yeah, I admit I managed to get disrobed by a coat hook. But that's beside the point. I'm here to let you know that I've paid Melissa's taxes. So you won't be getting your hands on that building."

"Oh, that's wonderful news, Jeff. I'm so pleased. I've been worried about Melissa. I know it's hard to let go of that bookstore, but once she realizes she can make money leasing out the space, I know she'll come around."

Wait a sec. What the hell was Pam saying? That she didn't want the building? That she cared about Melissa's future? "Wait. I'm confused. You don't want her building?"

"Well, if she wants to sell it, I'm ready to buy it. But

I'd rather see her join the rest of the property owners and participate in our downtown restoration project."

He stood there for a moment trying to figure out which Pam Lyndon was the real one, the woman who had threatened Melissa on Saturday or this sweet Southern lady.

"Sit down, Jeff. Lidia will bring us some tea, and we'll talk. I can see you're upset. But, truly, if you've paid her taxes, then that's good news." Her drawl was suddenly thick as a brick.

"I don't want any tea or talk, Aunt Pam. What I want is for you to call Melissa Portman and tell her you're sorry for the way you threatened her. I want you to make it clear that there is no truth to the rumors flying around town that you used me to soften her up so she'd sell out."

"What? Why are people saying that?"

"I don't really understand, except that when I introduced myself to her, I dropped the Lyndon from my last name. But now everyone in town thinks I lied because of some nefarious plan you set in motion. Honestly, you need to do some fence mending with some of the Liberty Avenue merchants."

Pam continued to look at him as if he'd blown in from Mars. "Why on earth did you drop the Lyndon from your last name?"

"Because I don't want anything to do with any of you, my father most of all. And just so we're clear, I've asked my attorney to begin the process of legally changing my name to Jefferson Talbert."

"Well, that's just ridiculous," she said. "Even if you change your name, you'll still be family. Don't let Tom manipulate you, darlin'. We all know your father is a dick."

"What?" Her words left him breathless.

"You heard me. He's an idiot and a . . . Well, I've already

used language I shouldn't have used, but in Thomas's case, it fits the bill. Thomas obviously hasn't said it recently, or maybe ever, but, Jeff, we're all so very proud of you."

Before he could collect himself, Pam stood up. "Wait right there, darlin'. Don't run away again, please. There's something you need to hear."

She left the room, and he started pacing. Had she even heard what he had to say? He didn't think so. Damn. He came to rest in front of a big window with old glass that gave a slightly wobbly view of the outside.

"Jeff?" an oddly familiar masculine voice said from behind him. Was his father here?

He turned. No. Not Dad. Uncle Mark.

The senator stood beside one of the comfortable easy chairs, wearing a pair of jeans and a golf shirt. The Senate was obviously not in session today.

"I'm so glad you came to find us," he said, resting his hand on the chair back. "Pam says you've been staying up at the fishing cabin. That's probably the last place any of us would have looked for you." He chuckled, his brown eyes dancing with some kind of merriment that eluded Jeff.

"What is it you want, Uncle Mark? I've already told Aunt—"

"I want to talk to you. First of all, I want you to know that the entire family was shocked by Tom's public statements about your story."

Jeff said nothing. His life had suddenly become theater of the absurd.

"I see I've surprised you," Uncle Mark said.

Jeff shrugged. "I don't give a flying fart what the family thinks about anything, really. I'm only here because Aunt Pam has gotten the Liberty Avenue merchants in an uproar. And they all think I'm part of some weird plan that she has to take over the real estate downtown. And, really, the only problem here is that I decided to drop the Lyndon from my name. And, you know, I'm not ever going to use that name again."

The senator's shoulders sagged a little. "I understand. And as for your aunt, she can sometimes be like a steamroller. I'll see what I can do to smooth things over with the merchants. It won't be the first time."

"Thanks. That's all I want. I'll be going now." Jeff turned and headed toward the door, but the senator blocked his way.

"Son," Uncle Mark said, "you have every right to be furious with your father. We're all furious with him. Family comes before politics, and Tom forgot that. So I just want you to think this through. If you want to strike back at your father, then you need to help me kill this nomination."

It took a moment for Uncle Mark's words to make it past Jeff's anger. "Wait a sec. Are you saying you believe the story I wrote about Joanna Durand?"

"Of course I do. Durand's family has a reputation for bending the rules when it comes to oil and gas. And her husband has more lobbying clients than a dog has fleas. I'm sure her husband and brother have been up to no good, and I could use your help in putting the kibosh on this nomination.

"By the way, I'm saying this, not as your uncle but as a member of the Senate Judiciary Committee. Her confirmation hearing is set for this coming Thursday, and I have every intention of giving her a hard time."

"Oh." The adrenaline in Jeff's body began to dissipate.

Mark Lyndon continued. "I'm not letting Joanna Durand's nomination get out of committee. So, I'd like you to give my chief of staff a call and help him hunt down the smoking gun that will simultaneously clear your name and sink this nomination for good and all."

Jeff stood there frozen. He hadn't expected this. Not in a million years. "Okay, I'll help, of course, but—"

"Son, if you want to change your last name, go right ahead and do it. No one could blame you. But it won't change anything as far as I'm concerned, and I suspect you'll discover that resigning from the Lyndon family is a whole lot harder than you might expect."

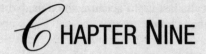

CHAPTER NINE

$\mathcal{H}$ugo jumped on Melissa's bed and settled on her pillow, purring like a finely tuned engine. That was unusual, since the cat hadn't been upstairs since Grammy died. And never, in all the cat's twelve years on the planet, had he ever jumped up on Melissa's bed. So why had he chosen this morning, when her head was pounding like nobody's business?

She batted the cat away and pulled the pillow over her head, hoping that would quiet the pounding. But the cat meowed loudly and then opened his claws on her shoulder.

She sat up. Her stomach lurched as she groped for her glasses. She should never have had the third margarita. The world came into focus as she settled her glasses on her nose. She picked up her cell phone and checked the time. It was well past noon.

So much for getting an early start on the rest of her life. She had barely enough time to take a shower before her one o'clock meeting with Walter Braden. She was about to put the phone down when she noticed that she had new voice mail messages—twelve, in fact—all from Jeff. She'd missed his calls last night because she'd inadvertently left her cell phone at home.

Damn.

She listened to his voice mail. He'd actually called last night to invite her up to his cabin. And then he'd called again in the morning to invite her to breakfast.

Double damn.

Maybe she should return his calls.

No. He needed to come to her. Most definitely. And in the meantime, she needed to take a shower and move on with her life.

She got up, fed the cats, made some coffee, but instead of taking a shower, she called Walter and rescheduled her appointment for the next day. Then she set up her laptop on the kitchen table and started searching Jeff's name. Wow. He had lied about a lot of things, starting with the fact that he was, really and truly, a published writer.

An hour later she was still sitting there reading Jeff's articles—not just the one on Joanna Durand, but a dozen others. The man was a talented writer with a knack for writing profiles of the rich and famous. She was totally engrossed when someone tapped on her back door. Her heart took flight. Maybe Jeff had come to explain himself.

But it wasn't Jeff.

Gracie Teague stood on her landing wearing her waitress uniform and a determined expression. She didn't wait to be invited in. She just took the territory like General Patton rolling over France.

"I brought you a bacon and egg sandwich and some serious advice." She plunked a sandwich wrapped in wax paper onto the kitchen table and eyed the computer, the empty bag of M&M's, and the wastebasket filled with used tissues. "I should have come sooner."

"I'm all right. Really. I didn't make my appointment with Walter Braden, but I did reschedule for tomorrow. I've decided to take your advice and sell out, take the proceeds after taxes and find a beach somewhere with hot, gorgeous, rich men."

She'd expected Gracie to be overjoyed with this news, but instead her mother's BFF frowned. "You will do no such thing," she said. "Sit down. I have something you need to hear."

Melissa sat, and Gracie took the other chair. "There was an emergency meeting of the Liberty Avenue Merchants Association at oh dark thirty this morning. You know how everyone loved Harriet. And everyone remembers you as a little girl, and we're all just a little overprotective of you, I guess. So this Jefferson Lyndon situation has gotten everyone into an uproar. Half the shop owners think Pam Lyndon sent that man to soften you up. To convince you to sell out."

"But—"

Gracie held up a hand. "I know, hon. Why would a man help you fix up the store if he'd been sent to convince you that keeping it going was pointless?"

Melissa nodded. "Exactly."

"Well, not everyone is as logical as you and I. Anyway," Gracie said with a little gleam in her eye, "at the meeting this morning, some of the merchants took up a collection to help you with your taxes. It's not much, but we figured it might be enough to buy you some time. I was nominated to go down to the county clerk's office to make a payment on your behalf. But when I got there, I found out that someone had already paid your taxes in full."

"What?"

"That's right. Paid in full first thing this morning, just an hour before I got there. The clerk wouldn't tell me who. She said it was a privacy matter or something. As if there's any privacy in a town as small as Shenandoah Falls."

"You think Jeff paid my taxes?" The weight in Melissa's chest began to lift.

"That would be my guess. Now, why would a man do a thing like that?"

Melissa tried to think of a good business reason and drew a blank. "Because he believes in independent bookstores?" It was lame.

"Or maybe he believes in you?" Gracie said, covering one of Melissa's hands with hers.

Melissa's eyes filled up, but this time the tears weren't angry. "And I believe in him, Gracie," she whispered, her lips trembling. "I've been sitting here reading the things he's written, and I can't help myself. I think what he wrote in that story about the Durand nomination is true. I think he ran away from New York because even his father refused to stand by him."

"You know," Gracie said, "if my daddy had publicly disavowed me, I think I might return the favor. You know, by dropping the hyphenated part of my last name."

"Really? Because now that I'm sober and I've read his story and the reaction to it, I've come to the same conclusion."

Just then Dickens jumped up on the kitchen table, sat down facing Melissa, and proceeded to meow at her as if he were scolding her or something. Hugo followed suit, only he yowled in a way that was practically mournful.

"Mercy," Gracie said. "I've never seen them do anything like that before."

Melissa got up from the table. "It's a sign, Gracie. They've been trying to tell me for days that Jeff belongs here. I just wasn't listening."

* * *

Melissa called Walter Braden back and canceled her meeting. Without a tax bill looming over her, maybe she could make a go of keeping Secondhand Prose alive, saving Hugo and Dickens's home, and preserving a little piece of Grammy for a while.

And all because of Jeff, who had walked into her store and insisted on fixing it up. Not because he was paid to do it. Not because she'd asked him to do it. But because he had simply belonged there.

The cats knew it. And now Melissa did, too.

She needed to talk to him, so she decided the ball wasn't in his court after all. The ball was in hers. She texted him.

Melissa: *We need to talk. Where are you?*

Jeff: *I'm just leaving Charlotte's Grove. Expect an apology call from Pam. I'll be at the store in ten minutes.*

Melissa: *No, not here. Too many busybodies. Where's your cabin?*

Jeff: *:)*

His emoticon was followed by an address in the Blue Ridge off Scottish Heights Road. She told him she'd meet him there in twenty minutes.

The cabin turned out to be high up on the ridge off a dirt road. Jeff certainly hadn't been exaggerating when he'd said that he'd been living back in the woods.

It was an old place, built years before people had started putting up luxury vacation homes in the area. Its weathered logs and rustic stone chimney looked as if they'd been there for a century. It sat in a clearing, nestled between two gigantic oaks, on a ledge that provided a commanding view westward toward the Shenandoah Valley and the Allegheny Mountains beyond.

Jeff was waiting for her, sitting in an Adirondack chair on the covered porch. He stood up as she pulled her VW in behind his shiny Land Rover, and he was right there when she got out of the car.

"Let me explain," he said before she had a chance to say one word of the speech she'd been rehearsing in her head. "I never—"

"You didn't tell me the truth," she blurted.

"I'm sorry. I didn't mean to mislead you. I just—"

"I know you didn't. I get it. If I had a father who issued public statements about me, I'd want to divorce him, too. But you could have told me that. You could have trusted me."

Jeff's gaze intensified, his brown eyes full of emotion. "Are you telling me that you actually understand why I didn't give you my full name?"

"Well, duh. I read what your father said about you. And it was brutal. But more important, it was just wrong. I spent a lot of time today reading some of the things you've written for *New York, New York.* They were wonderful articles, Jeff. You have a gift for words. So what he said was just not true. You're a writer—a really good one. But the thing is, you should have been honest with me from the start."

He let go of a long breath and closed his eyes for a moment. "I'm sorry I wasn't honest, but I didn't know you at first. And then...Well, I wanted to take care of your taxes before I said anything. Please tell me you never believed that crap that's going around town about how Pam used me to set you up, because that's just not true."

"Of course I don't believe that. If that was your purpose, you had a funny way of going about it. All that dusting and organizing and color coding. It didn't make it easier to decide to sell the place, you know."

"You aren't going to sell it, are you? I'd hate to see that bookshop go out of business."

Tears filled her eyes, and a lump the size of a peach stone swelled in her throat. She shook her head. "I never wanted to sell. I just had to."

He took her by the shoulders and pulled her right into his arms. Her head hit his strong, steady shoulder, and she leaned on him like she'd never leaned on anyone in her life. The emotions she'd been denying finally found their way to the surface. She had to take off her glasses when the tears came. She cried for Grammy and her parents. She cried because, standing there in the circle of Jeff's arms, she didn't feel alone anymore. And finally, she cried because she didn't have to close her store.

He held her tight, stroked her head, and gave her a place to stand, a place to be. Leaning on him was like coming home.

When the tears had run their course, she tilted her head up, but it was no use. She couldn't see him because her vision was still smeared with tears. But it was all right, because he came toward her and started kissing away the tears that had run down her cheeks.

She started laughing then, which was weird because her heart had swelled to the point where breathing had become difficult. He ignored her laugh and continued to dispense little kisses all along her cheeks and over to her ear, where he whispered, "Listen to me, Melissa, for just one minute. I went up to Charlotte's Grove, and I told Mark and Pam Lyndon that I was changing my name. I've already taken the first steps to do that legally. I also told Pam that she needed to call you to apologize for the way she acted the other day."

She pushed him back and gazed into his eyes. He was a complete blur, but that didn't matter. "You told Pam Lyndon she needed to apologize? Oh my God, I don't think anyone has ever told Pam Lyndon that in her entire life."

He laughed a little and put his forehead against hers. "Well, there's a first time for everything."

They stood like that for a long moment as the tension of the last few days melted away. "So, I have a million questions," Melissa said.

"About what?"

"About you, Jeff. I want to know everything. I want to know what your favorite color is and what you like for breakfast, and lunch, and dinner. And which vegetable makes you want to yak. I want to know your birthday and the worst and best Christmas present you ever got. I want to know it all because, damn it, I crave your body, and when that happens, it means my heart is automatically involved. You know? I don't do the whole friends-with-benefits thing well. So if that's all this is, I'll just get in my car and go now, okay?"

She was prepared to have her heart crushed when he said, "Brussels sprouts."

"What?"

"I hate brussels sprouts. How about you?"

She took in a deep breath filled with the woodsy scent of him. "It's cauliflower that makes me want to hurl. And, for the record, my birthday is the sixteenth of March."

"Really? Mine's on the seventeenth. Next year we should throw a big party."

Next year. She closed her eyes and rested her head

against his chest. His arms were still around her. She was safe here. She'd always be safe here. She may have met him only days ago, but he was "the One."

"I have something to seal this moment," he said, moving back a little bit. "I intended to present it to you last night. But you didn't answer my calls."

"I was getting drunk with the girls. Bad move on my part."

He laughed. "Put on your glasses."

She snagged them from her jeans pocket where she'd put them right before her crying jag. She slipped them on just in time to see him pull something from his pocket.

He held it out to her, nestled in his palm. "It's the arrowhead," he said. "Yesterday I bought a rawhide shoelace and made a necklace out of it. When I get a chance, I intend to take it to a jeweler for a proper gold chain. I thought you might like a little memento of our first time." He gave her a salacious grin. "Turn around. Let me put it on you."

She turned, and he pulled her hair aside and then fastened the necklace at her nape. He pressed his lips to the spot right below her ear, and she groaned out loud.

"Our first time, huh? That implies there will be a second time," she said.

"Yeah. And many, many more, I hope." And then he did the most romantic thing ever. He lifted her into his arms and carried her over the threshold of his cabin.

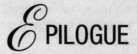

EPILOGUE

Three Months Later

*M*elissa was manning the checkout at Secondhand Prose and reading a murder mystery when the front door jangled. She looked up in time to see Jeff strolling through the door, carrying a cardboard box that looked as if it had come from an online bookseller.

Both cats immediately arrived on the scene and tried to trip him as he headed in Melissa's direction.

"Hey, you guys, give me a break," he said as he stepped over the felines with admirable grace—grace that hadn't yet failed to warm Melissa's insides.

"I bring gifts," he said, putting the carton on the counter and leaning across it to give her a kiss that left them both a little breathless.

"Hmm, nice. I like your gifts," she said.

He laughed. "I was talking about this," he said, nudging the box.

"This looks like a box of books," she said. "From the competition."

"Ah, but this isn't just any box of books. Look inside."

She opened the carton, and right on the top was a large-format paperback book titled *A Child's Book of Stories*. "Oh, how beautiful!" Melissa said in a rush as she opened the book and started browsing through. "I love Jessie Willcox Smith's illustrations. She's my favorite illustrator of all time."

"Yes, I know. That was one of the first things I learned about you. All those fairytale T-shirts."

She looked up from the book and gave him another kiss.

"There's another book in the box," Jeff said after a very long, hot moment.

"Another Jessie Willcox Smith book?"

"No, it's a hardbound copy of *Grimm's Complete Fairy Tales*."

She put her paperback on the counter and pulled the second book from the box. It was one of those leather reproduction books with a fancy embossed cover, gilt lettering, and a ribbon bookmark stitched into the binding. She wasn't fooled. The book probably retailed for less than ten dollars.

She glanced up at Jeff. There was a gleam in his eye, and the corner of his mouth was curling just a tiny bit, as if he knew a secret he was bursting to tell. Did he think he'd found her a special first edition or something?

"Oh, this is nice," she said, trying to sound super-enthusiastic, when she would much rather be hanging out on the beanbag chair drooling over Jessie Willcox Smith's illustrations. Or, better yet, upstairs in bed drooling over Jeff.

"Open it," Jeff said, "to the marked page." Was there a tremor in his voice?

She opened the book to a three-paragraph story entitled "Brides on Trial." Right below the story's final paragraph, the book had been horribly defaced. Someone had cut a deep hole in the pages to create a secret hiding spot. And in the spot, with the ribbon bookmark threaded through it, was a sapphire and diamond ring.

Melissa's breath caught in her throat, and tears filled her eyes as she looked up at Jeff, the man who had become, in just a few short months, her best friend and the love of her life.

"Melissa," he said in his deep, quiet voice, "I walked into this enchanted place, and the minute I saw you, I knew I'd come home. I've patiently spent the last few months waiting for the right time to ask this question, and I don't want to wait anymore. I think I know enough about you to say that I never want to leave your side. You love Jessie Willcox Smith, you know every story in *Grimm's Fairy Tales*, even the gruesome ones like the 'Heavenly Wedding.' You snore, you love margaritas, and you read romances when you think I'm not looking. Will you marry me?"

Like any fairytale prince, Jeff got down on his knee, took her hand, and kissed it.

"Oh my God, yes. Yes, yes." Melissa fell down onto her knees, too, and wrapped her arms around him. "I love you, Jefferson Talbert-Lyndon. And even though you are technically a member of the Lyndon family, I can't imagine spending my life with anyone else."

Jeff grabbed the *Grimm's Fairy Tales* off the counter and sat on the bookstore's floor. "Sorry about defacing a book, but I figured it was for a good cause. And we'll be keeping this book forever."

He pulled the ribbon bookmark through the ring. "Do

you like it?" he asked. "It's a family heirloom, but from the Talbert side of the family. It's my grandmother's ring."

"The cat-lady-on-the-Hudson grandmother?"

Jeff grinned. "The very one." He took her left hand and slipped the ring on her finger. It fit perfectly. "Grandmother would have loved you, Melissa."

And just then, Dickens and Hugo joined the group hug on the bookstore floor, one cat in each lap, proving—at least to Melissa's satisfaction—that Grammy would have loved Jeff too.

Acknowledgments

Some stories come very easily and some require a lot of patience and lots of rewrites. This story was more of the latter than the former. My thanks to everyone who held my hand and sometimes provided harsh critiques. This story would never have happened without you.

I would like to specifically thank my critique partners Carol Hayes and Keely J. Thrall, who read numerous drafts of this story and wouldn't let me off the hook until I completely rewrote chapters one and two—several times. Thank you, ladies, for sticking with me as I struggled to put the puzzle pieces together.

My thanks also to my fabulous editor, Alex Logan, who helped me put my finger on the things that didn't work in the first draft. Your red ink and tireless effort made the story (and my writing) so much better.

Finally, as always, my undying thanks and love to my husband, Bryan, who has to live with me when I'm working through the birth of a story. You are such a good listener, and sometimes that's exactly what I need.

About the Author

Hope Ramsay is a *USA Today* bestselling author of heart-warming contemporary romances set below the Mason-Dixon Line. Her children are grown, but she has a couple of fur babies who keep her entertained. Pete the cat, named after the cat in the children's books, thinks he's a dog, and Daisy the dog thinks Pete is her best friend except when he decides her wagging tail is a cat toy. Hope lives in the medium-size town of Fredericksburg, Virginia, and when she's not writing or walking the dog, she spends her time knitting and noodling around on her collection of guitars.

You can learn more at:
  HopeRamsay.com
  Twitter @HopeRamsay
  Facebook.com/Hope.Ramsay

Fall in love with these charming contemporary romances!

SUMMER ON HONEYSUCKLE RIDGE
by Debbie Mason

Abby Everhart has gone from being a top L.A. media influencer to an unemployed divorcée living out of her car. So inheriting her great-aunt's homestead in Highland Falls, North Carolina, couldn't have come at a better time. But instead of a cabin ready to put on the market, she finds a fixer-upper, complete with an overgrown yard and a reclusive—albeit sexy—man living on the property. When sparks between them become undeniable, will she be able to sell the one place that's starting to feel like home?

PRIMROSE LANE
by Debbie Mason

Olivia Davenport has finally gotten her life back together and is now Harmony Harbor's most sought-after event planner. But her past catches up with her when she learns that she's now guardian of her ex's young daughter. Dr. Finn Gallagher knows a person in over her head when he sees one, but Olivia makes it clear she doesn't want his companionship. Only with a little help from some matchmaking widows—and a precocious little girl—might he be able to convince her that life is better with someone you love at your side.

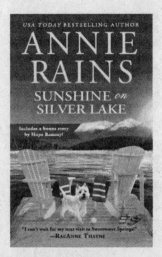
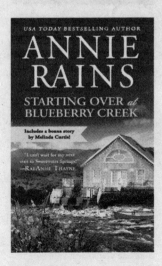

RETURN TO MAGNOLIA HARBOR
by Hope Ramsay

Jessica Blackwell's life needs a refresh. So while she's back home in Magnolia Harbor, she's giving her architecture career a total makeover. The only problem? Jessica's new client happens to be her old high school nemesis. Christopher Martin never meant to hurt Jessica all those years ago, and now he'd give anything to have a second chance with the one woman who always haunted his memories.

CAN'T HURRY LOVE
by Melinda Curtis

Widowed after one year of marriage, city girl Lola Williams finds herself stranded in Sunshine, Colorado, reeling from the revelation that her husband had secrets she never could have imagined, secrets that she's asked the ruggedly hot town sheriff to help her uncover. Lola swears she's done with love forever, but the matchmaking ladies of the Sunshine Valley Widows Club have different plans...Includes a bonus story by Annie Rains!

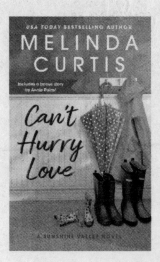

Discover bonus content and more on read-forever.com

THE SUMMER HOUSE
by Jenny Hale

Callie Weaver's too busy to think about her love life. She's invested her life savings into renovating the beach house she admired every childhood summer into a bed-and-breakfast. But when she catches the attention of local real estate heir and playboy Luke Sullivan, his blue eyes and easy smile are hard to resist. As they laugh in the ocean waves, Callie discovers there's more to Luke than his money and good looks. But just when Callie's dreams seem within reach, she finds a diary full of secrets—with the power to change everything.

PARADISE COVE
by Jenny Holiday

Dr. Nora Walsh hopes that moving to tiny Matchmaker Bay will help her get over a broken heart. When the first man she sees looks like a superhero god, the born-and-bred city girl wonders if maybe there's something to small-town living after all. But will Jake Ramsey's wounded heart ever be able to love again?